The King's Inquisitor

By Tonya Ulynn Brown

THE KING'S INQUISITOR
By Tonya Ulynn Brown

Published by Late November Literary
Winston Salem, NC 27107

ISBN (print): 978-1-7375561-4-5

This is a work of historical fiction. While parts of this novel, including certain character names and historical events, are derived from historical documents, the story itself is a work of fiction. Any brand names, places, or trademarks remain the property of their respective owners and are only used for fictional purposes.

Tonya Ulynn Brown.
The King's Inquisitor/Tonya Ulynn Brown, 1st ed.

Printed in the United States of America

~Praise for The King's Inquisitor~

The King's Inquisitor has everything a reader of historical fiction could wish for: a strong and intelligent woman; a man who is fair-minded and curious enough to challenge the barbaric notions of witchcraft that his monarch and country hold, and a fascinating glimpse into 16th century Scotland. This is a must-read for lovers of history and characters who forge their own paths through the injustices and bigotries of their times.

> ~Suzanne M. Wolfe, author of *A Murder by Any Name*,
> and *The Course of All Treasons*.

Beautifully written and meticulously researched, *The King's Inquisitor* provides powerful insight into one of Scotland's most shameful periods of history.

> ~Ailish Sinclair, author of *The Mermaid and the Bear*
> *Fireflies and Chocolate*

Sensuous. Evocative. And historically authentic. Talented writer Tonya Ulynn Brown rockets the reader back in time to the dark labyrinth of sixteenth-century Scotland's tumultuous Witch Craze. In her brilliant follow-up to the Queen's Almoner, Brown's new novel, *The King's Inquisitor*, follows the story of William, the ambitious courtier, notorious ladies' man, and companion to the Scottish King James, tasked with bringing witches to justice and protecting both King James and his queen from sinister plots whispering of the dark arts. And challenging him at every turn is Ailsa, the fiery and willful young woman determined to bring mercy to those wretched women blighted under the suspicion of witchcraft. As William and Ailsa's entanglement grows, so does the mystery surrounding the witch Geillis Duncan, and her compatriots, and their ties to the Scottish court. A riveting tale that takes the readers through as many twists and turns as the dark backstreets of Edinburgh!

> ~Heather E.F. Carter, author of *The Black Unicorn*

What a great story from Tonya Ulynn Brown! I enjoyed *The Queen's Almoner*, and this tale is even more captivating. In *The King's Inquisitor*, we get to know William, son of the loveable almoner from Brown's first novel. William is no carbon copy of his pious father, who sacrificed much in his striving to do the right thing. What the men do share in common is the war within their hearts concerning which woman is the one with whom they are meant to share their life. William is caught between a beautiful noblewoman, who has been hand selected for him by the Queen herself, and a feisty young woman he met only by chance. Drawn to each of them for quite different reasons, William tries to sort out his feelings while plots against the king also vie for his attention. King James sees enemies around every corner and puts his childhood friend in charge of questioning those accused of using witchcraft against him.
The story is exciting and entertaining without becoming implausible. This was a great read from Ms. Brown, and I look forward to reading what she writes next.
~Samantha Wilcoxson, author of *Plantagenet Embers* series

The Kings Inquisitor brings to life the perverse and dangerous world of the Scottish witch trials of 1591, when even well-intentioned persons needed to tread carefully and mind their tongues. The darkness of this story is leavened by the characters of Ailsa Blackburn and William Broune with their innate decency, charm, and light humor in their interactions. Tense, gripping, and, as the story progresses, a real page turner.
~Catherine Merrick, author of *The Bridled Tongue*

~*Dedication*~

For my mother. I think you would have liked this one too.

~Tonya

~*Author's Note*~

Although ***The King's Inquisitor*** is a work of fiction, much of the details concerning the North Berwick witch trials, the interrogations, and torture have been taken straight from contemporary sources of the time. The intent of this story is not to condemn nor condone the reported actions of many of the women, and even some men, who may have participated in the events surrounding the witch trials in sixteenth century Scotland.

Some Violent Imagery. Reader discretion is advised.

*What can be the cause that there are twenty
women given to that craft,
where there is one man? The reason is easy,
for as that sex is frailer than man is,
so is it easier to be entrapped in these gross
snares of the Devil,
as was over well proved to be true, by the
serpent's deceiving of Eve,
at the beginning.*

~King James, Daemonology

*...Be fire with fire;
Threaten the threatener and outface the brow
Of bragging horror...*

~William Shakespeare, The Life and Death of King John

~1~

December 1590

William

The business of witchcraft is a foul trade and only a scrupulous man is fitted for the task. Hunting down those blackened souls and preventing them from the Devil's work is not for the faint of heart. The weak in spirit need not apply. It is a foul business indeed. And one that I found myself entangled in, yet not entirely prepared for.

And so being inclined to do all that my sovereign asked of me, I truly was entangled, trudging along behind the Honorable Samuel Sheepshearer, and His Majesty, King James, making our way along Leith Wynd, a muddy, narrow road that led from the heart of Edinburgh to the outskirts of town. Sheepshearer was in the throes of keeping the hem of his ermine coat out of the muck. King James shielded his nose from the rotten smell that followed us.

The stench of putrid air truly burned the eyes as well as the nose. "This is wretched." James coughed, side-stepping a rat that cut across our path. In the falling daylight I saw his rheumy eyes follow the rodent as it slipped into a crevice at the corner of a house. Then he peered at me. "You are not bothered by the stench?"

"Aye, but I suppose I'm accustomed to the filth."

"How can that be?" He looked appalled. "I am sure your widower father, the almoner, would not have you living in such squalor."

"Ah, but you forget, Your Grace, I accompanied him on many an

1

excursion to visit the sick and poor of St Andrews parish. At a young age I learnt the trick of breathing through my mouth and not my nose, so as not to smell the stomach-churning miasma. This street we now make our way along is no different. Filth always smells the same." The king grunted something unintelligible but did not question me further. I wondered if he regretted his decision to come along.

The wind shifted, driving the stench away from us and making us clutch our collars even closer to our ears. We had been plodding along for the better part of a quarter of an hour.

"Your Grace," Sheepshearer spoke up, watching us from the corner of his eye. "Are ye sure ye wish to continue this course ye have set yourself upon?"

"Tis a dreadful trek," I added. "I would venture to say the inquiry will not be pleasant." I pulled the king around a drunkard that had fallen into our path only moments before.

"This woman is suspicioned to have cursed the travel of my beloved Anne before she even set sail for Scotland. I will hear her interrogation."

The rumors of witches causing storms that waylaid the queen's ships when she first sailed for Scotland had given the king more than one sleepless night. I imagined he needed this vindication.

We wound our way through the darkness, passing crude, wooden houses that leaned in on one another. The crumbling wattle and daub frames supported each other like staggering men on too much wine. From a window somewhere up above could be heard the threats of a shouting wife. A drunken husband responded in muted tones, then a bang, and peals of laughter. A battered tomcat, screeching into the darkness, skittered around us. Moments later, a barking dog scampered by, provoked by the cat, no doubt.

We finally drew near to a building, the purpose for which it served escaping me. There were no windows, thus erasing the likelihood that it had served as a shop for merchants. A darkened placard hung loosely from one lone screw in the wall, its markings scratched clean by the briny air from the sea just beyond.

The door was cracked open at our knock, and a tall, spindly man stood before us. Upon seeing Master Sheepshearer, he then opened the door fully to grant us entrance. The widening of his eyes led me to believe that he had not expected the king. With the removal of James's cloak, our host stuttered a greeting.

The room was dank, smelling of urine and ale, and not much of an improvement from the outside. The blackened walls seeped with an eerie perspiration that hinted at being the source of the smell. Once my eyes adjusted fully, I was able to see across the room. But what I beheld was more sickening than any smell I could inhale on the streets of Edinburgh.

In a corner of the room, a woman was sprawled upon the floor and whimpering like an injured animal. Long, blonde hair matted with dirt and blood fell over her face, but I could tell from the sound of her sobs that she was young, and not the old mother that we had expected. Her dress was missing; she wore only her shift, and it was bloodied and torn. I glanced at James to gauge his reaction, but he stood poker straight as usual, unaffected by the sight before him.

"Your Grace," mumbled the man whose name was Rupert Marley. "Allow me to introduce to you Deputy Bailiff David Seton. It is he who discovered the witch's activity. She is his servant girl."

A tall, brawny man stepped forward, his tiny black eyes shifting from left to right. His straw-colored hair fell loose from its queue, and he looked as if he had slept in the same clothes for a week. He bowed graciously, but his felicitous manner was negated by his audacity to look straight into the king's eyes. He straightened, then bowed again, this time touching his knee to the floor before standing up once more. "Your Grace, it is a great honor to be in your presence. I am humbled."

"And what have you discovered, seeing how you have apparently already begun your interrogations?" I interrupted. I couldn't decide if it was his sycophantic bowing, his faux humility, or his apparent disregard for his state of dress, but I immediately disliked him.

He turned his vulpine eyes on me and finally stopped bobbing like a duck on water. "The wench is sneaking out at night, sir, when her chores are done. She has a real knack for helping the neighbors when one of them ails. Several of them have recovered completely. It just started recently. There must be something secretive behind it."

I removed my cloak and threw it over a nearby chair. The air in the room was stale and flat, making it slightly hard to breathe. "Let me see if I understand. Your servant girl is a good healer, helping the neighbors when they are in need. She leaves your house on her own time, and now you think she is a witch?"

A choking noise came from the direction of the king, and I threw him a glance. A smirk lay hidden beneath the cynical brow and severely downturned mouth. "Perhaps there is more to this story, Sir William. Let us have a seat, and we can discuss what Bailiff Seton has discovered. Surely his suspicions are not totally unfounded."

The king pulled a chair out from the table and stretched out his crooked legs as he seated himself. The effects of a childhood disease that bowed his legs from a young age caused lingering leg and hip pain. But only his closest friends knew of this blight. I had known the king since I was ten years old and he nine, so I knew all about his infirmities.

I too pulled out a chair and settled in to hear the bailiff's tale. Marley produced a jug of ale, pouring the liquid into three mugs. Sheepshearer reached for his, pausing momentarily for a quick sniff of the fetid draught. Neither the sour expression on his face, nor the ale's apparent lack of appeal dissuaded him. He tossed back the wheaten liquid then held the cup out to Marley for another fill.

The young woman had stopped whimpering, but she had yet to turn her head so that I could see her face. She lay motionless on the floor. I might have thought her dead if it had not been for Seton striding to the pathetic form and jerking her up by her hair.

The woman let out a painful cry as he pulled her to her feet and shoved her in front of the king. "Aye, my fears are most certainly well-founded, Your Grace. For just this morning, we found the devil's mark upon her. We need a witch pricker to test her."

I watched the woman whom Seton had interrogated. Bloodied

finger tips, busted and bruised gave indication of the means by which he had obtained information. The pilliwinks had evidently been administered, the thumbscrew extracting confessions that interrogation alone could not obtain. Across her face were the markings of a rope, as if it had been tied around her head and squeezed. Her shift was also torn, a bare shoulder peeking out from a tear in her bloodied garment. I had no idea what benefit that type of abuse might produce; perhaps that's how he found the mark.

The look of horror on the woman's face at the sight of the King of Scotland sitting in front of her caused her lip to quiver. Yet, she made no other sound.

"What is your name?" The silk of Sheepshearer's words contradicted his steely eyes.

"G-Geillis Duncan, sir," she managed, a split and swollen lip making it difficult for her to speak.

"And what is it that ye do at night, when ye leave your master's house and venture into the dark?"

Her eyes darted from Sheepshearer to me, then to the king. One of the candles on the wall flickered and sputtered out just then, increasing the shadow on her already darkened and drawn face.

"Speak, woman. Ye must give explanation as to where ye go at night." Her interrogator barked out the order.

I watched as Sheepshearer wiped his brow on a piece of cloth. Hollow blue orbs stared at the magistrate without emotion. Then, as suddenly as her placid expression had appeared, it was gone.

"I was not aware that it be against the law to go where ye will when it is within your leisure to do so," she provoked. Gone was the whimpering girl, and in her place stood a defiant woman, evidently not so easily threatened. I had to wonder at the sudden transformation.

"Mind your tongue, witch." Seton jerked on a handful of hair again, snapping her neck backward. She winced in pain.

"Ye are at your own free will until it comes to the attention of your master that ye are up to no good." Sheepshearer was getting impatient. Usually, his size alone was enough to intimidate people. He stood well equal to a horse's head, and probably wore the same size coat.

"I have given no cause for him to accuse me so. Other than my refusal of his advances."

Seton pulled on her hair once more, anger overtaking him. He was seething, and spittle flew from his mouth as he said, "That is a lie! See how she lies, sir! Perhaps we should cut out her tongue and be done with it."

Sheepshearer held up his hand to silence the belligerent man. The king adjusted his seat but did not speak. Instead, Sheepshearer asked, "Where is this mark ye have found?"

The offended man jerked the woman by the arm and pulled her hair up to expose her neck. "There," he pointed with a stubby finger.

James and I both leaned closer to get a better look at the mark. Sheepshearer stepped closer, taking out a small lens and holding it in front of his eye. He didn't speak for a moment, then pulled a small leather pouch from inside his coat and walked to the table where we sat.

I stared in fascination. I had never seen a witch pricker do his work. I admit, that was one of the reasons I had agreed to accompany James this evening. I was intrigued at the method of determining who was a witch and who wasn't.

The witch pricker removed his coat then untied a thin strap and unrolled the pouch. Inside were all manner of instruments. Needles of various lengths, pointed rods, some straight and some curved, several surgeon's lancets with differing widths, a crude sort of pinching device, and a small rod with a severe hook on the end. I shivered as he selected his instrument of choice then turned and faced the woman.

"It looks like a lover's mark to me," I whispered to James. I eyed him to see if he understood my meaning. He was a recently married man after all, but the queen was the only woman he had been with in his twenty-four years. She had performed her duty, but whether it had been with enjoyment was not something he had shared with even me.

"Perhaps," he finally said. Yet, he did not move to stop Sheepshearer. I, on the other hand, shifted in my seat. I might have put a lover's mark or two on a woman. I shuddered at the thought that any woman I had been with would be subjected to such treatment. Still, any woman worth her weight in ale would never allow a bruise to be discovered. Apparently, Geillis Duncan had no choice.

He had chosen a straight blade. The likes of which a man would use to shave the hair from his face. *Surely, he did not intend to filet her alive?*

At the sight of the chosen instrument, Geillis too reacted. She tried to jerk her arm away from Seton but he held fast. Curling her toes in an attempt to dig her bare feet into the wooden floor, she pushed against Seton, bowing her back, and poking a boney elbow into his side. He almost lost hold of her until Sheepshearer motioned for Marley, who up until now had remained uninvolved in the shadows, to come forth and help restrain her.

Once subdued, the woman stiffened her body, straight as a branding rod. There was no pleading, no entreating for mercy, nor cry of innocence. She simply stood, looking straight ahead. The darkness that had overshadowed her face earlier seemed to have settled into a permanent mien.

"Marley, please find something else for your maidservant to do," Sheepshearer drawled as he stropped the blade on a piece of leather.

Marley, surprised by the order, shot a glance to the corner of the room, where yet another figure hid in the shadows, unnoticed.

She moved forward into the light, like a specter haunting a kirkyard. "Uncle, I want to stay. Why must I leave?"

"Well, now, child, if Master Sheepshearer thinks it best that ye go, then ye must." The pet name with which he addressed her was fitting for her short stature, but she was not a child. Her voice and figure testified to a maturity that her height did not.

"What do you intend to do to this poor woman? I have seen no evidence that she is a witch. Why torment her so? Can ye not see this man has abused her?"

At her words, Seton let out a low growl and Sheepshearer raised a brow and turned to her. "And are ye so well versed in witchcraft that ye can recognize a witch when ye see one, lass?"

His words were like a dagger, striking hot and fast. Or at least, they should have been. Instead, a fire ignited in the young woman's eyes, and she took another step forward.

"Sir, I do not know what ye are implying."

"Ailsa, please. Be a good girl and go fetch your mother home," Marley said nervously. "Give my regards to the McMurrays when ye see them." He took her by the arm and led her toward the door, reaching for a cloak that hung on the wall and shoving it toward her.

I didn't know who this glorious creature was, but she was enchanting. Perhaps *she* was a witch. Her amber eyes burned with what she perceived to be injustice. Her dark hair appeared to be lit with flame as well, for in the candlelight the copper locks that fell around her face shone brightly. Her passion burned on her cheeks, giving her an attractive, *well-worked* appearance. She may have been small, I dare say she would have been lucky if the top of her head reached my shoulders, but she was fierce. And needless to say, more than a little reckless.

She was already gone, and Sheepshearer ready to start his task by the time I came to my senses. Without a word, the witch pricker proceeded to hack at the woman's hair. Something seemed to break within her and she slouched, putting all of her weight in the hands of the two men that restrained her. When it was short enough, he then began to scrape the hair from her head until all that was left was stubble. The dirty blonde locks were now scattered about the floor.

When he was finished, I almost pitied Seton. Now he had nothing with which to jerk the woman around. *The prig.*

Next, Sheepshearer pulled a long, thin needle out of his pouch. With her hair removed the bruised skin lay exposed and damning.

"Now, herein lies the mystery of it all," he began dramatically. Without further word, he poked the needle into the woman's neck. She blinked twice, but no other reaction was notable. He removed the needle and tried again from another angle. There was still no reaction. He straightened, rubbing his chin in thought. Stepping back to the table, he explained, "When a person is pricked with the point of the needle, there will be one of two reactions. Either the subject will feel the pain of the prick and cry out, or they will feel nothing, or at least, not enough to solicit a cry. If the accused cries out, they are capable of feeling human pains and discomforts, and therefore must not be a witch."

I glanced at James again. He looked skeptical.

"So, you're saying that because the lass failed to cry out in pain, you are sure she is a witch? That simple?" I asked.

Sheepshearer looked perturbed. "The ways of the Lord are mysterious, my dear man. You, as the son of a man of the cloth, should recognize that."

"But I do not recall any sacred text that addresses how to go about finding a witch. Where did you come up with this method?"

Agitated now, his voice rose. "Master Broune, these ways are developed over centuries of experiment and research. When there is a proven way that works, we use it."

James finally spoke up. "Master Sheepshearer, I believe what my good friend here is trying to ask is against what have these methods been examined? Our kirk fathers have no scripture from which to pull information. It simply doesn't exist. Are you a student of the sacred texts, Master Sheepshearer?"

The man blinked in the face of this royal opposition, then replied, "I am just as much a student as the next man, I suppose."

James nodded, lost in thought. Finally, he said, "This is another reason why I say we need a standard text that men can study in their own language in order to know the illuminating scriptures. Have I not said so, William?"

"Aye, you have said so, Your Grace. I do believe it is something you should look into."

"Your Grace, Master Broune." Sheepshearer looked between the two of us anxiously. "Can we get back to the matter at hand? The witch?"

"Aye, but I fail to see how this woman's late-night excursions have anything to do with the Queen's voyage to Scotland," James said. "Ask her what she knows about that."

Sheepshearer nodded and picked up his bag of tricks. He tucked the needle back into his leather pouch and perused the instruments once more. I could only imagine what tool he would choose next, and I shivered at the thought.

~2~

December 1590

Ailsa

Never in all my days, no matter how short those may be, have I seen evil manifested as I did in Bailiff Seton.

I wrapped my cloak about my shoulders as I left the house, but the stifling heat inside that room had me gasping as soon as the brisk night air hit my face. I opened my cloak, letting the frosty air nip at my neck and ears. I sucked in the cold air in huge gulps, hoping that I wasn't cursed with the croupe in the days to come because of my negligence.

I looked up at the star-kissed sky. A faint sliver of moon hung suspended on the darkened canopy, a glowing aura of light leaking out of the orb that was hidden by shadow. Even in the blackest of night, there shone a light, a sliver of hope that the desperately wicked heart of man could find redemption. But what of those who claimed to already be in the light? What of those who thought they meted out justice in the name of all that was holy, yet they did it in the unholiest of manners? Who could hide from that scorching light?

The trickle of tears running down both cheeks brought a shiver to my bones, and it was then that I pulled the cloak tighter about me. I too noticed my hands were shaking, but it wasn't from the cold.

I picked my way along the muddy street until I reached Bess's home on Grey's Close, where I had left Mother a few hours before. I knocked lightly and waited for a reply. Within seconds the door flung open, and Bess, my childhood friend, stood smiling wickedly at me.

"Well, did the big, strong bailiff show ye how powerful he can really be?" Her words teased until she saw the tears glistening on my face and pulled me into the warmth of her home. "What has happened?"

I didn't speak at first, only removed my cloak and handed it to her as she held out her hand. She hung it up then took my hand, pulling me into the privacy of the little room she had shared with her older sisters until they had all married and moved away. She now lived in this home above her father's shop with only her aging mother and father, the last child to leave the nest.

The wooden planks creaked as we moved to her room, and I stopped to glance toward the hearth. "How is Mother?"

"She's all right. There have been no bouts of confusion. She took tea with my mother earlier, and now they are sitting quietly, stitching a new tapestry."

"Oh," I said with curiosity. "She hasn't done any stitching in a while."

"Mother has received an order from a Lady in Aberdeenshire and is anxious to complete it before Hogmanay. And your mother stitches so beautifully. She is a great help." Bess picked up a stack of linens from her bed and dropped them on a small table that sat two steps across the room. Even now, I was still amazed that she had managed to share this small room with three other sisters before they had all moved away. The bed, the largest piece of furniture in the room, took up most of the space, leaving room for only the table and a wash basin. Throwing herself down on the now too-large bed, she tucked her knees up under her chin and stared at me. "Well?"

I curled up on the bed beside her in the same position, dropping my head to my knees.

"I cannot believe Uncle Rupert wants me to marry that man." I shook my head. "Bess, he is the devil personified."

Bess furrowed her brow. "I thought he was seeking out those who had sold themselves to the devil. Is he a hypocrite?"

I did not lift my head to look at her, but instead, I spoke into my knees. "I don't know what he is, but I can tell you one thing. I am not going to marry him."

"Cannot your uncle make ye?"

"I don't think so." I lifted my head to look at her. "He tries to throw his weight around, as if he were the head of our family now that Father is gone. But Mother said she never let her brother boss her around before, and she isn't about to start now."

Silence perched between us as the unasked question hung in the air. I cringed when Bess finally put words to our thoughts. "What if something happens to your mother?"

I squeezed my eyes shut, willing the tears not to come. Flattening my lips into a straight line, I finally said, "I don't know." I looked at Bess again and saw such compassion on her countenance that the tears threatened to fall anyway. "Oh, Bess." The dam broke, and my tears finally escaped my eyes. My voice lost its bravado, and with barely a whisper's strength, I said, "She's getting worse."

Bess threw an arm around my shoulder and pulled me to her. "What does the physicker say?" She pulled a clean cloth from her sleeve then handed it to me.

"He says her mind is old." I took the cloth from Bess and wiped my eyes. "But I think there is more to it than that. It's more than just her forgetfulness. I've seen her become belligerent over the silliest of things. She explodes in a tantrum, then minutes later, acts as if nothing happened."

We sat in silence for a moment before Bess spoke again. "Perhaps it would be a blessing to have someone to care for ye and help ye look after your mother."

I jerked my head to her, spearing her with a traitorous look. "I hope ye are not referring to Bailiff David Seton."

She shifted her eyes away from me, having the good sense to at least *look* repentant.

"I admit, Mother's care is taxing. And with Nick away in London now, the responsibility falls on me alone. But if Seton's lewd words and lecherous stares during supper last night weren't bad enough, what I saw this evening confirmed that which I already knew. The man is a blackguard with a heart as wicked as the witches he claims to hunt. The witch pricker may not have wanted me present to see his deeds, but my uncle and Seton did not seem to be bothered by my presence. They did not send me away before Seton began his interrogation. I got a glimpse of the man that my uncle brought into his home and dined with the day before. I knew him to be an odious man, but the depths of the blackness of his soul had not been made manifest to me until Geillis' interrogation began. No, he would not make a loving husband, nor a good caretaker for my mother."

I spared Bess the details of how Seton had extracted the young woman's confession before the king had arrived. Her screams when he applied the thumbscrews to wring out her admittance still echoed in my ears. But even I did not know how her clothes had come to be torn and missing. Some things had happened before I had arrived, and I was sure the blame fell entirely on Seton.

"I met the king tonight," I said, changing the subject.

Bess's eyes widened as she drew in a breath. "Ye did?"

"Well, he wasn't introduced to me personally, but he came with the witch pricker to observe the interrogation. He and another one of his men. I think the man might be a magistrate. He asked a lot of questions." The visage of the young, dark-haired man who had come with the king invaded my thoughts, and I could still see his perceptive blue eyes flash as he hounded the bailiff with questions.

"What was it like? To be in the king's presence?"

This was where Bess and I ceased to be kindred spirits. Where she was fascinated with the pomp and pageantry of court life, I disdained it.

"He is very aloof." I reached over and picked up the small hornbook I had loaned to Bess the week before. I was teaching her to read, and this was the tool my father had used when he taught me.

"Well, he is the king," Bess defended. I eyed her suspiciously. For a secret papist, she sure had an obsession with the Protestant king and queen.

"It isn't as if I expected him to acknowledge me." I ran my hand over the thin sheet of horn that covered the letters of the alphabet and the Lord's Prayer, smoothing the aged and darkened layer that protected the words. I began smacking the wooden board that the page was glued on against my left hand, while I thought about the king. "But I have heard he is a just sovereign. I guess I expected him to have a little compassion for the lass whom Seton had obviously abused."

"Seton abused the witch?" Bess leaned over and removed the hornbook from my hand, apparently annoyed by the sound.

"She's not a witch!" I immediately regretted my harsh words and stole a glance at my friend. I tried to amend my words, "I mean, it has not been proven." Bess looked at me but did not speak. I felt the need to explain. "Geillis Duncan said nothing that could be construed as devilish. She merely helps her neighbors with tinctures and poultices and the like, and her master was irritated at her that she left his house at night to do so. She said he made advances on her, and she refused him. I can believe that, for I know the things he said to me." When Bess still didn't say anything, I entreated her. "Do ye want to know what I think?"

"I think ye are going to tell me what ye think." Bess smiled.

"I think Seton tried to get Geillis to do something she didn't want to do and when she refused, his pride was hurt, and now he is retaliating. That's what I think."

The pallor on Bess's face spoke volumes, but she swallowed before speaking. "That is a dangerous opinion to have, Ailsa. David Seton is a powerful man. His position as Deputy Bailiff makes him almost untouchable. I would keep those thoughts to myself if I were ye."

She was right but I did not voice my agreement. Instead, I turned my attention to a flattened pillow at the head of her bed and fluffed it.

Bess quickly moved on to another subject. While she began to prattle on about a new dress her father had purchased for her, a little seed of a thought began to germinate in my mind. I wondered whether

I should share with her the idea that had suddenly sprung into my head. But Bess left her spot on the bed to retrieve her gown.

It was made of a dark green velvet with tiny roses embroidered in gold thread on the sleeves and around the neckline. She held it up to her shoulders for me to see.

"It's lovely." I forced a smile and tried to look interested.

She dropped the dress. "What's the matter? I know that look."

I feigned innocence. "What do ye mean?"

"Ye want to say something, but ye are violently fighting the urge. Is it the dress?"

I crawled off the bed and took the two steps required to reach her. Picking up the dress, I held it up to her again. "It's lovely, truly."

"Then what is on your mind? It's not like ye to hold your tongue when ye have something to say."

I chuckled. She knew me well.

"What if I were to tell ye that I have an idea?"

"About what? How to alter the dress?" She looked down at the gown and ran a hand over the soft fabric.

"Nay, about Geillis Duncan and her predicament."

A dark look covered Bess's face. "Ailsa, this isn't your problem to solve."

"I can't stand by and watch these monsters torment innocent young women. It's not right."

Bess laid her gown on the edge of the bed and looked at me, the corners of her mouth pulling into a sorrowful curve. The sliver of moon that I had admired earlier shown dimly through her window, casting dark shadows across the delicate features of her face. "Ye have to trust the king and his process. He is a wise sovereign. All of Scotland knows him to be a man of wisdom and justice. He will do the right thing."

"If the king feels she had anything to do with the storms that prevented his queen from making her journey here, he will see her punished." I held her gaze. "Geillis is a young woman with no one to protect her from men such as Seton. I know not whether he seeks retribution or promotion, but I have no doubt that he will stop at nothing until he gets it." I paused and considered my next words. "If that were me getting the bones of my fingers crushed and having my head bound and wrenched, would ye stand up for me?"

Bess flinched at my words. "Don't say such things," she whispered, her voice catching.

I caught her by both arms and pulled her closer to me. "Bess, it could happen to me. I have no father to protect me from such men, and if Uncle Rupert has his heart set upon me marrying the bailiff, how long could I refuse before he seeks retribution from me as well? I must do the right thing. I must try to help Geillis Duncan."

"What are ye planning?" There was fear in her voice.

I paused briefly and contemplated if I should say the next words. Knowing I could trust my best friend, I said, "I need to find a way to help her escape."

~3~

December 1590

William

"Here's to the successful inquisition of the witch from North Berwick!" Thomas Hamilton, one of the king's advisors, lifted his cup in the air, and the other men toasted his pronouncement.

The king and those of us who made up his closest companions sat at supper in his private chambers. The winter wind blew outside, rattling the windows and forcing frigid air through the cracks around the panes. A fire crackled in the hearth, warming the room, and driving away the gloom that typically haunted these old, drafty castles. Yet, I couldn't shake the chill that had settled on me since visiting Marley's warehouse earlier in the evening.

I stiffened at Hamilton's assessment of the interrogation. "I do not think it is something to celebrate, Hamilton. I do not care for Master Sheepshearer's methods of obtaining information." As an afterthought, I added, "Nor Seton's." I took a sip of my wine but did not salute with the others.

The king agreed. "Aye. We still do not have enough information about her involvement with Anne's voyage from Denmark, nor our subsequent mishaps at sea when I joined her in Norway." He brought his cup to his lips then paused and raised a finger. "But I am convinced that it was witches that had a hand in the storms that prevented the queen from reaching me and also causing our delay in returning to

18

Scotland."

"Still, you did get a confession of several names out of her, did you not?" said the Keeper of the Privy Seal, Walter Stewart. The lord, better known amongst his friends as Blantyre, entered late to the conversation as he seated himself at the table and perused the fare with a judgmental eye.

James took a bite of pheasant, the juice dripping down his chin and onto his doublet. I imagined Queen Anne chiding him for his lack of table manners had she been here, for she had already fallen into the role of nagging wife rather nicely. Still chewing his bite, he said, "I too am a little skeptical of Sheepshearer's methods, but if I can discover the root of this melee, it will be worth it."

Blantyre picked at a piece of boiled egg as I chose a honeyed roll and began to slather butter on top of it. I continued, "Don't you think it was odd that her clothes were torn and bloody before we arrived? What did Seton do to her exactly? Besides the pilliwinks, that is. And do you believe her claims of his advances?"

The king did not answer straight away. Instead, he took a long drag from his cup before dropping it onto the tabletop with a *thud*. Swiping the back of his hand across his mouth, he said, "I think that Seton had to use whatever means he saw fit to get the information from her that he sought."

I eyed him, waiting for him to address the more pressing of my two questions. When he did not continue, I prompted, "And her accusations?"

"That is the only defense a woman of her character has," tossed Blantyre.

I shot him a withering look. "A woman of her character? How do you know what sort of character she has?"

"William, don't get your codpiece in a bunch. Blantyre has a point," James chastised. "A woman's only defense in situations like this, time and time again, is to toss accusations back at her accuser. In most cases they come to naught." James selected a spiced pair and forked it with the enthusiasm of a hound on a fox.

"Aye," agreed Hamilton. "Did you see any evidence of her accusations on her person?"

I looked at him as if he had grown another nose on his face. "See any evidence? Other than the fact that half of her clothing was missing, her body was partially exposed, and there was blood all over what little clothing remained? What other kind of evidence is it you suppose I am to witness?"

Hamilton opened his mouth to reply, then abruptly closed it, looking very much like a fish out of water. He bowed his head to me in acquiescence.

"Ever the champion of the oppressed, William," Blantyre laughed. "In that you remind me of your father. But only in that."

The others laughed at Blantyre's gibe, and even I smiled at his jest.

"Ah, do not harass my friend on account of his sense of justice. It is an admirable quality and one I hope to emulate," James defended. "But as far as that being the only quality he got from his father, I'm afraid I'd have to agree."

"Hear, hear!" the other men raised their cups once more and drank to my debauchery.

"I'll have you know that I picked up several qualities from my saintly father." I took another swig of my wine.

"Well, it certainly wasn't his chastity!" This time all three men, which included the king, were moved to tears with Blantyre's joke. Hamilton pounded the table, and Blantyre gleamed at his own wit. I just shook my head and let them laugh. For that was a fact I could not deny.

"Speaking of chastity," began the king. "A little birdie told me that there is a certain lady-in-waiting in the queen's court that has her eye set upon you, William. She is of noble blood and may be persuaded to take you on, should she find you agreeable."

"Agreeable?" laughed Hamilton. "Do you mean like a lap dog or a riding pony? Sounds promising."

"You are just jealous because you and I are in the same boat, my friend. Without a good marriage, we will continue to have to slave for every shilling that comes into our hands," I goaded.

"And who is this lovely poppet that has her eye on our dear William?" Hamilton questioned.

"Ah, he did not say she was lovely, only chaste, and rich. Two out of three isn't bad, aye William?" Blantyre pounded me on the back in encouragement. He was on a roll tonight. Perhaps it was time to cut off his wine.

"She is lovely, I suppose," James reasoned. "That is, if you can get past the frivolity and feather-brained conversations. Anne assured me that she is considered a real catch."

"Your wife assured you, Your Grace? You cannot tell for yourself?" Blantyre teased.

"He only has eyes for Her Majesty. They are newly-wed. Give him time," Hamilton defended.

Now that the tables were turned, and the jesting was targeted at the king and not me, James appeared a little uncomfortable. It was no secret that he never had much interest in women until it came time to marry. Perhaps it was a result of him being raised in a castle full of men without a mother or some other member of the fairer sex to dote on him. Still, James and his new bride appeared happy enough.

"All right, out with it," I interjected. "Who is this chaste maiden that I am to be introduced to?"

"Her name is Lady Beatrix Ruthven."

My fork suspended just before reaching my mouth. *Oh, I knew Beatrix.*

Hamilton let out a groan. "Ah, the Ruthven sisters. What heavenly blessings. You could do with either of the Ruthven sisters, for her sister, Barbara, is equally as lovely." He leaned back in his seat, draping an arm haphazardly across the back of his chair. His eyes blazed with the thought of the two beauties.

"Ruthven, as in the daughter of William Ruthven, the Earl of Gowrie executed for treason years ago?" Blantyre asked, sobering.

"Ruthven as in the sister of the current Earl of Gowrie, John Ruthven. So, aye, same family," James confirmed.

Blantyre said no more about the suggestion, but I noted his apparent dislike of James's choice of bride for me. I made a mental note to ask him about it later. Instead, I innocently asked, "Is that the blonde beauty that always wears the little baubles nestled in her hair?"

"You should have never mentioned Lady Ruthven in front of Thomas Hamilton." I smirked as I handed James a cup of wine. We were alone now, for the others had finally gone to their chambers. "I do believe Hamilton is in love with her. Perhaps you should have appointed her for him."

"Pish," he replied, taking a sip of the wine before setting the cup down and taking up a book that lay close by. "He likes anything dressed in a skirt and corset. Besides, I have someone else in mind for him."

My brow shot up involuntarily. "You do? Whom?"

He waved my question aside with a brush of his hand. "We can talk about that later. Right now, I want to discuss what happened tonight at Marley's."

I settled into a chair across from him, relieved to finally be able to speak about what we had witnessed without the joking banter of the others.

I wish we hadn't.

"William, do you even believe in a thing such as witches?"

I ran a nervous hand through my hair. It was true; I did not hold the same religious convictions that my father did, but I still considered myself a man of conviction nonetheless. But what the king was asking went beyond conviction. It flew in the face of all that was reasonable and scientific. Did I believe that unwise souls could devote themselves to the Prince of Darkness as much as a more intelligent soul would devote themselves to the Prince of Peace? I suppose. But to harness the power of the devil and wield his authority as the prince of this world, to work their own sinister deeds, was something of which I wasn't sure.

I chose my words carefully. "Your Grace—"

"No, no," he interrupted, holding up his hand in protest. "Do not address me as just another one of my courtiers. We have been friends since we were bawdy lads. Speak to me plainly as the close friend of fifteen years that ye are."

"James," I began again. "It may be so that a wayward soul may turn from their Lord and Savior and serve the god of this world. But to have the capabilities to brandish the power of Satan to use for their own interests? Is that even possible?"

James rubbed his hand over his chin, deep in thought. "I have asked myself that same question."

"To sell one's soul to the devil is a serious offense. But 'tis not against civil law. What we are talking about here is using the power of the devil to work evil against our fellow man. If that is possible, then that is a problem."

The king stood again, his awkward gait carrying him across the room. We were staying in Edinburgh Castle tonight before heading back to Stirling in the morning. He leaned an arm on the mantle of the massive hearth, resting his head thereon while poking the fire with an iron rod. James stood like that for a long spell until he finally straightened once more. This business with the witches troubled him deeply, but I didn't speak. Instead, I watched him and waited.

"It is a problem, and I want to get to the bottom of it." He paused for another moment before turning toward me. The long shadows cast by the hearth elongated his face even more, giving him an almost jester-like expression. "Do you remember the first time I met you?"

Surprised by the abrupt change in topic, I ran a hand over the short hairs at the nape of my neck as I thought about our first meeting. "Aye, how could I forget?" I grinned involuntarily, thinking about our introduction.

"I had taken a tumble from my pony and lay sprawled upon the grass like a spilt bundle of straw," he said with a laugh.

I chuckled at the memory too. It was my first day at court. Father said it had been the wish of the deposed queen that I be raised like a brother to her son, for she and my father had been close friends also when they were children. I had not even been formally introduced to the young king when I saw him fall from his pony in the courtyard of this very castle. Two older boys had stood nearby, laughing at the sight of young James, flailing his legs in an effort to sit upright. The taller of the two, a rotund boy with red, pudgy cheeks, and sausages for fingers, reached a puffy hand out to the king as if he intended to assist him in his recovery. But the young king swatted his hand away and cried that he wanted nothing to do with him and did not need his assistance. I had watched as the other boy, about the same height as James, hovered over the king, taunting him, and asking him to whom was he going to go cry. "You've no mother. Who will listen to your lamentations?"

"Those boys were boors," I said. "All you needed to do was wave a finger, and their families could have been exiled. I, for one, would not have minded."

James smiled, turning back to the hearth, and poking it once more. "What made you set your book aside and come to my defense?"

"I myself had no mother, as you know. She died when I was only a few hours old. I had endured many a gibe about my motherless state, and the thought of a king enduring such suffering was more than I was willing to bear. I took it personal."

"I was really hoping you would pummel that boy." James laughed with dry humor. "Both boys were older than us, but you were so much taller than they. When they turned their taunts on you, I feared for your safety. But you held your own rather well. That is until Master Buchanan came upon us."

I shivered at the mention of our old tutor's name. Taking a sip of my wine, I said, "Master Buchanan may have been harsh, but he saved me from making a grave mistake. I would have been severely punished for attacking an earl, no matter how young we were. I don't know what came over me. I don't like to fight."

"It was your thirst for justice," James interjected excitedly. "That is what I have always admired and respected about you, William. You could not stand by and allow someone, in this case *me*, to be wronged. And at the risk of bodily harm, you stepped in, going against your own nature, to right the wrong."

I nodded, thinking about his words. It was true. And although I had always preferred to talk my way out of conflict, I could not stand idly by while someone suffered injustice. That was another quality I had gotten from my father.

"This was a nice jaunt down memory lane, Your Grace. But why do I get the distinct feeling there is a reason you brought up our first meeting?"

The seriousness in his drooping eyes told me what he was about to say was no jest. "I want you to be my inquisitor in these matters."

"Inquisitor?" I choked, practically spitting out the sip of wine I had just taken. "In these witch inquiries?" I shook my head. "I am not qualified. I'm not even sure Sheepshearer is qualified."

"He's not. And his methods are, shall we say, barbaric. But I'm not asking you to be a witch pricker. I just want you to interrogate. Use your knowledge of the law, evaluate whether those who are being brought in for questioning have broken any laws. Then, persuade them to confess. If a confession cannot be obtained through reasonable means, then Sheepshearer, or his apprentice, can do their work."

"Sheepshearer has an apprentice?" I asked, surprised.

"Aye, David Seton will train under him and see to the work in North Berwick. I will determine from there if more men need to be trained."

"David Seton is a barbarian!" At this news I rose to my feet and found myself standing in front of the king before my senses could advise me otherwise.

"I found him to be a practical man, if not a little overzealous. His enthusiasm could stand to be curtailed, but I think he will do a fine job."

I shook my head at the king's pronouncement but dared not dissent. Of all the men in Scotland, I found the king to be one of the most sensible. He was educated, and reasonable, choosing sides based on facts and reason, more so than congruent views. But this decision astonished me, and I could not see from whence it came. This issue with the witches must be driving him mad.

"Your Grace, I am most satisfied with my position as an advocate. I have no wish to entangle myself with this witchcraft scheme. I will take on more of your financial affairs if you wish." He was walking away from me now, and I found myself talking faster in an effort to keep up with him.

He stopped at the door of the privy chamber and turned abruptly toward me. I could feel an icy chill flood my veins as his cold blue eyes fell on me. I had seen that look before, just not usually directed at me.

"William, I think you have misunderstood me. Do let me clarify. I am not asking you to be my inquisitor. I am commanding it. You are the best man for the job."

"But Your Grace—"

"I have a mind to make you Chancellor." His eyes softened, and he patted my cheek with his cold, skeletal hand. "It is the highest office with which I can appoint you since you are not a peer. Nothing would make me happier, my dear friend. But the Lords will want some proof of your worth. This should do the trick."

Chancellor? To be the head of all judicial matters in Scotland was truly an appointment that I could have only dreamed of when I first began my legal studies at university eight years prior. I didn't know what to say. Father would be so proud. Drawing myself out of my thoughts, I opened my mouth to speak but found my tongue tied as if with a string. James took advantage of my impediment to offer his pièce de résistance.

"You give me what I want, and I shall make sure you get what you really want in return, in the form of one Lady Ruthven."

I stared at him, still unable to form the words that I wished to say. In an instant the moment had passed, and it was too late. He turned and walked stiffly out of the room, leaving me to consider my next course of action with the weight of this new responsibility pressing heavily on my chest.

~*4*~

December 1590

William

I was up before the king the next morning, having little sleep the night before. Truth be told, I was more than a little irritated with James, and I had no desire to break my fast with him. He had made several promises to me the night before, but they came with heavy attachments. And although he had presented it as if he were doing me a favor, I recognized it for what it was: an underhanded attempt to make me do his bidding. The king and I may have been childhood friends, but that didn't mean I enjoyed being manipulated.

I decided a brisk walk into town might clear my head, so I set off down the High Street, the road that led from Edinburgh Castle straight to the heart of town. I had no particular destination in mind, and I soon found myself amongst the Luckenbooths, where the venders of Edinburgh sold their wares.

A light snow flitted about and the smells of roasting meat mingled with Venetian spices and sweet Spanish wine wafted through the air as merchants called out their goods to passersby. Hogmanay would soon be upon us and that brought a deluge of townspeople into the mercat cross, anxious to make their purchases before the New Year celebrations began.

That is when I saw her. The fiery chit that had been at the witch's interrogation the day before. Marley's niece. She was dipping out a hot broth and giving sup to those who were ahungered. I caught her attention as well, for I saw her eyes open widely in apparent recognition.

I weaved my way through the crowd, squeezing past a woman haggling over a goose, and getting cut off by two boys horse-playing while their mother was occupied with a merchant. I continued my pursuit until I stood a few feet away from her as she stirred her pot.

"I don't believe we had the pleasure of being properly introduced yesterday."

The smell of cooked vegetables and herbs drifted up in little tendrils from her pot and hung suspended in the heavy winter air. I bowed politely, hoping she could forgive my forward manner. But she straightened, tossing down the ladle with which she had been stirring. She picked up a knife and began slicing away at some shriveled vegetables that lay upon a small table in front of her.

"I don't believe there was a need for introductions," she said curtly. She continued to chop away at the carrot in her hand, then tossed the small pieces into the pot that hung above the fire. Picking up a parsnip, she then began her assault on it without another word.

I would not be dissuaded. Propping my boot on a wooden beam that held the rough table up, I leaned in. "Ahh, but a proper introduction would make our meeting here now a little less awkward."

She hmphed, and I noticed the little smirk on her face as she tossed the vegetables into the pot. Lifting a bucket of water, she carefully poured the liquid into the pot as well, then threw the bucket down, dusting off her hands afterward.

"The only thing making this meeting awkward is ye, sir. Now, if ye are in need of a bite to eat, I can oblige ye, otherwise, good day."

I watched as she brushed a wisp of hair out of her eye, then turned and inspected the remaining withered vegetables in her pile. Her hair was not as dark as it had appeared the night before, but even the lack of sunlight could not dim the copper flecks in her chestnut locks. Her hair was tucked into a linen caul that hung to the nape of her neck. But the tiny, loose wisps around her face rebelled, being drawn incessantly toward those alluring, amber eyes. I opened my mouth to speak to her again, but before I could utter a word, an elderly woman wrapped in a tattered shawl shuffled up next to me.

"Good day, Goodwife Gibson. Would ye like a bowl of stew?" I watched as the young woman's face transformed into an angelic visage that the other woman returned with a toothless grin.

"Aye, I was hoping ye would be here this morning, Ailsa." She handed the young woman her vessel, a small bowl fashioned from wood. "Would ye mind putting a little extra in it? My Robert says he feels up to eating a little something this morning, and I want to make sure he gets his fill."

"Certainly, ma'am" Ailsa filled the bowl up with the steaming soup until it was almost overflowing. Turning back to the old woman she said, "Now, this is very hot, and 'tis filled to the brim. I'm sure this nice gentleman wouldn't mind carrying it home for ye, so ye don't spill any." She flashed me a sweet smile, but I noticed the gleam in her eye.

"By all means," I said, removing the bowl from her hands and looking about me. "In what direction do you live, Goodwife?"

"Just around the corner there." She pointed with a crooked finger. The smile on Ailsa's face had faded. Apparently, she did not expect me to acquiesce so readily.

I was back in less than fifteen minutes, and Ailsa's face shone with aggravation upon my return. Her ire was my motivation, and I smiled as I spoke to her again. "I think I shall like a bowl of that soup."

Another smirk lifted her lips as she stirred the pot slowly. "Aye, well, unfortunately, I don't have a bowl for ye to put it in."

"No mind, Ailsa, he can use mine." An older woman stepped up beside her, and I reasoned from the shape of her face and same fiery eyes, that she must be Ailsa's mother. Her once darkened hair was now a spindly gray and the lines of age branched out from her warm brown eyes. But it was apparent she had been just as beautiful as Ailsa in her younger years. Dusting off the piece of crockery with her earasaid, she thrust the bowl toward us.

"How fortunate that your sister has a spare," I said. The older woman giggled like a young lass, covering her mouth with a withered hand. Ailsa rolled her eyes at my flattery as she reached for the offending object. It was my turn to smirk.

Lifting her chin in defiance, she turned back to the pot.

"I'm Mistress Blackburn, Ailsa's mother," the woman said kindly. Her eyes twinkled with merriment, the remnants of my compliment still warming her.

"William Broune, my lady." I swept her a deep bow as I took her hand in mine and brushed a light kiss across the bony knuckles.

"Oh," she cooed. "My lady? Is your sight spoiled, sir? 'Tis no lady that stands before ye." She grinned and turned to look at Ailsa as she dipped the hot liquid into my borrowed bowl.

Handing the bowl back to me carefully, Ailsa said, "That will be sixpence."

I snapped my head up in surprise. "Sixpence? But you didn't charge Goodwife Gibson anything."

"That's because she cannot afford it. Ye evidently can." She looked me up and down, then lifting her face, rested her eyes boldly on mine.

"Oh, I'm sure we can forego the charge just this once dear," Mistress Blackburn tried. But Ailsa stood staring, arms crossed over her chest, waiting. I fished in my pocket for the payment and handed her the coin. She looked at it then stuck it between her teeth to test its worth.

"It's real." I pretended offense. She nodded but said nothing more as she shoved it into a pouch that hung at her side.

Mistress Blackburn moved to speak to another passerby. As far as Ailsa was concerned our business had concluded. She turned back to the bubbling pot over the fire and stirred it again. I stood, sipping at the hot liquid, and eyeing her over the rim of my bowl. She wore a plain russet gown of worsted wool with a pale green kirtle beneath. A whey-colored cloak covered her shoulders and prevented me from seeing any further details. Yet a fine chemise, embroidered with intricate blackwork around the collar, enshrouded her neck. Though simply dressed, her clothing was of fine quality, and she looked almost out of place in the workings of the mercat cross.

She dropped the ladle into the pot, and without turning to look at me, she huffed, "Are ye going to stand there all day staring at me?"

I chuckled. "How do you know I was looking at you?"

"It doesn't take the sixth sense to tell when someone is ogling ye," she retorted. She turned then and shot me a cutting glare. I choked on my broth and wiped my mouth on the back of my hand before speaking.

"I wasn't ogling you, Ailsa. I was merely observing."

Her face drained of color, and she said shakily, "How do ye know my name?"

"Goodwife Gibson. She spoke your name when she got her soup. And your mother said it too."

The color immediately returned to her cheeks. "Well, that is quite ignoble of ye to speak to me as if ye know me when I don't even know your name."

I was thoroughly enjoying this little exchange, even if it was at her expense. "My apologies. But I do believe I tried to introduce myself to you earlier before you volunteered me to carry Goodwife Gibson's bowl for her." I then winked at her.

She pressed her lips together, obviously tamping down her irritation. "Oh, for the love of..." she said under her breath, not finishing her sentence.

"As I told your mother, my name is William Broune." I bowed to her again, but she didn't reciprocate the gesture. Instead, she stood with her hands planted firmly on her hips, a wary expression on her face.

"Ye be the king's man," she stated more than asked. I took another sip of the hot liquid before answering.

"I'm not sure that I understand your meaning. I am an advisor to King James, yes. But my principal job is an advocate." I took another sip from my bowl.

She nodded her head as if it all made sense now. But what sense she was making of it, I knew not. Finally, she said, "Are ye pressing legal charges against that poor woman who was brought to my uncle's house yesterday? Will she even get a legal trial?"

At her words, my broth dribbled down my chin, and I barely missed dripping it onto my doublet. I wiped my face again and looked at her in surprise. Her disdain for me was finally becoming apparent. "What concern is that of yours? Is she a friend of yours?"

"I do not know that woman. But I can tell she has been abused. And I believe it was at the hands of that snake, Seton. I truly hope that ye will see to it that she gets justice." She quickly clamped her mouth shut, then turned away from me as if she had said too much.

"You know Seton's actions toward Mistress Duncan to be dishonorable?"

"No, but I caught him eyeing me when my uncle was not looking. And I don't mean like ye were eyeing me." She waved her hand at me. "He eyed me like a hungry wolf looks at an innocent lamb. He also said some things to me that a man ought not be saying to a lass. I very much believe he made advances on that poor woman. I'm glad he is no longer under my uncle's roof. He made me feel uncomfortable."

I hated to break the news to her that she would be seeing a lot more of Seton now that he had been appointed as Sheepshearer's apprentice. Instead, I chose another vein of thought. "What did he say to you?"

Her eyes shifted away from me uneasily, and she began to look around for something to occupy her. "'Tis not appropriate to repeat what was said to me. Especially to a stranger. I fear I have misspoken." She picked up another carrot and poised her knife to begin her assault.

Oddly, my heart sank into my gut. I couldn't explain it, but I didn't want to be a stranger to her. I wanted to protect her from Seton and any other rakes like him. Yet somehow, I got the feeling she didn't want my protection. I could tell she had already decided she didn't like me. Perhaps I ranked right up there with Seton on her list of people to dislike.

"How long have you known Seton?"

She stopped chopping and looked at me oddly. "I don't know Seton. I know *his kind.* He is the kind of man who believes that women are put here on this earth for one purpose—for him to enjoy. Any woman who opposes, or rejects him, stands a chance of becoming a victim of his overwrought, power-hungry deeds. But he has taken a very interesting approach to his punishment. Using the king's emotions, and his desire to avenge his young bride, is very clever. The witchcraft claim is genius."

"You don't believe Geillis is a witch?"

"Ho there, Mistress Blackburn!" A middle-aged man approached, and Ailsa blinked quickly, turning her eyes toward the disfigured man, his twisted back taking on an ophidian shape. He hobbled closer, and Ailsa managed a slight smile at him. "I will be having your yule log ready the day after tomorrow. Do ye need one of my boys to bring it to ye, or will Marley's wagon be available to retrieve it?"

"M-master Campbell," she paused slightly, flicking her eyes back to me before continuing. "My uncle has been very busy lately. Perhaps Angus could bring it to us?" Her voice wavered, and she shifted in apparent discomfort.

"Aye, aye, that will be nay a problem. Nay a problem a 'tall." He bowed profusely this time, taking her small hands in his gnarled ones. "Thank ye kindly for all ye do for me and my boys. I'm sure my Jean will be sending blessings down to ye from above. She always did speak kindly of ye and your mam."

"Ye are too kind, Master Campbell." Ailsa pulled her hands away gently and twisted them into the folds of her skirt. She looked to me again then back to the older man.

Understanding took light in his eyes as he glanced at me. "Oh, I apologize. I did not mean to interrupt." He bowed slightly, as much as his twisted back would allow.

"Nay, Master Campbell. Master Broune was just leaving." She

turned to me again and shot me a hopeful look.

"Actually, we were in the middle of a most interesting discussion."

"Aye, well, don't let me keep ye. Good day to ye, Mistress Blackburn. Sir." He nodded to include me. Then the older man turned away and shuffled off to another destination.

Ailsa turned toward me abruptly. "Master Broune, about the yule log, the Campbells have been long time family friends. When Master Campbell's back began to twist like an ancient tree trunk, we have tried to help the family as much as we can. He refuses charity but allows us to buy a yule log from him each December. I know the kirk is opposed to the burning of the yule log—"

"Ailsa, please don't worry yourself. I won't tell the king, nor the kirk." Relief flashed in her eyes, and a feeling of satisfaction welled up within me. "My father is a man of the cloth." She let out a little gasp, but I held up my hands to sooth her worries. "Do not fear. What I meant to say is my father is a man of the cloth, but even he enjoys the age-old traditions of Christmas and burning the yule log." Leaning into her a little closer, I whispered, "He was very fond of our former Catholic queen and didn't always follow the kirk's rules when they abolished the celebration of Christmas. When I was a child, we always celebrated the mass, even though he was a converted Protestant. It is one of the few rules that my pious father ever broke."

She smiled insecurely, and I noted the lines of tension on her face had begun to ease. I hoped that sharing this private little secret would earn me some trust with her.

"Aye, 'tis hard to break old habits, I suppose. But I don't remember a time when Christmas celebrations were permitted."

"Nor do I. I am not that old." I grinned at her, and this time her smile seemed genuine.

I would have liked to continue our discussion of Geillis Duncan, but we were suddenly converged upon by several people who had come to get sustenance from Ailsa's pot. The opportunity for more conversation was gone. That was unfortunate. For I sensed there was something she wasn't telling me and not just the words that Seton had spoken to her. She appeared fearful of something, or someone, and I was determined to get to the bottom of it. Perhaps I could make my excuses to the king and find a reason to stay in Edinburgh a little while longer.

~5~

December 1590

Ailsa

"I don't care what ye say. I like him."

Mother had been lecturing me, off and on all day after Sir William had left us. I rolled my eyes as she yet again reiterated to me how much she liked the young man that had stopped to chat with me that morning.

"When one with honeyed words but evil mind persuades the mob, great woes befall the state," I cooed over my shoulder as I bent to pick up our cat, Sadie, who had greeted us at the door.

"What?" Mother crinkled her brow at me in confusion as she continued to arrange the wood in the hearth in preparation to light the fire.

"Euripides, Mother," I explained. "He recognized that men with evil intentions use sweet words to deceive many and bring down great nations."

"Oh poo," she responded, waving my words away with her hand. "You and your father's philosophical ramblings." She shook her head as she picked up a rug to beat the dirt from it.

I rubbed my cheek against Sadie's smokey gray fur as I watched Mother flit about the room.

"That man did not just stop to chat. He wants something, and we must be very careful as to what we say or do around him." I set Sadie

37

down and took the rug from my mother's hands. Picking up the beating rod, I stepped outside to pound the dirt from the rug. I watched as gray specks fell from the woven carpet and sprinkled onto the white snow below. *Just like the man's intensions, filthy specks dirtying an otherwise beautiful vessel*, I mused.

He was beautiful, I'd give him that. And he knew it too. Only men who possessed a certain aura of confidence would dare to wink at a lass he didn't even know. I could feel my cheeks warming again at just the thought. Yet, dark, wavy hair with a lock that fell over a broad forehead in a rather unruly fashion. The slight indentation in his chin gave him a mature, serious air, but his bright blue eyes lined with dark lashes hinted that he probably got whatever he wanted. And from the few times I had seen him, he appeared to be impeccably dressed. Today, his coat covered his apparel, but the ruff of his collar was a pristine white that contrasted starkly against the dark blue velvet of his overcoat. His chain of office hung heavy about his neck, the ample golden links glinting boldly in the morning sun. And that little lock of hair seemed to hang there to remind me that he wasn't as put together as he would like everyone to think. I smirked at the thought, imagining him to be one of those people to have all his flotsam and jetsam shoved under his bed in secret, while on the outside looking so perfectly put together.

"Are ye beating a confession out of the thing?" Mother's words startled me out of my daydreaming, and I looked down at the rug still in my hand. "I think ye've got it all." She stood eyeing me as I ducked back into our house: a small, two-story stone structure that sat a short distance from St Giles Kirk.

I placed the rug back down on the floor and watched Sadie pounce on a stray thread as if it were the tail of a mouse. She batted at it for several minutes until she realized it was no longer a threat then curled up on top of it. I surveyed the small living quarters that we had managed for ourselves since Father had died. He had left a small dowry for me, an inheritance for my brother Nick, who now lived in England, and a beautiful home that sat on the outskirts of Edinburgh with a decent income for Mother. But she and I had decided to sell the house and move into this smaller one to be closer to town and have a little extra to help others who were more in need than we were.

"I've been around the mill a time or two, Ailsa. I know it's hard for ye to imagine this old crow knowing anything about men, but I do know when a man is just blowing hot air." She picked the conversation up right where we left off, even though I had hoped it was finished.

"You're not an old crow," I said gently, moving to her side and brushing a strand of hair out of her face. "But this isn't just any man. He's a king's man, and he is involved very heavily in this witch business that has come out of North Berwick. So, we must be careful."

Mother let her eyes fall closed as she stood silent for a moment. "I understand. I suppose ye are thinking of my blunder. I am sorry about that." Mother had already let it slip to a neighbor that I was sneaking food to the prisoners at the tolbooth.

I rubbed my hand over hers. "I know ye are. We both are. And I know ye couldn't help it. It's just that—" I couldn't finish the thought. One wrong word, one hateful person hearing that wrong word, could send her—us—to the tolbooth, and I wouldn't allow myself to think about that. Patting her hand, I pulled her toward the small table that stood in the corner of the room. "Come, let us prepare ourselves some supper now that the poor of Edinburgh have had their bellies filled."

She wiped at her eyes with the corner of her apron, even though I saw no tears there. Mother cried a lot without tears lately, and I watched her as she moved to pull a small black pot off the shelf. "I'll fetch some water," she began.

"Oh no, ye don't." I protested. "It's too slippery out there. I don't want ye falling. I'll fetch the water while ye start chopping vegetables."

"I'm a little tired tonight. Do ye think we could just have some parritch? Goodwife Douglas gave me some jam today at the mercat cross. Perhaps we could make some bannocks to go with it."

Parritch for dinner did not sound appetizing, but I smiled and nodded to her before ducking out the door with our bucket. Mother seemed to grow tired a lot easier these days, and I feared it had to do with the confusion she had been experiencing of late.

The temperature had dropped, making all the slushy snow created by the tramping of feet earlier in the day harden into a slippery mound of ice. It took a little longer to retrieve the water, and I was happy to retreat into the warmth of our little house. But as I hulled the bucket in to sit it on the table, Mother's still figure hovering over the supper preparations halted me. There on the table sat a parsnip half cut and covered in blood.

"Mama!" I dropped the bucket of water and rushed to her side. "What happened?" Mother stood, staring down at her slivered finger, blood dripping from the gaping wound. "Ye are hurt! Come away from the table into the light of the fire, so I can see what ye have done."

"I am sorry," she lamented, following me listlessly across the room. I grabbed a piece of cloth to stay the bleeding. "I am sorry," she said again.

"Shh." I soothed, kissing her on the forehead and dabbing at her finger until the blood seemed to slow. I sat her in a chair by the fire. "Mother, what were ye doing? I thought we were going to have parritch tonight for supper. Ye were cutting parsnips."

"Was I?" She looked up into nothingness as if trying to remember what she had been doing. I stifled a cry that fought to tear from my throat.

Mother indeed was tired, for she fell asleep in her chair by the fire after supper as she read her book of hours. I lifted the brown, velvet-covered book from her lap, closing it and placing it back in the trunk that she kept it hidden in. It had been a gift to her from my father upon their wedding day. I smiled every time I heard them tell their story. Mother had been a young woman about to take her vows when she met Father on his way to university. To hear him tell it, he had stolen her heart, and she never gave her vows another thought. According to her, she refused him twice and only gave in a third time because he promised her a ride on his pony.

Not wanting to disturb her, I wrapped her shawl about her shoulders and laid a blanket on her lap. I straightened, stretching my back muscles, and rubbing a hand over my tired eyes. The short December days made me sleepy too, but there was too much to do before considering sleep just yet.

I began plucking the herbs from where they hung above the fireplace when there was a soft knock at the door. Glancing to Mother to gauge her condition, I tip-toed quietly to the door. Our neighbor stood before me, wringing her hands, and stamping her feet in an effort to warm herself.

"Janet, do come in." I opened the door to allow her entry, and she stepped warily inside. "Is something amiss?"

Janet moved slowly into our house, the anxious look on her face easing. That is, until her eyes fell on my mother. Her back stiffened, and her face fell blank. "Perhaps I should not bother ye. I do not mean to be a pest."

Looking to my mother who still slept peacefully, head lulling to the side, I whispered, "Ye are not a pest. Mother is simply sleeping. She was very tired after our day at the mercat cross."

Janet nodded but still did not move further into the room. Keeping a watchful eye on Mother, she finally said, "It's my Robert. His stomach ails him again. This is the third day in a row he has complained of pain."

I bit my lip in concentration, reviewing in my mind what I had available that I could give her for her child's pain. Sweeping across the room, I picked up a few leaves and wrapped them in soft cloth. *"Salvia officinalis."* I let the Latin words quietly roll off my tongue. I enjoyed the sound of the foreign words on my lips. They had become like a second language to me over my years of study.

"Here is some sage. Boil it in water and have Robert drink it every four hours. I'm sorry I do not have any fennel to give ye. I am starting preparations on the seeds. We didn't even have anything to sell at market today, our supplies have been depleted."

Janet took the cloth from my hand and bowed slightly. "Bless ye, Mistress Blackburn."

"Please, call me Ailsa, I am not much younger than ye." I smiled at her, and she handed me a coin for the herb.

Just then Mother stirred as if a sleeping giant had been awakened.

"George, who's there?" She slurred, trying to unwrap herself from the blanket that I had lain on her lap. Janet took a step back, looking like a rabbit about to fall into a snare. I noted her fear, then looked to Mother in concern.

"Do not fret, Janet. Mother gets confused sometimes when she has been awakened suddenly. She is speaking of my father."

The woman looked at me then back to Mother again, and it was then that I noticed it wasn't fear on her face, but distrust.

"Forgive me Mistress Blackburn, but I have taken up too much of your time. Thank ye kindly for the herbs. Have a good evening." And with that she swept out of the house, the door slamming in conclusion.

I looked to Mother again and noticed her still struggling to get herself free from her blanket. "Ailsa, who was that? Was that the pesky neighbor woman again?"

"Mother!" I scurried to assist her before she fell flat on her face in a tangle of blanket and skirts. "What has gotten into ye? Ye know that Janet is the sweetest of women. She only comes when her son is ill."

"Och, her son is always ill," Mother scoffed.

"Mama!" I chastised. "Why are ye being so cruel? This isn't like ye." I turned my head and stared into the space that Janet had occupied, replaying in my mind the scene that had just transpired. "Mama, have ye had a run around the coop with Janet?"

Mother didn't answer at first, but instead occupied herself with a loose thread on her dress. The hard set of her mouth told me she was biting her tongue.

"Mother, look at me." She rocked herself back and forth in her chair, even though the legs of the seat stood firm on the floor. "Mother?" I tried again, but this time she turned her head and looked away from me completely.

My heart sank to the pit of my stomach. I had seen my mother become forgetful, and tired, and even a little distant of late, but the behavior that I feared the most was the turning of my sweet-natured mother into a hateful, old crone. If she had words with Janet, it was hard to tell what sort of damage she had done. I would have to be sure to talk to Janet as soon as I could and see if I could smooth things over.

"Would ye like a cup of tea, Mama?" I tried to pull her back to me, the trick of using something familiar clinging to my efforts.

She shook her head then went straight to her bed. I picked up her shawl and blanket and tucked them both around her as she lay down. Sadie hopped onto the bed with Mother and curled up by her head. The feline had been waiting for someone to go to bed, so she could snuggle with them. When they were both settled in, I began a little tune:

Lullay, mine Liking, my dear Son, mine Sweeting,
Lullay, my dear heart, mine own dear darling.

It was a simple lullaby; one she had sung to me and my brother when we were babies. Her mouth began to move as if she sang with me, but there was no sound coming forth. I continued the sweet refrain:

I saw a fair maiden, sitting and singing,
She lulled a little child, her sweet Lording:

Faintly, the soft sound of the song brooked her lips, but so lightly the words could not be made out, only the melody. By the time I reached the last lines, she was snoring softly.

Pray we now, to that Child, and to his Mother dear,
Grant them His blessing that now maken cheer.

I kissed her brow and patted the blanket down once more. Turning back to my tasks, I readied our herbs to be sold at market the next day.

~6~

December 1590

William

"What have you brought me, my friend?" The king sat on the dais in the Palace of Holyroodhouse with legs outstretched and an arm lounged across the back of this seat. His queen sat beside him. She was just a girl, really, aged almost sixteen years. Her fresh, milk glass skin and fair hair gave her the appearance of one too young to be exposed to such affairs of state. Yet, she watched with interest as His Majesty held court and made judgements on the business brought before him.

I waved my hand in indication to the guards to bring the accused forward. "Your Grace," I said with a sweeping bow. "This is Goodwife Agnes Sampson. Bailiff Seton arrested her on charges of witchcraft. He claims that she has already confessed, but when I questioned her yesterday evening, she seemed to have no knowledge of why she was even arrested."

James regarded the old woman as she approached, his eyes sweeping her form from head to toe. When he didn't say anything for a moment, Seton stepped forward to speak. I felt the hair on the back of my neck rise.

"Your Grace, I questioned her yesterday as to the charges brought against her per the testimony of Geillis Duncan. The witch assured me she understood the charges and confessed she was aware of the storm that waylaid our queen."

"That's not a confession to being party to it." I resisted the urge to raise my voice.

"My ways are quite persuasive, good sir. Perhaps she forgot what we talked about." His eyes swept over her in sinister examination, and I felt my stomach tighten.

"If you mean starving and freezing an old woman to death, then aye, I can see how she might have forgotten."

"Gentlemen, let us have no more of this bickering. We shall simply interrogate the mother again." The king rose to his feet and walked closer to us. Queen Anne sat, wide-eyed and curious as to what was about to happen. She was an intelligent young woman, but I was sure her young mind had never witnessed the likes of a Scottish witch interrogation.

Agnes stood silent and stiff before the King of Scotland. I made sure she ate again this morning before bringing her to Holyroodhouse and confirmed that she remained undisturbed the whole of the night prior. She should be well-rested and satisfied and be able to speak with a clear mind.

"Goodwife Sampson, are you aware of why you have been brought before me?" The king twisted a button on his black doublet, the straight line of his mouth accompanying his sinical eye.

"Aye. I borrowed a cup of flour from Mistress Dutton and have not had a chance to pay it back."

The king raised an eyebrow then flicked a quick glance at me for assistance.

I continued the interrogation. "Goodwife, has Mistress Dutton asked for her cup of flour back, since the time you borrowed it?"

"Aye," was her simple reply.

"And what did you tell her?"

"I told her I didn't have it to give back. She'd have to wait for it."

"Was she satisfied with that answer?"

"Nay, she was put off by it."

"So, has anything been said between the two of you since?"

"Aye." Her short answers were beginning to make me feel like a barber charged with extracting a tooth from an ox.

"What was said?"

"She threatened to get the law involved. I called her a ronyon and told her to take her hedge-born children and leave my cottage at once."

His Majesty's brows shot up immediately, pushing his forehead into his hairline. Coughs and snickers followed, as the woman's insults on her neighbor spread throughout the throne room. I felt my own lip twitch in an impeded smile.

"Goodwife Sampson, your insults are colorful. Insinuating that Mistress Dutton's children were born under illegitimate circumstances is harsh. Are you aware that slander is a serious offense?"

"Aye, isn't that why I'm here?"

More laughter snaked its way through the room, and the woman looked about her in confusion.

"Your Grace, if I might interject here?" Seton interrupted.

"No," the king and I both said at the same time. The king continued, "Bailiff Seton, I pay Master Broune an exorbitant amount of money to do his job. You have had your turn already. Now let him take his."

Seton glowered, crossing his arms in apparent agitation.

"Goodwife, did you threaten Mistress Dutton in any way?"

"Aye, she threatened to have me arrested, and I told her I would make her well bitter if she brought about her threats."

"And how would you go about doing that?"

"A simple charm would do the trick."

The onlookers gasped in surprise at the old woman's admittance, and I quickly moved to clarify her meaning. "Do you mean an herbal concoction that you would spread in the well to turn the water bitter?"

Agnes lost all color in her face as the realization of her admittance became clear to her. She closed her mouth in silence and refused to answer any more questions. Sighing, the king turned and walked away. The queen's inquisitive eyes followed him, and his back straightened when he saw her watching him. He immediately turned back to us. "Send her to the tolbooth. Her charge is slander. Perhaps a few days in the tolbooth will give her an inclination to talk again. We have a birthday celebration upon us. I don't want this mess overshadowing the queen's party." He waved a hand at the guards to remove Agnes from the room.

I took a step forward. "Your Grace—" The king held up a silencing hand then shook his head slightly, putting an end to my objection. The two guards who had brought Agnes in seized her arms, pulling them behind the old woman and roughly pushing her toward the door. A weak, high-pitched wail escaped her twisted lips.

"Where are ye taking me?" Her cry was desperate. "Goodwife Combs is expecting a bairn any day now. She be needing my help. I must return home." She struggled weakly to remove herself from their grip, and one of the guards lifted a beefy hand and slammed it against her mouth.

"Your Grace!" I clenched my teeth so hard that my jaw began to ache.

James turned back to me. "Let it go, William." The hard set of his eyes assured me there was no turning his mind. It sent a chill down my spine. "See if you can get her to talk in a day or so. I want to know what she knows about the storms that beset the queen's ships. We need to get to the bottom of this ridiculous farse."

"I have ways of making her talk, Your Grace," Seton interjected. "If only ye had allowed me."

"Aye, Bailiff Seton. I know you can be extremely persuasive. But I wanted no such display in front of my lovely bride. She is such an innocent." Seton bowed in acquiescence, and the king said, "See to it."

Seton's smirk when he glanced at me was enough to make me want to hit the beast right between his eyes. I watched as he strutted out of the throne room, his gait taking on a new confidence not previously noted.

"You know his persuasive ways are barbaric," I reminded the king.

"There won't be anything left of that poor woman by the time he is done with her."

James looked at me with a curious stare. "Why William, I do believe you are going soft. Have you forgotten our Lord's example of vengeance on the money-changers in the temple? Where is your righteous indignation toward this witch and her evil doings?"

"What proof have we of her witchcraft? You know those old wives use herbs and concoctions to do all manner of healing. How is that entering into a pact with the devil and selling her soul?"

"But she wasn't offering to heal, was she?" He cocked his head as if considering me. "William, I know that you did not want this job, but you are the best when it comes to the legal questioning. However, I don't mind sending Seton to do the dirty work when the need arises."

"I will not have this woman injured just to coax a confession," I said vehemently.

"Sometimes that is the only way to obtain it." He turned from me as Queen Anne approached and offered her his arm. He dismissed me out of hand. "See what you can accomplish with your gentle tactics of grilling, and your knack for making people uncomfortable. If that doesn't work, I'll see what Seton can do." And with that, he left me standing in the throne room, an ache starting in my head.

~7~

December 1590

William

The tinging of a prong from the king's fork rang out as he tapped his goblet. "Ladies and gentlemen, and esteemed guests, even you, Hamilton," he said bowing to Thomas Hamilton as everyone laughed. "I have some wonderful news that I am excited to share with you." The supper party quieted and turned their attention on the king, curious at his announcement. "In honor of our lovely queen, and just in time for her birthday celebration, I have secured the rights to a certain English tragedy that shall be performed three nights hence."

Exclamations of enthusiasm began to ripple across the supper table, with the majority of excited squeals coming from Queen Anne's ladies-in-waiting. The ladies clapped their hands in delight, and Queen Anne beamed, her bright eyes shining with pleasure.

I, on the other hand, was not so thrilled. I had known James long enough to know that nothing he did was half-hearted.

Catching Blantyre's attention across the table, I widened my eyes at him. He understood my purport, for he rolled his eyes at me in return.

Girlish squeals were not in the queen's nature, but she did lay hold of the king's arm and exclaimed, "Dear husband! Will the actors be from London? Perhaps one of the playing companies?"

"Nay, even better, my love. For they will come from right here in

Scotland." The queen's face fell momentarily, her disappointment apparent.

"A playing company from Aberdeen then, Your Grace?" The melodic voice of Beatrix, Lady Ruthven, rang out sweetly across the table. I turned my attention on her at her question, and she blushed prettily when she saw me looking at her.

"Nay, wrong again," he gloated. "These players come from Edinburgh and are in fact amongst us as we speak."

The supper party looked about at each other, trying to understand the king's riddle. I could take his jesting no longer.

"What His Majesty is trying to say is that we are the actors that will be performing this play." All eyes turned toward me at my pronouncement, and then more excited exclamations ensued.

"What a wonderful idea, my lord." The queen had quickly recovered from her disappointment. She clapped her hands together in approval.

At that, the king produced a stack of paper pamphlets, upon which was printed the drama that was to be ours for the next three days. "May I present to you, The Spanish Tragedy," he announced, holding the pamphlets up and waving them above his head. Shouts of glee once again followed until the king motioned for silence. "Now, the next order of business is to decide who shall play what parts." He began passing around the scripts, and we all took what was offered to us.

"I've only read this play, I've never seen it performed," said Barbara, the other Lady Ruthven, and Beatrix's sister. Her eyes and hair were much darker than Beatrix's, and if I hadn't already known they were sisters, I would have never been able to guess. Barbara possessed a low, umbral voice, sultry and seductive. Coupled with her dark, thickly lashed eyes, she was a minx. The woman every man dreamed of at least once in his life. I know I had.

But it was her sister sitting next to her that James had spoken to me about. Golden haired and blue eyed, she shone like a phoenix next to her raven-haired sister. Friendly and warm, I snuck a glance at her again, as everyone talked of the parts they wished to portray.

"Of course, my lovely queen will play Bel-Imperia, and I shall play Horatio."

"Oh poo, my love. I somewhat had my heart set on the Spirit of Revenge." The king looked askance but did not object. "Why not let Barbara play Bel-Imperia, she has that dark, Spanish look about her," the queen suggested.

"I mean no disrespect to Lady Ruthven, but if you are not playing Bel-Imperia, my dear, then I shall play another character. I only chose Horatio so we could play at lovers." The queen's cheeks pinkened at James's intimate words, and she lowered her eyes, her girlish embarrassment accentuating her age.

"I had rather hoped to play the suicidal wife of Hieronimo. Would you play my heroic husband, Thomas?" said Barbara Ruthven. Hamilton looked to her in surprise.

"Only if His Majesty does not wish to play the hero."

"I shall play the Spanish king, for he is one of the few that do not die," James said dryly. The irony was not lost on those of us who had known the king a long time. Between successful and attempted kidnappings, he had developed a healthy fear of death and bodily harm.

In the end there were only two parts I cared about: I was Horatio and Beatrix would play Bel-Imperia.

***

"Shall we practice our roles, sir?"

Beatrix stood before me in a pale dress with little pink pinwheels sewn down the front. A high lace collar enshrouded her ivory neck, but the bodice of her dress was cut to mimic the latest fashion; a low neckline that dipped well below the top of her breasts. Creamy, porcelain flesh peeked out at me below the lace collar, bringing about pleasant memories from the last time I had the pleasure of stroking her skin.

The sound of her voice drew my attention away from my conversation with Blantyre, but the sight of her made me forget my words altogether. I soaked her in, every soft curve and womanly inch of her. "Aye," was the only response I could muster, my mouth watering from the memory of her. She giggled, and the sound of her breathy laugh made my heart pound harder in my chest. She was divine, and I felt as if I were the Devil himself being given another chance at eternal life.

She turned, pushing her skirts behind her, and I offered my arm to lead her to a small alcove where we could rehearse our lines in solitude. Queen Anne was busy speaking to some musicians about the music she desired for her birthday celebration, and James was instructing porters where to place the trunks of costumes that we were to use for the performance. Everyone seemed to be otherwise occupied, working out their part in this drama, so we were left alone to scheme our own portrayals.

"Her Majesty was almost giddy with excitement over the play." I tried to break the awkward silence as we sat down on a crane-colored chaise longue at the end of the great hall. James had spoken to me of Beatrix, but we had already met. Yet, now she seemed tentative and shy, and I felt as though I must approach as if luring a kitten.

"Yes, it is her most favorite thing in the whole world. Dramas and music and fashion and parties." She twisted a row of delicate amethysts that hung from her neck around a long, slender finger. "His Majesty could not have suggested a better activity to celebrate her day of birth."

"Do you suppose she enjoys those frivolous activities because she is yet a child?"

"I don't know. I enjoy those things and I am one and twenty." She looked up at me with her big blue eyes and blinked at me, her long eyelashes fluttering.

Oh, dear God.

Taking a ragged breath, I turned to the page where Bel-Imperia's lines were first spoken and directed her attention to the spot where we should begin.

She slid her delicate finger between the pages of the pamphlet and turned to the instructed page. "I'll warn you now," she said in a light voice, "I am not a very good actor."

Actually, she was an excellent actor. And her play at shyness was most certainly appealing. I steadied my breathing. "'Tis all right. This will be a very slipshod play, there is no need to be nervous. We are all amateurs." I leaned toward her to direct her to the correct lines and I heard her slightest intake of breath.

"I'm not nervous because of that," she said. "But you are too modest, Sir William. For I know that you are anything but an amateur." She smiled at me, and I somehow got the feeling we were no longer talking of acting. She reached out and ran her finger over the stubble along my jawline, then rubbed the pad of her thumb over the slight indentation in my chin. "I do not know how I feel about these whiskers. For they are beginning to cover that glorious dimple in your chin."

My eyes fell on her lips, pouty and full. A little pink tongue darted out and wetted them and my nostrils flared as I took another deep breath through my nose.

She continued. "You didn't have those whiskers at the Midsummer's Eve feast."

"My whiskers weren't the only thing I seemed to lack at the Midsummer's Eve feast. I seem to recall a deliberate lack of self-control."

She laughed softly again, and it sounded like the whispering of a breeze through summer leaves. "I rather enjoyed your lack of self-control."

I coughed to clear my throat and my mind. My eyes darted across the room to see if we were being observed, for there were far too many people around. Changing the course of the conversation, I said, "Bel-Imperia does not come in until act one, scene three. Start here." I pointed once more to the appropriate lines. We then took turns reading the parts, she playing the Castilian duke's heart-broken daughter, and I, Horatio, her dead lover's comforting friend.

At the end of the scene, Beatrix stopped reading, and I considered the lines she had spoken. "I should think 'twould be hard to love another so soon after your lover was killed."

"I agree," she said. "But keep in mind, she did it out of revenge for her lover, Andrea's, murderer. I don't think she really fell for Horatio."

"You don't?" I asked in surprise.

Beatrix blushed and lowered her eyes, looking away from me with an adorable little smile pulling at her lips. "No," she said, dragging the syllable out a little longer than necessary.

Perception alighted on me. "Ahh ha ha! I think I understand your meaning, you little minx. That is just like a woman, using us poor men for their own deceitful ends," I teased. She huffed, pretending to be offended, but I saw the smile pulling at the corners of her lips again. By now we sat with our backs against the wall, leaning into each other, shoulders practically touching, heads almost together. I found her to be most delightful company, and the strong urge to touch her hand that rested so dangerously close to mine was forever beckoning me to oblige.

"I could be wrong though," she continued. "Horatio was noble. What woman wouldn't be moved for the man who wept over his best friend's death?"

I watched her and considered my next words for a moment. "Do you prefer a lover to a fighter, Lady Beatrix?"

Her cheeks turned a pretty shade of pink at my question. "I like them both in equal measure, sir." She watched me intently. The little gems that lay against her milky white skin bobbed up and down as her breath increased.

"That's good," I conceded. "Because I don't think I could be a fighter."

She looked up at me, surprised. "But I took you to be an excellent swordsman, Master Broune. Could I have been mistaken?"

"I can swing a sword well enough. My father made sure of that. But I prefer the act of love to the act of war, Lady Ruthven." And with that, I lightly brushed a finger down her shoulder feeling her tremble under my touch. Her lips parted slightly, and I leaned in just enough to tease her. The art of allurement was to leave them wanting. "Who is playing your beastly brother, Lorenzo?"

She breathlessly said, "I-I am not sure."

"I believe Blantyre is to portray the murderous prince, Balthazar. I shall enjoy watching him grovel at your feet in hopes of winning your love."

As if summoning him from thin air, Blantyre suddenly appeared at my shoulder. "Did I hear my name?" He grinned wickedly, propping himself on the arm of the chaise longue and inviting himself into our little tête-à-tête.

"You are to be the Spanish prince, sir. Be prepared to try to win my heart," Beatrix bubbled, her round eyes shining in amusement.

"Rest assured, madame, that I am already prepared for that challenge." He lifted her hand and brushed a kiss across what I knew to be velvety skin. The devil take him. I had not even enjoyed the luxury of a stolen kiss yet this evening, and he acquired one within minutes. And what was he about, anyway? He had showed such a distaste for James's choice of woman for me, and now here he sat flirting with the very woman that he had disdained.

"Are you going to run your lines with us or not, Blantyre? Either retrieve your script and prepare or leave us be. We have work to do."

Blantyre's mouth fell open at my brusqueness. I had known him almost as long as I had known His Majesty. I always put up with this jesting in good nature. But he was an interloper here in my territory now, and for once, I feared that I was not so hospitable. Sensing his intrusion might not be welcome, he said guiltily, "I shall retrieve my script and return momentarily."

"What do you think of William's little witch?" Blantyre blurted as we were finishing up our practice. I jerked my head up in time to see the mischievous little gleam in his eyes.

"First of all, she is not my witch," I corrected. "And furthermore, we've gotten very little information out of her. I do not see how anyone can pass judgement on her yet."

"Aye, but she is a curious little creature, is she not?"

"I think she is guilty," Beatrix exclaimed.

Shocked at her plain opinion, I questioned her. "What has she done that makes you so sure of her guilt?"

"She has a look about her. And she is a known healer in North Berwick and has had several run-ins with town folk thereabouts."

Blantyre looked at me, a wide grin overtaking his face. "You should hire her, William," he said thrusting a thumb in Lady Beatrix's direction. "It seems that she knows how to dig for information that you have yet to discover."

"She has not shared any more than what Goodwife Sampson has already divulged herself."

"I am sorry, Sir William. I meant no offense," she offered.

"There is no offence taken, Lady Beatrix. Blantyre just needs to worry about his own job and quit trying to rid me of mine."

Blantyre laughed heartily at that. Indeed, I meant the words in jest, but somehow still felt the tinge of irritation at his bringing up the matter in front of Beatrix.

"William, there you are," James cried from across the hall. "I am in need of your assistance. Do come immediately."

I looked to Beatrix apologetically. "Forgive me," I said, taking her small hand in mine and brushing my own kiss across the top of her knuckles. The scent of lavender water faintly filled my nose, turning my insides to liquid warmth. I bowed but was hesitant to leave her in Blantyre's company.

"Oh, you go on, William. Do not worry yourself on Lady Beatrix's account. I shall see that she reaches the queen's antechamber safely."

I narrowed my eyes at him in distrust. "You do that, Blantyre. And see that you don't dally." He barked a laugh, and I bared my teeth at him in a forced smile, sure that he understood my meaning completely.

~8~

December 1590

William

The mercat cross was the center of Edinburgh and was the heart of the activity that flourished there. From here to the Lawnmarket that stretched all the way to Castlehill, shopkeepers pushed their wares on daily visitors. Here, deals were struck and bargains were made all within the shadow of the towering St Giles Kirk beside which the Luckenbooths had been built. It was also here that the tolbooth stood, dark and looming over any happiness that might be bought or sold in Edinburgh. Within its walls, judgements were passed. Outside, sentences were carried out. A turn in the pillory, or when the need arose, an execution, all fulfilled within the reach of the tolbooth.

I made my way once more to the dreaded establishment. Ten more witches had been arrested, and I wanted a chance to question them before Seton got his hands on them any further. The morning was bitter, and I cursed having to leave the warmth of my bed. The biting wind, blowing in from the Firth of Forth, brought gusts of snow. Unfortunately, it wasn't the soft, fluffy snow, but tiny ice crystals that stung the face and threatened to burn one's ears off. I pulled my collar tighter about me and kept my head down. But as I drew closer to the daunting structure of the tolbooth, a small figure wrapped from head to toe in a brown earasaid bent, shoving a tiny, wrapped parcel through a hole in the tolbooth wall.

"What in the name of all that is holy do you think you are doing?"

The woman jumped at the sound of my voice, but otherwise did not acknowledge me. She continued to shove the package through a crumbling hole in the wall. Passersby shuffled around her, clearly uninterested in the woman's activities. However, grubby fingers reached from within and removed the package from her hand. I sprang into action.

Only a few strides were needed to be at her side. I grabbed the woman's arm in annoyance, irritated that she chose to blatantly disregard me.

"Unhand me, ye beast."

I stepped back abruptly. It was Ailsa. Her voice was low and passionate, and her eyes shown with a rebellious fire. I instantly released her and held my hands up, palms facing her. "My apologies. I meant no harm."

"I will not be manhandled thusly. I am not your property, Master Broune, therefore ye cannot command me as ye will."

"Even if you were my property, I shouldn't have grabbed you. It was a reaction."

Her right eyebrow shot up in irritation. "So, ye think a woman can be your property then?"

"I, no, of course not. That's not what I meant at all." She was twisting my words and that irritated me even more. I had apologized and had already shown this chit much more tolerance than what she deserved. I stepped closer to her. She *would* hear me.

"I just caught you scheming with the prisoners." I jabbed a finger toward the hole in the wall. "That is my business to command." I stood so close to her now that I could see the faint hint of freckles scattered across her nose. They were charming, and I had to resist the urge to brush the pad of my thumb across her cheek to catch one or two of them. Her cheeks were rosy, more than likely from the fierce wind, and tiny ice crystals clung to her long dark lashes. Even her adorable button nose was red. She'd been out here for a while; I was sure of it.

"I am not scheming," she whispered harshly, looking about her. "Is it a crime to show the compassion of Christ to these poor starving souls?" She reached into her basket again, pulling out another small bundle.

"It is when they are witches."

She scoffed at that then turned her face on me fully. "Master Broune, I am disappointed. I thought ye a man that might be prevailed upon to do the right thing. Ye are the arm of justice for His Majesty, the King, and all power is in your hands to help these poor victims. They are accused, not convicted. Any advocate worth his salt would justly want to find the truth, not just believe tainted accusations from a sadist whose position has gone to his head. Perhaps that is your affliction as well?" She looked up at me then, all innocence.

I flinched at her words. I was not intoxicated with the power King James had bestowed upon me. And I certainly gained no pleasure from it. In fact, I loathed it. But she had no way of knowing that. If only I could make her see that I wasn't the blackguard here.

A gaggle of children went bustling by, screeching at the top of their lungs as they clung to a wagon that pulled them along the High Street. The puddles of water on the road had frozen overnight and the children found great delight in slipping and sliding along behind the wagon as it pulled them across the icy road. Ailsa's expression also showed smug delight in the noisy interruption of my lecture.

When the commotion had died down, I turned back to her. "I beg to differ, you, you—" I searched my mind for an appropriate way to address the little chit. She was mouthy, and opinionated, and all the things that a lady of the court was taught *not* to be. And I was fascinated with her.

"I think the words ye are looking for are, *Mistress Blackburn.*" There was that smirk again. I felt my body tense at its appearance.

"Listen, *Mistress Blackburn*," I said, irritated. "I am not a sadist, and I'm certainly not on some kind of power-hungry rampage."

"I was referring to Bailiff Seton." She brushed her comment away with the wave of her hand.

Irritation pulsed through me at her comparison of me to David

Seton. I straightened. "It just so happens that I prefer to seek justice for the accused, not swift punishment without a trial. But I also recognize that there must be no contact with outsiders while the prisoners are in our custody. What is in the package, Ailsa?"

"It's a wedge of cheese and a small loaf of bread. These prisoners are starving." She pulled the paper open to reveal the contents and shoved the fare toward me. "They are also exhausted and freezing. And the longer they are tortured, the more likely they are to say something, anything that will bring relief from their affliction. Ye would do well to find a different way to obtain the truth ye seek."

"What do you suggest?" I truly was curious as to her opinion. She seemed to have a lot of them, surely there was something of use amongst the many.

She closed her eyes for a moment. "I don't know," she breathed, barely above a whisper. Her frosty breath rose above our heads and hung suspended as if it too awaited her suggestion. Opening her eyes to look at me again she said, "But if there is truth, there has to be some humane way to find it."

I watched as a horde of emotions flickered across her face. Hurt, anger, hopelessness, and an emotion that made my blood run cold: defiance. I opened my mouth to say something, but nothing came out.

"If the accused truly had something to do with Queen Anne's storms, do ye really think it was on their own volition? The devil goeth about as a roaring lion, seeking whom he may devour," she quoted the Holy Writ. "They are as much the victims as Her Majesty."

"Are you sympathizing with the witches?" I stepped back, feeling as if she had slapped me.

She sighed and looked away from me. "Men like you will never understand."

"Try me."

Raising her eyebrows, she looked at me with amusement. "You are so cut and dry. Black and white. Right or wrong." She cut her hand through the frozen air, chopping at nothing as she tried to make her point. "Will you never understand that some things just aren't that easily explained?"

"You speak as if you know me, *Ailsa*." I closed the gap between us again, but she took a step back. I wasn't sure if it was the use of her given name that alarmed her, or my closeness, but if we were going to speak as if we knew each other, then I would address her as such.

Puffs of warm air escaped her parted lips, curling into tiny spirals that dissipated into the air. "Ye mean to intimidate me."

"Not at all." I studied her, noticing her shoulders rising and falling more rapidly and the puffs of air increasing as she took quicker breaths.

"Then why do ye stand so close to me? And why do ye call me by my given name? I gave ye no such permission."

"I stand close because I do not wish our conversation to be heard by every wagging tongue that passes by." Then, allowing a smile to spread across my face, I said, "And I use your given name because you presume to know me so well. I thought perhaps we were on more familiar terms than I had previously realized."

Balling her hands into fists, she let out a short grunt that sounded a mixture of clearing her throat and huffing, similar to my mare, Cleopatra. Pulling her earasaid tighter about her face, she said, "I have nothing more to say to ye, Master Broune. Good day."

I fought the urge to let out the laugh that I held inside. I enjoyed teasing this woman, for her reactions were so tantalizing. But the seriousness of our conversation soon resurfaced, and I was left to ponder what she had said. *Will you never understand that some things just aren't that easily explained?* She was right about one thing: I saw only the black or white, right or wrong. Evidently another quality I inherited from my devout father. And I served a king who ruled in the same manner. Even if I had the ability to see the gray areas, how could I convince James of such? No matter. I didn't see the gray. I was committed to justice, but that could only be obtained by finding the truth. And I was determined to do just that.

I watched as she gathered her earasaid into her fist and lifted it to keep from tripping. She made her way across the street, gingerly stepping to avoid a fall. I watched until she passed St Giles, and soon she was out of sight.

~9~

December 1590

Ailsa

My heart was racing as I hurried along the High Street and past the kirk. I fought the urge to turn around, to see if the king's man followed me, or even watched me from a distance. *I must be more careful,* I chided myself, *especially if I am to carry out my plan to help Geillis.*

But things had become more complicated. More people had been arrested, including a well-respected doctor, and it was becoming harder to plan any type of escape. I also had to ask myself: do I assist all of them, or only Geillis?

The young woman's plight had struck me with such sorrow the night I first saw her at Uncle Rupert's storehouse. I truly believed her to be innocent, to be a victim of that monster, Seton. But then Agnes Sampson was arrested, and although she seemed a sweet old woman, there was something different about her that I couldn't put my finger on.

Then came the arrest of Barbara Napier, who supposedly bewitched the Earl of Angus. Then Margaret Thomson. And soon there were too many to count.

I hadn't dared share all my plans with Mother; she only knew I fed the prisoners. She was becoming increasingly volatile, and I never knew when she would become confused and blurt out something in the company of others that I did not wish for her to share. Therefore, my only confidant was Bess, and even then, there were times when I got the impression that she did not agree with my scheme.

I slipped into Grey's Close then dared a peek around the corner. William had not followed me, and I sighed in relief. I stood watching for several minutes, waiting to see if he would come into view. When no sign of him was apparent, I leaned my head against the cold stones of the building, closing my eyes and focusing on calming my nerves. When my heartbeat slowed and my breathing became easier, I turned to make my way to Bess's house.

"Hiding from someone, Mistress Blackburn?"

I cringed at the sound of David Seton's voice and felt the muscles in my stomach immediately tense. "Wh-what are ye doing here?"

He let out a low chuckle then stepped closer. "Your uncle was concerned about you. Seems you didn't come to his shop at the time you were appointed. He sent me to fetch you because I'm very good at sniffing out people who are trying to avoid others."

"I don't know what ye are talking about." I tried to keep my voice level. The thunderous pounding in my ears from my beating heart practically drowned out my words.

"Aye, you do, Ailsa." He reached up and took a strand of my hair and ran it through his fingertips. "You're a bonny little lass, you know that?"

Pulling my hair free from his hand, I took a step back. I tucked my shaking hands into my cloak to hide my distress. "Well, ye've found me now, Bailiff Seton. Ye can tell my uncle that I will be along shortly. I made no promises to him that I would come today, and I have a visit to pay first to a friend. Thank ye for your concern." I moved to step around him when he caught my arm in his large hand.

"You cannot blow me off so easily, lass. You'll find that I generally get what I want. And when I don't, there is a price to pay." He flashed a crooked smile at me, his yellowing teeth baring down on his thick lips.

"I've no doubt that ye take what ye want without regard to the wishes of others." I silently cursed myself for my brazen words and steadied myself for his next move. His eyes widened, and he let out a deep, guttural laugh. I realized then that this was a game to him. A game of cat and mouse, and my words were the bait. He lowered his face to mine, and for a moment, I thought he would kiss me. I had never been kissed before, but I was sure I did not want this man to be my first. He stood so close that I could see the tiny black pores of his oily skin. When his hooded eyes closed completely, I saw my chance.

Yanking my arm free from his slackened grip, I darted around him and ran as fast as I could toward Bess's house. I had only gone a short distance when I slid on the frozen stones and went down, hitting my knees and catching myself with the palms of my hands to prevent my face from hitting the ground. I could feel the rock and debris imbedded in the icy path dig into my skin, and the impact sent shards of pain through my limbs. I pushed myself upward to stand on my feet once more and continued running. I could hear Seton laughing from a distance.

"Ah, come back now, Ailsa. I meant no harm." His sweet coaxing as if I were a child made my skin crawl, and I was glad to put more distance between us.

I arrived panting at Bess's house, and when her father opened the door to me, his face revealed his alarm. "Come in, child." Placing his hand under my elbow, he ushered me into the warmth of their home and sat me down in a chair by the fire. "Ye have fallen, haven't ye? Bess, Margaret, come quickly." His voice cracked with an age and frailty that I had not noticed until recently.

He moved aside when Bess and her mother entered the room. My friend let out a gasp at my bloodied hands and clothes. She then flew into action, placing a pot of water over the fire, as Mistress McMurray gathered some scraps of cloth to wrap my wounds. My stockings were torn, along with a gash in my dress. However, the dress could be savaged. I wasn't sure about the stockings.

"Pull the stockings off and we'll soak them in cold water to remove the blood," she said as if she could read my mind. "I can darn those, and they'll be good as new." Bess was never of a sounder mind as when she was barking orders and taking care of someone. She would make a fine goodwife when her time came.

Bess cleaned my knees, then with a needle she picked out the dirt and stones that had torn at my hands. Her father paced as she doctored me. "'Tis treacherous out there, lass. Why don't ye allow us to walk ye home, so ye don't fall again?" The faded blue of his aged eyes implored me, and I was warmed by the old man's concern. Master McMurray and his wife had been very kind to Mother and me since my father had passed away. He and father had been schoolboy friends, but when Father moved on to university, Angus McMurray went into business with a skilled trade. His own father had been a candlemaker, and Angus had developed his own recipe for beeswax that would burn twice as long as other types. It had raised their status as merchants and given them a comfortable living that the average chandler would not have had.

"That's not necessary, sir. I'll go slow the next time."

He heaved a sigh as Mistress McMurray wrapped a gentle arm around his waist. "Let's leave the girls to talk, my dear. I want to finish my sketch before all the light is gone, and I can't do that without my subject." Her eyes twinkled as she pulled her husband back into their sitting room. Mistress McMurray had recently begun drawing lessons, and her husband and remaining child at home were the helpless victims of her endeavors.

"Ye should have let Father walk ye home. I think it is supposed to snow again." She looked out the window, but the air was clear and crisp now without another snowflake in sight.

"I'll be fine. I won't have to run the next time I go out."

"Why were ye running? Was someone chasing ye?" Concern wrinkled her brow and she came and sat at my knee. I was more than a little embarrassed now at the incident. Perhaps Seton hadn't intended on kissing me. But if that wasn't his intention, then why did he stand so close? I shivered when I recalled how his head had dipped, and his eyes had closed. *Isn't that what people do when they kiss?*

I lingered a moment longer before voicing my question. Bess had never been kissed either, but she had three older sisters who had married. Surely in such confined quarters the girls must have talked amongst themselves. I was confident she would know the answer to my question. Finally, I said, "Bess, when someone is about to kiss ye—"

She gasped. "Did someone kiss ye?"

"Nay, but—"

"Was it the king's man that stopped and talked to ye that day ye were at the mercat cross?" At this, Bess's eyes turned dreamy, and she looked as if she were far away, anywhere but right here in front of me.

"Bess! Nay!" I said impatiently. I waited for the turning of my stomach at that thought, like the repulsion that I felt when Seton made to kiss me. But it didn't come. In fact, I was more than a little perturbed at my body's betrayal, when a warm sensation began to fill my belly. William had also stood close to me. Yet, his intentions had not been as those of Seton. And although I had indicated I was disturbed by his apparent effort at intimidation, the feeling was actually the opposite.

She frowned then, the dwindling choices of suitors becoming apparent.

"Ye didn't have a run in with Seton, did ye?" When I hesitated again, she leaned closer, grabbing my face in her hands and pulling my eyes from the fire. "Did Seton act dishonorably toward ye?"

I forced myself to look at her. Swallowing hard, I said, "I'm not sure. I believe that was his intentions, but—" My voice trailed off.

"That cad," she whispered, sitting back on her heels. I could have sworn I saw her shiver too. Neither of us thought him to be a particularly fine catch.

"Aye, well, I have bigger concerns at the moment. The king's man that ye so dreamily made reference to, caught me poking my little food packages through the holes in the wall at the tolbooth."

The color drained from Bess's face. "He didn't…he didn't find the note, did he?"

"Nay, it was hidden. Baked beautifully within the bread. I tested the method with a few scraps of paper before taking it to her. When he demanded to know what was within the package, I opened it for him to see. He was oblivious to my little Trojan horse."

Bess giggled nervously. "This is a dangerous game, Ailsa. What would ye have done if he had insisted on taking the package from ye and then tried to eat it later?"

My smile vanished. "I hadn't thought of that." I chewed on my lip as I pondered what had transpired. In frustration I said, "May he choke on it!" Then I remembered, "He caught me before I could pass the parcel for Geillis through. Now I'm going to have to go back and try again and hope I don't get caught." I let out an exasperated huff at the thought of William's interference. That irritating man.

Bess frowned. "Ailsa, please be careful. Are ye sure this is what ye want to do?"

I thought about this little hiccup in my plan, and suddenly felt anxious. I no longer wished to talk of Seton, nor William, nor my plans to help Geillis Duncan escape. I just wanted to go home. I stood and said, "I need to see to Mother. Thank ye for taking care of my wounds."

Bess stood as well. "What about your stockings?" She picked the garments up from where I had laid them and inspected the shredded fibers.

My heartrate had finally slowed, and with it, my energy had dissolved. My shoulders slumped in resignation as I stifled the urge to cry. "Can I borrow a pair of yours?"

"Of course." She hurried off to her bedchamber, taking my torn and bloodied stockings with her. When she returned, she held a clean pair of stockings in one hand and a small sgian dubh in her other. "Tuck this into your belt and cover it with your earasaid," she whispered.

I gaped at the weapon that lay in her palm. "Where did you get that?" I whispered back.

"It's Father's. But he won't notice it's missing." She shoved the small dagger toward me.

"I can't take that. I'm not sure I would even know what to do with it. I certainly don't think I could actually stab somebody with it." The thought sent a wave of sickness roiling through my stomach.

She knelt again on the floor beside me and motioned for me to sit so she could put the stockings on my feet. "Well, if David Seton tried to kiss me, I don't think I would have a bit of trouble poking that into his arm." She pushed the second stocking up my leg, then twisted it to straighten the seams.

"Into his arm?" I said with alarm. "Do you really think a knife to the arm would stop such a man?" She halted her efforts and looked up at me sheepishly.

"Ye don't suppose?" Her innocent eyes were as wide as a newborn bairn's.

"Nay, I don't. Men are not so easily dissuaded."

She tilted her head and looked at me in confusion. I couldn't help it then, the laugh that slipped out of me sounded foreign to my own ears. It had been a long time since I had reason to laugh. Bess began laughing too, and soon, we were both giggling uncontrollably. Another round of laughter ensued when Bess said innocently, "Well, I should think a stab to my arm would cool *my* ardor."

At last, I slipped my boots onto my feet and donned my plaid. "Thank ye for the doctoring, Bess, and for the laughs. I need to remember sometimes not to take life so seriously." I kissed her cheek and then headed back out into the cold. But the memory of my encounter with David Seton still haunted me, and I wondered if I should have accepted the sgian dubh after all.

~**10**~

December 1590

William

I had hoped that Lady Beatrix would be seated close to me at the queen's birthday celebration. Instead, I found myself sitting two seats away from the king. Still, she sat on the opposite side of the table, a few seats down from me. Through a bountiful centerpiece decked with sugared fruits and flowers that stood between us, we had an alluring, if not partially hidden view of each other.

"Don't be surprised if Lady Barbara and I flub your whole play this evening, Your Grace." Hamilton picked apart the meat of a partridge and threw the bones down on his plate. He winked at Barbara across the table, and she stifled a smile pulling at her lips. "I'm not confident that we know all our lines."

"You should have been practicing." The king licked the grease off of his fingers from his own meal and grabbed his cup. "What have you been doing for the past three days?"

Ahh, James, such an innocent still in so many ways.

Hamilton turned his gaze on Lady Barbara, and I was almost certain that the woman's ears turned pink. Blushing was not her habit, but coloring ears were definitely a good sign that whatever it was they had been doing, it was not something she wanted announced. Aye, they most certainly had not been practicing their lines.

I snuck a peek at Lady Beatrix between a branch of greenery. Her eyes sparkled with secret delight. We, on the other hand, had been practicing our lines. And we were more than prepared for tonight's entertainment. I felt confident that even if we forgot a line here or there, we would pull it off magnificently.

"What's that grin for, William?" Blantyre asked between bites of parsnip. I turned to him abruptly, as if I had been caught making faces at the bishop during benediction.

"I'm sure I don't know what you mean." I took a quick gulp of wine from my cup, spilling the crimson liquid onto the front of my doublet.

"Drink much?" Blantyre teased, eliciting howls from our friends.

I smiled at my own expense, then rose to my feet. "Gentlemen, ladies, if you'll excuse me. Perhaps I should clean myself up."

"Ahh, sit, William, no one will notice a little dribble down your chest." The king waved for me to sit.

"Your Grace," I dared. "If you please, you know better than anyone here how much this is going to bother me for the rest of the evening. I need to change my doublet."

"All right, all right." He waved a dismissive hand at me, and I stepped away from the table.

The hallway was cold and drafty, and I picked up my pace as I made my way down the dark corridor. When I was a child, I always hated the eerily darkened walkway that led from the Great Hall of Edinburgh Castle back to our rooms at this old, stalwart castle. It was hollow and silent, with only the echo of my boots clicking on the stones to signal any bodily presence. The ghosts, on the other hand, needed no boots, so their manifestations were usually *felt* more than heard.

It took only a minute or two to change my clothes, and I was soon on my way back to the gathering. However, a slight lifting of the hair on the back of my neck indicated to me that I was not alone in the hallway. I turned and looked over my shoulder just in time to see Francis Stewart, the Earl of Bothwell, stepping out into the dim light. Candlelight bathed his face in a warm glow, but there was nothing warm about his company. I stiffened at the sight of him and resumed my walk toward the hall.

"William Broune, just the man I wanted to see." He caught up to me and matched his stride with mine, keeping pace with my quickened steps.

"Bothwell, what are you doing here? I'm sure you did not receive an invitation to the queen's birthday celebration."

"Ah, is *that* what is going on? And here I thought perhaps it was a welcome home party for me. I've been abroad, you know."

I didn't bother to answer him. His company was about as welcome as a burr in one's shoe. Only, the burr could be removed and discarded. We could never seem to rid ourselves of the earl completely.

I sighed. "What do you want?"

He chuckled, scratching his chin. "Such a friendly greeting from an old friend. I'm touched."

I stopped abruptly and turned to him. He took two steps further before he realized I had paused. "I would hardly call you an old friend. I don't make a habit of befriending men who make sport of kidnapping our king and terrorizing the nobility."

A grin crept up his face, but the look in his menacing eyes was anything but jovial. "Aren't we the sycophant. You are no more noble than the Holyroodhouse maid your father married."

I drew my clenched fist back. I didn't like to fight but speaking of my dead mother was too much. He flinched but smiled again when he realized I hesitated. He was an earl after all, and I merely a servant of the crown.

"You've gone too far."

"Oh, come now, William. You know I meant no offence. I'm merely pointing out that you are not nobility and therefore shouldn't be troubled when one of the noble class is ruffled. I know I'm not bothered, and I'm as noble as they come." He inspected the nails on his upturned hand, and I started walking again.

When I didn't speak, he hastened his pace to catch up. "I was hoping to speak to you about a business proposition. Then again, perhaps you are too busy with the witch trials."

I ignored him. It unnerved me how much this man always knew about the king's business. Besides, I was too busy. There had been many more arrests and another interrogation awaited me tomorrow with Doctor Fian. But I wasn't about to tell him that.

"It is a chance to make a lot of money, and I thought perhaps you would be just the person to assist me."

"Not interested."

"But there may be a wench or two in the kitty as well."

"Still not interested."

He reached out and grabbed my arm, stalling me once more. "Since when is William Broune not interested in a good roll in the hay and a chance to make some loot?"

"Since I am actively pursuing Lady Beatrix Ruthven, and I have no desire to attach myself to the likes of you." I jerked my arm from his hand which still held fast to my coat.

"Lady Beatrix? Ah, but she is a fine, *fine* prize." His voice turned husky, and he cocked his head. "Yes, a marriage to her will certainly enhance your prospects. But this is money in your pocket, man. Immediate money. And there's no need for her to know about the wenches." He lifted and dropped both eyebrows in one swift motion, and I caught a glimpse of how persuasive he was capable of being.

"I'll go into business with you when hell freezes over." I was just inches from his face, close enough to smell the whisky that clung to his breath. I tapped the side of his face playfully, then resumed my walk. He did not follow.

"I can barely resist your sweet talk, Broune," he called as I continued walking. "But when you realize that you need a little capital, and your new bride is suffering from a headache again, as all new brides do, come find me. I'll be more than happy to accommodate you."

"I suggest you make yourself scarce, Bothwell." I called over my shoulder. "If His Majesty were to find you here, you may not escape as easily as you did at your last trial."

I couldn't imagine what kind of business proposition the Earl of Bothwell could possibly have in mind. The man was a notorious blackguard who killed practically anyone he ever had a disagreement with. He had been arrested on charges of treason and plotting to kidnap the king a year earlier, yet somehow managed to escape a harsh sentence. Perhaps it was the family ties that benefitted him. For although James hated the man, he was his cousin, even if illegitimately, they both being grandsons of the fifth King James.

I, on the other hand, had no such blood ties to the man and a very good reason for disliking him. His uncle had been the very Earl of Bothwell who had kidnapped and married our beloved Queen Mary. My father loathed him, which was of some consequence seeing how he is a man of the cloth. I grew up hearing of the treachery the man had caused the woman whom my father loved. Evidently the depravity ran in the family.

When I reached the great hall, the supper party was moving toward the makeshift stage that had been built for the occasion. Beatrix caught my attention from across the room then moved quickly to stand by my side.

"Oh, thank God," she said. "I was beginning to think you had abandoned me."

I looked down into her bright blue eyes. "Never, my sweeting. I was merely waylaid by a monster lurking in the shadows of the corridor."

Her brows furrowed, and she looked at me with concern. "A monster? Surely you don't believe in such childhood tales?" She wrapped her arm around mine, and we walked toward the stage. I looked at her out of the corner of my eye, debating on how much to tell her about Bothwell.

"I believe in the human kind," I finally said. Perplexed, she opened her mouth to speak again, but I was saved by a footman shoving a costume into my hand.

"Horatio?" he asked. I nodded dumbly, not realizing that someone had actually taken the time to figure out costumes for each character. James really was taking this seriously.

"I'll just go slip this on," Beatrix said, lifting the costume for Bel-Imperia that was draped across her arms like a sacrificial offering. I watched her hips sway seductively as she sauntered off. This play acting couldn't be over soon enough. I had other plans for this evening, and it didn't involve silly costumes.

~11~

December 1590

William

"You look like horse manure." Blantyre's voice pierced my ears and sent a sharp pain straight into my skull.

"Good afternoon to you too." I sat with my head in my hands, wishing that the king's chamber in which I sat did not look as if it were about to tilt onto its side.

He stopped and stared down at me. "You must have had a very eventful evening. Where did you and Beatrix disappear to last night?"

"I'd rather not talk about it." I waved him off, hoping he would let the subject drop. Of course, this was Blantyre. He wasn't going to let it drop.

"I gather it didn't go as planned." An annoying grin lifted his mouth. "She sure *seemed* like she was in a good mood after the play."

"Aye, well, so was I until she started asking me questions about Fian and today's interrogation. She said she heard the man was a sorcerer, and she hoped he would just confess to the charges to prevent the interrogation from being prolonged. I told her I wanted to go into these interrogations with an unblemished opinion and would rather not talk about it, but she persisted. The night ended with her fleeing in tears and me drinking myself to sleep."

Just then the door opened and Master Sheepshearer entered the room. He was followed by two guards that led a young bound and fettered man into the room.

In true prisoner fashion, his clothes were torn and his fingers bloodied. But it was plain to see that his fingers had not been crushed as with the pilliwinks, but his fingernails had been torn completely off.

I stood in protest. "Master Sheepshearer, I was under the impression that we were to interrogate the prisoners first before torturing them. I haven't even had a chance to question the prisoner yet, and already he is bleeding and bruised."

Sheepshearer shifted his eyes to Seton, who had entered the room behind the prisoner. He spoke up. "We had some questions of our own for the school master. But alas, he will not confess. It seems he is a glutton for pain."

"I want this prisoner cleaned up and tended to before any further questioning."

"There is no time for that, Sir William." The king's voice rang out across the chamber as he stepped into the room. "Now that everyone is here, let's just get on with it."

I stared at the king. The silence in the room was awkward until someone cleared their throat. The king spoke again. "Proceed."

With a pounding headache, I stepped closer to Fian. Upon additional scrutiny, I noted that his face bore the markings of a thrawing, the act of twisting and squeezing a victim's head with a rope.

Fian's eyes were bloodshot, as if he hadn't slept in several days, and his hair was matted to the side of his head. Tear stains smudged his cheeks, and for a moment I forgot that this man had been accused of pillaging tombs in order to supply body parts for his various charms. This was someone's son. What would his parents and the rest of his family think if they could see him now?

When I came and stood before him, he didn't even look up at me. "Doctor John Fian, you have been formally charged with treason. You have been accused of various charms including but not limited to the tossing of a dead cat into the ocean with the intent of conjuring up storms that would bring about the death of Their Majesties. On the lesser charges of intent to do harm, eyewitnesses have claimed on more than one occasion you have been known to rob the graves of the local dead in order to obtain body parts for your spells. We also have the testimony of a man who claims that you have bewitched him, causing him to behave with bouts of lunacy for the space of one hour, every day. What say you to these charges?"

Silence. The man did not speak, neither to deny nor admit to the charges. I could see Seton out of the corner of my eye. He stood to his feet then spoke up. "This is the same response we received. I think it is time to administer new tactics."

I held up a hand to silence him. Walking around the young man I inspected him further. A tiny trickle of blood seeped out of his ear and had dripped onto the white ruff of his collar.

"Doctor Fian, are you employed as a school master in Saltpans?"

"Aye," he said faintly.

"And how is it that you came to be employed in this position?"

"My uncle got me the position."

"Are you married?"

The man shifted in his seat as if the question made him uncomfortable. I doubted he would answer, but he surprised me when he finally said, "Nay, she would not have me."

"Who? Who would not have you?"

He didn't answer. Instead, a faint sniffle was his only response.

"Did she say why she would not have you? Did she have another lover?"

His eyes shot to me, and with a terrible undercurrent to his voice he said, "They say she does."

"Who says?"

More silence.

This went on for another hour, with me bombarding the doctor with questions, and he answering in vague, unexplained answers, if he even answered at all. But at no point did the man confess to anything with which he had been charged.

"Master Sheepshearer, you need to find the witch's mark on this man. I am growing weary of this interrogation." The king stifled a yawn as if to make his point.

The man was stripped and the witch pricker conducted a thorough inspection of the doctor. When nothing of note could be found, Sheepshearer turned toward the king.

"There is another means by which we might be able to obtain a confession. If it please my lord, let us call for the boot to be brought."

The king looked to me, and I thought for a moment that he would refuse this barbaric means of torture. The instrument was a contraption into which the victim's legs would be placed. A mechanism within the boot would squeeze the leg and continue to squeeze until the bones of the leg were crushed, or the victim confessed.

James raised a skeletal hand and motioned, giving approval for the device to be employed. My stomach turned. I had hoped we could obtain a confession without such horrific means.

But even the boot would not loosen the man's tongue. And about a half an hour into this, Sheepshearer received a missive, which he shared with Seton. The two men conversed momentarily before Sheepshearer brought the note to me.

I glanced down at the writing. There were two simple sentences scrawled across the note in a hand that looked to be untrained.

Now is the charm stinted. Search his tongue.

I stood to see what they meant as Sheepshearer walked back to Fian.

"Open your mouth," the witch pricker commanded.

Like a bairn who had just been caught with a bannock in his mouth, the doctor pressed his lips together, refusing the command. Sheepshearer motioned and with a flick of his wrist, Seton twisted the device, putting more pressure on the boot.

Fian tried his best to keep his mouth clamped shut. Great drops of sweat had already beaded on his brow and were now dripping down his face.

"We can do this all night, doctor." Sheepshearer motioned again and Seton obliged his request for more pressure.

Finally, the doctor broke, and Sheepshearer was waiting there, ready to force his hands into the man's mouth once he let out a scream.

"Ah!" he cried, nodding at me to come and look. There under the man's tongue were two pins, pushed up to the heads. Sheepshearer released the man's mouth and went to the tools he kept tucked away in his leather pouch.

Once the pins were removed, the floodgates of hell had been opened. Fian confessed to everything. He told how he was the man responsible for registering all the names of the witches who pledged their allegiance to the Devil. He explained how he bewitched another young man in town, who also had an interest in the lass Fian was in love with. The man would fall into a trance every twenty-four hours, bending himself and leaping to high heights and doing all manner of things that were beyond his control. For one hour a day this would persist until the spell ended, leaving the man no wiser to his curious feats.

Fian even explained how he had tried to put a love spell on the lass. He had enlisted the help of the girl's brother, to obtain three hairs of her privities. But her mother caught wind of his intent and instead she sent three hairs from the udder of a heifer. When the spell was cast, it was the cow that showed up at Fian's door.

All this was written into a confession which Fian signed. He was then dragged off to the tolbooth to await his assize. It would be a simple conviction.

Everyone had left the chamber except for the maids who had been sent to clean up the blood left behind. I could not bring myself to leave the room. I sat pondering the depravity of man. His quest for power and the lengths he was willing to go to obtain it. What I couldn't devise was which was more disturbing. Men like Fian who found power from some supernatural means that helped him obtain the things he wanted? Or men like Sheepshearer and Seton, who used their natural strength and would go to such lengths to maintain their positions and give the king what he wanted?

And then there was me. How was I any different? I did the king's bidding, though it chafed at my very being. With each interrogation, I shuttered yet proceeded. I grew more sickened with each head twisted and finger pinched. Yet, I stood silently by, never dirtying my hands, but allowing it to happen all the same. Like Pontius Pilot, I had washed my hands of it all, yet allowed it to happen under my watch. And for that, I felt truly depraved.

~12~

December 1590

William

And so it continued. It seemed every day a new victim was arrested. And at every turn, I found myself attending another interrogation. This time it was a third questioning of Agnes Sampson.

The woman that stood before the king was not the same woman that I interrogated a fortnight before. Patchy wisps of whitened hair stood out all over Agnes Sampson's otherwise bald head, her hair having been shaved in like manner as Geillis Duncan's. Sagging skin replaced her finely wrinkled face, and her large cow eyes now sunk deep into her head. Purple smudges lay beneath her hollow eyes and evidence of thrawing, which left a mark across her face.

The small chamber which had been secured for this interrogation was hot, and I pulled at my collar in an effort to catch my breath. Heavy smoke hung above our heads due to an unkempt flue, and the smell of stale smokehouse odor choked our lungs. Agnes lifted a hand to wipe her brow, her bruised and bleeding fingers hanging like limp twigs from her battered hands. She stood in complete silence until James called for her to be brought to stand before him.

"I have been informed, Goodwife Sampson, that the Devil's mark has been found upon your person, and that you have confessed to having knowledge of the storms that, had it not been for the grace of God, would have taken the life of my dear queen." He brought a copper cup to his lips and took a long drink. Agnes' eyes followed his every movement, her tongue darting out involuntarily to wet her parched mouth.

When she did not respond immediately, Seton poked her in the back with his staff, and she shuffled forward another step. Her voice was weak now, and she could barely be heard above the simple scuffling of feet and occasional clearing of the throat. "Aye, my lord. Ye have been informed correctly."

"And what exactly was your role in these events?" James set his cup down beside him and adjusted his doublet, aligning the buttons and straightening his cuffs. Agnes did not answer him until he looked at her again.

"Upon the night of All Hallows' Eve last, I and those accompanying me that ye have already been told of, with a great many other witches, went together into the sea in a sieve."

"How many other witches?" James asked, alarm clouding his voice.

"About two hundred."

"My God," he muttered. The color drained from His Majesty's face, and a great murmuring rose up within the room.

"When you say a sieve, you refer to the kitchen utensil used to drain water away from food stuffs?" I interjected.

She turned then and looked at me. She smiled strangely, and I felt my blood turn to ice. "Aye, the same."

I cleared my throat. "And what did you do while you were on the water?"

"We took bottles of wine with us and made merry, all the way to the Kirk of North Berwick."

Before I could ask another question, a great squawking sound emanated from the smokey fireplace. All in the room turned to look at the hearth. It sounded like someone had their hands around the neck of a bird and was squeezing the life out of it.

"See to it, Hamilton." James motioned to the grate. But Hamilton stood frozen to his spot, eyes wide with terror. The screeching continued to grow louder, and a few began to back away from the fireplace. "Silence that bloody racket!" James shouted. He too looked terrified. In fact, the only person in the room who seemed to be unaffected was Agnes.

I walked to the hearth and grabbed a long metal poker that stood propped beside it. I knelt and began jamming the rod upwards, hitting it against the flue while trying to stay clear of the fire below. The squawking continued, and I scooted closer to the chimney in order to reach my hand further into the gaping smoke hole. I thrust the rod once more, and felt it scrape against the flue. Thrice I shoved the poker through the flue in an effort to clear any nests or debris that may have been caught in the chimney. By this time, I was covered in black soot, and I could feel my patience quickly wearing away. The unmistakable cawing of a crow grew even louder. The cry began to sound more like a cackling laugh, and I turned to Agnes. I don't know what I sought in her eyes, or what I expected her to do, but when I looked at the old woman's face, I knew what I must do. I began banging the rod against the flue, clanging it like a kirk bell in a tower. I smashed my knuckles against the side of the chimney and felt the blood immediately breech the lacerations on my skin. With one final clang, a large black crow fell from the chimney, flapping its wings and scooting itself across the floor on its side. The neck looked broken, but the bird continued to squawk and cry as it pushed itself across the floor. It finally came to rest at Agnes' feet and only then did it cease its noisy protest.

No one spoke, only stared at the bird in amazement. Agnes stood looking down on the sorry creature, but she made no motion to pick it up or try to comfort it.

"What the devil was that, Agnes?" I finally bawled.

She slowly lifted her eyes from the bird. Staring at me momentarily, she said, "The steps of a good man are ordered."

I recognized the portion of scripture from which she quoted. I stared back at her, feeling the hair on the nape of my neck lift in response. I thought witches couldn't read the Holy Writ. Wasn't that one of the tests the witch pricker always used, amongst others, to try the abilities of the witch? I pushed myself up off the floor and brushed off my hands as best I could. My legs were trembling, but I focused on my shirt and doublet. They were ruined and there was no hope of remedying the soiled clothing. Bowing to the king, I said, "Excuse me while I go clean myself up." He nodded his release, and I went to wash my hands.

"And take that disgusting creature with you and dispose of it."

Heeding the king's command, I scooped the bird into my hands and held it away from me as I walked toward the door. I was shaken. The others appeared terrified, but they had not come face to face with the demonic creature.

"I don't get paid enough to deal with this nonsense," I grumbled as I tossed the bird across the road and then broke the thin layer of ice that lay on top of the bucket of water that stood outside the door. Splashing the freezing water on my face, I rubbed the water across my brow and swiped it through my hair.

"Having a bad day?" I turned abruptly at the familiar voice to see Ailsa holding a pail full of withered vegetables.

"Off to make soup for the poor of Edinburgh?" I asked with a bite to my words.

"Aye, but what of ye?"

"As a matter of fact, I *am* having a bad day, but you don't have to look so happy about it."

She took in the scowl on my face and softened her brow. "I'm sorry."

"Nay, you're not." I dipped my hands into the bucket again and scooped out another handful of water to splash on my face.

"Aye, I am. Here." She pulled a piece of cloth from her sleeve and handed it to me. "Use this to wipe your face. Is that *soot*?"

"Aye," I took the cloth from her hand. "Thank you," I held the piece of cloth up and nodded my head in thanks, then dipped the cloth into the bucket.

"Ye are interrogating the witches again, are ye not?"

I nodded but didn't speak, instead choosing to focus all my efforts on ridding myself of the black grime.

"Have ye any success?"

I looked at her expecting to see the same smug expression she always held when discussing the witches. But instead, I saw only concern. The fire I normally saw in her light brown eyes was replaced with empathy, and for a moment, I wished that it were me she empathized with. But I knew better.

"Have a look." I tilted my head toward the dead bird lying in the ditch on the other side of the road. The twisted black body starkly contrasted against the freshly fallen snow.

"Oh, dear." She stepped closer to the lifeless crow and stared at it for a moment. Turning back to me, she said, "Where did it come from?"

"From the chimney. But don't ask me how it got there. Nor why it chose to make its presence known at the exact moment we started interrogating Agnes Sampson. The fire had been lit for nigh on half an hour."

"That is most extraordinary. Perhaps it is a sign?"

I closed my eyes briefly and took a deep breath, recalling Agnes' cryptic words. I wasn't in the mood for another battle of wits with this enchanting creature. "Believe it or not, Agnes Sampson has indeed confessed to being a witch." I studied her, looking for any reaction that told me I had hit a sensitive spot.

"Indeed. It is no wonder, after all she has endured in the tolbooth."

I pressed my lips together in consternation. This woman tried my patience every time I was around her. "If it is simply a confession given under duress, then why the need to tell such tall tales in her confessional? For I can guarantee you, she has some cock-and-bull stories."

Worry clouded her eyes. "What kind of tall tales?"

"My apologies, but I am not at liberty to discuss this inquiry with you. May I just say, pray for her soul, Ailsa. This woman is going to need it."

I moved to return to the chamber, but Ailsa stopped me, putting her small hand on my arm. "Wait." I turned and looked at her, noticing once again the adorable freckles that lay scattered across her nose. "You still have some soot on your face." She dropped her pail and took the cloth from my hand, wiping it gently across my brow.

She handed the cloth back to me, but I stopped her. "It's yours, remember?" The air suddenly grew thick between us, and I found it difficult to catch my breath.

"Aye, but ye might need it again. Keep it." She shoved it into my hand, then quickly retrieved her pail as if I had the plague, and she needed to get away from me.

As she hurried off, I called after her. "Pray for their souls, Ailsa."

She turned and looked at me again, nodding silently.

~13~

January 1591

William

Assuming the interrogation would carry on without me, I was surprised to see that James had awaited my return before he began questioning Agnes again. I shoved the handkerchief that Ailsa had given me into my pocket. She had actually been half-way civil toward me during our little exchange. I wanted to take the offering of her handkerchief as a token of friendship, an extending of the olive branch, so to speak. But I wouldn't get my hopes up. This woman sympathized with the witches, and therefore, I needed to be leery of her. She might even be one of them, for all I knew. So, why did I find myself wishing more and more that she and I could be friends?

"Now, what did you and the other witches do when you arrived at the kirk in North Berwick?" The nasally sound of James's voice cut through my woolgathering, and I was brought back to the matter at hand.

"We all took hands and danced a reel." She lifted the hem of her skirt with busted fingers and began kicking up her feet as she twirled around in circles. From deep within the shriveled creature, the sounds of a tune came to her lips, and she pushed out the noise almost effortlessly.

"Visitor go ye before, visitor go ye,
If ye will not go before, visitor let me."

She stopped abruptly, breathless, and dizzy and would have collapsed if one of James's guards had not caught her under the arm and pulled her upright again.

"That's when Geillis Duncan went before us playing the reel on her Jew's harp until we entered into the kirk."

Interest piqued, James sat up straighter. "Her Jew's harp? I have heard of such an instrument but have never heard one played. You say that Geillis Duncan can play one?"

"Aye, she played for us as we danced a reel."

Motioning to another guard, James demanded, "Bring Geillis Duncan and her Jew's harp. I want to hear her play." The guard bowed then turned to fulfill our sovereign's command. "And make it hasty, I don't want to wait all day."

Since Geillis was in the tolbooth, it didn't take long for the guard to return with her in tow. He shoved her toward the front of the room, and James eyed her suspiciously.

"Play us a little reel, Mistress Duncan," the king commanded. She looked about her in bewilderment, not sure what to make of the odd request. "You play the Jew's harp, do you not?"

The room, still filled with smoke and the foul stench of body odor, grew quiet.

"Your Majesty, I, I have been stripped of all my earthly possessions. I do not have—" A small metal instrument, the size of a child's palm was produced as if by magic, and Geillis stared at it as if it would bite.

"Well, go on then." The king pointed at the small object. "Play us a reel."

Geillis took the instrument that was offered to her and turned it over in her hand several times. Her bloody fingers had been wrapped with a crude cloth and she began to slowly unwrap the binding from around her hands. She let the cloth drop to the floor, then laid the harp in her palm, wiggling her torn fingers and getting a feel for the pain that must still shoot through her appendages.

"Mistress Duncan?" Geillis looked up suddenly at the king. "Play."

She lifted the Jew's harp to her mouth and gripping it as best she could with her left hand, she clenched the harp with her teeth. Plucking the small metal prong that protruded outward, she began to make a strange sound with the instrument. Using the fleshy part of her palm, she plucked faster as she became accustomed to playing it without her busted fingers.

The tune picked up, and Agnes began shuffling across the floor again, skirts slightly lifted and eyes closed as she danced the reel that Geillis now played. Soon, she parted her lips, and her throaty voice began singing once more. Like the first song, the lyrics were nonsensical, and she soon lost herself in the rhythm of the vibrating sounds.

The king sat transfixed until the song was finished, and then he replied, "Fascinating." Then, as if he hadn't just sat in admiration for the last ten minutes, he began his interrogation again. "Goodwife Sampson, this has been most enlightening. But what does the Devil have to do with any of this?"

"Oh aye, the Devil met us at the Kirk of North Berwick, and seeing we made a merry sight, enjoined us to a penance."

"And what penance did he ask of you?"

"We were to kiss his buttocks as a sign of duty to him. He sat bare upon the pulpit of the kirk, and each took their turn pledging their devotion to him with the sign of a kiss. He then began to protest vehemently against the King of Scotland and therefore was happy to receive our fealty."

At that the king's face turned a most uncomely shade of purple. He stood and took a step toward Agnes. "Why did the Devil protest against me?"

"Because he said ye are his greatest enemy in the world."

A look of satisfaction overcame James's face. It appeared that being the greatest enemy of Satan was a holy compliment. He lifted his chin and with a slight smirk on his face, returned to his seat.

He stroked the whiskers on his chin for several minutes but did not say a word. When his contemplation came to an end, he finally spoke, but it was not the words anyone expected to hear.

"Goodwife Sampson, you have told some of the most far-fetched tales this day. Your stories fly in the face of reason, and I find them quite unbelievable. I am inclined to believe that you and your cohorts are complete and utter liars."

The hush was broken by gasps, and everyone began speaking at once. I moved toward James in order to counsel with him on his conclusion, but a motion from Agnes turned the room quiet again. She stood with her hand upraised in an effort to quiet the room.

"I would not wish His Majesty to suppose my words to be false. Rather, I would that ye believe them, and to that end, I will discover such matters to ye that will leave no doubt."

She began to approach the king, but two guards stepped forward with halberds in hand and stopped her.

The woman lowered her voice. "It be a private matter, Your Grace."

James motioned for the guards to move and allow Agnes to step forward. She moved closer and closer until even the look on the king's face took on one of concern. She then leaned forward and whispered something to the king that no one else in the room could hear. I watched as the king's countenance went from smug disbelief to utter shock. All color drained from his cheeks, and his eyes grew as round as goose eggs. A choked sound escaped his lips, and he looked about him as if to gauge if anyone else had heard the old woman's words.

Straightening in his seat, he bellowed, "Guards, remove this woman at once!" A great commotion ensued as the guards grabbed Agnes by the arms and dragged her away. Geillis was also dragged off, and those remaining were left to wonder at the curiosity of it all. I turned toward James once more, but he had already risen from his seat. "That will be all for today."

The stillness in the room at the king's pronouncement was palpable, and only after James had departed in great haste, did anyone dare to question what Agnes had said.

"There was mention of his wedding night," whispered Hamilton as he drew near to me. I turned and looked at him with concern.

"Do you suppose she threatened him or the queen?"

"It's hard to say." Hamilton stroked his beard. "The old hag is as crazy as the stories she tells."

I didn't respond, but instead I looked at the floor where the old woman had stood only moments before. There truly was something odd about the exchange that had taken place here today, but I didn't know what to make of it.

"It is no wonder after all she has endured in the tolbooth." Ailsa's words came back to me. Had the woman truly been driven mad by Seton's interrogations? I ran a hand over my face. After what I had seen at Fian's interrogation, it wouldn't be hard to believe.

I looked around for Seton, but it appeared that he had slipped out when Agnes had been removed from the room. I would speak to him again and express my concern at the brutalness of these interrogations. I also wanted to talk to James. What had Agnes said to him that had upset him so much?

But the person that I wanted to speak to the most was the one person that was probably least likely to want to speak to me. Ailsa seemed to be very concerned with these witches, even though she claimed to know none of them. Why was she so interested? And why was she convinced that none of them were guilty?

I stepped out into the cold and glanced about. The street was busier now but I looked to see if I could find Seton in the crowd. When I didn't see his broad figure pushing his way through the throng, I decided to check the tolbooth. More than likely, he was heading that way to wreak more havoc with the prisoners.

That is when I noticed it. The crow, whose broken body I had discarded in the snow only an hour ago, was gone, and there was no trace of it having ever been there.

~14~

January 1591

Ailsa

It had been a couple of weeks since I had tried to sneak a message to Geillis through a package shoved into the wall of the tolbooth. William had caught me the first time before I had completed my task. I was hoping that he wouldn't be around this time. I would get a note through to Geillis one way or another.

I wrapped the small loaves in pieces of heavy cloth and tied them with jute. I had spent the morning baking the loaves of bread with messages in them. The most important message was the one I had jotted for Geillis, relaying to her that I wanted to help her.

I kissed Mother on the head and gave Sadie instructions to keep an eye on her. It was getting increasingly difficult to leave my mother alone, but she had seemed clear-headed again this morning, so I hoped that I would not regret my decision later. I wrapped my cloak about me and stepped into the cold morning. The tendrils of fog that clung to the distorted shapes of buildings and wagons were a blessing. Hopefully that would keep me from being seen again.

I managed to get all the packages in through the tolbooth wall without getting caught. I breathed a prayer of relief that I had not been discovered. But as I gathered my basket and wrapped my earasaid tighter about me to go, a soft hissing noise caught my attention and I paused to listen again.

"Mistress," the voice whispered. "Mistress, please."

I bent to peer into the hole. A dark eye stared back at me and blinked when I drew near. "What is it?" I regretted the sharpness of my tone. For although I wanted to help in any way I could, I didn't want to draw attention to myself. The fact that at any time, anyone could be accused of witchcraft for the most trivial of things was a constant threat.

"The king is in danger," the eye said to me. "Ye must tell the king that he is in danger."

"In danger of what?" I asked, feeling my blood quicken. Witchcraft wasn't the only dangerous crime. Threats against the king were treason, and treason could be just as deadly.

"The Devil wants his throne."

The Devil? This time my blood turned to ice. Had these accused witches really been practicing their craft in order to depose the king?

"What do ye mean?" Uncertainty shook my voice.

"The Devil wears black and has lots of friends. He is rich in houses and land. He says the throne is rightfully his, and he will have it, no matter the cost."

"Of whom do ye speak? This sounds like no devil to me, but a greedy man."

"Aye. He is a greedy devil. Tell the king he will be taken. Tell the king!"

Something black was shoved through the hole of the wall toward me, and in an instant, shouts could be heard from inside the tollbooth, and the eye suddenly disappeared. I straightened and moved away quickly so as not to be found in league with this disembodied voice. My heart was pounding, and I looked around to ascertain whether I had been seen. When I was sure no one watched, I looked to see what had been pushed through the wall. There on the ground lay a large, black feather, like that from a crow. I picked up the feather and stuffed it into the folds of my skirt. I wanted no evidence left behind of this encounter.

I walked some distance before I felt confident enough to remove the feather and look at it. The large plume shone in the morning sunlight as I ran my fingers over the silky strands. For a moment I almost wished that William had come after all. He was the only person that might be able to do something with the information I had been given. I wasn't sure how true the accusation was, but it might be worth looking into.

I meandered up the High Street and soon found myself standing in front of Gordon's Bookshop. I tucked the feather back into my skirt and felt for the weight of my coin purse, debating on whether I wanted to spend my extra coin on a new book.

Making a decision, I stepped through the door of the shop, the tinkling of the brass bell above the door notifying Master Gordon of my entrance. The smell of fresh ink on paper sent a thrill through me as I inhaled the rich aroma, closing my eyes to thoroughly enjoy the pleasure. The musky odor of binding glue, though not as fragrant, also shot a jolt of excitement straight to my bones.

"Good day to ye, Mistress Blackburn. How may I be of service to ye?"

Martin Gordon was a short, rotund man with thinning hair and a large knobby nose. I had made a comment once to Father about Master Gordon's nose, and he had rapped me on the knuckles for my impertinence. "Don't get on the bad side of the local bookseller, Ailsa," he had chided. "There may come a time when ye will need his kindness. Ye don't look a gift horse in the mouth."

I hadn't understood the adage when Father had first spoken it, but in the ensuing years, I had come to understand his meaning. It had indeed paid off to stay in Gordon's good graces. For on more than one occasion he had loaned me one of his used books with the understanding that I would take extra special care of it and return it to him in the same condition as he lent it to me.

"May I take a look around, Master Gordon? I'm not sure what I want yet."

"Of course, take your time." The bookseller adjusted his spectacles, the tiny, round lenses sliding down his nose as soon as he pushed them up.

I browsed the shelves of books, resisting the urge to run my hand over every copy presented to me. A sea of deep burgundies, russet browns and rich blacks sang out to me as their supple leather coverings beckoned me to touch them, stroke their coverings, smell their pages and drink in their alluring words. It was a feast for my senses, yet one that I partook in painfully. For along with the enticing sights and smells came the overwhelming tinge of memory. Memories of Father bringing me along as he sought out a book he needed for study. The recollection of times spent together browsing the shelves and soaking in the captivating draw of a good story.

I picked up a copy of a new book called *Astrophel and Stella*. It looked to be a collection of love sonnets. I read several lines and thought it would make for great entertainment on the coming long winter nights when Mother and I would retire to our spots by the fire for quiet reflection. No matter that Mother's idea of quiet reflection was the reading of her book of hours. Perhaps I could convince her to listen to a few sonnets, for they did sound lovely when I glanced through them. I carried the book for a while until I spied a copy of *Tamburlaine the Great*. My heart began to pound as excitement rushed through my veins. My brother, Nick, had mentioned seeing Christopher Marlowe's play of the same name in London two years before. His letter made it sound so exciting, and I bemoaned the fact that I would never get to see such entertainment the likes of what Nick got to experience in London.

I grabbed the book and quickly put *Astrophel and Stella* back on the shelf. As much as I thought I would enjoy the sonnets, I couldn't resist a good tragedy. And Nick's description made me to know that I would thoroughly enjoy this book.

I took my selection to the counter and placed it on the smooth, worn surface in front of Master Gordon. He took one look at the book, eyeing the title over the rim of his spectacles.

"Are ye sure, Ailsa? The players in London have put out some questionable material over the past decade. I'm not sure this title here is fit for female consumption."

"Nick said it was a wonderful play, and he highly recommended it."

Just then the little bell above the door rang. Gordon's face lit up as he moved to the new customer. "Jean, can ye assist Ailsa with selecting a book, please?" he called over his shoulder.

Selecting a book? I already selected a book. I didn't need Mistress Gordon's assistance in selecting a book. I crossed my arms in agitation. Out of respect for Master Gordon I would wait for his customer to leave before confronting him about his opinions on my book choices.

A stout woman came through the doorway and greeted me with her usual cheerful self. "Ailsa, dear! How are ye? How is your mother?"

But her greeting went unanswered when the voice of the new customer spoke up from the other end of the counter. I would recognize that voice anywhere.

"Master Gordon, good day to you. I had a few minutes and thought I would stop in to see if those books were in that you ordered for me."

My fingers instinctively went to the feather, tucked safely within the folds of my skirt. Now I could speak to William when he had finished his business with Master Gordon. But as I rehearsed what I would say to him in my mind, Mistress Gordon noticed my distraction and leaned in closer so she could whisper to me. "He is a fine specimen, is he not?"

I felt heat flush my face as I tried to nonchalantly ask, "Who?"

A grin spread across her face, and her eyes brightened. "The king's man, at the end of the counter. I know ye noticed him. How could ye not?"

I picked up my book and flipped through the pages in a fluster. "I hadn't noticed," I lied. "Can I pay for my purchase, please? Then I'll be out of your way."

Mistress Gordon reached for the book, and then said, "He always looks so impeccable. And that dark hair. If I were thirty years younger—"

"Jean," Master Gordon interrupted. "Excuse me for a moment, sir." He nodded at William then approached Mistress Gordon and me, a look of consternation on his face. "I do not think this is the wisest choice for Mistress Blackburn. Can ye help her pick out something else?"

The heat that burned on my face moments before was now a flaming fire. I could feel William's eyes on me as he listened to the exchange between Gordon and his wife. I silently wished for the floor to open up and swallow me. I needed to speak to William, but I did not wish for this kind of attention. And I certainly didn't want Gordon's interference with my book selections.

William drew closer to us until he stood hovering over me. My skin turned to gooseflesh at his nearness, and I struggled to keep my breathing even. I did not need his opinion either. He would surely side with Gordon, and that would be the end of it.

"What seems to be the problem?" William asked, leaning over my shoulder to peer at the book that lay before me.

"I-I don't think this is a suitable choice for a young woman, Master Broune. I have known Ailsa and her father for years, and I'm sure her father would agree."

"With all due respect, Master Gordon, I know my father better than ye do. He would not object. And my brother gives his blessing." I spoke with feigned calmness, trying desperately to maintain my composure in the face of this unwelcome opposition.

Gordon looked desperately to William. "What think ye, Master Broune?"

I shut my eyes to his interference. The anger bubbling within me was now palpable, and I feared that if I lost my temper, I could do irreparable damage to my relationship with the bookseller. I did not care about any damage between William and me.

"You can read, lass?" His question was a legitimate one, yet it irritated me like a pinprick to my eye. I took a deep breath through my nostrils and tried to calm myself before answering.

"Master Broune, I know ye find it very difficult to believe that a woman could be useful for anything more than adorning your arm at court and perhaps providing ye an heir when the time is right. But some of us do actually have competent minds, capable of reading and writing, and even holding intelligent conversations now and then." I looked at him finally, fluttering my eyelashes in mock adoration.

He took a step back, a patch of color staining his cheeks. "I meant no offense, Ailsa. I am well aware that women are capable of reading and writing. I am always delighted to meet a woman with whom I can hold an intelligent conversation."

"Because intelligent women are so few and far between, ye mean?" I stared him down, watching the injury blaze in his eyes.

"You insist on twisting my words, Mistress Blackburn. I find that very off-putting, as this is not the first time that you are guilty of it."

My stomach tightened as I watched the irritating grin fade from his face. I almost felt sorry for the loss of his pleasure and feared that I may have overstepped my bounds. Now I felt awkward and stupid.

Master and Mistress Gordon stood with mouths agape as they watched our conversation. I suddenly felt the air tighten between us, and I couldn't breathe.

"Ye know what, I think I'll hold off on my purchase for now, Master Gordon." I pushed the book toward him and his wife, as I reached for my purse, making sure it was still attached at my hip. Pushing past William, I pulled my cloak tighter about me as I braced for the cold January air. "Good day to ye all," I said as I stormed out of the bookshop.

That insufferable man. He had turned a beautiful, almost spiritual experience of a trip to the bookseller into an embarrassing catastrophe. Or perhaps it had been Master Gordon that had done that, but William certainly had helped. I set off down the street, pushing the fact that I had wanted to see him, to speak to him about the danger the king was in, to the back of my mind. I needed to calm down before sharing any insight with him. The information I had was important, but it would just have to wait.

~15~

January 1591

William

By the time I reached the street, Ailsa was nowhere to be seen. I looked up and down the High Street, searching for her chestnut locks or the whey-colored cloak she had wrapped about her. Seeing nothing that looked familiar, I chose a direction and started walking. I gathered from snippets of conversation that she may live nearby to St Giles Kirk, but I had no idea where exactly she lived and knew choosing a direction would be a shot in the dark.

I had only walked a block when I spotted her petite figure wrapped in blue, haggling with a merchant at the Luckenbooths. I stepped up behind her and watched as she immediately straightened, her back going rigid, and her hands stilling.

"You really shouldn't run off like that," I said under my breath, not wanting to frighten her. She did not turn around, but I suspected she heard me for I saw her head tilt slightly to the side as if listening to my words. She finished her transaction, then turned toward me, fire still burning in her eyes.

"Come to ruin the rest of my shopping experience?" She spat out the words, and I could see that she was still angry with me. She had a right to be. I had been a heel.

"I've come to offer my apologies," I said, handing her a package wrapped in brown paper. She looked down at the parcel but did not take it.

"It will take more than an apology for me to forgive your interference."

"Which is why I hope this will suffice." I nodded to the package still in my hand and pushed it toward her again.

She extended a tentative hand, then took the object from me. Her eyes darted around us, and I motioned for her to follow me in an effort to guide her away from the merchants and booths. When we were out from amongst the crowd, she stared down at the package in her hand.

"Why did ye do this?" she asked, irritation etching her voice. The unopened parcel measuring the length between us.

"You don't even know what it is." Amusement lit my voice.

"I know what it is." Her voice caught, and I could see tears fill the rims of her eyes. "I can tell by the weight of it." She slid a small finger beneath the string and slid it off the package. Slowly, she unfolded the paper and turned the object over to see the front. *Tamburlaine the Great* was etched across the cover in intricate gold letters. "Why?" she asked again, her voice softer this time.

"Because I'm a prig sometimes, and I don't think before I speak."

She tilted her head up toward me, brows furrowed. "Ye recognize that?" A slight smile curved her wine-colored lips. I nodded but did not speak. "Ye didn't tell Gordon it was for me, did ye? Ye don't want to get on his bad side."

"I most certainly did. I told him that I thought you were more than capable of making a sound decision on your own and that your Father could take it up with me if he had a problem with it." She tore her eyes away from the book and pinned me with a hollow look.

"My father is dead."

"I know. Gordon told me as much. I'm sorry." I wanted desperately to make things right between us. I didn't know why this woman's opinion of me mattered, but the more I saw of her, the more I realized I wanted to be friends. She was making it extremely difficult.

"I can promise ye he will not come back to haunt ye from his grave," she said, sniffling. "He believed that women could have as much intelligence as men, and he taught me to that end. He always let me make my own reading choices. If it was something he thought questionable, he made sure to discuss it with me. It made for very lively discussions, as ye can imagine."

I smiled at her memory of her father, recalling my own memories of times spent under my father's tutelage. "Was your father a tutor?"

"He was a scribe. He scribed for several of the Archbishops until he became too sick to do the work anymore."

"He worked for the Archbishop? At St Andrews?"

"Aye. He worked for several of them."

I wasn't sure why that sent a warmth to my chest. She and I had common roots. I had lived in St Andrews the first ten years of my life until Father had sent me to court to serve King James.

"My father must have known your father. He is the Dean of Theology at the University of St Andrews and has taught there for many years. I don't recall the Blackburn name, but then again, I left St Andrews as a young boy. We must have lived there at the same time. How old are you?"

"I'm one and twenty."

The button of her nose had turned crimson and a soft pink had tinged her cheeks. Ailsa stamped her feet in an effort to warm herself, tucking her new book under her arm and rubbing her hands together.

"You're cold. It's freezing out here." As much as I longed to talk with her more, I did not wish to see her catch her death when she was clearly suffering from the effects of the frigid air. Reluctantly, I said, "I should let you go."

"Actually," she said, hesitating for a moment. "There was something I was hoping to talk with ye about." Her eyes slid from mine and I noted the nervousness with which she spoke.

"All right," I said without question. Turning to look over my shoulder, an idea struck me. "I have a room a few minutes' walk from here. We can get out of the cold and talk privately."

"I thought ye lived at the palace?" She turned and followed me as I motioned to her the direction that my room lay.

"I do. Most of the time. But I wanted to be closer to the tolbooth and to the prisoners whom we are interrogating. And sometimes I just want the privacy."

At the mention of the prisoners, I saw Ailsa's back stiffen. It was a sensitive topic with her, and one I really didn't wish to broach at the moment.

"Aye, the witches." Her voice strained with emotion.

I stopped walking and reached out a hand to stop her too. "Ailsa, can we call a truce for the afternoon? Let us not speak of the witch trials today. I finally feel like I'm building some solid ground here. I don't want to knock this foundation down before I've even had a chance to stand on it."

She cocked her head and looked at me with confusion. Then without a word she nodded and continued walking. Finally, she said, "I'm very opinionated, if ye haven't figured that out." She huffed a small laugh, hugging the book I had given her to her chest as if it were protection from the cold. I didn't say anything as I was learning very quickly how precarious this little friendship of ours was. If one could even call it a friendship. If I could just figure out the right things to say and do around her, then maybe the friendship stood a chance.

We reached my room within minutes, and I stopped once more. "Here we are."

She looked up at the building, suspicion wrinkling her forehead. "The bookshop?"

I chuckled. "I stay above the bookshop. It's very convenient." I motioned for her to go before me as I opened the door that led to the upper floor. The smell of aging wood enveloped us and the warmth of the building, without the winter wind blowing against our faces, was a welcome benefit.

I moved to her side, laying my hand against the small of her back to help guide her up the steps. It was dark in the musty hallway, with only a little window at the top of the stairs to let in the bleak, winter light. The first—and last—time I had touched her had resulted in a tongue lashing, the likes of which even my old nursemaid Suzanne couldn't compete with. I felt her muscles tense beneath my touch, and I removed my hand as soon as we had reached the second landing, where I was sure our footing was secure. I ignored the tingling in my fingers and fumbled for my key instead.

~16~

January 1591

Ailsa

I was curious to see William's room. I had imagined him to be a man of flawless outward beauty, while all the while living in quarters equivalent to a pig stye. How wrong I was. Although the room was occupied with the barest of necessities, I still found nothing out of place. Nothing shoved under the bed in hurried tidiness. No clothing strewn about as if rushed to his next appointment. I frowned. All those imagined faults that had given me more reasons to dislike him didn't exist. Mistress Gordon had the right of it—he was impeccable. From his cleanly starched ruff and immaculate boot buckles to the neatly laid bed linens. Everything was in clean and perfect order. That in itself was almost a fault. Unnerving perfection.

I watched as he removed his chain of office then unbuttoned the ornamental braided toggles on his blue cloak, his deft fingers maneuvering its workings with precise dexterity. Broad shoulders stretched beneath a finely embroidered linen tunic, covered with an equally stunning brocade doublet. He wore black paned trunks trimmed with fine gold threading of the same brocade and knee-high boots of leather to cover his calves. An onyx leather jerkin completed the attire.

"May I?" He caught me staring and reached for my cloak.

"Aye, of course." I hurriedly removed my cloak and handed it to him. He hung it on a peg on the wall next to his own.

"Would you like some tea?" He moved to the hearth and hung a small brown kettle on a hook that hung above the grate.

Clearing my throat, I said, "That would be wonderful." I stood awkwardly, still clutching the new book in my arms. My hands felt moist as I clasped the volume, a looming sense of dread beginning to creep up my neck. What was I doing here? I had just slipped a message to one of the prisoners in the tolbooth, plotting her escape. Now here I was about to have tea with one of the most dangerous men in Edinburgh, the man overseeing the witches' interrogations. What a treacherous game I played.

I tried to swallow the nervous lump that had formed in my throat, feeling any words that I might have spoken in casual conversation get stuck in the roof of my mouth. I couldn't stop my hands from shaking and found myself clenching the book even tighter to me in an effort to ease my nerves. Coming here was a mistake. True, he had suggested we not talk about the witch trials, but I couldn't shake the feeling that I had forced my way into a den of vipers.

He turned back to me, and I saw his bright blue eyes sweep over me. "Please, have a seat." He pulled a chair out from the small table that sat in the corner of the room and motioned for me to sit. "Are you hungry? I have a meat pie, or some boiled chicken."

"No, please don't trouble yourself." I laid the book on the table, then regretted having nothing to occupy my hands and therefore shoved them into the layers of my skirts.

"It is no trouble. I'm feeling a little hungry myself. It is well past noon."

I shot a glance out the window, but the sun that had peaked the horizon this morning had turned into a hazy gloom that settled on the town like a wet sea mist. My mind went to my mother, and I wondered how she was getting on. Thoughts of her drove my anxiety and spurred my mind back to why I had come. But William was busy slicing bread and had laid out cuts of cold chicken and walnuts on a plate.

He seated himself at the table, placing an empty plate in front of me. "In case you change your mind," he said. But no sooner had he sat down when he remembered the water that he had put on for tea, and he was back on his feet again.

Turning back to me abruptly, he said, "Have you ever tasted cacao?"

I blinked at him several times, puzzled at his random question. "N-no, I don't believe I have. I've never even heard of such a thing."

He pulled a small red tin from the shelf and gathered two cups in his hands. Placing the items on the table, he went once more to the shelf and pulled down a bowl and two spoons as well. Finally, he grabbed a bottle of cream and pulled the kettle from the fire and set it on a wicker plate he had also placed on the table.

"It is an acquired taste, and one that His Majesty has decidedly not obtained. That is how I came to be in possession of such a precious commodity. The king did not like it and therefore gave it to me."

"Ye look like ye are about to indulge in an alchemy experiment." I laughed, indicating all the containers he had laid out on the table. A slight smile curled one side of his mouth, but he didn't answer. Instead, he lifted the lid from the tin and pulled out a flat, round cake that had been hardened into a brown disc. "Have ye been making mud cakes, Master Broune?"

He laughed at that and dropped a fragment of the disc into both of the cups. Pouring hot water onto the darkened pieces, he began to stir the liquid until the heat had dissolved the disc and turned the water a dark, rich color. A spicy, nutty aroma filled the air between us and I found myself leaning in to see his creation.

"When the Spanish conquistador, Hernando Cortés, returned from his travels, he brought back a supply of beans known as cacao. The natives he met in the New World would drink a concoction made from this bean, and the Spanish fell in love with it. The beans are crushed and grounded into a paste then poured into the round cakes you see here. They are left to dry for months before consumption. The cakes are very expensive, as the beans are only grown in the New World.

The Spanish ambassador brought a gift of cacao cakes for His Majesty, but he did not care for it."

He added a spoonful of sugar and stirred the mixture again. An ample dose of cream was his finishing touch. Pushing a cup full of the dark liquid in front of me, he said, "Drink carefully. The Spaniards add crushed Jamaican peppers to their cacao. The sugar and cream will offset this a bit, but it is still spicy." He nodded toward the drink then picked up his cup and carefully took a sip.

I picked up the cup offered to me and smelled the brew. The scent was enticing, but I blew cool air along the surface of the liquid to calm the steam. Carefully, I lifted the cup to my lips and took a drink as well. Fire shot through my tongue and burned a hole straight through to my nose. Tears sprang to my eyes immediately, and I began to choke as I tried to swallow the remaining liquid trapped in my mouth.

William grinned and took another sip. "I told you to drink it slowly," he advised.

"Ye told me to drink it carefully," I corrected, one arched brow reprimanding him. "There is a difference." I lifted the cup and took another drink, this time squeezing my eyes shut as I swallowed the searing liquid.

"You don't have to drink if you don't like it," he said.

I didn't speak for a moment as I considered the rich, spicy flavor. It had a tinge of bitterness to it, but the faint taste of sugar gave it just enough sweetness to make it enjoyable.

"I actually like it," I said, surprise shading my voice.

His blue eyes lit up in apparent approval. "I'm pleased to hear it."

I drank the cacao slowly and even took a few bites of chicken to offset the heat on my tongue. Before I knew it, our drinks and meal were almost finished, and I hadn't even told him yet why I had come.

I drained the last drop of dark liquid from my cup and dabbed at my mouth. The warmth of the liquid filled my belly, giving me a satisfied feeling and maybe even a little boldness.

"I have some information to share with ye. It is concerning the king. But I need a promise from ye that I will not be held responsible for the information, nor accused of accessory to the crime due to my knowledge of it."

William raised a brow, and I noticed his eyes darken to a turbulent shade of blue, the color of the North Sea before a storm. "A crime?"

"Aye," I said, suddenly not feeling so sure of myself. "That is, the crime has not been perpetrated yet. What I have is knowledge of a crime that will happen in the near future."

He stopped twirling his empty cup and let the vessel come to a rest on its own volition. Sitting back in his chair, he draped an arm across the back of it. "And how have you come to be aware of such knowledge?"

I closed my eyes in regret then blew out a long breath. "I guess I should have added that to my list of disclaimers—no asking where the information came from." My attempted smile felt more like a plea.

But any friendly banter that we may have shared over the meal had disappeared like the cacao in our cups. He dropped his arm from the chair and leaned on the table toward me. "Ailsa, you cannot tell me there will be a crime committed against His Majesty and not tell me how you came about this information."

I dropped my eyes to the table. I could not meet his blue-black gaze. Taking a deep breath, I began, "I heard it from a prisoner at the tolbooth."

He narrowed his eyes on me momentarily. "What have you done?" he asked in an accusing tone.

I lifted my chin. "I've been feeding the prisoners, as ye know I am wont to do. Ye cannot stop me."

"Actually, I can," he shot back. "But I'm more concerned with what you heard while you were there."

I watched as he strode across the room. Picking up a bottle of wine, he poured himself a drink, then set the bottle on the table with a heavy *thunk*. "Proceed," he said, motioning with a wave of his cup as he seated himself once more.

"The king is in danger." William stared at me, and I felt the heat creeping up my neck in an uncomfortable prickle. I swallowed, then looked at him again, expecting to see impatience on his face. But he just gazed at me with his darkened eyes, waiting.

I relayed the incident that had happened at the tolbooth, telling him of the Devil and his desire to remove the king from his throne.

When I finished William sat up straighter. "So, the devil they refer to is not some spiritual being but a man of flesh and blood?"

"I cannot tell ye any more than I have already shared, for that is all that has been revealed to me."

"They said *he will be taken*. That sounds like a kidnapping plot. When? When will this scheme come to fruition?"

"I do not know."

William rubbed a hand across the back of his neck. "Was this a witch that told you this?"

"I'm not sure. The conversation was short but before they were dragged away, they shoved this through the tolbooth wall." I pulled the feather from my pocket and laid it on the table.

That's when the color drained from William's face.

~17~

January 1591

William

God's teeth. Not another crow.

I shoved myself away from the table. "Is this a jest?"

Ailsa stared at me in confusion. "Nay. That is, I do not know. What does it mean?"

I reached across the table and carefully took the feather between my thumb and forefinger. It looked like any other feather, just like the crow that had fallen from the fireplace had looked like any other bird. But still, there had been something other-worldly about the thing, just as this feather here before me now.

"Do you remember the dead crow that lay outside in the snow on the day you saw me at Agnes' interrogation?"

Understanding alighted her face. "Aye. Do ye think there is a connection?"

I studied the object for another moment before a shiver caused me to drop it onto the table. "'Tis very strange."

Ailsa, too, stared at the feather. She had grown very quiet, and I wondered if the talk of witches was bothering her.

"I promised you we would not speak of the witch trials."

"'Tis all right. Do ye think this schemer has something to do with the witches? I'm not sure with whom I was speaking through the wall."

I moved to begin cleaning up, and Ailsa stood with me. "It certainly warrants looking into."

I set the tin of cacao back on the shelf, but when I turned around Ailsa was behind me, holding the flask of cream. We bumped into each other, and the flask crashed to the floor, the contents slushing out all over the place.

"I am so sorry!" Ailsa cried as she immediately stooped and tried to sop up the spilt cream with her skirts.

"Please, don't use your clothing," I said as I reached for a drying cloth and knelt to clean up the mess. "Here, allow me." I knelt beside her, but she reached for the cloth and wouldn't let me help. Instead, I found myself looking at the intricate lacework of the ruff she wore around her slender neck. I resisted the urge to curl the little wisps of hair at her nape around my finger.

"I am truly sorry. What a waste of good cream." She continued wiping up the liquid as she chatted nervously. "I'm usually not so clumsy."

"It was my fault. Please, don't worry yourself." I watched as she scrubbed the wooden surface until it practically looked dry.

"But you're so particular," she continued. "I can tell ye take great pains to be neat, and I imagine anything out of place probably drives ye mad."

I laughed at her assessment of me. "You're not wrong," I began. "But it's rather unsettling to know that I can be read like an open book."

"Aye, well, I have a bad habit of judging a person before I even get to know them. For instance, I had ye all figured out. Ye dress so immaculately, but I was sure ye had some fault, hidden beneath your bed, or shoved in a closet somewhere."

She wasn't making any sense, and I truly thought she would rub a hole in the floorboards if she continued scrubbing. Reaching for her hand to stay the cloth, I said, "You can stop now. It's perfect."

I simply meant to take the cloth from her, but when I touched the soft skin of her hand, my blood heated and I felt a thrill of *something* shoot up my arm. I expected her to recoil from my touch, but when she only stilled her hand, I looked at her in disbelief. Her eyes searched mine, and I suddenly felt very aware of our situation.

Taking the cloth, I whispered, "Forgive me. I know you don't like to be touched." I stood and laid the cloth on the counter, striding to the table to finish cleaning up.

She cleared her throat behind me. "I should go. I have stayed much too long."

I turned toward her. "It didn't seem too long. In fact, I rather enjoyed your company. I was going to ask if you wanted some tea."

She stood twisting her skirts in her hands. "'Tis kind of ye to ask. But ye see, my mother is not well, and it is not wise to leave her alone for long periods of time."

"I am sorry to hear about Mistress Blackburn. Is there anything I can do to help?" I reluctantly retrieved her cloak and wrapped it about her shoulders.

"Thank ye. I don't know of anything that I can ask of ye at the moment, but if I think of anything I will not hesitate to ask."

~18~

January 1591

Ailsa

I know you don't like to be touched.

William's words struck me like an ice-cold bucket of water thrown in my face. I actually did like to be touched, but I guess I hadn't realized that until his hand had covered mine, seeking the cloth that I used to almost demolish his floorboards with my incessant scrubbing.

It was bad enough that I had dropped the cream. But I couldn't stop talking. I sounded like a magpie with all of my chattering. And then, he laid his hand on mine to take the cloth. His warmth was comforting, as if wrapping myself in a woolen blanket that had been left to hang by the fire on a cold winter's night. I rather liked it, and that had sent this magpie to flight.

I hurried down the steps and out into the harsh elements, my mind a maddening blur. Thoughts of tight leather jerkins, cups of cacao, ravenous blue eyes and gentle touches all came whirling back to me, crushing my thoughts, and making it hard to breathe.

"Take care!" shouted a fishmonger, pushing along a cart of his wares and practically flattening me in the street.

"My apologies," I murmured, holding up my hand to stay his cart, as if I could stop him from running me over by my will alone. He nodded in acceptance of my apology and allowed me to pass before moving on.

Something had shifted between William and me. A bond of trust was being forged, but I was still unsure how much of that trust was on my part.

When I turned down Fishmarket Close, I immediately sensed something was not right. Several people congregated in the narrow alleyway in front of our home, an awkward stillness hanging heavily in the air. Fanny Haskins paced back and forth in front of the threshold, her babe on her hip, and Janet stood in front of the door, biting at her thumbnail. When she saw me, she quickly said something to Fanny and ran to meet me.

"Oh, Ailsa! Thank the Almighty ye are here!"

"What has happened, Janet?" I looked from her to Fanny, feeling as though a millstone had been tied about my neck and was pulling me beneath some imaginary firth.

"'Tis your mother, Ailsa. She has locked herself inside the house and won't open the door for anyone."

I chuckled nervously. "Why would she open the door to a crowd of people gathered outside of our home. Perhaps ye all have scared her."

"We are only here because we heard her cries for help. It began with an awful wailing coming from within. Then the wails turned to terrified cries as she shouted for someone to leave her alone. We thought a thief had forced their way into your home, but an ear to the door revealed no other occupants. Forgive me for saying so Ailsa, but I don't believe your mother is well in the head."

I turned on her. "I will not forgive ye for saying such a thing, Janet." Then turning to the small crowd, I said, "Now, leave us while I see to my mother and find out what has frightened her." Reluctantly, the crowd dissipated until only Janet stood with me on the doorstep.

"I did not mean to upset ye, Ailsa. I am only concerned for ye and your mother. I know she has not been herself lately."

I looked up to find a set of soft green eyes under a worried brow searching my face. Memories of her reluctance around my mother came back to me. Her kindness struck a chord in me, and I realized how awful I had been to her.

"'Tis me that should be seeking your forgiveness, Janet. Ye are right, my mother has not been herself lately. Thank ye for your concern. Now if ye don't mind, I shall see to her." She nodded, and I unlocked the heavy wooden door and slipped inside.

The first thing that caught my attention as my eyes adjusted to the darkened room, was the faint light glinting off of Sadie's feline eyes as she hid beneath my chair by the hearth. The fact that she was not curled up somewhere comforting Mother told me that she had been startled into hiding. I looked about, following the whimpering sound that came from the bed. When I reached her, Mother was curled up into a ball, her earasaid covering her head. When I pulled back her plaid, I saw her knees tucked up to her chest, and her arms wrapped about her. Her face was buried in her knees.

"Mother," I said softly, not wanting to scare her even more. But when she did not immediately respond, I reached for her, stroking her hair, and rubbing my hand down her arm.

When she finally recognized my voice, she peeked at me with one eye and let out a choked gasp. "Ailsa, my love. Are they gone?"

I looked around the room. "Are who gone, Mother? I see no one. Who was here?"

She lifted her head at that and looked also. When she didn't say anything further, I prodded, "Who was here?"

She shook her head as if clearing the fog from her mind and sat up. "The King's Guard. They were here to take me away."

My heart nearly stopped at her words. "What do ye mean, Mother? Why would the King's Guard take ye away?" She shook her head again but did not answer. I rose to put some water on for tea. The kettle reminded me of the afternoon I had spent with William. The afternoon I had *foolishly* spent with him. I had ignored my intuition and worry because I had been drawn into his perfect little world. With his perfect cacao drinks and his perfectly intriguing fear of crows. I had been stupid for lingering so long.

Why did Mother think the King's Guard had come for her? I shook the terrible sense that had settled in my bones and tried to busy myself with thoughts of supper preparations.

"Well, they are gone now," I said cautiously, wondering if it was a good idea to play into her imagination. "Why don't ye come sit by the fire while I prepare us something to eat." I helped Mother off the bed and into her chair. I would try to ask her again about the guard when she was less upset. Perhaps she would be more willing to talk about it.

A light tapping on the door the next day drew me from my bucket and scrub brush. I looked to Mother to see her reaction. She had sat quietly the rest of the prior evening and had shown no other indication of fear or confusion since.

I opened to find an exquisitely dressed William in front of me. A long, brocade cloak covered his broad frame; the ermine collar pulled up to his chin. His frosty breath partially hid his face until the condensation cleared, revealing clear blue eyes smiling at me. He held two packages in his hands.

"Sir William." I nodded at him, opening the door to allow him entrance into our home. When Mother saw who was at the door, she let out a delighted squeal and ran to greet him.

"Master Broune, to what do we owe this pleasure?" She curtsied to him, and he took her small hand in his, brushing a light kiss across her knuckles. Mother fluttered her eyelids and cooed. I just rolled my eyes.

"Mistress Blackburn, a little birdie told me that you have not been feeling well. I brought you some lemon glazed wafers in hopes of cheering you." He handed her one of the packages, and she took it greedily.

"That is kind of ye, but I've not been ill. Who told ye such a falsehood?"

His eyes swiped to mine questioningly, and I blanched. I shook my head slightly, hoping he would understand to not ask questions. "I'll explain later," I mouthed silently.

Mother set to work putting a kettle over the fire for tea and setting the wafers out on a plate for us to enjoy. William handed me the other package. "You forgot this yesterday," he said softly.

"Thank ye," I said, taking the book from him but not making eye contact. The circumstances for which I fled so suddenly yesterday were still raw in my mind. I motioned to a seat by the hearth as I took William's coat, running my hand over the silky fur collar before hanging it up.

When Mother came bearing a tray with tea and lemon wafers, William stood. "Mistress Blackburn, please take this seat. I can pull another one over to the fire." He took the tray from her hands so that Mother could get situated. When he set the tray down, he moved to get a chair from the table.

I watched and considered him. As with everything else about this man, his manners were flawless. No one could be that perfect. It unnerved me, and I was determined to find some character flaw or vice that proved this paragon was merely a man and not some god sent to torment us mortals.

Mother poured our tea, and I cleared my throat, searching for an excuse as to why William might be here.

"Mother," I started slowly. She looked up at me from her plate, a smear of lemon glaze stuck to the corner of her mouth. "Do ye recall how I told ye of a plot to put the king in danger and remove him from the throne?

Mother, to her credit, shot her eyes to William, then back at me. I was thankful that she was in her senses and knew enough to be leery of mentioning such things in front of people we barely knew. Especially when it pertained to the help we were trying to give the accused witches. A slight nod of her head told me that she knew exactly to what I referred.

"I had to share the information with someone we could trust. I told Sir William of what information I had in hopes that he could prevent the plot from coming to fruition."

Mother swallowed the bite of wafer that she had been chewing. "But Ailsa dear, I thought ye said that Master Broune was not to be trusted?"

William coughed, almost spitting his tea down his beautiful velvet doublet.

"I don't know that I said those exact words—"

"Nay, not those exact words. But ye said he wanted something, and we must be very careful what we say or do around him." She sat, wide-eyed, clueless as to the fact that she had just embarrassed me and shared something that I had spoken in private.

"Mother," I began, but William cut me off.

"Mistress Blackburn, Ailsa is right. I do want something. I want to be your friend. You can trust me. I will not betray any confidence that has been shared." He looked as if he would have said more, but he was suddenly taken with a sneeze that practically rattled our cups.

Mother was unphased. She fluttered her eyelashes again and said in a sickeningly sweet voice. "That is kind of ye, but ye might not say as much when ye find out how Ailsa came about the information."

"Mother!" I was horrified. What was she doing? William wiped his nose with a scrap of cloth he had tucked into his pocket and looked at me, the shock on his face reflecting my own. Mother said no more as she stuffed another wafer into her mouth and took a gulp of tea.

"I have already shared it with him, Mother."

"Aye, that is why I am—" Another sneeze overtook him, cutting his words short.

"Oh dear, ye aren't catching a cold, are ye, son?"

"Mother, don't call him *son.*" I was mortified. This visit was quickly turning into a disaster, as so many of my encounters with this man seemed to do. "He is the king's man. Ye must address him with respect."

"It's all right," he began before a third sneeze shook his body. His eyes were beginning to water, the rims reddening in irritation. Just then, Sadie mewed at him from below as she wrapped her tail around his calf and rubbed her head against the soft leather of his boot. "Ah, there is the culprit." He leaned away from Sadie as if she had the plague and tucked his legs beneath his chair.

"What do ye mean, sir? She is the sweetest feline ye will ever lay eyes on." I picked Sadie up and rubbed my cheek against her head.

"I mean I have a reaction to such animals. Their fur causes my eyes to itch, my nose to run, and a series of sneezes to ensue."

"Oh." I gulped, understanding taking hold. I quickly took the feline to the door and shewed her outside to get some fresh air. "I *am* sorry. I did not know."

"How could you know?" *Achoo*. Another sneeze bellowed forth.

"My, ye do shake the crockery," Mother observed. I giggled.

"My apologies," he said sniffling as he wiped his nose again. Inwardly I beamed; for once this man was not in full possession of his composure. *Finally!*

"Sometimes my eyes itch. In the spring when the flowers are at their first bloom. This always helps me." I handed him a cloth that I had wetted and rung out. I had folded it into a rectangle and motioned to his face. "Lay it over your eyes."

"Here now, Ailsa," Mother crooned. "Let him lay upon the bed for a moment. It's hard to keep the cloth over your eyes when ye are sitting upright." She grasped him under his upper arm and pulled him from his chair. I marveled that this small woman could lead such a large man, like an ox with a ring through his nose.

"I don't think that is necessary," William began.

"Ye will do well to just obey, sir," I advised, struggling to hold down my amusement.

"You're laughing at me," William accused, pulling the cloth from his eyes, and sitting back up on the side of the bed to glare at me. A red, glassy glare.

"Ignore her," my mother commanded, pushing him back down.

"Mistress Blackburn, my boots, they are dirty. I don't want to soil your bed linens."

"Oh pish," Mother waved away his concern with her hand. "Here, we can solve that." And with a huff, she pulled his boot from his right foot.

"Mother!" All decorum was completely gone.

"Mistress—"

"Shh," Mother hushed, but I could clearly see that William was uncomfortable.

"Mother, Sir William is very particular about his clothing. I don't think he wants his boots removed. Just leave him be for a moment. The wet cloth will help, and he'll be good as new."

Mother huffed in disagreement but said nothing more. I watched as William's chest slowed to a steady pace, his breaths calming and relaxation taking over. He was silent for several minutes, and I was afforded the opportunity to admire him unashamedly, without being seen. A dimpled chin and strong jawline, covered with the first appearances of dark whiskers could still be seen from beneath the cloth, and thin, smooth lips parted slightly as he pulled breath into his lungs.

Heat crept up my neck as the awkwardness of the situation began to take hold. I could have probably observed him for another hour or so and wished for an instant that I had taken up drawing lessons along with Bess's mother. He would have made a fine study in the human form, but instead I finally said, "At least ye aren't sneezing anymore."

"Aye, I do believe the warm cloth has helped." He sat up and removed it from his eyes. The rims had returned to a faint pink, and his cobalt blue eyes fastened onto me.

"My apologies for my mother's overbearing nature," I whispered, trying my best to tamp down another smile. "Sometimes she won't take no for an answer."

"She means well." He handed the cloth back to me and picked up his boot, shoving his foot into it. Something in my chest warmed to his gentleness concerning my mother. Most men of his position would have been put off by her antics. Indeed, I wasn't sure what had gotten into her. But I was thankful for his understanding, even if I didn't understand her myself.

A knock at the door summoned Mother, and she opened to find a friend of hers standing on the other side. "Ailsa, I'll be back in a bit. I'm going to walk with Maggie to the Lawnmarket."

"But Mother," was all I got out before she had grabbed her cloak and slammed the door behind her. I looked at William, an awkward silence enveloping us. We had been alone together in his room yesterday, but here, in my little neighborhood, I felt more exposed and more at risk of gossip than before.

He moved back to his chair by the fire, and I sat down in mine.

"I endured your mother's antics because I can tell there is something truly wrong with her."

My mouth fell open at his brash statement. "How dare ye!" I seethed, coming to stand over him in his chair. But he rose too, and I immediately felt dwarfed by his hovering bulk. We stood facing each other, he looking down his nose at me and I craning my neck to meet his surprised stare.

"Not the best choice of words," he whispered. His eyes searched my face for acceptance, but I was not ready to give it. "What I meant to say was that I could tell she is not well. She blurts out things that you do not wish for her to share, and she seems almost childlike in her mannerisms. Or forgive me, has she always been thus?" He swallowed hard, and I could see his throat working to keep his emotion at bay.

I dropped my eyes from his face, suddenly feeling weary. My shoulders sagged at the weight of the burden, and I realized how much I wanted to unload my problems onto him. He had not asked for that, but he was here, and he was asking questions, so I took that as permission to share my worry.

"No, she has not always been like this. She has become forgetful and often gets confused. It is not unusual for me to come home and find that she has done the opposite of something that we had discussed we would do. Supper plans change, chores get repeated or forgotten. One day she left the pot hanging above the fire too long and scorched our parritch. If I had not come home when I did the whole house probably would have been burnt down. It took weeks to get that awful smell out of here." I laughed at my words, trying to lighten the mood, but inside, I could feel my heart tearing in two. Massaging my fingers and palms, I worked the muscles as if I could ease the pain of the conversation with a stroke of my hand.

He laid a hand on my shoulder, and I could feel his warmth enveloping me. "I'm sorry," he murmured.

"She is not the same gentle woman that I grew up with. When I asked ye to please forgive her overbearing personality, ye have no idea how more untrue words have never been spoken. She's never had an overbearing personality. If anyone in our family did, it was my father, and now me. But not my mother. She was so gentle and sweet-natured. And now she has become a peevish woman who appears bitter and unhappy, yet she has nothing to be unhappy about."

I stopped talking and rubbed at my nose. I reached into my pocket and pulled out a piece of cloth.

"Perhaps it is unhappiness at the death of your father." Concern penetrated his eyes, and I felt a cry almost slip out of me at the gentleness of his gaze.

Shaking my head, I said, "I don't think so. My father has been gone for three years. Her episodes did not start until about a year ago. Don't get me wrong. My mother was devastated at my father's death. But she was a strong woman, who held her head high and carried on. She was strong for me and my brother, although my brother has since moved on to London and is no longer in need of her comfort." A tear finally slipped down my face at the mention of Nick. It was times like this that I still wished he were living with us and helping me bear the burden of caring for Mother and her illness.

William reached up and brushed the tear away with the pad of his thumb. I resisted the urge to lean into his warm palm even as his fingers brushed against the lobe of my ear. The touch felt so intimate that I shivered, and he pulled his hand back instinctively.

"I'm sorry," he said again, shoving his hands into the pockets of his jerkin. I felt another stone fall away from the wall of defense that

I had built around myself. But he didn't know that. As far as he was concerned, I had no wish to be touched, to be loved. My suspicion coupled with my insecurities had built that wall of defense. And even though I could feel that protective barrier crumbling, the effects of that fortification were resounding.

Pulling my senses about me, I straightened and wiped my nose again. "Well, I suppose ye want to tell me why ye have come." I stepped away from him, putting a safe distance between us.

The heat from his gaze burned into me, and I grabbed my bucket and brush to distract myself. When he saw me lifting the bucket to dump the water, he moved to assist me.

"I have an idea of someone who fits the description of your plotter. He is someone who is close to the king and has a claim to the throne." He opened the door and poured the dirty water out, careful not to splash his boots in the process.

"That was fast. How did ye find him so quickly?"

He handed the bucket back to me and brushed off his hands. "The man's name has come up a few times in interrogations. And he has made attempts to kidnap the king in the past. I don't have any proof yet, but an inquest with Doctor Fian brought about his name once more."

I had begun pulling stalks of heather that had been dried the September before from the cupboard when he mentioned the doctor. "Do ye mean the schoolteacher from Saltpans?"

William was watching me intently as I crushed the flowering buds into a jar. "Aye. Do you know him?"

I could feel nausea sweep over me. "Everyone knows of the hardships the poor doctor has endured since finding himself under the king's arrest." The fragrant *Calluna vulgaris* released its scent as I pinched the dried flowers between my fingers. I took a deep breath, drawing in the scent in hopes of calming my now churning stomach.

"The poor doctor? What this man has endured he has brought on himself."

My mouth fell open. "How can ye say that? I have heard that the man's fingernails were pulled out and his legs squeezed so badly in the boot that he couldn't walk for several days. Ye are telling me he brought that on himself?"

William fisted his hands then released them. "And have you also been informed that the man tried to bewitch a lass whom he was in love with and instead ended up bewitching a heifer?"

I snorted. "That's ridiculous. Where did you hear that?"

"With my own ears, at the man's interrogation. He is a sorcerer who is in league with the Devil himself. He confessed it, then recanted his pact with the Devil. But he escaped the tolbooth a few days ago, so it sure makes it appear as if he has returned to his devilish master."

"He is a human being that deserves some kind of civility while he is being questioned. If he is under some kind of evil influence, is he to blame? Please tell me that ye did not participate in this man's humiliation and suffering." I swallowed hard, not sure I could bear it if he told me otherwise.

"I do not participate in the torture. But I am the king's inquisitor. I have a job to do, and this is part of the ugly truth."

My heart sank. "How? How can ye stand by and watch such villainy? Do ye hold your position in such high regard that ye cannot afford decency?"

He looked at me then, and his eyes told me everything I needed to know. "Ailsa, I—"

"Don't." I held up a hand to stop him. "Don't give me your honey-covered words." He came to a halt in front of me, his mouth still agape with his unspoken sentence. "I have a lot to do. If ye will excuse me, I think it is best that ye leave."

"Ailsa, let me explain."

I closed my eyes and shook my head, willing myself not to cry.

He stared at me a long moment, then retrieved his cloak and tossed it over his shoulders.

When he reached the door, he turned around and looked at me one last time, but he didn't attempt to speak again. It wasn't until he closed the door behind him, that I allowed myself a good cry.

~**18**~

January 1591

William

I didn't recall ever being kicked out of someone's home.

Having been raised by a prince among men, my father, and then being sent to James's court at such a young age and learning the behavior of a courtier, I prided myself in my honor and my ability to always say the right thing. With the king, in a courtroom, and with women. I knew the limits and how much was too much. With the exception of the latter, perhaps. No, *especially* with the latter. They were my specialty.

I ran a hand across my forehead and squeezed where there was a tension pulling. I did not like the way my conversation with Ailsa had ended and wondered if I should have insisted on her listening to me. I had not participated in the torture, but my hands were tied when it came to how much was permitted at the interrogations. I didn't choose to be the inquisitor; it was forced upon me. So how could I defy the king? My loyalty was expected, demanded even. Yet, after speaking with Ailsa—after seeing the way she looked at me, like I was a monster—I felt the weight of my sins even more, and my involvement in these trials.

Snow had begun to fall again, and a light dusting covered the gray cobblestones as I made my way past the Luckenbooths toward the palace. Smells of roasting meat drew hunger pangs, and I quickened my steps, eager to reach my destination. However, a quick glance over the wares caused me to stop short at a jeweler I had done business with before.

"Signore Broune," the vender greeted me with his heavy Mediterranean accent. "I have several new pieces that you have not seen. Where have you been? I have not seen you in the Luckenbooths for weeks."

"Signore Bernardi." I grasped the Italian man's hand and shook heartily. "The king's business has not afforded me much spare time, I'm afraid." I swept a look once more over the brightly shining jewels he had on display.

"Ah, you work too much for His Majesty," the short man said with a twinkle in his eye. His black hair was streaked with silver and it reminded me that the jeweler had a family back home in Italy that he was never able to see.

"Aye, but you cannot lecture me, Signore Bernardi. You also allow work to take you away from more delightful pursuits. How is your family?"

The older man flashed me a repentant look before a shy grin crossed his face. "Signora Bernardi will be delivered soon of our sixth child. Alas, when I return home in the spring, it may be a great while before I make it back this way again." I nodded in understanding and opened my mouth to express my congratulations when he added, "Which is why you need to take a look at this piece I set aside for you."

With that he stooped and pulled a small, locked box from under his counter. Fishing for a key that he had tucked into his tunic, he unlocked the box and turned it toward me, displaying two pieces of exquisite beauty. The first, were two dainty hair combs made from what looked like iridescent sea shells. The tiny silver teeth of the combs were adorned with diamonds at each apex. "These are for another gentleman who was looking for something special for his mistress." We waved aside the combs and instead picked up a delicate pink pearl attached to a silver chain. "For your lady friend." He grinned holding the fine necklace out to me.

I took the jewel and examined it closely. "You've painted it," I accused.

"No, no. This pearl comes from the South Sea where others of like quality can be found. They are rare, however, and I only come across such jewels once in a great while."

I looked closer at the pale pink pearl. "Exquisite," I said, running my thumb across the bottom of the slightly tear-shaped charm. "Lady Ruthven would be pleased with this. I am sure of it."

The older man smiled broadly, flashing a set of perfectly straight teeth. "I am pleased that she will be pleased." He beamed. "I shall wrap it up for you, yes?"

I nodded but then turned my attention to the piece that had caught my eye in the first place. The jewel was of obvious lesser value, but the handiwork was so detailed that it begged to be considered. Two hearts, fashioned in brass, twisted within one another had been melded to a stick pin, allowing the piece to be worn as a brooch. In the center, where the hearts intertwined was set a small garnet. Above the hearts, a simple crown was set, giving the jewel a noble look. I picked the piece up and studied it.

"Ah, yes, that is a nice piece as well, though not as fine of quality as your pearl. But look closely. It has a love note etched into it."

I held the piece closer and studied the inscription. "*Of earthly joys thou art my choice*." The words seemed to thrum through my veins as I spoke them aloud.

"Sì, Signore. Would the lady appreciate the handiwork that has gone into it? For that is where the value lies, not within the tawdry jewel."

I weighed the brooch in my hand, considering the beauty of the craftsmanship. "I am not sure," I finally admitted. "But I like it and want this one as well." Signore Bernardi took the piece from me and set to work wrapping it up.

After we settled on the price and with purchases in hand, I turned my attention toward Holyroodhouse and picked up my pace. The snow had swelled, hindering my vision, and making my steps unsure. The sun, which had been but a soft orange glow in the sky, was sinking behind the ramparts of Edinburgh Castle, and soon darkness would reign over the city.

Holyroodhouse was a perfect mare's nest upon my arrival.

"William, where the devil have you been hiding?"

I turned to look over my shoulder at the accusing voice and saw Blantyre sauntering toward me, a goblet of something in his hand. His black jerkin was askew, with one of the buttons missing and his dove-gray doublet was covered in grime.

"What happened to you?" I asked in return. "You look like you've been dragged through a hovel."

"I have. With no help to be found from you, I might point out." He took a swig from his cup and swayed slightly as his throat forced the liquid down.

"Are you drunk?" I swept him with an assessing eye, noticing now a slight tear in his doublet at the apex of his right arm.

"Don't judge me," he complained, taking note of my measuring glance. "I have good reason to look so disheveled. But I will ask again. Where have you been? His Majesty has been in straights—until today—and your Lady has been worrying herself sick at her imagined demise of you. Do me a favor, will you? The next time you decide to disappear for a few days, tell Lady Beatrix where you are going. She could not be comforted, and I'll confess, I did my best to try to ease her worries."

With that, he took another drag from his cup, squeezing his eyes shut as the liquid went down, as if the effort pained him. I crossed my arms over my chest. "I dined with His Majesty only three nights ago and saw Beatrix then. What has happened within that short expanse of time that you felt the need to prevail yourself upon the Lady in whose company I have been keeping?"

He opened his blood-shot eyes and stared at me. As if he didn't hear my question he said, "We found Fian, holed up in a barn right outside of Inverness."

I blinked at the change of subject, and then sighed slightly, my shoulders relaxing. "That is good news. So why do you look as if you've been scrapping with a pack of wolves? And why would you need my help with that? You know I have no use for swords and confrontation."

He waved a dismissive hand. "Och, no need of your help with that. But I was getting tired of hearing His Majesty bemoaning the fact that he needed your assistance, and Beatrix sniveling every evening, imagining the worst for you. When are you going to seal that deal, by the way?"

I pressed my lips together, considering my next words. "I have not made a decision about that yet." He raised one brow at me in surprise.

"What's there to decide?" he asked almost defensively. "She is a beauty. And she is titled and rich. What more could you want?" He looked down distractedly and pulled at his crooked doublet, evidently noticing for the first time that he had fastened it wrong due to the missing button.

Resisting the urge to point out his mistake, I instead cast about for more explanation. "His Majesty has not given his permission yet. I think he is waiting for the conclusion of these witch trials. Besides, why do you care? You seemed to have had an issue with the king's choice of wife for me. I noted your lack of enthusiasm the night he mentioned her the first time." I studied his face, his thoughts unreadable within the darkened walls of the great hall.

He didn't speak for a moment as he twisted his goblet in his hands. Finally, he said, "Theirs is an old and influential family, are they not?"

Still not following his thoughts, I asked, "Are you concerned because of her father's involvement in His Majesty's kidnapping when we were still mere boys?"

He shot a glassy look at me. "Nay. She is innocent of that debacle. I am sure of it."

"Aye, that was a stupid fiasco her father plotted, kidnapping the king and holding him captive."

"He wasn't held captive. He was free to go wherever he wished."

His sudden defense of the man guilty of the king's kidnapping when he was fifteen years old was odd. But I had just begun my formal studies at St Andrews when it had happened. I never really knew all the details, so I couldn't argue them.

Blantyre drained his cup and mumbled something under his breath.

"I beg your pardon?" I turned an ear toward him to better hear his complaint. Behind us the loud crack of breaking wood sounded as two servants tried and failed to balance a very large wooden bench between them.

"I said, we are all at his disposal, are we not?"

I gaped at him, not knowing how to respond. He was in a rare mood this evening. Unlike his court jester persona that he usually kept up, tonight he was sullen.

"Come. His Majesty is in his antechamber. Perhaps I'll receive a reward for finding his lap dog."

"What the devil is that supposed to mean?" I stopped walking, irritated at his insult. "Look, you had a bad day. Perhaps you've had a few bad days. From your appearance that looks to be the case. But you don't have to take it out on me. What has happened that has put you in a foul mood?"

He scrubbed a hand over his face, then he ran it through his tawny hair. Releasing air forcefully through his nose, he said, "My apologies, old friend. I simply don't understand why His Majesty is so preoccupied with these witches. We all wait with bated breath, our lives put on hold, while he plays God, deciding who lives and who dies."

I was stunned at his words. "I suggest you get ahold of yourself, Blantyre," I said in a loud whisper. Grabbing his arm, I pulled him over to the wall for privacy. "You are playing a traitor's game." Color drained from his face, and he darted his eyes around the hall, looking for eavesdroppers. When he didn't speak again, I prodded. "What has happened? You were the first to condemn the witches when Geillis Duncan was arrested." I lowered my voice as two maidservants scurried by, carrying baskets of cloth and other sundries. "What has changed your mind?"

He pulled his arm from my grasp yet glanced around again before opening his mouth. "Doctor Fian has been condemned to death. His Majesty ordered it this afternoon."

I stiffened. "But we were to have another assize after his apprehension. I even arranged a trip to speak to the lass whom Fian was in love with, the one spoken of in the letters you forwarded to me. What brought this about?"

Blantyre shook his head in confusion. "He claims he feared the pains of death during the interrogations. He denies any wrong-doing now and says his confession was coerced, and he is not guilty of the crimes to which he confessed."

"By my troth. Do you think he renewed his pact with the Devil while he was away?"

"I'm not even sure there was such a pact."

Every muscle in my body seemed to stiffen. "God's teeth, Blantyre! You were so quick to disparage the women when they were arrested for witchcraft. Why are you having such a hard time accepting that this man was an instrument of the Devil? You were there, you heard his confession."

"But Fian is an educated man. It's all so odd. I think the lass is responsible. I think *she* bewitched *him,* and this has all been twisted somehow. The town folk claim her mother is a witch. That's how she was able to perform the bovine enchantment. Even James is of the belief that men do not normally participate in such devilish practices."

"Well, I don't know about that. I've seen some stunningly evil things done by men in my short lifetime. Take Seton for instance."

His mouth dropped open. "What do you have against Seton?"

I started walking again. I didn't want to get into that right now. "I need more time," I said, ignoring his question. "I need to talk with this chit. And her mother. I was going to leave for Saltpans tomorrow morning. It's already been arranged." I followed the cracked black and white checkered tiles that lined the hallway and led into the easterly rooms of the palace. "What is His Majesty doing at the moment?"

Blantyre followed me as I made my way to the king's antechamber. "I'm not sure, but I believe he is preparing for the supper hour."

"Good. He's always in a better humor when there is food and wine involved." I increased my pace, and Blantyre followed suit, handing off his empty cup to a footman passing by.

As he quickened his steps he said, "Do you think you will be able to rescue Doctor Fian?"

I stopped walking at that and stared down at Blantyre, not unlike the large portraits that hung on the walls behind us, the kings of old boring their oily black eyes into us unsuspecting passersby. "My aim is not to rescue, per se. I am searching for truth and justice. Those are the only acceptable outcomes."

Blantyre stared at me, dumbfounded. "Aye," he finally mumbled. "Truth and justice. You're a better man than I thought if you can discover those."

~20~

January 1591

William

A guard slouched outside the door when we reached the antechamber.

"His Majesty has given strict instruction that he does not wish to be disturbed." The sentry picked at his fingernails with a sgian dubh, his halberd leaning against his shoulder haphazardly. He didn't even look at us.

Blantyre snickered then moved as if he would shove past the guard. The man quickly straightened and with an unexpected move, flipped his knife to his other hand and pointed it at Blantyre's heart. "*Very* strict instructions." His eyes flashed in warning.

I cleared my throat. "Please tell His Majesty that William Broune and Lord Blantyre are here to speak with him." I inspected his shoddy uniform and worn boots wondering when he had last had a decent meal.

"Are ye deaf? I said His Majesty does not wish to be disturbed. Now run along and do whatever it is that ye noblemen do when ye aren't sucking—" The sound of scraping steel cut through his vulgar words as Blantyre drew his sword faster than the guard could spit out his insult. The echo of grinding metal bounced off the stone walls as the edge of his blade laid against the dirt ring around the guard's throat.

"I don't think you want to finish that sentence," Blantyre said with a growl in his voice.

The guard looked down his nose at Blantyre, but his jerky breaths led us to know that he took the threat seriously. "Do ye think that your demands eclipse those of His Majesty?" His words strained against the steel impediment.

"I think that you should watch your tongue and do as you are bid. If you spent half as much time keeping yourself clean as you did worrying about the deeds of others, we might be able to take you seriously."

The guard scoffed. "Says the man who can't even button his fancy doublet correctly."

Blantyre's eyes widened at the slight. "You filthy plague-sore." He pressed his sword further into the man's flesh.

"Wait!" I tried to intervene. "Let's not be too hasty."

"The time for diplomacy is over, Broune," Blantyre said through clenched teeth. "I'm done playing nice with this piece of dung." He pressed the sword deeper until I feared the guard's flesh would succumb to the sharpened blade.

"When was the last time you ate?" I tried, taking a gamble that he was just like any other soldier; always hungry.

"Half hour ago," he rasped.

"And ale?" I tried again. Surely the man wouldn't turn down a good drink.

"Not thirsty," he spat.

Sighing, I admitted defeat. "It is encouraging to know that His Majesty has such loyal keepers." I patted the guard on the shoulder then turned to Blantyre. "It is heartening, is it not, my lord?" My friend curled his lip but did not answer, his eyes never leaving the man's hardened face. "What we have to say to His Majesty can wait. Come, help me find Lady Beatrix instead." I laid my hand on his sword arm, hoping that my unhurried words would calm him. When I felt the slighted ease of his muscle, I tried again. "We'll speak to His Majesty about the necessity to have access to him at all times. Do nothing you'll regret later."

With a step backward and a swift removal of his blade, Blantyre sheathed his sword. His black eyes bored into the guard's defiant ones. "Don't think I will forget this. I forget nothing."

The guard blinked at Blantyre, then took a step back. "His Majesty will hear of this affront," he complained, lifting his chin slightly.

"Indeed, he shall." Blantyre turned his back on the guard and walked away.

"You are in rare form tonight," I said under my breath as we walked away from the guard. "And you left your flank wide open. You're lucky the guard didn't gut you when he had the chance." Blantyre only grunted, and I chanced a glance at him from the corner of my eye. "He was only doing the job for which he was retained."

He rounded on me. "How can you always be so bloody calm?"

I flinched at the vehemence in his voice. "So what? You want to off the king's guards now? That would not have boded well for you." The scowl on his face told me he knew I was right. "Besides, James has every reason to surround himself with protectors. The man has been the victim of more than one kidnapping attempt with one of them being successful."

"He lives in fear." Disgust laced his words. I studied his face and felt a shiver run up my spine at his heartless tone. "He does not even try to defend himself but stays holed up in his rooms, attacking innocent people when the real threat is those who actually have the power to end his reign."

Relief washed over me as the suspicion I had begun to harbor dissipated. He may have been frustrated and disappointed with our king, but he was no traitor. The relief loosened my tongue, and I was wagging it before I had time to consider my own words.

"There is a possible plot in the works to bring harm to His Majesty," I said, watching his face for a reaction. We had reached the stairway that led to the second floor where the previous queen's rooms had been housed. Queen Anne had chosen to utilize the lower-level rooms for her personal needs but entertained herself and her ladies in the upper chambers at times.

Blantyre stopped and gaped at me. "How do you know this? Who is your source?"

I swallowed hard, not sure that I was ready to reveal Ailsa and her tale. "I cannot tell you that right now. I am still looking into it. But I have reason to believe that the information is accurate, and I think it should be taken seriously."

"You're protecting someone." He stared at me, a muscle in his jaw tightening in nervous energy. "Who is it?"

It took all my strength not to look away. "I just want to make sure that the report has merit. Let me look into it a little further."

"But you said you had reason to believe the information is accurate."

I stiffened at his interrogation. "Just trust me on this. Give me time to get a little more information. I'll give you more details when I have them."

"When is this supposed to happen? Who are the people responsible?" He kept hammering.

"Give me time."

He stared at me a moment longer, then abruptly abandoned his questioning. "Fine. Keep your secrets," he said in dismissal. He turned and without another word sprinted up the steep, spiral steps. I followed more slowly. The stone spiraling of the ancient steps was stifling, and I always became dizzy when I had to employ them.

The stillness of the queen's outer chamber was an eerie contrast to the bustling activity below. Her Majesty was not here, but three of her ladies-in-waiting sat occupying themselves with needlepoint and quiet conversation. They stopped talking and lifted their heads to us when Blantyre's boisterous voice intruded on their peaceful enterprise.

My eyes immediately fell on a moon-kissed face with eyes the color of a summer sky and lips the shade of spiced wine. A brilliant smile dimpled her cheeks when she saw me, relief and excitement flashing in those azure eyes.

"Look what the cat dragged in," Blantyre chided as he strode straight for Beatrix's chair and seated himself on the arm. He leaned scandalously close to her ear and said, "Do I get a reward for finding the long-lost inquisitor?"

Beatrix giggled and placed her hand on his chest, pushing him away. "Have you been imbibing, my lord? You reek of prunellé."

"I may have had a drink or two, my lady. Did you know that I helped bring the scurrilous Doctor Fian back to Edinburgh?"

"Did you now?" She grinned sweetly at Blantyre, and he leaned toward her once again in an effort to receive his just reward.

I cleared my throat to interrupt the awkward display, and Beatrix turned her face toward me. Blantyre was drunk. He had already tried to kill someone this evening, and therefore, I was prepared to overlook his unscrupulous advances toward Beatrix. But he needed to control himself, or I may be forced to lay hold of my sword this time.

Laying her needlework aside, she rose and came to me. "William, where have you been? I was beside myself with worry for you."

"Lady Ruthven, your concern warms me, but it is unwarranted. I was merely at my private room on the High Street. I needed solitude to do my work. And I have been busy."

She stuck out her lower lip as if she were a petulant child. "I will be glad when the business with these witches is over, and we can go back to living our lives in peace. They have done nothing but cause grief to Their Majesties and taken you away from me." She stepped closer and looked up at me, eyes full of heat.

"Shall we walk, my lady?"

She nodded silently then turned and shifted her skirts behind her, clearing a path for her slippered feet to walk freely.

"Don't mind me," Blantyre called out to us as we took a turn about the room. The chatter of the other ladies pulled at him soon enough, and I could hear his jovial voice responding to them as we walked away.

The dark, elaborately carved ceilings hung heavy above our heads. Coupled with the dense, ceiling to floor tapestries that adorned the walls of the outer chamber, it felt as though the room was closing in on us. We walked the perimeter of the room in silence for a spell until we came to a crimson stain imbedded in the wooden floor boards at the far corner of the room.

"Take care," I pointed out, not wishing to step upon the sight where innocent blood had been shed years before, albeit just months before His Majesty had been born. Beatrix looked down to where I pointed, her face turning the color of milk glass at the sight.

"What is it?" She stopped, inspecting the wicked stain upon the floor.

"The place where Queen Mary's secretary, David Rizzio, was stabbed to death." Her eyes widened, but no sound came out of her mouth as she stared at the spot. I lowered my voice to a whisper. "My father told me that His Majesty's father, Lord Darnley, had the man killed, out of jealousy for his relationship to the queen. But never say that to the king." She tilted her head up and stared at me. "Let's move on," I coaxed, continuing our stroll.

We walked for several more minutes in silence. "I should be angry with you, William," she finally said in her breathy tone as we inspected a tapestry that had been hung on the wall. A unicorn and a fair-haired maiden, embellished with flowers and arabesques were woven into the heavy wall covering, the dark greens and golds contributing to the solemnity of this suffocating room. But as Beatrix spoke, she leaned upon my arm, and I could smell the faint scent of lavender on her hair. I resisted the urge to shove my face into her locks and inhale her floral scent.

"I will try to tell you the next time that I will be away from court for any length of time," I said, pulling her into the little oratory off of the outer chamber and out of the sight of prying eyes. The little alcove was nothing more than a box, a small room used for prayers when Queen Mary was in residence here. The smell of oak mixed with dust provoked our senses, the room having not been in use in at least two decades.

We stood facing one another, her eyes wide in anticipation, and my heart beating wildly as I pulled a small wad of cloth from my pocket.

"I have something for you." I unwrapped the pink pearl necklace and held it up for her to see.

The sun had set leaving only a soft glow of hazy moonlight filtering through the long window of the oratory. There were no candles in this little nook, and we were almost completely hidden in darkness, with the exception of the moonlight that lit upon Beatrix's golden curls and cast a shadowy halo about her head.

Her breath caught as her eyes landed on the dainty pearl in my hand. The scent of lavender was driving me to ruins, but I managed to hold myself together long enough to say, "Turn around."

She obeyed, and I wrapped my arms about her, pulling the delicate chain around her neck. Pushing the golden whisps of hair away from her nape, I clasped the chain together, then let the back of my hand brush the soft skin of her neck. It was so quiet here, within this little prayer closet, and only the sound of our breathing could be heard as I stood over her. I brushed a kiss across the slender column of her neck, and she shivered. She turned then, wrapping her arms around my neck, and pushing her hands into my hair.

"I cannot wait for all of this witch business to be over. They are putting a damper on my plans."

"And what plans are those, Lady Ruthven?" I brushed my lips across her forehead, finally allowing myself the indulgence of burying my nose in her hair.

"Why, my marriage plans, of course." I pulled away from her, running my hands down her arms and holding her at length, so I could better see her face in the moonlight. "Oh, I know you haven't asked me, but I want you to know that when you are ready to ask, I am ready to answer *yes*."

I leaned my forehead against hers and brushed another kiss across her brow. I opened my mouth to respond, but instead, she spoke again.

"I'm hoping the execution of the doctor will get things moving, and His Majesty will just declare them all guilty so we can get the whole thing over with. That way you won't be tied up with all the legal matters, and we will be free to marry as soon as possible."

I felt hot bile rise in my throat. How could she be so callous and wish for the deaths of so many people—possibly innocent people— just for her own convenience?

"You do realize that some of those accused may not be guilty?" I studied her, looking for compassion or understanding to alight in those beautiful eyes.

She didn't speak for a moment, and I should have been thankful. For when she did finally answer my question, I felt as if I had been punched in the gut.

"Does it really matter if they get a trial? They have all been seen performing acts of witchcraft, or they have been duly pointed out by concerned neighbors. The king should assert his authority and take care of them all with the swipe of his pen."

I pulled away from her. "You sound as if you have been talking with Blantyre."

She looked away from me momentarily, then found her voice once more. "Lord Blantyre has been most accommodating to me since your departure from the palace."

"I was only gone two and a half days," I said, incredulous.

The injury in her eyes was genuine, yet a slight irritation pricked me over the whole affair.

"He kept me company and entertained me with stories from when you and he and His Majesty were boys. His attentions were most felicitous as I worried myself sick over your absence, for I did not know where you had gone."

"Indeed?" My brow lifted in suspicion, and to her credit she caught my meaning. Her mouth fell open in innocent ignorance and fumbled for her next words.

"I…you don't think…" Her cheeks pinkened, and she hurried to explain. "Lord Blantyre has been an exemplary gentleman," she finally managed. "No one takes his flirtations seriously, least of all me."

"Perhaps you should. He has made it apparent that he desires your attentions."

"I have not encouraged him. Please don't think that I have betrayed your trust, William. I would never—" She stopped speaking and with lips trembling, moved toward me, pushing her face into my chest. I stroked her shoulder in soothing circles.

"Of course," I said, the words strangled in my throat. I trusted her, but it was Blantyre whose loyalty I was beginning to question. "Come now, do not cry. You do not want to redden those beautiful sapphire eyes." I reached into my pocket to hand her a piece of cloth to wipe her eyes, then remembered I had already used it. Had that been just this morning that I had reacted with sneezing to Ailsa's cat? The turn of events and loss of her welcome in that regard still stung a bit. I shoved the cloth back into my pocket.

"Now my nose is running," she complained, pulling away from me. "May I be excused to see to my personal needs?"

"By all means." I released her and watched as she hurried off to blow her nose. This night had not gone as planned. In fact, the whole day had not gone as planned, and I was a little more than irritated about that. Beatrix rushing off was just the final disappointment. I had hoped to spend a little time with her. I didn't even get to enjoy seeing my gift on her. Then there was James, ordering Fian's execution. So much effort had gone into this investigation, and even more was planned. But I had no idea if I should pursue those plans since I couldn't get in to see James and get his orders. And finally, there was my argument with Ailsa, resulting with her not-so-kindly command for me to leave her home.

I sighed heavily, pressing my back against the wall of the oratory, and leaning my head back. I stared up at the ceiling where the Cross of St Andrew encircled with a crown had been carved. The emblem reminded me of my father who had committed half of his life to the university at St Andrews. How I wished he were here now that I might seek his advice.

My thoughts returned to Ailsa's news about the plot against the king. That whole situation bothered me. Not only that there was someone out there plotting to overthrow James, but that we had no clues to go on, no way of knowing who it could possibly be, except the fact that they were of the peerage. Ailsa had said it was someone who could actually claim a right to the throne. There were relatives by blood and relatives by marriage all over Scotland and some in England too. Any of those could claim some kind of royal connection. Yet, there was only one relative that stood out to me as a possible culprit: James's cousin, Francis Stewart, Lord Bothwell. He had attempted the king's kidnapping before. And he most certainly fit the description of a devil.

My mind wondered back to my conversation with Ailsa, and I thought once more on the look she had given me right before telling me to leave. And that was truly the crux of my problem, although I was hesitant to admit it. I should be focusing on Beatrix, working on getting James's blessing. She already made it clear she was willing to marry me. With her family connections and the king's appointment to Chancellor, I would be lacking for nothing. I just needed to get past these trials so we could move on with our lives, as Beatrix said. So, why was I allowing Ailsa to distract me?

I counted the leaf motifs on the ceiling before pushing off from the wall and letting out a harsh breath. I would make one more attempt to see James this evening, then I was going to bed. It had been a long day.

~21~

January 1591

William

It was early still, and only the faint glow of a winter's sun on the eastern horizon gave hint that morning would soon arrive. The city streets were normally barren this time of day, but word had quickly spread that there would be an execution on Castlehill today, and no one wanted to miss the spectacle. By sunup, the victim would be on his way to the hill.

The rock in the pit of my stomach had not dissipated by the time I reached Edinburgh Castle. I looked about for a familiar face, wondering if any involved in this horrific farce of justice had deigned to show themselves on the hill. For my part, I had not been asked to defend nor judge the proceedings, or what there was of it, for James had declared Fian guilty and pronounced his judgement after the doctor had been put to the boot one last time.

The tolling of the bell of St Giles Kirk sent the hovering crows into a cacophony that beat the air above us and announced the coming of the accused witch. The broken silence was followed by the cries of a frenzied crowd as they converged upon us, pushing the cart that bore the doctor barreling down the cobblestone street. It should not have come as a terrible surprise, but nonetheless, the appearance of Seton at the front of the procession sent shards of fire coursing through my veins. His face shone with exaltation as he single-handedly led the way from the tolbooth to Castlehill with Fian lying in a broken heap upon the cart behind him. I moved closer to speak to Fian. I didn't know what I would say. Offer words of encouragement? Persuade him to repent? I wasn't a clergyman, and that wasn't my forte, yet I felt compelled to speak to him. If nothing more than to sooth my own conscience of any part I played in his demise.

"Sir William," Seton greeted me as if we were old friends, slapping me on the back and shoving his hand out for a shake. "We have done it. Retribution for His Majesty and his queen. The fight has only just begun, but I am confident that we shall see all of the witches brought to justice in due time."

I did not acknowledge his offer of comradery, nor shake his hand. With measured control, I said, "There is no *we* in this scenario. I had nothing to do with this sentence, nor will I take credit nor blame for the outcome."

He pulled away from me and blinked. "Am I to believe that you disagree with His Majesty's pronouncement?"

"You may believe that I had nothing to do with it. That is all I'm saying." I looked to Fian who had not stirred since I reached them. "Is he conscious?"

"He's alive," Seton pronounced, pulling a pike from the cart and poking Fian with it. "Alive enough to feel the flames of hell." Fian winced but did not open his eyes.

The sight of Fian's legs turned my stomach inside out. The boot had been administered for a second time since he had been captured, and this time Seton made sure he could never run away again. His legs were crushed beyond use, squeezed within the confines of the metal brace until a confession could be extracted.

"Did you get the information you wanted out of him?" I nodded toward his legs; a look of disgust surely apparent on my face. I could not hide my revulsion. I didn't even try.

"Doesn't matter." Seton tossed back. "He sealed his fate when he escaped prison and proved his confession and repentance were for naught."

"Then why use the boot again? What were you trying to accomplish, if not to get more information out of him?"

Growing tired of my questions, Seton pushed me aside. "We have an execution to see through, Broune. Either you are for us, or you're against us. Shall we proceed?" He turned his black eyes on me, and a chill ran through my blood. His unspoken threat was not lost on me.

I stepped back, allowing the cart and the procession to continue. A sweat broke out on my brow as I realized this execution would happen, whether I wanted it to or not.

When they finally reached the end of Castlehill, Seton flicked a finger, drawing the cart to a stop and bringing forth two castle guards to do his bidding. A rope was tied around Fian's neck, then a discussion ensued as to how they would tie him to the stake. He could not stand; the boot had secured that fact.

"Devil's tool!" shouted an onlooker from behind me. I ducked as he laid a hand on my shoulder to shove me aside. A rotten plum went flying over my head and landed at Fian's mangled feet. A woman nearby screamed curses at the doctor and invoked the wrath of God on him. Her child, a boy of about eight or nine years old, hurled a chunk of potato at the accused witch.

"You would throw away food just to express your displeasure at the doctor's misdeeds?" I asked. The woman turned a cruel eye toward me and with a gaping hole where a tooth used to sit, spewed her venom.

"'Tis rotten, sir. Just like the heart of that witch. He can feed on the rot in hell." She then turned, grabbing her child by the hand, and moved to another spot across the street, where they could get a closer look at the pyre.

The din of the crowd grew louder as Seton and Sheepshearer discussed the best way to carry out the judgement. It was finally decided that an iron chain would be wrapped around the doctor's waist, securing him to the stake to hold him upright. The attempt was made, but when Fian's body slumped and slid to the bottom of the stake against the crush of his battered legs, they finally retrieved a chair to prop his body up.

When Fian's body was finally secured, his head was held to the stake by the rope around his neck. Bundles of sticks were laid about the doctor's crushed feet in preparation for the pyre to be lit. Only one time did the doctor open his eyes to behold the crowd, but the pain in his legs proved too great, and his lids fluttered shut as the last bits of wood were laid in place.

The time had finally come. Flint was brought forward and a spark lit the twigs that surrounded the doctor's body. A guard held the rope tied around Fian's neck and began to pull on it as the fire began to take hold. When the rope began to cut off the doctor's airway, he finally opened his eyes in panic. Wriggling in the chair with his hands tied behind his back, he was unable to clutch at the rope. His raspy calls for help could be heard above the crackling flames. I stood watching, grief-stricken and conflicted as Fian's cries were soon cut off by the noose as the loss of air rendered him unconscious.

I was torn. There was no doubt in my mind that the man had engaged in some questionable activity in Saltpans before his arrest. But the lack of a fair trial bothered me. Would James take matters into his own hands for each of the accused? And what would that mean for other individuals accused of crimes in the future?

The flames began to climb higher and soon Fian's body was engulfed. The pyre burned at some length until a coppery tinge of aroma eventually filled the air, causing the crowd to begin to disperse at the unpleasant odor. My eyes had strained, long and hard at Fian's body, calculating any missteps and weighing any mistakes I may have made in the investigation. I had not been permitted to complete my examination, but it still did not keep me from feeling the guilt of this failure, nonetheless. The image of Fian's burning body would forever be embossed on my memory.

The sting of the smoke burned my eyes, and the sulfuric stench of burning hair pulled me from my trance. When I turned away from the flaming pyre, my attention was drawn across the street. There in the shadows of taller figures, stood a maiden with dagger-shaped eyes and hair of flaming chestnut. The anger in her eyes coupled with the tremor of her lips struck me like a blow to the gut.

I pushed through the crowd, quickly making my way toward her. But too soon she caught sight of me, and her eyes widened. She pulled her earasaid over her face and turned and fled. Picking up my pace, I quickly overtook her, but she would not halt as I called out her name. I was left with no choice but to seize her arm to bring her to a stop.

"Ailsa." The sound of her name on my lips broke something within me. "Ailsa, please, wait."

"Kindly remove your hands from me, sir," she said, the emotion in her voice on the brink of breaking.

"No." Far be it from me to force a lady. To make her feel uncomfortable was the last thing I would ever want to do. But I couldn't let her go. Not with this anger between us. Somehow, I sensed she blamed me for Fian's execution, and I couldn't let her leave without an explanation. "No, Ailsa, I will not let you go while you still believe that I had something to do with the punishment meted out here today."

She looked down at my hand on her arm then squeezed her eyes shut. Two tears leaked from beneath her thick lashes and my heart broke.

"Didn't ye?" The words were a strangled question.

"No," I choked out. It seemed we both felt the pain of Fian's demise, even if for different reasons. I pulled her into me, and she buried her face in my chest, her sobs shredding me to pieces.

"It's all right to cry," I soothed, rubbing my hand gently down her back. The small notches of her spine felt like pearls beneath my fingertips, and my breath caught as I realized the jewel that I held within my arms. This woman was passionate and profoundly moved by injustice. She concerned herself with the troubles of other people and saw it as her duty to help when she could. She would love hard and love deep, and I couldn't help but feel a little twinge of jealousy for the man who would be the recipient of that love.

Pulling myself from dangerous waters, I said, "It was an unfair sentence for a citizen to face without a fair trial."

She looked up at me then, tears still forming glassy pools at the corners of her eyes. "Without a fair trial?"

I nodded. "I was unable to complete my investigation. His Majesty pronounced judgement on Fian after he was caught the second time. I guess he felt Fian's flight was proof of his guilt."

"Don't make excuses for the king. It isn't right that he was executed before all evidence could be gathered. Ye might have found something to acquit him. He might have yet been innocent."

"Shh, don't excite yourself. The odds were stacked against him from the start."

"Don't excite myself? A man was killed here today because ye were unable to complete your investigation. Does the king intend to pronounce judgement on all those still held in the tolbooth without a trial?" She pulled away from me, and I immediately missed the feel of her in my arms.

She suddenly seemed desperate, wringing her hands, and mumbling something under her breath.

"William, ye have to allow me to see Geillis. Please, is there any way that I can get in to see her, to talk to her?"

The sudden change in topic had my head spinning. We were still speaking of the witches, but her mind seemed to be on a different path now, and I wasn't sure I followed.

"Prisoners aren't usually allowed to have visitors unless it is a family member," I started.

"Yes, but ye have authority. Ye can grant special permission. Ye could get me in to see her if ye really wanted to help me."

"Help you do what, Ailsa?" She chewed on her thumbnail for a moment, not answering. "Help you do what?" I took a step closer to her, closing the gap, the vast chasm between us. If I could help her, I would. I'd do almost anything.

Her brown eyes took on a trusting look that I had never seen before, and the soft light of the mid-winter's sun melted them into pools of liquid amber. I could feel myself sinking now, and the feeling alarmed me. How easy it would be to give in to this woman. I was treading dangerous ground, yet I proceeded headlong anyway. Tumbling further into this hole I was digging for myself, I said, "I don't know what you are planning. And I have a feeling I don't want to know. But I will see what I can do to get you a visitation."

Her eyes lit up then, and it was the most glorious feeling I had ever experienced.

"Oh William, thank ye so much!" She threw herself into my arms and kissed me on the cheek.

I froze, like the idiot that I am, as if realizing for the first time that we stood in a public place. A man consoling a crying woman distraught over the events of the morning was one thing, but a man holding an excited woman in his arms who just kissed him was an entirely different thing. I pulled away from her awkwardly, wishing I had the courage to reciprocate. But thoughts of Beatrix abruptly flooded my mind, and I felt a sense of duty that I should have already thought about.

The look on Ailsa's face as I pulled away from her caused my heart to kick against my chest. I couldn't breathe, and I wanted desperately to kiss away the disappointment that splayed across her face. Before I could change my mind and pull her back to me, she spoke.

"My apologies, Sir William." Her sudden turn to formalities emphasized the neanderthal that I was. "I shall await a note from you that I may see Geillis." She turned away from me and darted, not giving me a chance to say anything more.

~22~

January 1591

Ailsa

Stupid, stupid, stupid! My footsteps against the cobbles pounded this word into my brain and I felt like even more of a ninny with every step. How could I be so stupid?

I was overwrought, I told myself. *It had been a traumatizing day*, I soothed. Surely William would understand it was my joy at the possibility of seeing Geillis that spurred me to such actions. A simple kiss. It was just a simple kiss on the cheek between two friends in payment for a favor.

But that was not a simple kiss. At least not to me. When I was far enough from Castlehill, I paused, leaning against the side of a row of shops to catch my breath. I closed my eyes and pushed my palms flat against the stone wall behind me. The roughness of the stones reminded me of the scruff of William's whiskers against my lips. The smell of soap and something spicy lingered on me, sending an unwelcome thrill through me. It would not have been unwelcomed, if I hadn't seen the look on his face, and if he hadn't stepped away from me in shock.

I could feel the tears building behind my eyelids again. This had indeed been a trying day, and I had gone and complicated it even further. It had been a simple kiss, given out of gratitude for his help, *hadn't it*? No, I was lying to myself. I had misinterpreted the touch we had shared in his room the day I visited with him. And when he pulled me into his arms today and let me cry all over the front of his velvet cloak, I imagined more than what was there. I had committed a terrible indiscretion. But the one good thing about me was this: I never made the same mistake twice. The queen of England would have to marry and effectuate an heir before I allowed myself to show William affection again.

I had just finished setting up the herbs and tinctures that Mother and I had prepared for sale at the mercat cross when a prickly sensation overcame me. Like that of insects crawling under the skin, the feeling overwhelmed me, and I immediately looked up to see the cause of such discomfort. I looked about me but saw no cause for anxiety. The butcher, Master MacElhaney had opened his stall, with slabs of pork ribs and sides of beef hanging from large hooks screwed into the top of his windowsill. Then there was Mistress Kincaid. She always had the nicest ribbons and buttons for frocks and coats. Her wares were lain out in nice, neat rows, ready to be picked over. Everything looked as it should be. I turned my attention back to my task.

The errand boy that I had hired to fetch water for the vegetable broth returned with buckets overflowing. I dumped one of the buckets into the kettle and handed it back to him for one more haul. "Fill this one, Gerald, and I've got a little something to add to your coin when ye return." The boy nodded eagerly, then took the bucket and dashed off again.

Still, I couldn't shake the uneasy feeling in the pit of my stomach. I felt as though I was being watched. I looked over my shoulder but saw no one for just cause.

"Ailsa, I promised Margaret that I would bring the mending to her as soon as I finished it. Would ye mind too terribly much if I ran these linens over to her? I'll be back in two shakes of a lamb's tail."

I searched Mother's eyes for signs of confusion. I was starting to recognize some of the signs that popped up before her disoriented episodes, such as a cloudy gaze, weakness in her limbs, and irritability.

"That should be fine, Mother. But try to be back before the crowd thickens. You know the demand for remedies is high this time of year, and anytime we have herbs, they go quickly."

"I'll be back before you can say, '*Sir William Broune is a charming grandee and would be the perfect man for me*'." I rolled my eyes at her ridiculous statement. Mother had talked nonstop about William since he had visited with us the day he brought her lemon wafers. If I didn't know any better, I would think she was infatuated with him herself.

"Here ye are Mistress." Gerald handed the last bucket of water to me, and I set it down beside the fire. Reaching into my basket, I withdrew a cloth-wrapped bundle tied with jute. I untied the string and opened to reveal two golden brown bannocks, still warm from the stone they were baked upon. Gerald's eyes widened, and he licked his lips. I took one of the oatcakes, broke it in half, and handed it to him. He hesitated. "Do I get the whole thing?"

"Aye, the whole thing. But don't eat it all at once. Break this piece in half and ye can have some for later."

He nodded eagerly, then took the bannock from my hand.

"Here," I said, lifting the other bannock from the cloth and laying both pieces in my basket. "Ye can wrap your other half in this cloth to save it for later."

"Thank ye, Mistress," he said around a mouthful of cake. "If ye don't mind, I might share a little bit of it with my little sister. She loves bannocks."

I smiled at his generous suggestion. "I think that is a wonderful idea, Gerald." Tying the jute around the cloth again, I handed the child his reward along with the coin I had promised him.

"That's very thoughtful of you, Gerald."

At the mocking words spoken to the boy, I jerked my head up. I had been too busy with the child to notice David Seton approaching. Now he stood right behind the child, and there was no avoiding him.

Gerald squinted up at Seton. "Do I know ye, sir?"

Seton smirked then broke a piece of oat cake off of Gerald's share. Popping it into his mouth, he said, "Nay, but you will. I shall soon be promoted to witch pricker, so that old goat Sheepshearer can retire."

"Och! Ye ate my bannock!" Gerald cried, and Seton looked down his nose at the boy. Seton dug in his pocket and produced a half penny. Flipping it at the boy, he said, "Now get lost."

"This isn't enough to buy more bannock," Gerald complained.

"I said beat it." The boy turned and scampered away, clutching his small bundle in his arms.

"That was rude, Bailiff Seton." I now knew where the uneasy feeling had come from, and it was standing right in front of me.

"I wanted to speak to you alone, my bonny lass."

"I can't imagine what ye would need to speak to me about unless ye are in need of some herbal remedy. A salve for your grandgore pustules, perhaps?"

He ignored my insolence and cast his eyes upon the goods that I had laid out upon the table. Picking up a small bundle of fennel seeds, he dropped them back on the table in what looked like pure disgust.

"I am in no need of herbal remedies, lass. But it will be convenient to have a healer in my bed for times when my gout ails me."

I turned my nose up at the mental picture that popped into my mind upon his words. "Whatever do you mean?" I asked with a pasted-on smile, all the while struggling to keep my breakfast from splattering Seton's boots.

"Your uncle has finally signed the betrothal agreement. We are to be wed."

"What?" I was sure I had heard him incorrectly. "My uncle has entered into an agreement on my behalf?"

"Aye. As soon as banns can be read."

I swallowed hard. As soon as the banns could be read? That only required three Sundays to be considered legal. This could not be happening.

"Sir, I hate to inform ye, but my uncle has no legal right to make those kinds of decisions for me. My father left him no such rights, and my mother will have something to say about her brother making legal decisions for me."

Seton leaned toward me, his yellowing teeth grinding together in irritation. "And I hate to inform you that the documents have already been signed. There is no way out of it now, Ailsa. You should have broached the subject with your uncle before he made pains to marry you off."

I took a step back, tripping over one of the water buckets and falling onto my backside. Seton stepped around the table and stood over me. With a wicked laugh, he said, "That's it, just as you should be. On your back beneath me."

"Ye wretched man," I yelped, rolling to my side before he could reach me. I scrambled to gain purchase, digging my heels into the frozen snow to try to escape him.

It was no use. I couldn't move fast enough. I felt Seton's heavy hand on me, grabbing my arm and pulling me upright to stand in front of him. He released my arm, only to grab my partlet instead. I stood before him. With his hand still gripping my clothing, and his arm wrapped about me, he pulled me against him. The stench of his ale-soaked breath, coupled with the bulk of his ingloriously large body, turned my stomach, causing bile to rise in my throat. I twisted my head involuntarily and coughed, choking on the unpleasant sensations.

"Sir, my uncle does not hold that authority. If any man did, it would be my brother."

"Your brother?" He grunted.

"Aye, my brother. Now please unhand me this instant. You will need to discuss this conveniently forgotten fact with my uncle." Never mind I might be putting my uncle in danger. At this point I didn't care what consequences he may suffer for this presumptuous act.

But Seton didn't release me. Instead, he leaned closer. This time I knew for sure what it was he intended. I turned my head once more, avoiding his lips and causing his kiss to fall on my ear.

"You little minx." But before he could make another attempt, a woman's voice came crackling through the cold winter air. It was sharp enough to set birds to flight and perhaps break glass.

"Get your hands off of my daughter, ye filthy, lily-livered beast!" My mother came storming toward us, broom in hand. She was waving the bristled end at Seton, the most shocking and filthiest of insults spewing from her mouth. He finally released my clothing and shrank back several steps. Who would have thought that a little old woman could set this goliath of a man to flight?

A crowd had started to gather as my mother continued to flail with the broom in her hand. "This isn't the first time ye have menaced my daughter. Now go on with ye, and don't show your face here again."

Seton's face turned scarlet. He pointed a finger at my mother. "You," he bellowed, pausing to catch his breath, "are mad!" Spittle flew from his mouth as his voice shook the Luckenbooths.

"Aye!" Mother shouted back. "And if ye show your face here again, ye shall see just how mad I can be." I stood wide-eyed at Mother's declaration. She had never spoken with such anger nor made such threats.

A clump of icy mud hit Seton in the middle of his chest, and the crowd began to jeer. "Leave 'er be, ye monster!" came the cries of Mistress Gibson. An elderly man pushed his way to the front of the crowd, and I immediately recognized Master Campbell, his twisted back preventing him from standing as tall as he would have wished.

"Sir, ye have been asked to leave the lass be." Campbell's frail voice defended. Seton looked about at the crowd that had gathered then back at my mother.

"Have you bewitched the whole town to stand against me?" Seton's nostrils flared in anger, and a red rash that stained his cheeks crept down his neck, shading his skin in burning flame. "You shall pay for this interference, Mistress. You can be assured of that."

He turned and stomped away, swiping his arm across the table, and knocking all of the contents onto the ground. I scrambled to rescue the herbs before dirt and melted snow could ruin them.

"Are ye all right, lass?" Master Campbell bent to retrieve a stray bundle of yarrow that I had missed.

"Aye, thank ye. There was no harm done."

"Who is that man, Mistress Blackburn? I've not seen him around here before."

My mother began, "That is the man who has been harassing—"

"Mother, please," I interrupted. Turning back to my elderly friend, I said, "That is Deputy Bailiff David Seton. He is an apprentice to the witch pricker and a very dangerous man. Ye will do well to steer clear of him, for he likes to prey on those weaker than he."

"Och, I've got three sturdy boys at home. I'm not afraid of that man."

"Aye, well. He warrants being careful. Ye can never be too sure of what he intends. I don't trust him, and neither should ye."

Master Campbell nodded his head then bid us a good day after ensuring that all was well. I then turned to Goodwife Gibson and warned, "Ye be careful too. Ye have marked yourself as an enemy of the bailiff for standing up for me. Be sure to stay away from him, and don't let him learn your name."

"Aye, Ailsa. I'll be sure to keep my distance," her frail voice promised.

I patted the older woman on the hand then sent her off with a blessing. Turning to my mother, I unleashed my worry and fear.

"Mama, what have ye done?"

"I have chased off the lout that has been pestering ye, Ailsa. I doubt he bothers ye again."

"Ye have made yourself a target. David Seton is a dangerous and powerful man. He holds the authority in his hand to arrest ye for witchcraft, and he as much accused ye of it here today."

"Oh pish," Mother scoffed. "Everyone here knows I am not a witch."

"The king doesn't know it. And neither do any of the men who would be judging ye. Even Sir William would be called upon to assist in a trial if ye were brought to court under accusations."

"Then Sir William can vouch for me. He knows I am not a witch."

"Mama, Sir William does not know us that well. And it is his *job* to make inquiries and prove innocence or guilt. Don't lay that burden on him. He may not be able to assist ye."

"Hmph," she protested, saying nothing further. Instead, she set to chopping vegetables as if nothing had even happened.

For my part, my head swam, and my stomach objected to my refusal to release its contents. All I wanted to do was go home, crawl into bed, huddle under the warm blankets, and have a good cry. But there was something that I would need to do first, and I was anxious now to see to it.

When we arrived home later that evening, I immediately set to the task that had plagued me all day. I pulled a piece of parchment from Father's desk and removed a readied quill and ink pot from the drawer.

I penned a letter to Nick, telling him of Seton's claims and how Uncle Rupert had given Seton permission to marry me and signed legal documents to that end on my behalf. When I was finished, I sealed the letter and set it aside, determined to post it first thing in the morning.

Now all there was left to do was to worry about whether the letter would reach Nick in time. The banns only needed to be read for three Sundays prior to the marriage ceremony. Could a letter reach Nick in London and give him enough time to make it to Edinburgh before it was too late? I did not know.

With my letter to Nick completed, I sat down to stitch my torn partlet which Seton had ripped during our scuffle. A knock came at the door just then, and I opened to find a young messenger, bearing a note.

Meet me at the tolbooth after the curfew bell rings tomorrow night. Haste must be made, for there is to be another execution before month's end. ~W

Another execution? Panic seized me, and I wondered if it were Geillis who was to face the flames. And month's end was only a few days away. I crumpled the slip of paper and tossed it into the fire. William had not signed his name to the missive, which led me to believe he may be at some considerable risk for assisting me. With renewed vigor I stoked the fire then set about preparing for my meeting with Geillis.

~23~

January 1591

William

I stood beneath the shelter of the tolbooth regretting my decision almost as soon as I had made it. The gibbous moon was hidden by cloud cover, providing no light to illuminate one's path should they desire to move about the city. House lanterns had been lit, but the moisture that hung heavy in the air was visible, making the darkened corners of the city consume what little light there was. I should have offered to meet Ailsa at her home instead of requesting she traverse by herself in the dark to the tolbooth.

And then there was the decision to allow Beatrix to come with me.

Earlier in the evening I had sent a message to Bothwell, asking him to dine with me at my room on the High Street. I had a few questions for him, and I wanted to make sure we had complete privacy.

He had arrived in fine form, already in his cups.

"Sir William, I was delighted to receive your invitation to dine. Although I must admit I was already settled in for a long night with my companions at the Hoary Oak. I do hope you make it well worth my change of plans." He removed his cloak and tossed it over a chair, not waiting for me to hang it up. With shirt askew and doublet missing, he did indeed look as if he had been occupied for some time with his companions. He pulled out another chair and dropped himself into it, looking about him with an air of interest. "I say, you do have yourself quite the private little place here."

At that a knock sounded on the door. "That will be Mistress Kennedy with our food."

I opened and allowed the goodwife to enter, her servant girl trailing behind her with a large tray. The housekeeper began unloading plates of roast mutton, turnips and parsnips, a cream soup, and a bottle of wine. Bothwell took the bottle and immediately grabbed a cup. "Do you have brandy, my good lady?"

"Nay, my lord," Mistress Kennedy bowed apologetically. "I have ale and a fine bottle of whisky."

"I'll take the whisky." He poured himself a generous portion of wine and swallowed it in one gulp.

"Aye, my lord." The housekeeper curtseyed then departed, her little maid shadowing her mistress once more. Bothwell's hungry eyes followed the lass until she could be seen no more.

The earl turned his attention back to me. "I can always rest assured that the eating will be excellent at your table, William. But what is it that you want? It's not like you to be so generous with me."

I watched him down another cup of wine, his throat bobbing in greedy consumption. "Tell me about this business proposition you approached me about." I began scooping food onto his platter, then served myself.

His eyes tapered into tiny slits as he considered my words. "Why this sudden change of heart?"

"I've got my reasons. You needn't know my personal affairs. Either tell me the particulars or we can eat our meal in silence, and you can be on your way."

A slow smile curled his lips, and it took everything within me not to knock it off his face. I prayed I could get this meal down. I had spent a good part of my adult life avoiding the king's cousin, even when he was in James's good graces. He was a snake, and I had to remind myself why I subjected myself to him now. If the king was in danger, I would do what I had to do to uncover the truth.

"I'm not asking for your friendship Broune, I simply wondered at your change of heart."

I took a swig of wine, and a sharp knock announced Mistress Kennedy. "Enter," I called.

"Here ye be, my lord." She fluttered into the room. Quickly assessing Bothwell's drinking habits by the nearly empty wine bottle she asked, "Shall I pour ye a dram?"

The earl bellowed with laughter. "A dram? No, my good woman. I want the whole bottle." He took the bottle from her hand and unstopped it, pouring the contents into his empty cup.

"Thank you, Mistress Kennedy. That will be all."

"For now," Bothwell tossed in, flashing a smile at the housekeeper.

When she had quit the room, he turned back to me. "Now, where were we?"

"You were about to tell me what grand scheme you had for me."

"Ah, yes. I am in need of an advocate to draw up some legal documents for me. Alexander Home and I have reconciled and have some business plans in the works. I am on the verge of taking on a more, shall we say, powerful role, but I fear there may be some contestation of the transfer of power once it happens. I also need a bond of manrent drawn for a couple of lords along the border." He ran his tongue over his lips when he had finished, tilting his head to look at me from under his drooping lids. "It will, of course, take a modicum of discretion."

I lifted a brow in curiosity. "Transfer of power?" This was exactly the kind of information I had been searching for but didn't realize I would hit upon it so soon. "You mean, being High Admiral of Scotland and the Sherriff of Edinburgh are not enough power?"

Bothwell took another drag from his cup before answering. "Perhaps you are content with being His Majesty's runabout, but I have higher aspirations."

"Is that why you are flirting with Spain? Everyone knows you are still in contact with the Spanish governor, the Duke of Parma."

He dropped his cup onto the table and rolled his eyes heavenward. "And everyone knows I was in correspondence with Parma by the king's directive. I merely continued our communication after the king decided the scheme with Spain wasn't to his liking. The plan was to attack the town of Berwick in retaliation for Queen Mary's execution. Obviously, it did not come to fruition. Parma was too busy preparing his armada for his own attack on England." He leaned forward with his elbows on the table. "He is of no use to me now. I turned over the last missive that I received from Parma to the Reverend Bruce. No one, least of all the Scottish lords, can accuse me of hiding anything from His Majesty. The Reverend will be sure of that. And if Parma writes to me again, I shall notify the Queen of England."

I scoffed at that. "You see, Bothwell, that is where I am a little confused. Are you a Catholic sympathizer or a Protestant hero? I cannot determine which."

The slight on his motives had the desired effect. His face darkened at the challenge, and his eyes bore into mine with an icy stare. The air in the room had turned thick and stifling, but I resisted the urge to take a drink. Instead, I met his glare with one of my own and waited for his explanation.

As quickly as his hardened face had appeared, it was gone and instead an amused expression lifted his brow. "You of all people should understand how a devout Protestant could wish to avenge the offense caused by the execution of our Catholic queen. Do you mean to tell me that your Protestant father never spoke to you of his Catholic love affair?"

I hadn't noticed when the muscles in my jaw had tightened, but at the mention of my father, I could feel the tension pulling there. "You leave my father out of this." The growl in my voice was low, but the threat was there, nonetheless.

He chuckled. "Aww. I heard he was a broken man when he returned from England." He clicked his tongue against his teeth. "I wasn't here to see him of course, but it is well known the love your father had for our Catholic queen and the contempt he holds for her son, seeing how His Majesty did nothing to prevent her demise."

I stood abruptly and grabbed Bothwell's collar. I pulled him across the table toward me until his face was a hair's breadth from mine. A plate of something skidded across the table and crashed onto the floor. "My father is a saint," I said between clenched teeth. "He may have loved her deeply, but it was not tainted as you insinuate. And he would never sacrifice his principles for mere ambition. That is something that you will never understand."

His eyes danced with mirth. "I will not argue that. I will never understand a man who has all the brains and brawn that Providence could bestow upon him yet does not take advantage of those gifts to further his own cause. But I did not come here to talk about your pious father. I have laid out a task before you, and it is now time for you to tell me whether you will oblige me or whether I need take my coin elsewhere." As quick as it had come, his merriment was gone, and his voice was laced with controlled contempt. Then, as if sensing my ability to read him, he said, "I do say, Broune, I believe you have dragged my tunic through the soup. I am soaked through."

I released my hold on him and shoved him away. He straightened his garments before sitting back down in his chair as if nothing had happened. I needed to get control. The earl was a powerful man, and I did not want to get on his bad side. Truth be told, I was surprised he didn't retaliate with a pistol or dagger that he kept tucked away for just such an occasion.

"Such a shame. That was the parsnips you sent tumbling to the floor. I have an unusual fondness for parsnips." He picked up his fork and stabbed the mutton with ravenous enthusiasm.

We ate in silence after that until the burning question that had been pressing me for some time now finally had to be asked.

"Why me? You know James and I have been friends since we were boys."

Bothwell looked up from his charger. He swiped the back of his hand across his mouth then took another swig of whisky.

"I never said this had anything to do with my dear cousin. Besides, what's that old adage? Keep your friends close and your enemies closer. Nonetheless, you're the best there is. And, you have not entangled yourself with the squabblings and churlish behavior of Scottish lords. I trust that you will be an unbiased participant who will simply do the job and not interfere. Although now I'm not sure. You ask a lot of questions, and that can be dangerous."

"That is my job."

A low chuckle slipped from his mouth. "Aye, and you do it so well. For example, look how close you were to convicting Dr. Fian. If he hadn't escaped the tolbooth, you may have actually had some evidence against him."

I stiffened. What a strange topic to breach. "You are intimate with the details of Fian's case?"

He put down his utensil and reached into his pocket. "You are an intelligent man, Broune. I know that you understand if I show this to you, there will be a certain comradery between us from here on out. A tie that is not so easily broken. An obligation and a loyalty not to be taken lightly."

I watched as he produced a piece of metal and laid it on the table. I tried to school my reaction, but it had to be written all over my face. The traitor. He had just laid a key in front of me, as if it were a flower he had picked from a field.

"Please tell me that isn't what I think it is."

His brow shot up in innocence, and then a smile slowly crept onto his face. "It depends. What do you think it is?"

I had my suspicions. "The key to Fian's cell," I said more to myself. But would he be so careless as to actually confess his involvement in Fian's attempt at escape? How badly did he need my help? But I would never know, for once again, there was a loud knock on the door.

"Sir, there be a Lady here to see ye," Mistress Kennedy announced.

I stood abruptly, my thoughts immediately going to Ailsa, but when Beatrix stepped out from behind the housekeeper, I realized my mistake. I ignored the slight disappointment I felt.

With the interruption from Beatrix, Bothwell and I could not continue our discussion. He made a quick work of his exit and left

Beatrix and I standing there in my chamber.

"I did not mean to interrupt," she began, eyeing the parsnips on the floor.

"Thank you for rescuing me," I said lightly. I turned back to the table and noticed that Bothwell had left the key. Was it a sign of some sort? A warning for my silence or a reminder of the bond he perceived we now had? I knew not, but I quickly picked the key up and tucked it into my desk drawer.

I had already sent Ailsa the note to meet me at the tolbooth, and now there was nothing to be done for it. I had to either persuade Beatrix of some other business that I needed to take care of, or I could bring her with me. I thought it might do her some good to see the conditions within which the witches were kept. Her innocence was admirable, but it also made her clueless as to the suffering around her.

Now here we stood in the cold night air waiting for Ailsa. Beatrix had begun shivering within minutes of stopping, and I pulled my cloak from my shoulders and wrapped it around her.

"When did you begin keeping company with the Earl of Bothwell? I thought you didn't care for him?" Her teeth chattered as she asked the question, and I tugged my cloak tighter about her before answering.

"We don't keep company. Not normally. But he needs the help of an advocate for some legal work and has asked me to assist." I didn't think that was too terribly revealing, but I didn't wish to discuss him further.

"And what of this lass you are meeting here tonight? Who is she?"

I shifted on my feet. This was a topic that I wished even less to speak with Beatrix about. I rubbed my hands together and blew into them, trying to warm myself. "She is the niece of one of the men who has been assisting the Deputy Bailiff with the witches." Not a lie, but probably not something Ailsa would be proud of.

"And tell me again why you are meeting her here after curfew? What if we get caught?"

"I have a question for you instead," I said, interrupting her thoughts. "How did you find me this evening?"

She blinked twice, staring at me with mouth agape, as if my question were a jest.

"I, I asked Lord Blantyre. He told me where I could find you. But don't worry," she rushed to add, lowering her voice, "I won't tell His Majesty. That *is* whom you wished to hide from, is it not?" She blinked again, sounding as if the thought of me hiding from *her* would set her to tears.

I chuckled. "Not exactly hiding, but I do like to get out from under his thumb every now and again." She laughed too then her voice caught, and her teeth set to chattering again. I pulled her closer to me, wrapping my arm around her. If Ailsa didn't come soon, we would need to abandon this scheme altogether.

I had almost given up hope when I saw a figure in the shadows moving toward us. Her shapely hips could have been any number of women skulking about between ale houses, but her shortened stature, making her look more like a child than an adult woman lurking in the dark, led me to know it was her. I chastised myself for my lecherous thoughts, admiring one woman while I stood with my arm around another.

She carried a basket on her arm, and her earasaid was wrapped so tightly about her that she looked like a walking cocoon. She came to a stop in front of us, eyes wide and breath coming at quickened intervals, the wisps of expelled air curling between us.

"Are you all right?" I inquired, after running an examining eye over her.

"I'm fine."

"My apologies, I should have offered to bring you here." I moved to step forward but felt Beatrix's eyes on me and changed my mind.

"I said I'm all right," she said with a bite to her words. She looked then for the first time at Beatrix and curtsied slightly. "My lady," she mumbled.

Clearing my throat, I said, "Lady Beatrix, this is Ailsa Blackburn. Ailsa, Lady Beatrix Ruthven." I motioned toward Beatrix.

"'Tis a pleasure to make your acquaintance," Beatrix began. "Tell me, Mistress Blackburn, what are we doing here? For Sir William refuses to make it plain to me."

Both women looked to me for an answer. I felt stuck between fire and ice. Beatrix's eyes pinning me with an icy blue stare, and Ailsa's stabbing me with flaming amber.

"We are here to see Geillis Duncan."

Beatrix's sharp intake of breath sliced through the night air. "The witch?"

"Aye."

I turned both women about and led them to the entrance of the tolbooth.

"Wait," Beatrix said in a panic. "I do not want to see the filthy creature. If I had known this is what we were doing, I would have never agreed to come." She dug her heels into the stones beneath us and refused to move further.

Ailsa opened her mouth to say something, but I stepped in before she could brand Beatrix with her striking words.

"You do not have to accompany us. I will understand if you wish to remain in the receiving area. I will see you back to the palace when we are finished."

She looked to Ailsa and then back to me, eyes wide with worry. "Well, I certainly do not wish to remain outside in this frigid air." She looked over her shoulder then, making it plain that the cold air was not her only concern.

"You can stand inside the door. We will meet you back here in a few minutes."

"Perhaps you will reconsider, my lady." Ailsa began. "I'm sure Geillis could benefit from your prayers and a little Christian charity." I turned my head toward Ailsa as she spoke. The edge in her words was unmistakable, and Beatrix appeared torn.

"This must be done in great haste. There's to be another burning soon."

"Geillis?" Ailsa's voice caught on the word. I could barely see her face in the dark, but I imagined it was drained of color. She was on the verge of tears.

"Agnes Sampson," I said. "We must hurry. Beatrix, what have you decided?"

"I'll go," she said, her voice wobbling. I moved them toward the door, and we slipped inside.

It was even darker inside the tolbooth than it had been outside. Within the tiny receiving room sat a woman behind a wide podium, head bent and dozing. A small candle sat dangerously close to where her head bobbed, her wheezing breaths moving the flame each time she exhaled. At the sound of our voices, she awoke with a start.

"Who goes there?"

"'Tis I, Mistress McCullum." I moved toward the woman, so the light from the single candle could illuminate my face.

"Och, Sir William. I had not expected to see ye again, and this late at night." Her eyes sagged in exhaustion, and the beginnings of lines creased the sides of her mouth.

"How much longer until your shift is over?"

"Only another hour." She yawned then looked around me at the two women standing behind me. "Ye brought visitors?"

"Mistress McCollum, this is Lady Beatrix Ruthven. She is in my charge and is waiting for me to see her home as soon as I can conclude some business here. May she sit with you until I return?"

"Aye," the older woman nodded toward Beatrix and motioned toward another chair that sat across from the podium.

I reached into my pocket and discretely withdrew a small bag of coin. "And this is Mistress Blackburn. I have brought her to see one of the prisoners." I set the bag on the desk in front of her, and the gaoler raised her eyebrows.

"Ye've got an hour and a half before Sheepshearer returns. But I can make no guarantees about Seton. That lecher comes by at all hours to torment the prisoners."

"I understand," I said, lifting her hand to my lips and dropping a soft peck. "You are a jewel."

"Och, go on now before I change my mind." She chuckled, tucking the bag of coin into the folds of her skirts.

I turned and motioned to Beatrix to have a seat in the vacant chair, but she seized my arm and clung to me. "I wish to stay with you, William," she whispered, the darkened shadows of the receiving room barely allowing the candlelight to touch her face.

I turned back to Mistress McCollum. "Apparently there has been a change of plans. If you don't mind, Lady Beatrix will accompany us as well."

"Suit yourself," the older woman said, tucking her chin into her chest and settling in for another nap. "Have ye got a candle?"

"Aye," I said, reaching into my pocket again. Lighting my candle from the one that sat on her desk, I led the ladies to the iron door of the receiving room and stopped. "What you are about to hear are the sounds of desperation, agony, and misery. Prepare yourselves for it is not for the faint of heart."

~24~

January 1591

William

I swung the heavy door open, and we stepped into an alcove. To the right was a long, barren passageway with wooden doors lining the hall. Painful groans came from the cells. Further down the hall, a low hum, like that of a song being sung, drifted through a cell door. A screech rang out closer to us and sobbing came from every direction.

"Is that a child?" Beatrix stiffened at my side.

"There are several children in residence here. Victims of a father or mother who could not pay their debts."

To the left was a spiral stone stairway, leading to the upper floor. I chose the stairs and led the way. Ailsa had been so quiet since we had entered the tolbooth, I finally looked at her to measure her thoughts. When she saw me looking at her, she lifted her chin to convince me she was strong. But I could see the fear in her eyes.

"I thought that Geillis was on the first floor?"

"She was until a few days ago. She was moved up here to make room for some new inmates."

She didn't speak again until we had reached the top of the stairs. "Why is Agnes the next person to be executed?"

"She gave a splendid performance at her inquisition before the king a few weeks ago and sealed her fate when she told the king of some words that had passed between himself and Her Majesty on their wedding night," I whispered back. "And her assize was held this morning."

Ailsa looked at me aghast. "What did she say to His Majesty about his wedding night?"

"No one knows. But whatever it was, it shook the king to his very core and convinced him right then and there that she could be none other than the witch that she was accused of being. She must have spoken true. For if it weren't witchcraft, then how did she know the intimate words spoken between a king and his queen?"

"Servants talk, ye know. And no one is ever truly alone. There is always someone about to prattle," Ailsa defended.

"That is true," Beatrix added. "I know at least half a dozen servants who would share good gossip if given the right amount of coin."

"But the king had nearly dismissed her for a liar only moments before. Why would she dissuade him with such a confession?"

"I don't know," Ailsa admitted.

Our conversation was interrupted by a mournful sob. Someone begged for mercy. They became more intrusive and shouting broke out from somewhere down the hall. Both ladies stopped walking when a cackling laugh overtook the crying.

"I don't think I can go any further." Beatrix's voice shook as another wave of sobs overtook us from a cell somewhere down the corridor.

"It's just around this corner." I pointed to another hallway that intersected with ours, and we turned to the left. A guard stood at the end of the passageway and watched us by the light of a torch that hung above his head.

"Sir William Broune here to see Geillis Duncan," I said as we drew up before him.

The guard stood to his feet then scratched in the most inappropriate of places, eyeing Ailsa and Beatrix like a dog eyes a scrap of meat. Spitting a wad of blackened birchbark at our feet, he said, "And who are they?"

"This is Lady Beatrix Ruthven. She is under my protection and is simply waiting for me to see her home safely. And she," I said pointing to Ailsa, "is a healer come to check on the prisoner."

I could sense Ailsa's quick intake of breath and prayed she didn't give us away. We hadn't discussed a cover story, but it seemed the most logical.

"I've not heard of any prisoners being sick. Not beyond the typical ailments, at least. What makes this one so special?" He crooked a thumb at the large wooden door that stood between us and Geillis.

"I have reason to believe the witch might be ill. You don't want a plague breaking out in your prison, do you? Now grant us entrance, or I shall be forced to tell the king of your lack of cooperation."

"All right, all right," he said, waving his hand in the air dismissively. "Ye tell His Majesty that he needs to communicate these orders better in the future. With all the comings and goings between ye, the bailiff, and the witch pricker, I don't get a moment's rest."

"If you value your head, I'd advise against you sending that message," I counselled.

The guard grunted and begrudgingly removed a ring of keys from his belt and unlocked the wooden door. My mind went back to Bothwell's key, and I wondered how he knew which one would open Fian's door. They all looked the same. The creak of the hinges reverberated off the stone walls, alerting the prisoner to the intruders.

Ailsa started for the door then stopped abruptly when she saw me following. "Are ye coming in too?"

"Of course." I breathed, noticing a tinge of uncertainty in her eyes.

"But I thought ye didn't want to know what I was doing?" she whispered.

"Is it something illegal?"

She opened her mouth to respond when the guard bellowed.

"Go on with ye then. If the prisoner is sick, I don't want any part of it. Get inside so I can shut the door."

I turned to Beatrix, "You stay here until we are finished."

She looked at the guard in disgust and shook her head. "I'll take my chances with the plague."

Ailsa and I looked at each other, then she slid inside the cell. I placed my hand on the small of Beatrix's back and guided her into the cell in front of me. I ducked through the doorway behind her.

Only one of the candles that had been lit on the walls still burned. That lone candle gave off a faint glow of yellow light, clinging to life until the sun rose again. A strong stench accosted us upon entry, and as our eyes adjusted, we could see the source of the smell. A bucket left for the prisoners to relieve themselves had been kicked over, and the filth had spilt out onto the floor. I observed Ailsa and Beatrix, gauging their reactions to the sites we beheld. Beatrix covered her mouth and nose with a piece of cloth, but Ailsa immediately rushed to Agnes and eyed the bridle that had been placed in her mouth.

"Sir William, remove this instrument from her at once," she demanded. When I did not heed her command, she looked at me, releasing a cry of aggravation. "Sir William!"

"That is beyond my authority to do so, Mistress." A garbled cry escaped her lips as she brushed a wiry gray lock of hair from the old woman's face. Agnes moaned at the gentle touch and shifted on her feet as best she could. The rings of the shackles that held her to the wall bore most of her slight frame.

"Can ye at least demand some water from the guard?" she said in disgust.

I considered her words momentarily then went to the cell door and banged on it. This time, the creaking of the hinges was followed by curses from the guard.

"What is it now?"

"Bring some water and some clean cloths."

The guard looked at me as if I had gone mad. "Och, we ain't a hostelry."

"Just do it." I shoved a coin into his hand and pulled the door closed in his face, Ailsa's unspoken chastisement spurring me on.

There were three prisoners in this cell: Geillis, Agnes, and a woman named Barbara Napier. Barbara was another soul that Geillis had condemned with her testimony. She was a bit more well off than

Geillis and Agnes, although the satin ruffles of her dress were dirtied now and the French lace that had encircled her wrists and the collar of her frock this morning had been torn off. I had questioned her earlier in the day, but apparently, she had been interrogated again after I left.

Moments later the door swung open, and the guard stood there with the requested items.

"Would you be so kind as to remove the scold's bridle from Mistress Sampson so she can be examined properly?" I inquired.

The guard propped a hand on his hip in rebellion. "She ain't to be released from that bridle until her execution." He huffed. "Them's were my instructions from Bailiff Seton."

"Fine. Let her spread plague to the rest of the inmates and you as well." I turned back to Agnes, but the guard had a change of heart.

"If Seton catches wind of this, I'm sending him straight to ye," he balked, fidgeting with his ring of keys to find the one that unlocked the scold's bridle. Once the device was released, Ailsa lifted it from the old woman's head. The bridle was designed with a long, narrow plate that fitted into the prisoner's mouth when the metal cage was placed over one's head. It was intended as a punishment, and to keep the victim quiet. Agnes licked her dry lips with her thick, swollen tongue, and moaned in relief. Ailsa immediately gave her a drink of ale then pulled out a small loaf of bread that she had brought in her basket.

"Loosen her hands as well," I commanded. The guard glared at me but said nothing. I wondered just how far I could push it.

He released the locks on the rings that held the old woman upright against the stone wall. She immediately fell to the floor, rubbing her hands against the paper-thin skin that crinkled across her legs.

"Hers too," Ailsa instructed, pointing toward Geillis.

His lip curled. "I don't take orders from the likes of *ye, Healer.*"

"Then take them from me," I said, stepping between the guard and Ailsa. "Loosen Geillis' hands from the wall." He rolled his eyes toward the ceiling and mumbled something under his breath before unlocking the shackles that held her to the wall. Then without another word, he left the cell, slamming the door behind him.

Ailsa washed the old woman's face and arms and administered some ointment around her wrists that she had stored in her basket.

"I thought we were here to see Geillis," whispered Beatrix, watching the scene before her in astonishment.

"We are, but I suspect once Ailsa heard of Agnes' plight, and saw her condition, she couldn't help but be moved with compassion."

Beatrix sniffed at that but didn't speak again.

"What an odd turn of events, Sir William," Agnes croaked, looking from Ailsa to me.

I stood frozen, watching as Ailsa ministered to the broken woman. I didn't realize she even knew my name, but she had seen me several times, the last being at her assize. I was part of the commission of justiciary council that condemned her. Ailsa looked to me puzzled, then Agnes spoke again. "The steps of a good man are ordered."

I shifted on my feet but did not answer her. It was the same words she spoke to me at her interrogation with the king. I wondered now if she thought of my involvement in her conviction. I had not been the deciding vote, but there was no way around the guilty verdict after her confession to the king. How could I have decided any differently?

Ailsa finished with Agnes and moved on to Geillis. "I'm so sorry this has happened to ye," she soothed as she ran the cloth over the young woman's face.

"Don't be sorry for her," the third woman cried, the hoarse sound scraping past her lips. "If it weren't for her, we wouldn't be here."

Ailsa looked to the woman, her mouth gaping. "What do ye mean?"

Barbara swung her head toward Ailsa. Her sunken eyes were red from weeping and perhaps a lack of sleep. Deep purple smudges stained the hollows under her eyes, and her nose was swollen to twice its normal size. "What I mean is that this stupid girl gave Seton our names and told him we were involved in some sort of witchcraft." She paused, dragging a sharp breath into her lungs. "I have never practiced witchcraft. All I wanted was some help repairing my strained relations with Her Ladyship, the Countess of Angus. I went to Agnes in hopes that she could help. My husband was a burgess of Edinburgh. I have properties left to me by him after he gave up the ghost." With that she broke off her jumbled thoughts, a strained cry slipping off her tongue.

"Aye, and it was at that residence that ye boast about that ye allowed the witches to gather to discuss your plans." Geillis accused.

Ailsa frowned. "How do ye know this, Geillis?"

"I was told," she said simply.

"You were lied to!" shrieked Barbara. At the angry woman's words, Geillis began to sob.

"Ye did more than that, Barbara." Agnes spoke, her weakened voice barely audible above Barbara's cries. Five sets of eyes turned toward the old woman in surprise. "Ye took the wax figure that I gave to ye and used it for ill."

Barbara's face twisted in anguish. "I did not know. I only did as Lord Bothwell instructed."

At the mention of the earl's name, my head jerked to Barbara. "What does the Earl of Bothwell have to do with all of this?"

Ailsa tilted her head, and I could feel her eyes boring into me. "Perhaps he wishes ill toward someone too. Someone who stands to lose a great deal."

I understood immediately what she meant. Or rather, who she meant. And after the conversation I had with Bothwell earlier in the evening, my suspicions were confirmed. Bothwell had attempted to kidnap the king before. It would come as no surprise that he would attempt it again. But to use witchcraft as a means to achieve his goal? He was more depraved than I thought.

"Barbara, what part does the Earl of Bothwell play in all this?" I tried again. When she didn't answer, I walked toward her. She was the only one of them chained to the floor instead of the wall. "It would benefit you to tell me what you know. How is he involved with the witches' plot to kill the king?"

"I know of no plot!" she cried, shrinking away from me. "I don't know what the earl's plans are. I took the wax figure and said some words and hid it under my bed. It was supposed to protect my husband while he was away from Edinburgh on business."

"But instead, the Earl of Angus ended up dead," taunted Agnes, her voice gaining strength. "If ye had followed *my* instructions, perhaps the countess would be here to defend your innocence, and your own husband might have made it home alive."

"What went wrong, Barbara?" I stood over her now and watched as she curled further into herself, drawing her knees up to her chest and burying her face in her bloodied hands.

"William," Ailsa said in irritation. "Ye are scaring the poor lass. She has been through so much. Ye will not get the answers ye seek employing Bailiff Seton's tactics."

I ignored her. Turning back to Barbara, I said, "Did the Earl of Bothwell procure your help to put a hex on Angus?"

"No. That is, I didn't know."

"Did Bothwell seek your help in putting a hex on His Majesty?"

"No!" she screeched, the word slipping out on the tail of another sob. "I don't know what his intentions were. The Earl of Bothwell visited me the day that Agnes gave me the image. He said he had further instruction for me and told me what to do with the statue. I only followed his advice to ensure that the charm would bring my husband home safely."

"But he didn't come home safely, did he Barbara? From the sound of it, he didn't return at all. What were the instructions that Bothwell gave you?" I knelt down in front of her, my face so close to hers that I could feel her ragged breath on my cheeks. She trembled under the sound of my angry questions.

"I don't want to talk about it anymore," Barbara wailed, turning her face toward the wall.

"That is enough for now," Ailsa said as she moved toward the disgruntled woman and began to wash her face as she had done for the others. She handed the woman a small loaf of bread. The sound of iron shackles scraping across the cold stone floor echoed through the cell in the ensuing awkward silence.

Then Geillis spoke up. "Ye are the woman who sent the bread. With the message." Her face lit up. "Are ye here to rescue me?"

Beatrix gasped. I stiffened at the feeling of betrayal that coursed through my blood. Ailsa looked at me uncomfortably then back to Geillis. "I'm afraid not, love."

"But ye said ye wanted to help me. I thought ye meant ye would help me get out of here."

"I—" For the first time since I had met her, Ailsa seemed completely without words.

"I think it is time we be going," I said. "Sheepshearer will be returning soon."

"The witch pricker?" Barbara squalled, kicking her legs, and scooting her body backward in an effort to push herself further into the corner of the room. "Please, don't let him touch me again. His prickings are painful."

"Be thankful for that dear heart," Ailsa soothed. "That means you're not a witch."

I rapped on the door, signaling for the guard to come and lock the women back up.

"Please," Geillis entreated. "Please take me with ye."

"I'll come again as soon as I can or send ye a message if I am unable to." She cupped the young woman's bruised cheek in her small hand, then released her, wiping a tear from her eye.

The guard shoved passed us, jerking Agnes first to her feet. The old woman cried out in pain as he locked the rings around her wrists once more.

"Be gentle, ye brute!" Ailsa moved to throw herself at him, but I caught her by the arm.

"Ailsa," I warned. "Let him do his job."

She glared at me, pulling her arm free and pressing her teeth into her bottom lip in an effort not to cry. But a tear ran down her cheek all the same, and that was my undoing.

~25~

January 1591

Ailsa

Now that the curiosity of seeing Geillis was satisfied, the fear of being discovered by Master Sheepshearer sent my heartbeat into a whirl. I did not like the man, and I definitely wanted to be away from the tolbooth before he came back.

But William stopped me as we reached the stairs before I could flee the tolbooth and the possibility of seeing Sheepshearer.

"What did Geillis mean? The messages?" His voice was strained, and I fought the urge to look away from his piercing eyes. In the light of that single flame of his candle, I felt his eyes burning into me, and I couldn't bear the reproach.

"Were you going to help that witch escape the tolbooth?" Lady Beatrix's tone was accusing and gave me just the iron I needed to face William's wrath. But before I could defend myself, William spoke again.

"Why did you want to see Geillis? Did you actually think you were going to help her escape right under my nose?"

"Nay," I said, more forcefully than I intended. I put my hand out to steady myself with the wall, but the cold, damp stones felt slimy to my touch, and I recoiled in repulsion. "I merely wanted to speak to her. I wanted to find out for myself whether or not she was a witch."

William sighed and scraped a hand across his burgeoning

whiskers. "Let's keep moving. I don't want to see Sheepshearer and have to explain my actions this evening."

We tread quietly down the stairs, the scuffing of our shoes echoing off the walls. The smells of excrement and vomit, coupled with William's reproving tone, made me feel faint. I stumbled twice on the steps; once when my toe caught on a lose stone, and then again when the slick surface of the rock broke the traction on the bottom of my boot.

"Will you suffer consequences if it is discovered that you were here tonight?" Beatrix asked. Even her concern for William's well-being grated against my nerves. He didn't answer her at first, and I felt a sort of satisfaction as he ignored her question. "Surely, you have more authority than Sheepshearer, my love. You are the king's friend."

A choking noise escaped my lips before I could stop it. *My love.* I rolled my eyes but then caught William looking at me.

"The only authority that matters is the king's. If something displeases him, that is what I will need to worry about."

We reached the bottom of the stairs but not before I felt the walls closing in around me. A tightening in my chest squeezed my heart, and I found myself gasping for breath.

"Are you ill, Ailsa?" William cupped my elbow in his hand and tried to steady me.

"She should be," Lady Beatrix reprimanded. "She could have gotten you into serious trouble with this scheme. This was very foolish, and I'm not sure—"

"Enough," William commanded. Lady Beatrix and I both jumped at his words, but I noticed that his hand still held my elbow. It sent a comforting feeling straight to my belly. Like warm milk on a cold winter's night. "We will speak no more of this. It is done and cannot be changed."

Lady Beatrix closed her mouth and looked at me from the corner of her eye. I could not hold her gaze. I felt like an interloper now. Everything suddenly felt awkward.

William waved to the woman behind the podium as we reached the tolbooth door. I couldn't wait to take a gulp of the cold night air and let it freeze my lungs if it must. This new epiphany was unsettling. My budding feelings for William accosted by the apparent feelings that he and Lady Beatrix must hold for each other. I felt as though my stomach was going to overturn, and I couldn't get out of the tolbooth fast enough.

But as I reached to push on the door, it opened on its own volition. Tears were pushing at the back of my lids, demanding to be freed, but I would not let William see his effect on me. I was so busy trying to get away from him, away from *them*, that it took me a moment to realize why the door opened so easily.

"How fortuitous," said the voice that accompanied the bulk that stood before us.

I looked up into the black eyes of David Seton.

"I must say, but this is a surprise." He stood in the doorway, refusing to move. I could not get around him, and with William behind me and Seton before me, I felt like a caged wildcat.

"Aye, well, we were just leaving," William said. His hands were on me again, but this time it was to move me aside, so he could look Seton in the eyes. He was half a head taller than Seton but where Seton's bulk came from extra meat on his bones, William's was well-worked muscle. Sword play and horseback riding were my guesses.

"And why is it exactly you are here at the tolbooth in the middle of the night? And with my betrothed?"

"Your betrothed?" William repeated. I almost thought he stuttered over the words, but I knew better. He was too perfect in looks and mannerisms to let a few unimportant words throw him off.

"Aye, my betrothed." Seton pounded William on the chest in a hearty, celebratory sort of way.

"I am not your betrothed," I said, annoyed.

Seton looked at me, his eyes round in innocence. "Why, my little dove, I thought we had already settled this? You are my betrothed, and we shall be married in," he paused, looking toward the sky as if he were calculating, "a little less than three weeks."

"Ye blackguard." I tried my hardest not to draw attention to us. "Ye know good and well that we are not betrothed. As I have already told ye, my uncle has no legal rights to enter into such agreements. Least of all, not while my brother is alive."

Seton opened his mouth to speak, but William spoke first. "Your Uncle Rupert betrothed you to this man without your consent or proper authority? Was it set about in your father's will?"

"Nay. My father would have never given my uncle such authority. He and my uncle didn't get along. My older brother Nicholas Blackburn would have the say, if anyone. And my brother would never force me to marry someone so loathsome as the Deputy Bailiff." I wasn't sure where my bravery came from. Perhaps standing behind William gave me courage. Whatever it was I felt safe and maybe a little reckless.

"I have a signed legal document stating that you are to be my wife. I will hold you to this betrothal or else."

"Or else what, Bailiff Seton? You clearly have a document that is worthless. It will not hold up in court." William took a step forward as if in a challenge.

Seton turned his anger on William now. "I don't believe this concerns you, sir. You don't want to cross me. I have ways of making people pay."

William took another step closer to Seton and a thrill coursed through me as I watched Seton take a step back, craning his neck to look into William's eyes. "Legal matters, especially those of my friends, do concern me, bailiff. And if I were you, I would think twice before threatening the king's advocate."

Seton's eyes sharpened on William, and he chewed on the inside of his cheek before speaking again. Finally, he said, "If you can prove that this Nicholas Blackburn actually exists, and that Marley has no legal authority to make agreements on his niece's behalf, then I will give up my claim. But you have three weeks to do it."

Seton took a step aside, holding the door open for us to walk through. But as I stepped forward to leave, he seized my arm, his tight grip digging into my flesh. "You're staying with me, my little dove." He pulled me to his side, making room for William and Lady Beatrix to leave.

"Nay, she is coming with us," William said. "She and I had some business to finish, and I will see her home safely."

Seton's nostrils flared, and he took a deep breath. "Aye, what business exactly was that that would require you to be at the tolbooth in the middle of the night? You never did say."

"Bailiff Seton," Lady Beatrix spoke up for the first time since William reprimanded her. "This night air is not good for my delicate constitution. We must be on our way, so I'm afraid I'm going to have to ask you to excuse us. You'll have to see to your betrothed at another time. Right now, *my betrothed* needs to see me back to the palace. Her Majesty will be wondering why it has taken me so long to return."

Seton planted a sour, ale-soaked kiss on my forehead before releasing his grip and shoving me forward into William's chest. William threw a protective arm around my shoulder, and I heard Seton let out a low growl. "This isn't over, Broune."

"You are correct, Seton. I'll be serving you a petition in a day or two concerning your betrothal. Be on your watch for it." And with that William motioned for me and Lady Beatrix to follow him.

~26~

January 1591

Ailsa

We hurried along in the shadows of the Luckenbooths until we were far enough from the tolbooth and Seton's glare. When we slowed our pace, I turned to Lady Beatrix.

"I cannot thank ye enough for stepping in and putting Seton in his place."

The beautiful woman pulled William's cloak around her tighter. She looked at me, annoyed. "Let me make this perfectly clear to you, Mistress Blackburn. What I did back there was not for you. It was for William. I do not like Bailiff Seton, and I do not trust him. What we did tonight was very stupid and has the potential to get William into a lot of trouble. I was merely trying to put an end to Seton's questions, so William will not be suspected of something. You are lucky that William considers you a friend enough to go through such great lengths for you, but he is *my betrothed,* and I couldn't bear to see something happen to him."

He is my betrothed. Her words hit me as if I had been pushed into the Water of Leith with the icy depths of the river swallowing me up and pulling me under.

"Beatrix," William's low reprimand pushed me further into the frigid waters. I didn't want his sympathy. And I certainly didn't want to feel like the kitten between two hounds.

"Aye, of course," I said instead. "Well, thank ye all the same. Now, I'll see myself the rest of the way home. Sir William, thank ye for arranging this meeting with Geillis. I realize now how foolish it was, and I'm sorry to have put ye in danger. I'll be going now."

"Wait," William shifted, reaching out to stay my steps. Between he and Seton, I felt like a piece of dough being kneaded. "You will not be walking home by yourself. I made that mistake once, and I will not be doing it again."

Lady Beatrix cleared her throat. "My love, perhaps we should let her go. If she is not going the same direction, we will be delayed."

I noticed the tone with which she spoke to William was totally different than that she used with me. Of course, he was her equal, and I was just a scribe's daughter. Why would she speak to me any differently than she would a servant?

"Lady Beatrix, I realize that you desperately want to get back to the palace. And I do not blame you. Like you told Seton, this night air is not good for your health. I'm sure Mistress Blackburn will not mind to accompany us to the palace first to see you home safe and sound, then I can take her home." He still held my arm, and I felt his hand tighten on me at his words. It wasn't a grip like Seton's. It seemed to me he wanted to relay a message to me of some sort. But I wasn't sure what he was trying to say.

"Actually—" I began, but I was cut off by Beatrix. She sounded distressed.

"William, my love. It is not safe for you to be out past curfew. There is already a cloud of suspicion hanging above your head."

William frowned. "There is no suspicion. I have as much a reason to be at the tolbooth as Seton. Besides, the curfew is more for the villagers to bank their fires and for ale drinkers who tend to flit from ale house to ale house. I will be safe enough. But I will not have Ailsa walking home alone. It is different for a woman. Surely you understand that."

"Aye, my love," she acquiesced. But she was not happy. Of that, I was sure.

When we reached the gates of Holyroodhouse, the need to fall back into the shadows overwhelmed me. I slowed my step in hesitation, the great stone edifice towered over us like a bird of prey. My eyes fell upon the fires where the guards stood to keep warm.

"Heat," I whispered, and William looked at me.

"Aye, but it will be much warmer inside the palace, no need for you to stand out here."

I moved to protest, but once again his hand was on me, on the small of my back, guiding me toward the palace doors. I had never stepped foot inside the palace. I had no need to, and I suddenly felt very much out of my realm.

We entered into a small receiving room, and he immediately swept us up the great stairs, the stairway being wide enough for a horse-drawn carriage. Once upstairs, we walked through the dining hall, where large Ionic columns stood at one end of the room. I marveled at them and fought the urge to reach out and touch the beautiful ivory-colored pillars. However, we did not stop, but instead he led us next into a drawing room, where a large fire was crackling in the hearth.

Pulling me toward the fire, William said, "You wait here and warm yourself by the fire while I see Lady Beatrix to her chambers." He turned then, with her Ladyship on his arm and gave a command to the footman to bring me something hot to drink.

Lady Beatrix turned and looked at me once more before floating away on William's arm. I nodded to her, pressing my lips together in a solemn line of indifference. But once they had quit the room, I felt my shoulders sag, and all I wanted to do was cry.

Minutes later, a maid came scurrying in. She carried a large tray bearing the accoutrements for tea and a bottle of whisky. A plate of biscuits also accompanied the drinks. The maid curtseyed before setting the tray on a nearby table.

"I know that Sir William ordered something hot for ye to drink, but Barnes said that ye looked as though ye could use something a little stronger." She smiled then and motioned to the whisky.

"Aye, I do believe I'll have a little."

She picked up the kettle, then paused. "Do ye want the whisky, then the tea, or the whisky in the tea?" She grinned, and I felt the tightness in my chest ease a little.

"Both," I said, returning her grin. She poured two fingers worth of whisky in the cup and handed it to me. I tossed the amber liquid back, feeling the burn in my eyes, nose, and throat. I then held the cup out to her.

"More?" She asked, her eyes as big as the plate of biscuits. I nodded my head.

"In the tea," I gasped, still feeling the effects of the whisky searing my throat.

She added the tea leaves to the cup then poured the hot water over them. Then, adding two large dabs of whisky, she stopped the bottle and set it back on the tray.

"What is your name?" I asked, as I sipped the hot liquid.

"Mary, ma'am."

"Thank ye, Mary. Ye are a life-saver."

"Will there be anything else ye will be needing, ma'am?"

I had closed my eyes, letting the warmth of the drink soak into me. When I opened my eyes once more, Mary stood over me, wringing her hands and looking like a mother hen worrying over her brood.

"Have ye ever made a complete and utter fool of yourself, Mary?" I looked up into her curious green eyes, hoping to find commiseration. Nay, I doubted she had ever been as foolish as I had been. Letting yourself fall for a man that was beyond your equal was one thing, but allowing yourself to fall for the king's man was an entirely different kind of foolishness. Lady Beatrix had been right. What I had done tonight was stupid. But she didn't know the half of it. My recklessness began way before the notion of saving Geillis had come into my mind. It began the moment I allowed myself to have a second thought about the king's advocate.

The maid's brows scrunched together, arching into a concerned peak. She looked as if to answer, but just then William entered the room. She curtseyed again and departed, sneaking a sympathetic smile to me before she left.

"Do you feel better?" he inquired, grabbing the other cup from the tray, and pouring a little whisky into it for himself.

"Aye, much better." I continued to sip the hot tea, watching William as he pulled up a chair and sat down across from me.

"Do you want to talk about this betrothal with Seton?"

I felt the color drain from my face. "Not really," I said. "There is nothing more to say about it that I haven't already said."

He ran a hand over his jaw, and I could hear the scrape of his fresh whiskers against his palm. "Your brother, Nicholas, he lives in London, correct?"

I nodded. The thought of Nick always made me emotional and after the night we had had, if I spoke, I'd lose all composure.

"Is he a good man? Will he defend your right to choose your own husband? Or will he force you into a marriage for what material gain it might have?"

"Nick would never do that," I said, my voice shaky with emotion. "I've written to him about the situation, but I don't know if he can make it here in time."

William rose and walked across the room, looking deep in thought. "I can draw up a document, contesting the betrothal but that only extends it another week or so. If Nick cannot make it within the confines of the legal limits, I'm not sure what other options we will have. I'll have to do some research."

"What do ye mean, *we*? This isn't your problem. Ye have your own betrothed to worry about." There was a little too much bitterness in my words, and I hoped that it had not sounded in William's ears the way it sounded in mine.

"Ailsa, about that," William began, but we were interrupted by a man who had just stepped into the room. He wore muddy brown woolen trunks and matching hose and his doublet was of brown leather was well. His slender form, coupled with his choice of unremarkable color, gave him the appearance a tree branch, tall and willowy. He certainly did not cut the striking figure that William did, yet he bore himself with even more composure than William. And at first, I thought him to be the king.

"William, I see that Beatrix found—" he cut himself off when he saw that I was not Lady Beatrix. "A thousand pardons, my lady. I didn't realize—"

"It's all right, Blantyre. Beatrix did find me and accompanied me to a meeting that I had planned. Lord Blantyre, this is Mistress Blackburn, Mistress Blackburn, the Keeper of the Privy Seal, Lord Blantyre." He moved his hand back and forth between us, the sound of his voice waving the rules of introduction aside.

"Lord Blantyre," I said, bowing my head. "A pleasure to meet ye."

"Oh, come now, William. Must we toss about such formalities?" The man picked up my hand and brushed a soft kiss across my knuckles, tickling my skin with his short beard. "The pleasure is all mine, Mistress Blackburn." He looked up into my face, his sparkling gray eyes dancing in mischief.

"All right," William interrupted. "Mistress Blackburn has had a long and eventful evening. I was just about to see her home.

"So soon?" Lord Blantyre raked his eyes from the waves of my hair to the soles of my boots. When his eyes drew back to mine once more, he trapped me in a stare that made heat rise to my cheeks. Either that or the whisky was finally catching up with me.

"Aye," William confirmed. "As I've said, it's been a long night." He offered his hand to assist me to my feet.

I pulled my earasaid up around my face once more in preparation for the frigid air. Blantyre, still staring, said, "I say, Broune. It's really not fair. You always manage to find the prettiest little morsels. I do think if you bring home one more fair maiden, I will be forced to steal her from you."

The flush on my cheeks burned hotter, and I turned away from him to prevent myself from saying something rude. He was William's friend, and the king's Keeper of the Privy Seal. A powerful man. I did not need to make another enemy.

"Blantyre, as always you have managed to make my guest feel like a piece of meat at the mercat cross. You really do have a way with the ladies."

The man let out a laugh, laying his hand upon his chest in amusement. "My apologies, Mistress Blackburn, if I have made you uneasy."

I curtseyed to him, dipping my chin in acceptance of his apology, but I did not speak.

William offered me another shawl to throw over my own covering. It was a beautiful lawn of purples and greens, with delicate fringe hanging from the edges on all four sides. "Take this, it is warmer than it looks and should help keep out the cold air for a few more blocks."

"God's teeth, Broune, how far do you have to go?" Blantyre spoke up. "Why don't you take one of the palace carriages? It's freezing outside."

"Nay," I blurted, not intended to sound so harsh. "That is, I don't want to be any further trouble." In reality, I didn't want to draw more attention to us than what we already had with Seton.

"It would be no trouble—" Blantyre began, but William cut him off.

"We'll walk, it's not far." And with that he reached up and pulled the soft shawl over my other shoulder and tucked it into my belt.

"My apologies. I hope I didn't sound too rude to Lord Blantyre." I side-stepped a large mud puddle that had frozen over into a block of ice, meeting William on the other side of it and picking up my pace in an effort to match his long strides.

He shot a look at me out of the corner of his eye, then chuckled. "No one has ever apologized for being rude to Blantyre. He's a notorious nuisance." We walked along in silence for another moment before the weight of what had passed between us earlier was too heavy, and I finally had to speak again.

"William, I am sorry for putting ye in danger this evening. I tend to do things in a headlong fashion, and sometimes I don't stop to think about how others might be affected."

The crunching of the snow beneath our feet seemed to shout accusations at me. *You fool, you fool, you fool.* Each word pounded into my head with every step we took. William did not speak for a moment, and his silence seemed to confirm my imprudent deeds.

I gingerly picked my way around the patches of ice—or at least the ones I could see—before stepping blindly upon a slick spot that was covered in freshly fallen snow. My feet started to slide apart from each other, and William stretched his arm out, snaking it around my waist to steady me and hold me upright. The warmth of him felt like molten lava against my icy skin and I wondered how he stayed so warm.

"Anything I did this evening, I did on my own accord," he finally said, drawing me out of my woolgathering. He released his arm from around me and straightened his cloak, pulling at his cuffs as if nervous. With each word a little puff of heat floated into the air and I watch his breath crystalize before me with every word he spoke. "My only regret is that you did not trust me enough to tell me what your intentions were."

His words condensed before us in vapor, and I imagined that I could reach out and take them in my hand. Hold them like a skein of wool or a hot roll. I could even clutch them to my heart or rub them against my cheek. When the frozen puffs ceased to expand before us, I realized he had stopped talking. That is when I understood what he had said.

"I wasn't going to try to help her escape right under your nose," I rushed to point out. His words from earlier and those of Lady Beatrix smothered me in guilt. *"What we did tonight was very stupid and has the potential to get William into a lot of trouble."*

"But you *were* intending to help her escape at some point." His words were more a statement than a question, and I looked at him, a giant lump forming in my throat. I could not lie to him. He had risked too much for me already. He deserved to know the truth.

I took a deep breath. "When I first saw Geillis that night at my uncle's warehouse, I was appalled to see the treatment she received. I was sure she had been molested, or at the very least, she was propositioned by Seton. The man is a beast, and after the run-ins I have had with him, I do not doubt that he mistreated her in some way."

"You have had unpleasant encounters with him on more than one occasion?"

"Aye, but that's an entirely different story." I wrapped my arms about my waist, feeling suddenly colder just speaking of Seton. "I was determined to help Geillis. Since my father died and Nick moved to England, my mother and I have had no one to protect us, should we meet the likes of David Seton. I imagined that Geillis probably had no one either, to stand up for her, to protect her."

I stopped talking for a moment, taking a look around me to gauge where we were. I could see the apothecary shop up ahead, its beaten brass sign swinging from its hinges squeaking past the icy wind that stung our ears. We were getting close to my house.

"I sent a note to Geillis in a baked loaf of bread. The note was just some words of encouragement and told her that I believed she was innocent and wanted to help her."

"That is what you were doing the day I caught you sticking parcels through the tolbooth wall, isn't it?" We passed under a lantern that hung from a shopkeeper's door, and the light illuminated his face for a moment. His cobalt blue eyes were curious, but I sensed no anger in them.

"Aye, that is what I was doing. But after more and more people began to be arrested, and after Doctor Fian's execution, I began to have doubts. There are so many stories flying about and so many confessions and denials of witchcraft and other wicked deeds, that I was confused and didn't know what to believe anymore. I had to meet with Geillis. I had to talk to her and see for myself whether I thought she was a witch. Whether I thought she was worth saving." The final words felt brittle in my mouth, and I found that when I tried to swallow, I choked on the bitterness of them.

"But you do realize that you have to let justice run its course, right?

You cannot go around with this vigilante attitude, taking legal matters into your own hands."

William's chastisement plucked at me like little pinpricks under my flesh. Shame burned hot on my face. I was mad at every person in my life who had let me down. Mad at Nick for leaving Mother and I unprotected while he went off to see the world and have a grand old time at it. Mad at Father for dying way too soon and taking away any further chances for me to enrich my education. Mad at Mother for putting us in danger with David Seton, even though in my heart I knew she couldn't help it. And even mad at William for breaking down my protective wall, wheedling his way into my heart, when he had no intentions of returning the affection. Unfortunately, only one of these people were here in front of me now, and I decided that he would be the recipient of my wrath.

"Well, I'm sorry," I started, feeling my muscles begin to quiver and my stomach tie itself into a knot, "that I have made some foolish choices the past few months. I am doing the best I can with what has been left for me." I pushed my finger into his chest as I spoke the words. "And I'm sorry that I have been worried out of my mind that my mother was going to have one of her episodes and say something crude or do something rude or wonder off somewhere and forget how she got there and how to get back home." I slammed the palms of my hands against his chest as I spoke the words, trying unsuccessfully to give him a little push. "And I'm sorry, that I thought I was doing the right thing by trying to help someone whom I believed to be a victim." I curled my fingers into a ball and smacked William in the chest with the blunt end of my fist. "And I'm sorry that I can't just up and move to London and study theater, and literature, and the arts with some of England's greatest playwrights, and lay about all day and carouse all night, and drink wine until the sun comes up." I pounded my fist into William's chest now. At some point, tears had begun to stream down my face, but I didn't care. The dam had burst, and there was no stopping it now.

I opened my fists and flattened my hands against William's chest once more. I could feel the pounding of his heart against my palms, and the warmth of the blood flowing through his veins seeped into me through my fingertips. I leaned my forehead against his chest and finally let the sobs overtake me.

William wrapped his arms around me and pulled me to him. He smelt of the hearth and Spanish tobacco, and for a moment, all my other senses eluded me as I thrilled at the heady sensation. Then a faint, familiar feeling scratched at the back of my mind. The last time we had been in a similar situation, I had done another foolish thing by kissing him on the cheek. But his feelings for me were not the same as what I felt for him, and that wrenched my heart even more. Giving in to more tears was the only thing I could do.

"Shh, there now," he soothed, rubbing his hand in soft circles over the crown of my head. After a few minutes I tried to pull away, but he held me firmly in place, gently kissing the top of my head through my earasaid.

The tender gesture broke me, and I couldn't take it another moment. I pressed my hands against him again in an effort to push away. "I should go," I said, my voice feeling like broken glass in my throat.

"You carry a load of burdens, Ailsa." He lifted my chin with a finger, forcing me to look into his eyes.

"I should not have unloaded them all on ye." The cold air burned my skin where my tears washed my face, and I quickly tried to wipe them away. William ran the back of his fingers across my cheek, and his touch burned with a heat hotter than what any fire or frost could produce.

"I'm glad you did. It gives me a glimpse inside that perfectly chaotic mind of yours." The side of his mouth quirked up, and I attempted a smile, but he stared at me so intensely that I couldn't seem to catch my breath.

"It's a chaos that ye don't want any part of," I said, in self-deprecating fashion.

"It is a beautiful chaos."

He cupped my cheeks with both of his hands then gently ran one of his thumbs across my bottom lip. I watched his mouth too, silently willing him to touch his lips to mine. The ache in my chest was so strong, that when he finally brushed his lips across mine, I felt the burst of sweet relief through every muscle in my body. I could still taste the whisky he had drunk earlier, and the taste of him made me hunger for more. His kiss was soft and unhurried, and his lips were like smooth, rich honey pouring over me. I stood on my tiptoes, clutching the collar of his cloak, and stretching to reach him, to consume as much of him as he would give to me. My lips parted eagerly to show him, convince him, that I wanted this—I wanted him— with everything within me.

The night watchman called out the time, and we both startled at once.

"I," William began, but closed his mouth after a moment of speechlessness. I flinched, anticipating an apology. Perhaps he had remembered he was betrothed. Resentment coursed through me, bursting the dream bubble I had been living in for the moment. I would not allow his regret and thoughts of *her* ruin my first real kiss.

Pushing away from him was easier this time, and I took a step back. Lifting my chin, I said, "Well, Lady Beatrix sure has something to look forward to."

I was sure his face blanched, for although I could not see the color drain in the darkness, I could tell by the appalled expression on his face that I had struck a nerve.

"I best be getting home," I said, turning in the direction of Fishmarket Close. I shuffled my feet along the icy stones, determined to reach home without any further assistance.

"Not without me, you're not." His voice rumbled sending dark vibrations thrumming through my blood.

I turned and looked over my shoulder. William stood in the darkness; the faint light of the moon that had been hidden by cloud cover earlier, now shed a soft glow on his dark hair. That one devilish curl fell over his forehead again. He squeezed his hands into fists, but

I couldn't tell if it was irritation or frigid temperatures that had him on edge.

"Aye, well best ye hie. I'm freezing," I said, then turned and plodded away.

~27~

February 1591

William

I did not see Ailsa at the execution of Agnes Sampson. I was glad she had stayed away, for the old woman's demise was much more disturbing than the doctor's had been.

"His Majesty has asked that you lead Agnes to the pyre, Sir William." I turned to see the hint of a smile pulling at Seton's lips.

I glared at him. "I did my part. I gave the king the guilty verdict he wanted. Someone else can have the glory for it." As part of the legal counsel, I was supposed to show my support of the sentence. I was expected to be a part of the procession as the prisoners were led to their deaths. But after tending to the old woman last night, I found the duty difficult to maintain.

"I don't think you have a choice." Seton patted me on the back, but the tone of his voice told me he had not forgotten about our dispute the night before.

"We always have a choice." Rolling my shoulder and throwing his hand off of me, I stepped away. "The first and greatest punishment of the sinner is the conscience of sin."

Seton's eyes grew round. "Are you a preacher now, Broune? I have heard you are the son of a saint." His grin widened, and I fought to find the strength to resist hitting him.

"If you count the words of a Neronic advisor equal with the Holy

Writ, then you are stupider than I thought."

He wasn't stupid. He caught my meaning exactly. I watched as Seton's face turned a deep shade of red, and his eyes blacken to burnt peat. "The stupid one is the man who dares to go against the king's orders."

"I don't take the king's orders from you," I said, ire in my voice.

Now I watched as Agnes stumbled her way up Castlehill, her spindly legs wobbling as they carried her shaking body. Her eyes like a caged pine marten, darted to and fro about the crowd. When her eyes fell on me, they widened in recognition. She did not blink, only stared at me while Seton laced the rope that was around her neck through the ring on the stake. My heart lurched, and I felt the condemnation of my part in this ordeal. I reminded myself that she had sealed her own fate, but that didn't keep me from the bitter taste of involvement. With a crazed stare, her eyes bore into me. Unable to tear my own eyes away, I stared back until hers closed under the force of strangulation, her repeated mantra still ringing in my ears. *"The steps of a good man are ordered."*

My steps didn't feel ordered. In fact, every step I took seemed to end in some kind of disaster. Which is why I needed to find Ailsa. I needed to at least try to make that mistake right, to speak to her about what had happened between us the night before. I stayed only until the pyre was lit. There was nothing more I could do for Agnes, so I turned my attention toward Fishmarket Close.

"William, you might want to make yourself scarce. At least for the rest of the day." Blantyre greeted me in the west drawing room with a cup of wine outstretched to me and a smirk on his face.

"What do you know that I have not been made aware of yet?" I crossed the room and took the cup from his hand.

"Only that Seton high-tailed it back to the palace this afternoon after Agnes Sampson's execution to tell His Majesty that you rejected his orders and did not lead the procession as was requested."

I swallowed the crimson liquid in one gulp then held the cup out for a second drink. I had been looking for Ailsa all morning with no success. Now my patience was in short supply with none left for the likes of David Seton.

"I told him that I don't take orders from him. His Majesty did not relay to me that he wanted me in the procession. I was not proud of my involvement in that sentence, so I wasn't about to participate in the execution. Especially at the command of David Seton."

Blantyre refilled my cup then set the decanter back on the tray. "Aye, but you need to watch your back with Seton. The toad has it out for you, for some reason, and he is taking great pains to blacken your name with His Majesty. What is it that has crossed between you two?"

I turned the cup in my hand, swirling the liquid within and watching the red substance turn into a tiny whirlpool within my grasp before tossing the second nip back.

"I've never liked him."

Blantyre waited for me to continue, but when I didn't say more, he prompted, "And?"

"And what?" I crossed the room and poured myself another tot of port. Blantyre's raised eyebrow gave me pause, and I set the cup on the table instead.

"And there is more to it than that," he explained. "There is a difference between not liking someone and wanting that same someone to go hang. He has it out for you, and I want to know why. So, you don't like the man. I get it. I don't care for him either. But neither you nor I are trying to get the man under the king's suspicion. Or did I miss something? Should I be trying to get Seton arrested?"

I laughed dryly. "This is not your problem, Blantyre."

"Nay, but your enemy is my enemy, my friend. If he is causing you trouble, I want to know, and I want to be involved in helping bring him low. So, what is going on?"

I sighed then turned back to Blantyre, feeling a little awkward for Ailsa's sake. I still wasn't sure how the turn in our relationship would affect my standing with Beatrix, for I was trying to avoid her at the moment, not sure I was ready to face my guilt. And given Blantyre's affinity toward Lady Ruthven, I wasn't sure how much I wanted to tell him.

"The man has always rubbed me the wrong way. And now I have recently found out that he is harassing my friend, Ailsa, and he has entered into an engagement with her against her will."

Blantyre stared at me blankly. It was clear he didn't remember the woman to whom I now referred. "Your friend, Ailsa?"

"Aye, my friend Ailsa. The woman you met last night."

Understanding lit up his face, and a sly glimmer caught his eye. "Ah, yes. The enchanting Mistress Blackburn." He picked up the cup of wine that I had poured for myself and downed it swiftly. "But if she is betrothed to him, it sounds to me like it should be none of your concern. You know better than to come between a man and his lover."

"She is not his lover," I said too quickly. My sharp tone gave Blantyre a start, and he gawked at me momentarily.

"I see," he finally said. "Well, perhaps she is not his lover, but I know another lover that will be despondent to find her betrothed so besotted with another woman."

"I am not besotted," I said through clenched teeth. "And I am not betrothed either. Lady Ruthven has made some hasty declarations."

This time both of Blantyre's eyebrows shot up in confusion. "Well, this conversation has taken a turn into the unexpected. I think I am beginning to get a clear picture of the true problem with Seton. Sit and tell me everything."

An hour later I was no closer to solving any of my problems, but it did feel good to get everything off my chest. At the conclusion of our conversation, I said, "I need you to look into an issue for me."

"I'm not going to be a liaison between you and Ailsa. I couldn't do that to Beatrix."

I snapped my head up. "I have no need of a liaison between Ailsa and me. And this is of an entirely different matter. I need to get some eyes on Bothwell."

Blantyre coughed in surprise. "Bothwell? What has the rogue done now?"

I picked up a trinket that sat on a nearby table and turned it over in inspection. "I know I need not remind you of the delicacy of this situation, but I'll say it anyway. This is between you and me and is to be shared with no one. Not until I say so."

"Not even His Majesty?"

"Especially not His Majesty." I sat the trinket back down. "I don't want him worrying if there is nothing to worry over."

"All right. What is it that you suspect Bothwell of this time?"

"I believe he may be plotting another kidnapping attempt."

He held up a hand as if to stop me. "Would he be so foolish as to try that again? Did he not learn his lesson the last time when he ended up in the tolbooth awaiting trial?"

"Apparently, he believes it is worth the effort. Especially if he can depose James and take the throne for himself."

"And even more so if the king pardons him after his foolish attempt, evidently. What makes you think he has something planned? Wait. Is this the kidnapping you spoke of a while back?"

"I have a source who is privy to the information. And, Bothwell has spoken to me twice about doing some legal work for him. Apparently, he and Alexander Home have affected a reconciliation, and he wants me to draw up a bond between the two of them. He also mentioned needing a bond of manrent drawn for a couple of lords along the border."

Blantyre let out a disbelieving laugh. "He and Alexander Home? That won't last. You know it won't. They have been enemies for years."

"Aye. But he approached me concerning it, all the same."

"He is a professed papist and has given His Majesty almost as much grief as Bothwell has. I would not doubt if there were something brewing between the two of them. However, I'm not sure I understand why this leads you to believe there is a kidnapping plot looming."

"It's just some information that has come into my hands. I don't have enough evidence yet. That's why I need him followed."

"I can do that. I'll look into it right away." Blantyre rose to his feet, ready to begin his task.

"Why don't you engage Hamilton as well. He has connections that might be able to get information for us also."

Blantyre nodded then turned on his heels to go. He suddenly turned back to me and said, "William, when you realize that your feelings for Ailsa are more than you are currently willing to admit, please let Beatrix down gently. I would hate to have to hurt you for hurting her."

I opened my mouth to defend myself, but he was already gone.

~28~

February 1591

William

I woke to an incessant pounding. Pulling on my breeches, I lit a candle before making my way to the door. Anger and impatience must have registered on my face, for when I opened the door, Mistress Kennedy's expression looked fearful.

"Forgive me sir, but there is a young woman here that begs to see ye. I told her to go away and not disturb ye, but she is delirious and refuses to leave. She said you knew her and her mother."

Ailsa.

A mixture of feelings surged through me. I was elated to know that she was here. I had not been able to locate her all day, and when His Majesty called on me for some menial task, I was unable to continue my search for her. I could only hope that she was truly all right. But the fact that she was here now, in the middle of the night, frantic and refusing to leave, did not bode well.

I pushed passed the woman. "Thank you, Mistress Kennedy. I'll see to her."

"I put her in the kitchen," she called out.

I was not prepared for what I saw when I entered the kitchen, for Ailsa was indeed wild with grief.

"William!" she cried as she rushed toward me and threw herself at my feet, grabbing hold of my legs and practically toppling me with the force. I put out my hand and touched the top of her head to steady myself.

"What has happened?" I spoke barely above a whisper, unsure of my own voice and my ability to control it.

The fire on the hearth had already been banked, but the moonlight shining in through the window cast a faerie glow upon her face. Her eyes were wide with fervor and wet with tears. Her hair was unruly, the glorious locks springing free from their mooring and framing her round face in a blazing nimbus of fire.

"It's my mother." It was as if the words strangled her.

"What about your mother? What has happened?"

"Seton!"

I took a deep breath. "What has he done?" Already I felt my body tensing, and I forced my fisted hands open.

She took a deep gulp of air. "He has arrested her. Already Sheepshearer has been called. He wouldn't let me in to hear the interrogation. I'm sorry. I've no right to trouble ye with such a trifle as this must be to ye. I just didn't know where else to turn."

"You did the right thing by coming to me." I touched her cheek, then retracted hastily. I had decided there would be no repeats of our encounter the previous night, and I wouldn't tempt myself by touching her. Instead, I said, "Wait here whilst I go and dress. I'll send Mistress Kennedy to you to get some bread and ale. You need your sustenance."

"Please don't trouble her. I have no need of food nor drink. Just hurry."

I nodded, then turned to retreat. Stopping at the bottom of the stairs, I encountered Mistress Kennedy. "Please get the lady a cup of wine to calm her. She has had a most disturbing evening."

The older woman nodded, and I left her then, bounding up the stairs two steps at a time. I thought of Ailsa while I dressed and gathered a few items. Since our kiss, my intentions had been to apologize then avoid her. I didn't trust myself not to let it happen again, and I didn't want to give her false hope of anything between us. Marrying Beatrix was the only way for me to elevate my financial status. Even with James's appointment as Chancellor, should he keep his promise, it would not give me the amount of coin needed to establish my family name and provide an inheritance for my children and my children's children. I didn't want my progeny to be indebted to the crown and the only way to guarantee that was by making a powerful match. I couldn't deny there was something about Ailsa's wild and carefree spirit that drew me in. She was not confined by the same courtly rules as the queen's ladies-in-waiting. And it didn't seem to bother her.

Now I was putting myself into the worst possible position. Being in close proximity to Ailsa was maddening. But this was a desperate situation, and one that I could not turn my back on.

When I returned a short time later, she was pacing in front of the dying embers. "Come," I said hastily. When she reached the threshold of the doorway, I grabbed her wrist and pulled her along behind me. Heading to the stables, I quickly saddled Cleopatra. Ailsa stood watching me as I labored, chewing her thumb nail, and pacing once more. "The king has gone to Craigmillar Castle. We'll ride there and petition him."

"Nay!" she cried. In an instant she was beside me, pulling on my arm in protest. "The king has blood in his eyes. He is determined to rid the country of witches and will stop at nothing until he has found them all."

"Is your mother a witch?"

I heard the slap before I felt its sting upon my cheek. The pain was sharp and brought water to my eyes, unbidden. I blinked in shock, but when I looked at Ailsa, I saw she was shocked as well.

"I am so sorry. P-please forgive me." She covered her mouth with shaking hands, her eyes wide with fear. Then the tears began again.

"Hush," I soothed, pulling her to me. I wrapped my arms around her, and she pressed her face against my chest. "It was insensitive of me, I'm sorry. But you must tell me why Seton thinks your mother a witch. I need as much information as you can give me but we must make haste."

I could have stayed like that for an eternity. I buried my nose in her hair, drinking her in. Her nearness intoxicated me. But we had little time before the witch pricker would begin his interrogation. I quickly lifted her onto the horse then mounted behind her.

"Seton sent me a note early this morning. He spoke of our betrothal and threatened that if I did not follow through, he would see to my mother's arrest. He said he had enough evidence against her to prove that she was involved in witchcraft, especially with the way she flew at him the last time we were in the mercat cross. Did I tell ye of that incident?"

I shook my head, afraid that if I spoke, she would hear the absolute rage in my voice. She turned her head and looked at me over her shoulder. "Nay," I finally whispered.

I grabbed Cleo's reins and adjusted my seating before sending her off in a gallop. The force pushed Ailsa into me and I could feel her body stiffen in an effort to avoid the contact.

"He said that I *would* marry him, and if I didn't, he would make sure my mother burned."

"So, what did you do? Where were you all day? I looked for you but couldn't find you."

"I went to find Seton. To try to reason with him."

"Ailsa." I sighed. "There is no reasoning with that man, and he is dangerous. That wasn't wise."

"I know that now."

I felt her courage seep out of her as she slumped against me. But I was enlivened. Why did my courage rise whenever I felt hers wane?

"So, what happened? How did you find him? I don't even know where he resides."

"I found him after Agnes' execution. I followed him home."

"You were at the execution?" I choked. "I had hoped you would stay away." I snapped the reigns at Cleo, driving her into a faster gallop. Her flanks tightened under my legs, and her exerted breath blew out in frosty puffs of air that danced across the moon-kissed night.

"Aye. Well, somewhat. I came once I thought the deed would be completed. Seton was in a good mood, it seemed, and I thought that perhaps he would be level-headed. I followed him to Geddes Close before he caught on that he was being followed and turned on me."

"He stays on Geddes Close?"

"I don't know. That's as far as I made it before he caught me following him. Ye should have seen the look on his face. I wouldn't doubt if he thought I sought him out to make good on his promise." She shivered again, and I reacted by wrapping my arms about her tighter. The soft curves of her body relaxed into me, and I breathed a prayer of thanks that she no longer resisted our closeness. "I tried to explain to him once again that my uncle had no right to enter into an agreement on my behalf. He became angry when I wouldn't see things his way, and he tried to grab me. So, I spat on him. It was stupid of me, I know. I should have guessed that would make him even more irascible. But I didn't know what else to do."

"Aye, that is a difficult situation in which you found yourself." We approached Duddingston Loch. I pushed Cleopatra harder, spurring her to go faster. The cold wind cut into our faces like icy fingers and stole the breath from our lungs as her speed increased.

Ailsa continued her tale. "Well, let me tell ye. That was the absolute worst thing I could have done." She sliced her hand through the air in her animated fashion, and I couldn't tamp down the smile that pulled at my lips. The situation was serious, but I loved to hear her tell a story in her spirited way. However, my thoughts were pulled back to the present when I heard her say, "He lunged at me so quickly that I didn't have time to even think. He grabbed my arm and twisted it behind my back. I honestly think if we hadn't been in public, he would have taken me right there. But of course, by then a crowd had gathered, just like the last time, and he had no recourse. One of the King's Guard happened upon us with the gathering crowd and Seton released me and ran away before the guard could confront him."

"You said, *just like the last time*. The night we were at the tolbooth you mentioned that you had run-ins with him on more than one occasion. He has done this before?"

"Aye. Once on Fishmarket Close and once at the mercat cross. At the mercat cross he became belligerent and almost attacked me there. If it wasn't for my mother, sweeping in like an avenging angel and scaring him away, who knows what he might have done? She shamed him and almost set the whole town upon him. I've never seen her so angry. Nor Seton. He was truly humiliated at mother's interference." She went silent at that for a long while. When she spoke again, it was with a trembling voice. "This is his retaliation."

By the time we arrived at the castle, the round moon was covered with clouds, turning the chilly night into a blackened blanket that enveloped us. I thought Ailsa was asleep, for she had fallen silent after her story was told. But when I slid off my horse and reached up to help her down, her eyes were wide with fear, her tears frozen to her long lashes like tiny diamonds. Passing Cleopatra off to a sleepy stable boy, I led her, like a dream walker still sleeping, through the doors of the castle.

She finally spoke. "His majesty will not hear my complaint. I know it."

I laid my hand on her shoulder and gently pushed her forward toward the great hall. I deposited her in the massive room with unnecessary instruction, "Wait here."

I turned and made my way to James's private chamber. Rehearsing my approach, I considered my position. We had been friends since we were children. I ate with him, hunted with him, debated with him, but nothing more than any of his other close advisors had done. Yet, I had never asked him for anything, and I hoped that would work in my favor.

When I reached his chamber door, a guard with jowls like a mastiff and tiny black pebbles for eyes stood, halberd steady at his side. I blessed the Almighty that he looked familiar, so he must recognize me too. "I need to speak to the king."

"Aye, sir." He stepped aside, and I pushed forward, taking a deep breath as I mentally considered once again what I would say to him.

The king sat up, bleary eyed and bare-chested when the door opened. I knew him to be a light sleeper. Several kidnapping attempts had instilled that survival skill in him. Eyes wide with terror he said, "William, what is it? What has happened?"

Kneeling beside his bed and lowering my head in obeisance, I said, "Forgive me, Your Majesty, for disturbing your sleep and frightening you."

"You haven't frightened me," he snapped, feigning calmness. But I heard his voice catch. I watched as he wrapped a silk robe about his shoulders and threw his legs over the side of the bed. I forgot about his penchant for responding like a bear when he was awakened suddenly. "What is this about?"

"It has come to my attention that Bailiff Seton has arrested a certain person with the intentions of having her found guilty of witchcraft." I realized as I spoke the words, how unremarkable that sounded.

"That is nothing new, William." His voice cracked with sleepy strain, and he cleared his throat. "I must say that I am grateful for Seton's undying commitment to ridding our land of the wretched creatures. But is this worth waking me out of a most wonderful dream?"

I swallowed hard before continuing. "There has been a mistake, Your Grace. I know the family from which this woman hails. She is not a witch."

Something in my words ignited his attention, and he lifted his sagging eyes to mine suddenly. "Have you forgotten that family ties have no bearing on the oppressed of Satan?"

I wondered if he had been told of his cousin Bothwell's involvement with the witches. "No, sir, I have not forgotten. But I know the woman personally. She has been falsely accused to satisfy Seton's appetite for a pound of flesh."

James stopped suddenly. He had risen from bed and was padding across the room to retrieve his chamber pot. It hung limply from his hand. "You surprise me, William. I have detected a slight irritation between you and Seton for some time now. What has brought about this conflict?"

I stood to my feet and turned to face him fully. "Seton is a power-hungry, vengeful man. When he does not get his way, he uses his authority to achieve retribution. His pride was wounded by this old woman, and now he intends to punish her in the most horrific of ways."

A deep line of concentration creased the king's brow. He was a man of justice. Always seeking the truth in all manner of situations. It was upon this attribute that I hung all my hope.

"What exactly does that mean?"

"The old woman's daughter shared with me that her mother called Seton out in public a few days ago for his dishonorable actions toward the damsel. This is a deliberate attempt to make retribution for his injured pride."

The king made water and the awkward silence was palpable. I stared at the muted stones that lined the fireplace, waiting. Finally, he spoke. "This sounds like a lover's quarrel to me. Are you sure she wasn't caught in a dishonorable act and simply told her mother another story to avoid punishment?" He set the pot on the floor then turned to me, letting his robe fall back into place. I stared at him, sure the anger I felt in my blood was evident on my face.

"Your Grace, with all due respect, this woman is very put off by Seton's advances. He has shown unwanted attention toward her on more than one occasion and has made his intentions perfectly clear."

"Perhaps she is waiting for some proof of his affection?"

The vulgarity of the king's words and the tone in which they were spoken surprised me, and I clamped my mouth shut before saying something I would regret. I was trying extremely hard to think before I spoke, an attribute my father had always tried to pound into my thick head.

"Who is the young woman?" He questioned.

"Her name is Ailsa Blackburn. Her father was a teacher here in Edinburgh many years ago before going on to St Andrews to become a scribe for the archbishop. Perhaps you've heard of the family?"

James shook his head, scratching his chin in thought. Sighing, he finally said, "Allow me to dress, and I will accompany you to see what will become of the interrogation. Where is she being held?"

"At the tolbooth, I believe. I don't think he would have taken her to Marley's warehouse, for the old woman is Marley's sister."

James stopped and looked at me, his mouth gaping open. "Interesting," he said before calling for the Gentleman of the Bedchamber to come help him dress.

"Thank you, Your Grace." I bowed again to him and backed away.

"Do you have an interest in this young woman, William?" he said with curiosity. "I mean, in a marital sort of way?"

Halting, I looked at him, taken aback. "N-no, sir. Why do you ask?"

"Because I've never seen you so humble in all of your life. Perhaps there is some motive behind this?"

I stared at him momentarily. "I'm sorry to have bothered you, Your Grace."

I had almost managed to extricate myself from the room when he continued. "Her Majesty will be very disappointed to find out that her chosen bride for you might be in competition with a scribe's daughter."

I bowed again without word and turned to leave him to his dress. Heat burned on my face as I made my way back to where I had left Ailsa in the great hall. I pinched the bridge of my nose, hoping I had said the right words to the king.

Ailsa stood right where I left her. When I entered the hall, she rushed to me. "What did he say?" Her eyes implored me, begging me to give her good news.

"He's coming."

She let out a breath as if she had been holding it for an eternity.

Her eyes fluttered, and her body swayed under the anxiety. I reached out a hand instinctively to steady her, wrapping an arm around her waist.

"Do not worry yourself. We will get to the bottom of this mess."

She withdrew from me, and I felt my muscles tense. The blank look on her face as she pulled away from me was nothing short of a crucifixion, and I turned my head in frustration. I wanted to comfort her, but it was apparent she did not seek her comfort in me. It was my influence she needed, not my sympathy. It made sense. But that didn't make me feel any better.

~29~

February 1591

Ailsa

"Ye beast!" I lunged at Seton, anger surging through me. I had never known hatred until this moment, and it was an emotion I would have willing explored. But William seized my arm and held me fast to his side.

"Ailsa, be still," he whispered.

The small receiving chamber at the tolbooth where we now stood reeked of body odor and filth, and it was little more than a glorified version of Geillis' cell that we had visited just nights before. A large table stood in the center of the room with two chairs attending it, one empty and the other occupied by my mother. One long bench lined the far wall where iron rings hung from a screw in the stone wall. A rust-colored puddle of—something—covered the floor, making it sticky and slick to walk upon.

The small satisfaction I felt at Seton's surprise when William and I bounded in with His Majesty was short-lived. Mother was hunched over the table as she whimpered at her mistreatment. Seton on the other hand, hovered over Sheepshearer like a vulture awaiting a meal as the witch pricker painstakingly shaved my mother's long, silver locks from her head. They lay strewn across the wooden floor, like the wings of a beautiful bird clipped for captivity.

"What has she done?" I cried. "What proof have ye of witchcraft?

The whole town will testify that she is not a witch. She is an upstanding citizen of Edinburgh, and ye will be hard pressed to find anyone that will say differently."

"I say differently," charged Seton. "That woman flew at me like a demon from hell in the mercat cross. I have never seen the likes of it out of any woman before. She is mad, I tell you. She made the vilest of threats toward me; the whole town heard it. Words that any good Christian woman should not speak. She is surely under the Devil's influence." His tiny black eyes glowed with animosity, and he shook as he spoke. I was convinced that his pride had been wounded, and he was grasping at anything to get his revenge.

"That is a lie! She was defending me from your attack. I still have the bruise on my arm where ye grabbed me." I shoved my earasaid up to my elbow and revealed the faint bruise that was left behind from Seton's assault. I heard the quick intake of William's breath.

"Ailsa," he whispered, stepping closer.

"And here is the bruise this witch left on me after biting me." Seton too, pushed up his sleeve and revealed a mark that looked fresh and fairly large.

"Ye are a liar!" I shouted again. "My mother never laid a hand on ye, let alone her teeth! And that wound is fresh. My mother hasn't been near ye in almost a week."

The king turned toward me then. "Are you saying that your mother and Bailiff Seton did have an altercation at the mercat cross recently?"

"Aye, Your Majesty. But she did not bite him. She didn't lay a finger on him."

The king eyed the puncture wound.

"The proof is in the bite!" Seton shouted.

"Enough!" demanded the king. "This has turned into a farse, and I will not have interrogations conducted in this manner in my kingdom. Seton, leave. William, take Mistress Blackburn home. Sheepshearer and I will finish this investigation."

"But, Your Grace," William began.

King James turned his rheumy eyes toward us. His cold stare

stopped William from speaking further. "William, do as I command. Let me and Sheepshearer handle this. If the woman is not a witch, then there is nothing to fear."

A cry escaped my lips, and I shoved my fisted hand into my mouth to avoid further sound. I had no faith in this system and felt no assurance that justice would be served just because the king was going to oversee the interrogation. I felt sick and was glad I had not eaten anything all day for fear that it might show itself now.

"Come, Ailsa." William tried to move me toward the door, but my feet suddenly felt like clay, and I found I could not move. "Ailsa, please," he coaxed, desperation shading his voice. William tried again to guide me away, but panic seized me, and I couldn't leave my mother alone with these brutes.

"Nay!" I cried out, breaking free from William's hold, and darting to my mother's side. I ran my hand down her wet cheek, for she had been crying, and I kissed her repeatedly on the top of her head. Patches of fuzz dotted her head where Sheepshearer had hurriedly performed the deed.

"Come away, my dove." Seton stepped forward and grabbed both of my arms, forcing me away from her.

"Remove your hands from her," William commanded.

"She is interfering with the king's business," Seton said darkly. He turned then to the king and said, "Forgive me, Your Grace. My betrothed is overwrought. I shall see to it that she doesn't interfere again."

The king's eyebrow lifted in amusement, but William gave him no time to respond.

"The devil you will!" He sprang toward us and grabbed Seton by the collar of his shirt. I felt Seton's grip slacken, but he did not let me go.

"This is madness," grumbled the king. "William, please." William stared at Seton as his hold remained fixed. "William," the king commanded. He released his hold on the bailiff but did not step away. King James continued, "Are the two of you betrothed?"

"Nay!" I stated adamantly. I had not meant to shout, but I could not let the opportunity pass to plead my case to the king. However, Seton's voice drowned mine out.

"Your Majesty, I have signed a contract. We are to be wed in a matter of another week or so." Seton's voice had turned to silk, but I prayed the king would see right through his façade.

"Your Grace—" William began.

The king waved his plea away with a slender hand. "You have already explained it to me, William. Get the chit out of here. Seton, go home."

William shoved Seton away from me, and when the bailiff released his grip, I found myself sinking to the cold floor. "Nay, I will not leave. I cannot leave my mother alone with them." My desperation was rising, and I clung to her. Like a high tide, I felt the current rising and soon it would drown me altogether.

"And I will be a part of this interrogation. I take this personally," Seton complained.

Sheepshearer spoke up for the first time. "Dixon, remove Bailiff Seton from the tolbooth, please." At that, a gaoler stepped forward and apprehended Seton by his arm.

"Unhand me," Seton growled and managed to pull his arm free from the larger man's grasp. "I will leave on my own accord."

"Then do so, Bailiff Seton. I want this room cleared out immediately, or you will all be held in contempt." Spittle flew from the king's mouth in anger, and his words echoed off the unforgiving stones bringing the pandemonium to a halt.

I felt William's arm slip under my knees and across my back. All boldness that had bolstered me earlier had faded, and I was left with no strength to fight. He lifted me without a struggle as I buried my chin into my chest and sobbed.

William carried me to Cleopatra and lifted me onto her back. He was about to mount behind me when we heard the voice of Seton coming from the shadows of the tolbooth.

"This isn't over, my little dove. All you have to do is agree to marry me without further protest, and I will drop all the charges." He moved into the moonlight, and I felt my blood turn to ice at just the sight of his face.

"Never," William answered for me, and then he snapped the reigns to kick Cleopatra into motion. I turned my head away from Seton as I pushed down the bile that rose in my throat. Would it be that simple? Just marry the man and this nightmare would all be over?

My head was heavy with ache and my vigor spent by the time we reached home. William lifted me from the back of Cleopatra and carried me into the house where he laid me on the bed. He made quick work of the hearth, building a fire, and placing a kettle over it to heat water. When the water was ready, he made a warm compress to lay over my eyes. He even picked up Sadie, who was standing at the foot of the bed, and gingerly set her beside me, before brushing off his hands and moving quickly away.

"I don't know how to thank ye," I whispered, folding the warm cloth over my forehead.

"Don't thank me yet. I haven't done anything worthy of thanks. But I'm not finished trying. I am going to return to the tolbooth and see what I can do. Will you be all right here by yourself?"

"Of course." I tried to show bravery, but on the inside, I was dying. "William, do ye think I should just marry Seton? He will stop at nothing to get what he wants. I cannot allow harm to come to my mother because of my stubbornness."

William stood staring at me for a moment. "I would never advise you to do such a thing. He is a wicked man. Who's to say that you marry him, and he won't ask some other dreadful thing of you and threaten you until you have acquiesced? You and your mother will always be in danger with that man as your husband."

He was right. But that didn't keep me from the frightful consideration of just giving in.

"Ailsa, give me a chance to intervene. I don't believe Seton has a leg to stand on. Don't do anything overhasty until you hear from me again."

I nodded at him then reached out a hand, wondering if he would take my offer of thanks anyway. He reached for me, wrapping his larger hand around mine. Then lifting my hand to his lips, he gently kissed my fingers before placing my hand back in my lap. "I'll do everything I can," he assured before leaving me to Sadie's care and rushing back out the door.

The sun had not yet risen when I heard commotion at the door. Sadie stood and stretched her back then mewed at the figure who kicked the door open. William stood with my mother in his arms, her head rested upon his shoulders and her eyes were closed.

"Is she dead?" My voice shook with terror as I jumped from the bed to make room for her to lay on the vacated spot.

"Nay, but I'd venture to say she is likely traumatized." William laid her gently on the bed then brushed a hand across the stubble that now speckled her head. I watched as he wiped a smudge of something from her cheek with his thumb then pulled the blankets up over her and secured them under her chin. The gesture was deeply moving, and I wondered at his actions seeing how he had never had a mother of his own to care for.

"Mother," I whispered, afraid that a louder voice may startle her. She was so volatile, and who knew what havoc this interrogation might have wreaked on her weakened mind?

She didn't answer but lay quietly as Sadie snuggled up against her chin. I turned to William then, anxious to know everything that had happened.

"How did you get her out of there? Is the interrogation over? What was their verdict? I'm assuming they found her innocent since she is not still at the tolbooth."

William blew out an exhausted breath. "They could find nothing. They even brought in Mistress McCullum to look for—" William's eyes cut away from mine in apparent discomfort. "To look for a

Devil's teat in her privy places." He scraped his hand through this dark hair, but he did not look back at me.

"What a dreadful thing to do to an innocent old woman! Of course, they didn't find anything." I was horrified at the thought.

"I didn't stay to watch. But no, I do not believe they found anything of concern. Afterwards, I asked your mother to speak of the confrontation with Seton at the mercat cross. Ailsa, you would have been so proud of her. She spoke with a clarity of mind and gave a believable testimony. I then requested your mother make an impression with her teeth onto the flesh of a pear. We measured the circumference of the bite mark against the mark on Seton's arm. They did not match. His Majesty observed that the bite mark on Seton was also too new to be your mother's. I think the man actually bit himself to try to provide some sort of evidence. Can you believe that?"

"Aye, the man has a heart as black as birch tar."

"Well, that was a point in her favor. His Majesty is a just sovereign, and since this accusation had nothing to do with what happened to Queen Anne, he was weary of the whole ordeal and just wanted it over."

I sighed in relief, but it came too soon. William cleared his throat with one more thing to say.

"Ailsa, there is something that you should be aware of. Your mother, she did speak of the plot you have been told of concerning the king's danger. I fear there may be an inquiry into that when the king has gotten some rest."

I squeezed my eyes shut in dread. It didn't surprise me that Mother should tell this tale when she was under such duress. I couldn't blame her. Yet, fear still coursed through me, and I couldn't help but shiver under the consequences of her actions.

"Ailsa, listen to me." William moved closer, taking my hand in his and rubbing his thumb across the back of my fingers. "I have a lead on someone that I think may be involved in this kidnapping scheme. I have someone looking into it already. We will get to the bottom of this, and if the culprit is apprehended, King James will not care *how* you knew about the information, as long as he is safe."

"*If* the culprit is apprehended," I repeated. "And what if he is not? Then what?" I searched his weary face wishing that he could give me an assurance that he could not give.

"We'll cross that bridge when we come to it," he promised. "For now, sit, rest. You look as if you did not get much sleep."

"Nay, but it is more than lack of sleep that burdens me."

With that he moved me toward the chair by the hearth then turned aside and set to work building the fire back up. When it was aflame, he hung the kettle once more over the fire. "Where do you keep your tea leaves?" he asked, finally removing his cloak, and turning toward the kitchen.

I rubbed my hand across my brow, trying to force myself to think. *Melissa officinalis* and *Valeriana officinalis* came to me from rote memory. "Use the lemon balm leaves. There is a small bundle wrapped in jute on that shelf." I pointed to the intended leaves and watched as William unwrapped them gently from the string that held them together and gingerly laid them on the table. "Open that cupboard, and you will find a small jar with valerian root in it. It is a brown substance. Pinch two, no, your fingers are larger, pinch one helping from the jar and crumble it into the tea."

When the water was ready, William did exactly as instructed, placing the lemon balm leaves into a cup and pinching a small portion of valerian root on top. He brought the cup to me then pulled a chair up beside me in front of the hearth.

"I'm assuming these herbs serve some purpose. You were very specific."

I took a sip of the hot tincture, blowing gently on the tea as not to burn myself. "The lemon balm calms the nerves and the valerian root helps one to sleep." I took another sip before folding my hands around the cup and warming them with the heat.

"How do you know so much about herbs? Did you learn it from your mother?"

"Nay. Mother learned it from me." I smiled, remembering our

painful lessons. "Mother is not good with numbers and therefore was not a very fast learner. She used to get so frustrated when she would mix up a measurement and ruin a concoction." I laughed lightly then cut a look to Mother who was still sleeping soundly on her bed. "Father always teased us about it. And along with my love for herbs and learning their medicinal uses was my love for words. I used to keep a journal of all the Latin words for each herb. I collected them like I collected flowers. I did that a long while until Father bought me a book with beautiful illustrations, each painted with their names in several languages. Of course, I always liked the Latin names." I rose to retrieve the *Tractatus de Herbis* from my bookshelf. Running my hand over the well-worn book, I handed it to William.

He took the book from my hand and began to gently flip through the pages. The sight of his careful hands turning the precious pages of my favorite book set a horde of butterflies lose in my stomach. I bit my lip to keep from smiling.

"If it wasn't your mother, then who taught you?"

"I learned it from a neighbor woman who lived across the way from the house we lived in while my father was still alive. Goodwife MacGregor was an elderly woman whom all would seek assistance from whenever they had an ailment or needed help in childbirth."

"That sounds like Agnes Sampson. She was a healer and midwife."

I turned back to him suddenly, irritated at the thought of my gentle, elderly friend being compared to an accused witch. "Well, Goodwife MacGregor was no witch, if that is what ye are inferring."

"I wouldn't dream of it," William said softly.

"She was a kindly old lady whom I looked up to. She never turned a patient away, even if she wasn't sure how to help them. On the rare occasion that she didn't know how to help, she would offer them a watery soup made of chicken broth and vegetables. It always seemed to make us feel better, even if there were no healing properties within." I smiled at the memory of the aged lady dispensing her chicken soup to her patrons, her shaky hands carefully filling our bowls with what we thought was a magical elixir. "I adored her and wanted to be like her. She was such a caring woman. Everyone looked up to and depended on her. To a young girl as I, there was nothing better in the world than to be loved by all." I took another sip of my tea then fell into thoughtful silence. It had been a long time since I had thought on Goodwife MacGregor.

"Is that why you serve soup at the mercat cross? Did you get the idea from Goodwife MacGregor?"

I lowered my cup, pausing before taking my next sip. "Ye know, I never thought of that. I just saw a need and wanted to help. Perhaps I did take inspiration from her. I didn't realize the similarity. But I did learn a lot from her about herbs and medicinal cures. Father thought the lessons were useless until he came down with a severe belly ache one day, and I cured it with some *Foeniculum vulgare*, fennel seed."

Sadie rose from mother's side and stretched generously. When she saw William sitting in the chair, she immediately hopped down from her spot on the bed and headed toward him. William turned his head at the sound, and his eyes widened when he saw the cat moving in his direction. I shoved my cup toward him. "Hold this!"

I intercepted Sadie before she could reach her destination: William's leg. Instead, I picked her up and brushed her against my cheek. "That's a good girl. Why don't ye take a stroll and come back when ye've caught me a mouse." I opened the front door and set her down outside. I watched as her tail stiffened in the cold, morning air. She turned her head to look at me and mewed a mournful protest.

"I'm not afraid of her, you understand." William defended when I returned and took my cup from him.

"Aye, ye just melted into that chair as if she were the plague. I think I'll need a chisel to pry ye out of it." I teased him, and I could see him struggling to repress the smile that pulled at his mouth. He closed my herbal book and handed it back to me.

"I don't like cats," he said, as if that would explain everything.

"Well, she likes ye for some reason. And it's not her fault she makes your eyes itch."

"Then whose fault is it?" He ran a hand over his eyes as if speaking of it were bringing it to pass.

"Stop that," I said, rising from my chair again. I wrapped my hand around his wrist and pulled his hand away from his face. "Ye will bring about an itching fit if ye keep touching your eyes." He let me pull his hand away from his face easy enough. But when it came to releasing his wrist, I found that I could not let go. I felt his blood quicken where my fingers lay across his wrist, and I moved my smaller hand upward until it slid into his.

I stood over him and forced myself to look into his eyes. He stared back at me in question. I couldn't read his face. I had no idea if the thoughts going through his mind were anything like the ones that had plagued me since the night we kissed. I had thought of nothing else until Seton had arrested my mother. In fact, I had thought of him at every turn since the day he gave me *Tamburlaine the Great*. He had shown such kindness to me, time and again, even when I had treated him horribly. And more importantly, he had shown compassion toward my mother, even in her unstable state. He gave us gifts and overlooked my suspicious activities concerning Geillis. He tolerated Mother's doting and my sharp tongue. He even risked his own head to free my mother. But I reminded myself that he was betrothed. And he was the king's inquisitor. We lived worlds apart. It was for those reasons that I tried to step away.

"Ailsa." His voice was so low and husky that I wasn't sure at first if he had spoken at all or if I had imagined it. But when I took a step back to put some space between us, he gripped my hand tighter and would not release me. "We need to talk."

I pulled my hand from his and moved away. I felt the air rushing back into my lungs and realized that I hadn't taken a breath since I had grabbed his wrist. I shook my head and turned away from him, fearful that my face would show all the emotion I was hiding. Somehow, this man had broken down all my defenses, swept in and stolen my heart, and now sat here, wringing the wretched thing between his hands. He was in love with Lady Beatrix. They were to be married. But I hadn't found those things out until he had already stolen into the secret places of my heart and pilfered my emotions. And so, the only thing to do now was change the subject and not give him an opportunity to talk at all.

"Sir William, I thank ye for bringing my mother home to me safe and sound. Ye have been a great help, and I will never be able to repay ye for your kindness, even if I spent a lifetime endeavoring to do so. But ye look tired. I think ye should go home and get some rest. Now ye can focus on the king's enemies and finding those who wish to do him harm. I can take care of my mother from here."

I picked up my cup and walked toward the kitchen, putting more distance between us. But he followed me there and cornered me, not giving up so easily.

"So, it's *sir* now?" When I didn't respond he continued. "Ailsa, we need to talk about what happened between us the other night."

"Why? It was just a kiss. It was cold outside; we'd had a long night. The excitement of breaking the curfew law probably rushed through our veins. I don't know, but it's nothing that needs to be talked about now."

"Just a kiss?" Out of all the nonsense I had spewed, those were the words that stood out to him. "This is your inexperience talking. That was not just a kiss." He had me trapped between the counter and the wall, and he leaned now, his arms imprisoning me on both sides, and I could not escape.

Embarrassment burned on my face. "Aye, I'm inexperienced. There is no need to throw that up in my face," I tossed back at him. "Thank ye for the practice. I'm sure David Seton will appreciate ye teaching his betrothed how to kiss before he takes her to bed."

I was horrified by my own words. I wasn't even sure where they had come from or why I had spoken them, other than in retaliation for his comment about my lack of experience. But I had considered, for an insane moment the night before, that I should marry Seton to put an end to his threats. However, now that I could think clearly, there was no way on my father's grave that I would marry that man, unless it were the only way to save my mother.

"The only way you will marry Seton," his voice shook and his face contorted into what looked like a painful ague, "is when I am buried in my grave."

I stared at him. His face was so close to mine that if it had not been for the heated discussion, I would have thought he may kiss me again. He had loosened the ruffle at his collar sometime during the night, and it was untied at the neck. I watched as his faintly protruding Adam's apple bobbed in his throat. I resisted the urge to reach up and run a finger down the slight protrusion. Now was not the time to be distracted.

"Why do ye care? Ye will be marrying Lady Beatrix soon." I pressed my palms against the wall behind me and tried to calm my throbbing heart. The mention of Lady Beatrix would elicit strong emotions in William, so I pressed on. "I imagine with her family's titles and money and your talent and connections, ye will have a joyful enough life together. A match made in heaven, is it not?"

He looked down at me, anguish twisting his otherwise beautiful features. I couldn't read the emotion that I saw flash in his eyes, but he suddenly grabbed my arms and pulled me closer to him.

"I would tell you that I am not betrothed to Lady Beatrix. I would say that she has misspoken and that plans have not been made as of yet. I would want you to know that I have not asked for her hand in marriage. But once these witch trials are concluded that is exactly what I plan to do." His clipped speech competed against the sound of my blood pounding in my ears, and I struggled to understand what he was trying to tell me. "You and I will not work." He hurried on. "I have to marry someone who…I *need* to marry someone who—" He stopped suddenly and an unintelligible gurgle escaped his throat. "Hang it all!"

And without preamble, his mouth was on mine, and he kissed me with a desperation that could be felt to the ends of every finger and toe. His lips, which had so gently touched mine the time before, now crushed against mine, his tongue brushing hotly against my own and sending molten lava straight to my belly. He tasted of pomegranates and exotic spice, and I was immediately reminded of the cacao he had shared with me just weeks before when I first realized that I could trust him. When I realized that he was someone I wanted to trust. I wanted to let him in, and I wanted him to want me too. He released my arms and pushed his hands into my hair, pulling the already falling locks down around my shoulders and giving his hands free-reign to caress the flowing tresses.

I grabbed the front of his doublet, holding myself up as my knees turned to butter. When he pulled his lips free from mine, I gasped, taking in much needed air before my eyes fell on that coveted flesh that lay right beneath the slight knot of his throat. I kissed him there, in that little concave at the base of this throat. He let out a low groan and twisted the locks of my hair tighter between his fingers.

The gesture sent little pulses of pleasure through me, and I leaned my head back against the wall to catch my breath. William stooped and kissed me at that tender spot just below the ear. I wrapped my arms around his neck as a whimper escaped my lips. I immediately felt my limbs burn with wanton desire.

"Ailsa," William whispered in my ear. "You make me want to do things that we shouldn't do." He tugged at the lace ruff that was still tied around my neck and pulled it free, exposing the neckline of my bodice. I felt my body straining to be free from the confines of my dress. From my ear he trailed a line of heated kisses down my neck and along my shoulder as I fought the urge to pull him closer to me.

"George?"

Mother's confused voice rang through the air like a night watchman's herald. I unwrapped my arms from around William's neck and grasped his shoulders to steady myself. He righted my dress, and I smoothed my skirts before stepping around him to see to Mother.

Over my shoulder, I said, "My mother gets confused when she is very tired or when something has upset her. Ye may wish to leave us, for she can be somewhat unlike herself at times."

"I have faced down lovesick sorcerers, deranged witches going to sea in a sieve, a demonic crow, and a clingy cat that loves my legs. I think I can handle your mother."

I chuckled, relieved he would stay, then reached out to tend to Mother.

~30~

February 1591

Ailsa

"George, is that ye?"

"'Tis me, Mother. 'Tis Ailsa. Father's not here." I ran a hand over her hairless head and choked back the tears that pushed at the back of my eyelids. "Are ye cold? Do ye want a kerchief for your head?"

Mother reached a shaky hand up and felt her head. Her brow crumbled when she realized—or remembered—that her hair had been shorn.

"My hair," she wailed. "They cut off all my hair." She began to rock back and forth, sobbing and lamenting the loss. I pulled a worn linen kerchief from our chest and wrapped it gently around her head. I tied it at the nape of her neck then kissed her on the cheek. She looked at me as if seeing me for the first time. "I have no hair, and yours is askew. Ye look like ye've been through a whirlwind. Why is your hair so tussled?"

Abashed at Mother's observation, I glanced at William as my hands flew to my hair. I quickly gathered my locks into a chignon as William turned toward us with a cup of tea in his hand.

"Should I give her the valerian root?"

I nodded as I continued to right my hair.

"Here you go, Mistress Blackburn. Here is some tea for you." William handed the brass-beaten cup to Mother, and her face lit up

230

instantly.

"Ye are a handsome one," she said as she took the cup from his hands. Mother shot a glance at me and immediately smiled a toothy smile. "Ah, that's why your hair is awry."

"Mother! Don't be vulgar."

"Well, he is a comely man. Such a strong chin and piercing blue eyes." Turning back to William and reaching out her hand, she said, "'Tis nice to meet ye. I'm Ailsa's mother, Naomi."

"Yes, ma'am. We've met before." He took her outstretched hand and deposited a soft kiss on her knuckles.

"Mother, this is Sir William. Don't ye remember? He helped ye last night—" I stopped before I could say something that may upset her. Perhaps she didn't remember what happened last night. If that was the case, I wasn't about to remind her.

"Sir William, aye," she murmured, but confusion still clouded her face.

"Just William will do, mistress." He released her hand, and she cupped it under her tea.

"Well, if I am to call ye just William, then ye must call me just Naomi." She took a sip of tea and closed her eyes as the liquid slid down her throat.

"Thank you, Naomi. That is a lovely name. It's from the Old Testament, is it not?"

"Aye," Mother yawned and handed the cup of tea back to William. "I'm tired," she said as she slid herself back under the blanket and closed her eyes. William and I looked at each other then back to Mother as she drifted off. She was practically snoring before her head hit the pillow.

"Well, that was interesting. At least she didn't become belligerent." I took the cup from William's hand and carried it back to the kitchen.

"It almost seems as if she has forgotten about the events of yesterday evening. Except for her hair being cut off."

"Aye, and we are going to keep it that way. Don't speak a word to her about it unless she brings it up."

"All right," William said, stifling a yawn himself.

"William, ye have been up all night. I do think ye should go home and get some rest."

"We haven't finished talking." He scrubbed a hand over his face and forced his eyes open wider.

"We weren't talking," I reminded him as I bent to retrieve my ruff from the floor. I felt heat burning on my cheeks as I recalled what we had been doing.

He covered what I perceived to be his own embarrassment with a cough then said, "About Beatrix."

Childishly, I covered my ears with my hands. "Don't." I did not wish to hear again how he planned to offer marriage to Lady Beatrix once the witch trials were over. I should have been offended, that he would throw himself at me so recklessly yet still be determined to attach himself to another. Yet, they were a better match. That was no secret. I was the daughter of a simple scribe and a runaway, would-be nun. He was a childhood friend of the king and lived at court. But that still didn't keep the rejection from stinging.

I went to the kitchen once more and stood looking at the darkened cabinets which held our normal staples. I heard William sigh behind me, but I ignored him as I began gathering flour, lard, and the utensils I would need to prepare a few meat pies.

"Do you think your brother will arrive in time to contest the betrothal agreement your uncle signed?"

I measured the flour and dumped it into a large bowl. Once I cut the lard into the flour, I replied, "I pray that he will, but my faith is small. We only had three weeks to begin with. It takes almost that long to get a letter to London. Then consider the travel time and the weather." I shook my head. "I just don't know." I added a splash of water and a sprinkle of salt then began kneading the flour and lard until a sticky dough began to form.

William dipped out a cup of water and washed his hands. He rolled up the sleeves of his tunic and joined me at the table. "May I?" He motioned toward the dough, and I gladly handed the duty off to him.

"I'll chop the mutton." I stepped aside to give him room and started on the next task.

"I filed a Stay of Pursuance against the betrothal agreement. Unless Seton breaks the law, you actually have a month to prove the illegitimacy of the betrothal."

"All right," I said, cutting the meat into bite-sized pieces. "But if Nick doesn't arrive on time, is there nothing else I can do?"

When William didn't answer, I swept a look to him. He was staring at the gummy mixture that clung to his hands.

"Ye need more flour." I wiped my hands on a piece of cloth then scattered another handful of flour into the bowl. I reached in and began pushing the glob of tacky dough down with my hand. William laid his dough-covered hand over mine and squeezed, sticking even more dough to my hands. "Ah! Ye did that on purpose," I said, laughing.

"I don't know what you mean." He then wrapped his hand around my wrist, adding the sticky residue to my arm.

"Ye don't want to start this war." I pulled my hand free from the dough. It only took a split second to decide my next course of action. I flattened my sticky palms directly on his shirt.

He stared down in shock.

I hooted loudly. "Ye don't like to get dirty, do ye?" I snickered watching him stand there with gooey hands raised in the air, not knowing what to do next.

"You know I don't," he replied, the low rumble of his voice warning me that he was about to do something I would regret. I backed away from him, still laughing. But it was a panicked laugh now. I had no idea what he was planning.

"Please tell me this will not stain." His calmness unnerved me as I watched him approach, hands still lifted in the air.

"It won't stain," I promised. "But it might take a little work getting that off." I watched him come closer, feeling like a doe before a hunter's bow. Before I knew it, he stood just a hair's breadth before me. My heart beat in anticipation, and I could barely breathe. "What are ye going to do?"

Without a word, he reached out and grabbed my face with both of his sticky hands. Pulling me toward him, he kissed me on the forehead, before sliding his hands upward into my hair again.

"Ye beast!" I screeched, laughing just the same. But the laughter died on my lips as he stood staring down at me, heat burning in his blue eyes. Pulling his sticky hands from my hair, he laid them on both sides of my face and pulled me even closer. He stared at my lips momentarily before bending and kissing me, weakening my knees once more.

"You deserved that," he said breathless, before turning back toward the table and retrieving the bucket of water to wash his hands.

"I suppose I do." I giggled nervously then smiled as an idea occurred to me. "William," I said, and when he looked up at me, I swiped my crumpled ruff across my face, wiping the dough from my cheeks. Shock and disbelief overtook his face. It was not something I would have ever dreamed of doing, and Mother would have scolded had she seen me. But the pleasure it brought at seeing the look on his face was worth the effort it would take to restore the ruff to its rightful condition. I grinned wildly then returned to my work chopping the mutton. I didn't want to begin to find out how much dough he had actually gotten in my hair. I'd deal with it after it dried. Once we settled back into our work, I said, "Ye didn't answer my question."

"What question is that?" With diligence he kneaded the dough, sprinkling a little more flour in and bringing it to a perfect lump.

"Is there nothing else I can do, if Nick does not arrive on time?"

William pulled the remaining dough from his fingers and stuck it to the larger ball now sitting in the bottom of the bowl. "Hide," he said simply, before looking up at me with compassion in his eyes. The fun and games were over now, and the seriousness of my situation had settled on both of us. "Find some way to disappear. Do you have any other family that you could visit until Nick can reach Edinburgh?"

"Nay," I whispered, all confidence evaporated. "Uncle Rupert is our only other living relative, except for my father's cousin who lives in London as well. Too far away to get word to him."

William washed his hands again then joined me on the other side of the table. "You may have to drop in on him unexpected. Surely, he will not turn you away when your lives are at stake."

"I'm not even sure where he lives. Nick has never even met him, and he lives in London too. I wouldn't know how to find him."

"There can't be too many Blackburns in London. It shouldn't be that hard to find him."

"I don't know, William. I don't think running away is the answer. I don't know what a journey like that would do to Mother."

William leaned against the table beside me and crossed his arms. "Perhaps you could stay in my room above the bookshop for a few weeks. Only a few people know about it. I think you would be safe there."

"A few people, including Lady Beatrix." I looked at him and pursed my lips together. Surely, he understood why I didn't trust her.

"She won't tell."

"William—"

"She won't tell if I ask her not to. You'll be much safer there than here."

"I'll think about." I looked to Mother who was still sleeping soundly. I didn't like the idea, but this may be our only option.

"Well, whatever you decide to do, you need to decide quickly. Remember, Seton will stop at nothing to make you his wife." He reached into his pocket and drew out a key. "Here, take this in case you change your mind. I can have Mistress Kennedy let me into my room until I can get another made."

He handed the key to me, and I stared at it momentarily before tucking it into my pocket. The brief weight of the warm metal in my hand turned my insides over like the dough William had just kneaded. I felt my cheeks warming again at the intimacy of the gesture. He wasn't inviting me into his bed, but the offer of refuge in his own private room gave me a warm feeling in my belly, and I was embarrassed by the implication of his concern.

I finished making the meat pies as William tended the fire again. The sun was already setting by the time we sat down to eat. We didn't say much as we supped, each lost in our own thoughts. I worried what I was to do about Seton. And I imagined William worried about what he would tell Lady Beatrix when it came to explaining where he had been all day. I secretly smiled to myself. She may win him in the end, but she couldn't take away the sweet memories that we had shared today. And that brought me a little happiness at least.

~31~

February 1591

William

"You are a hard man to find."

My father looked up from his task, eyebrows raised in surprise until he realized it was I who spoke. "William," he said in his delighted tone. "I had not expected you."

"Of course, you didn't, Father. It's called a surprise."

He rose to his feet and stepped from behind the large oak desk upon which he was busily occupying himself. Sheets of folded foolscap covered his desk, and a strong smell of glue permeated the air. "I've been right here for the past two hours," he said, tossing a thick brush onto the desk and letting out a strained breath.

"I tried your house. I tried the chapel. I even tried Queen Mary's hawthorn tree that you like to sit under." He looked up at me sharply at the mention of the Catholic queen's name. Four years after her execution, she was still a sensitive subject for him.

"Aye, well, the library is another home for me as well, so add that to your list of places to search for me when I cannot be found elsewhere." He wrapped his arms around me. "Son," he said, as if he were inhaling a scent of fresh flowers on a warm spring day. My father and I had always been close. My mother having died soon after giving birth to me, Father was left as sole provider of not only instruction and discipline, but of nurturing and compassion as well. Holding me for a second longer than necessary, he asked, "To what do I owe this pleasant surprise?"

"Oh, I-I just wanted to pay you a visit. It's been a while." I hoped he didn't hear me stumbling over the words.

"It's been one month and ten days. I keep track," he finished, as if needing some explanation for knowing the length of our separation. Turning back to his desk, he picked up a handful of pages to a book it appeared he was repairing.

"What has happened here?" I asked, curious as to the scattered pages about his desk. In reality, I imagined I was stalling.

"Dante's *Divine Comedy*. It fell off the shelf as I was trying to retrieve another book. When it hit the floor, the binding split and pages went everywhere."

"Well, it *is* old," I quipped. "It was probably printed by Gutenberg."

Father chuckled. "The story itself predates Gutenberg's printing press by at least one hundred years. Yet, this *is* a very old copy. I'm hoping I can repair it."

I picked up a page and looked at it. Picking up three more pages, I said, "There are no numbers on these pages."

"Perhaps that is the divine comedy here," he mused. "Hopefully, I can remember the order it goes in."

"I would help you, but it's in Italian."

"You can read Italian. I should know, I taught it to you."

"Aye, but only when I have to."

He shook his head at me, trying to stifle his amusement. Sitting back down at his desk, he picked up a small pile of pages that he had already ordered. Setting them to the side, he said, "William, you know I love you. So, spit it out. Why are you here?"

"You always did cut right to the chase, huh Poppy?" I used the childhood nickname that I had for him to try to lighten the mood.

"You are a busy man. That king keeps you hopping. You must have some important reason for being here."

Noting the offhanded way he said *that king*, and seizing the opportunity to stall yet again, I said, "Will you never find it in your heart to love our boy-king, Father? How long will you hold a grudge against him for what happened to his mother?"

"He could have done more." His voice caught.

Silence hung heavy between us for a moment until the bell that hung from the university tower chimed out the hour somewhere in the distance. I watched as dusty particles from age-old books, danced in the late afternoon sun that shone through the cracked glass of the library windows. Father continued to shuffle through his disseminated pages, occasionally muttering a line from a page he held in his hand. Like a child testing the ice of a frozen winter pond, I proceeded cautiously. "You really did love her, didn't you?" He didn't look at me, but instead, he began gathering the dismembered pages a little quicker.

"She didn't deserve that, William. She didn't deserve to die in such a way." He looked up at me then, his blue eyes turned to orbs of glass. We rarely talked about his childhood friend: the Catholic queen who had been beheaded at the hands of the Queen of England. It was painful for him.

"The thing I regret the most, the thing that eats away at me when I am alone and have all the time in the world to just think about my actions, is how I thought I was doing the right thing. In the end, it didn't matter. Following the rules didn't matter."

His broken words jarred me. My father was the epidemy of godliness and piety. I had never seen him go against his conscience and do something—*anything*—just to please himself. Did he regret that now, after all these years?

"What about Mother? Were you madly in love with her when you married her?" A change of subject was more comfortable. He always spoke of my mother with sweet reminiscences, not the torturous memories he had of the queen he loved.

Again, silence reigned as he gathered his thoughts. Then he sighed and said, "Not at first."

Taken aback, I gaped at him. "What do you mean? You didn't love her when you married her?"

He sat another small stack of pages to the side and folded his hands on his desk. Looking me straight in the eyes, he said, "I married your mother because it was the right thing to do."

I could almost feel the color burn on my face. "You didn't...she wasn't with child—with me—was she?" I swallowed hard, not sure I wanted the honesty that he was so prone to give me.

A smile spread across his face. "No, Son. But it was right for me to marry, to start a family. To forget about the woman who held my heart, the one I could never have."

There she was again. That specter that never left his thoughts. I never really knew Queen Mary. Father always said I was smitten with her the *one* time I had met her as an infant. But she was driven out of Scotland when I was barely weaned, and I had never spoken a single word to her. Yet, she was like a ghost watching over us. My mother may have been dead, but it was the exiled queen who had haunted our otherwise peaceful home.

"But you *did* love my mother, right?" I pressed, feeling a little betrayal for her sake. I had never known my mother either, but she gave up her own life in order to give me mine. And that alone was worth my loyalty.

"Aye, I grew to love her. She was a beautiful woman with a kind heart. She loved to help others and was the most selfless person I had ever met. She gave all that she had to give to me and to you. And I know that she would do it again if given the opportunity."

I reached over and picked up a handful of pages of his book. Without a word I began sorting the poem into three piles, *Inferno*, *Purgatorio*, and *Paradiso*: the three cantiche of the religious narrative.

"Did you come here to talk about love, dear son?" He didn't look at me but continued to study the pages in his hand. "How is the lovely Beatrix, by the way?"

"She is as beautiful as a summer rose," I said frowning, the comparison feeling trite.

"And yet, your face tells a different story. They say beauty is only as deep as the skin. Has she proven to be not as beautiful on the inside as she is on the outside?"

Finishing up my small handful of pages, I picked up the final few that still lay upon his desk. Continuing my task, I said, "There is no guile in her, as far as I can tell. She is as agreeable as a lady can be. She always seeks to please me and is very disappointed if she feels she has failed. It seems her happiness is solely based upon my satisfaction."

Father raised an eyebrow at that. "Well, it seems that the Almighty has blessed you in that regard. Ask any man who has attached himself to a discontented woman. The misery is sore, and there is no end to his regret."

"I suppose there are worse things," I said, a slight smile playing at the corners of my mouth.

"Yet?"

"Yet sometimes I wish she would oppose me even just a little. Get a little backbone maybe. Show a spark of spirit. Where is the fun in agreeing all the time?"

Father chuckled again, this time running his hand over his mouth as if he wanted to say something but wouldn't. In the end, he just said, "A woman with spirit can be quite satisfying." He reached for the twine that would be used to thread the pages of the book back together. Handing me the organized stack of pages, he indicated for me to hold them tight as he began the tedious process of binding the pages together with twine.

"Are you having second thoughts about this marriage, William? Hers is a fine, noble family. You would want for nothing the rest of your life. You would have the influence that so many men seek, perhaps even a title."

I thought about his statement for a moment. "There was a time when I would have given anything for those advantages you named. But I've seen too much, experienced too much. I realize now that none of those things can make you truly happy, if you're not satisfied within yourself."

"This business with the witches that His Majesty has tasked you with, it has affected you, has it not?"

"How could it not? I have seen some very bizarre things over the past several months. Things that I would have never dreamed that one human being could do to another. Some have been in the name of Satan, and some in the name of God. Both equally disturbing. I have tried to be that light, that beacon that drives out the blackness, but I fear my one little candle is not enough, and soon the whole world will be overrun by darkness."

My father didn't say anything at first, and when I finally looked at him to gauge a response, he was deep in thought. "It is always right to do the right thing."

"But even you doubted the rightness of following the rules and only doing what was right. In the end, you found it didn't benefit you. And you have lived with the regret ever since."

He forced his eyes to mine, this time with a look of resolution on his face. "I do believe we are talking about two different things here, William."

"Not that different," I said defiantly. Rarely did I contradict my father.

"Are you thinking of going against your conscience? Who will benefit from that?"

"I don't know," I said simply.

We spoke no more of it, and two hours later, the sun had set, and we were finally adding the last dabs of glue to the comedy's spine. "Are you staying for supper?" Father asked, wiping his hands on an old rag he had tucked into the desk drawer.

"If it is not too much trouble, I would like to stay the night." He nodded his head in affirmation, then stood, stretching to loosen his tensed muscles.

Patting me on the back, he said, "Suzanne will be happy to hear you are staying over. The maid has never fully recovered since you were sent away to court." Suzanne was Father's maid whom I terrorized during my childhood. She was forever scolding me, and I found it hard to believe any time that Father would comment how much she missed me.

"I shall be sure to find a toad to stuff into her pocket before we get home," I teased, helping Father don his cloak and cap.

"I'll never hear the end of it, if you do," he laughed, leaving *The Divine Comedy* on the large desk to dry.

The walk home was a quiet one, and we had almost reached my father's door when he suddenly said to me, "You never did truly answer my question. Are you having second thoughts about the Lady Beatrix?"

I opened the door and motioned for him to go first as we entered that old familiar place that I called home for the first ten years of my life. It always smelt of cedar and peppermint. A strange combination, but one in which I found extreme satisfaction and comfort.

It also boasted a faint smell of ink and books which permeated from the shelves of Father's library just down the hall. For although not as extensive as the one I had just found him in at the university, it was still impressive.

We had not arrived for more than two minutes, when a spry, no-nonsense woman of about forty years of age greeted us. "Would ye look at that! A king's man come to dine with us. I do hope we have fare fine enough to feed such a noble one as yourself." Her words were sardonic, but when coupled with a twinkle in her eye, it was obvious she teased me. Suzanne always teased me, and it probably came from the many tricks I played on her as a boy. She was only repaying me for all my games.

"Hello, Suzanne," I said, wrapping my arms around her and kissing her on both cheeks. The soothing source of the peppermint scent, she had been employed by my father since I was but a wee lad and was the closest thing I had to a mother. And though we had many an argument when I was younger, she was very dear to me.

"'Tis good to see ye, William." She seized our cloaks and caps, her eyes lighting up as she took in my apparel. Whistling, she said, "My, my, but that king does keep ye in fine attire." I smiled brightly at her. "Oh, ye have a spot." She pointed a finger toward the front of my doublet and when I looked down in alarm, she flicked my nose. "Got ye good," she guffawed.

I furrowed my brow, but Father patted me on the back. "You know she has to make up for lost time. And I do believe you deserve every bit of the teasing she is dishing out."

I hung my head, knowing that he was right. Still, under my breath I said, "Remind me again why I didn't get that toad."

Father chuckled and motioned for me to take a seat in his small drawing room, while Suzanne rushed off to retrieve refreshment. He settled himself into a chair and leveled a knowing gaze at me. It was the kind that looks right through you and lets you know that your parent sees and knows *everything*.

"Now, I'm going to ask you once more because I do believe you are avoiding the question. Are you reconsidering your betrothal to Lady Beatrix?"

I shifted uncomfortably in my seat. I wasn't trying to avoid his question, but now that he confronted me in such a forthright manner, I felt a little uneasy. Would he be disappointed in me if I told him I *was* reconsidering? Would he chastise me for all the good fortune I would be throwing away by not marrying Beatrix? And was I really reconsidering? I had told myself over and over that I was still going to go through with it, regardless of what happened between Ailsa and me. But as I sat here in front of my father, I couldn't help but be honest with myself and with him.

I swallowed hard, then straightened my doublet.

"You are nervous. Why?"

I laughed once again at Father's straightforwardness. "How do you do that?"

"Do what?"

"How do you always read me like one of those books in your vast library?"

My father's face softened into concern. "I have known you all your life. I can tell when something is bothering you." He paused as Suzanne entered with sweet wine and cranberry scones and set the tray before us without a word. When she had quit the room, Father continued, "Do you remember that time when you were about seven or eight years old, and you wanted a horse of your own?"

I stopped pouring my wine long enough to look up at him. "Aye, I remember."

"You wanted that old mare that Simms was selling. The jade was nearly 20 years old, could barely carry a saddlebag and had laminitis to boot. I told you we would not buy the mare but would find you a decent horse when spring came round."

"I loved that horse. Simms used to let me feed her carrots and apples and let me brush her until her hair shone."

He nodded. "I forgot about the horse until you stopped eating supper. You stopped coming to my study in the evenings to chat. Next thing I knew, you were acting out against the other neighbor boys. You even attempted to run away, but Suzanne found your satchel full of apples and carrots and stalled you until I came home."

"I wanted to save the mare from an uncertain fate. Simms said if he didn't sell her, he would rid himself of her one way or another."

A faint smile captured his lips. "You wanted that horse so badly that your behavior changed. Things you enjoyed, *like eating*, you stopped doing. And things you never liked, such as brawling with the neighbor boys, you began to do. Your behavior changed, and it still changes. The only thing I'm not sure of is if it is an attempt to change another person's mind, or a subconscious action because you don't know what else to do, or how else to get what you want. So, tell me, William. What is it that you really want? Or, a better question might be, *who* is it you really want?"

His question jarred me, and I dropped the scone that I was about to put into my mouth. So, he knew. He knew there had to be a really good reason for me to change my mind about the lovely and perfect Beatrix, and the only good reason would have to be another woman.

I set my crumbled scone down and brushed the crumbs from my lap. I started a little when Father said, "For heaven's sake, William. Out with it."

"I've met someone. A woman. I've met a woman." I was a bumbling idiot who couldn't put an entire sentence together. Why was this so hard?

Father sat back in his chair and clasped his hands in front of him. "Go on."

"Her name is Ailsa Blackburn. Perhaps you knew her father. He was a scribe for several of the archbishops here in St Andrews many years ago."

"Blackburn. Aye, George Blackburn. A very talented and learned man."

"Aye, that's him. Master Blackburn died several years ago, and his wife and daughter now reside in Edinburgh. He also has a son who lives in London."

Father listened patiently as I recounted all I knew about the Blackburns, the events that transpired allowing me to meet Ailsa, and the troubles she has faced at the hands of David Seton. When I concluded my tale, I braced myself for his many questions.

"And you feel this woman is a better match for you than Lady Beatrix?"

I stood and nervously ran a hand across the back of my neck. "I suppose that is what it comes down to, isn't it? A better match."

Father maintained his seat and continued his questioning, "She is not a better match?"

"I don't know!" I groaned. "There is no money, no titles, no connections attached to her. If I marry her, that is all there will be. She and I."

"Is she not enough?"

His question was simple yet so profound that I couldn't speak. When I did find my voice, it was to air another concern.

"His Majesty will not take too kindly to me throwing off Her Majesty's wishes. For it is she who first put forth the idea of a match between Beatrix and me."

"God forbid you displease the king," he said in the acerbic fashion he always used when speaking of James. He shook his head as he stood, coming to stand before me at the spot I had claimed at the window. From there, I could see the perfectly manicured garden that Suzanne maintained in the summer, though it was currently buried under a mound of snow. A robin pecked at something on the ground, chipping away the icy covering to get to what lay beneath.

Father turned me toward him, forcing me to look into his eyes. "Since I'm getting so good at repeating myself today, I'll ask you again. Is she enough?"

"I want her very badly."

Father frowned. "Son, I know your reputation is…less than chaste when it comes to the ladies." My eyes widened in shock and embarrassment. Father and I had never discussed my female liaisons. I didn't even know he knew. "But you are giving up much, if you are to set Lady Beatrix aside for Mistress Blackburn. You need to know that what you feel for her is more than lust. Whatever it is you feel, it will need to sustain you for years to come and satisfy you should your other ambitions not come to fruition."

I didn't answer him. I couldn't even look at him. Instead, I stared at the marbled tiles that lay so neatly jointed together beneath our feet. I traced one of the edges with the toe of my boot, considering Father's words.

When I did speak, I found my voice had lost its efficacy. "She challenges everything I ever thought I believed. She opens my eyes to new ways of looking at things and makes me question everything. She is fire, and she is compassion, and she cares dangerously about the well-being of others. She thinks nothing of herself or her own safety if she can help someone else. She says what she thinks and isn't afraid to contradict me. And when I am with her, nothing else matters but making her happy."

"Those are admirable qualities indeed. I can see why you are attracted to her. But I will ask you one last time. Is that enough?"

"Shouldn't it be?" I wanted him to tell me what to do, not create more questions in my mind.

"I cannot tell you what to do, William," he said as if reading my thoughts. "This is a decision you must make entirely on your own. But I can tell you that I think in your heart you already know the answer to all of your questions. And whatever you decide to do, I will support your decision, for I know that you have a good head on your shoulders, and you do not make the judgement lightly. The steps of a good man are ordered by God."

"What did you say?" I paused with my cup half-way to my mouth and gaped at him.

"I said that the steps of a good man are ordered by God. It's from the Holy Writ."

"Aye, I am aware." I managed a half-hearted smile. Is that what Agnes had been trying to convey to me? I thought I was writing my own story, but perhaps there was a greater power controlling the pen.

"Supper is ready, sir."

"Thank you, Suzanne." Turning back to me, Father laid his hand on my shoulder and squeezed. "I hope your appetite is intact. We are having roasted lamb for supper tonight."

~32~

February 1591

William

"I think your source may be onto something, William." Blantyre met me as I walked to the king's antechamber to join him for supper.

I turned my head to look at him, but the movement irritated a soreness in my neck that I had been feeling since returning from my father's house that morning.

"To what do you refer?" I ran my hand over the back of my neck, massaging the tender muscles while at the same time trying to stifle a cough.

"Are you ill, man?" Blantyre took a step away from me, eyeing me with suspicion.

"It is a little cough. Don't act like I have the plague, Blantyre."

"There is a throat sickness going around. Three of the palace maids and two of the footmen have already been sent to their rooms to rest, and one of them is in dire need of a physicker's attention. You haven't been tupping any maids, have you?" He grinned, but his usual lighthearted teasing sounded strained.

I scowled. "I've tupped no one."

"Pity," he tossed back, turning his head to get a longer look at a young woman as she passed us in the hallway.

"Focus, Blantyre." I snapped, feeling a bit irritated today. "What might my source be onto?"

He lowered his voice to just above a whisper. "You asked me to check on Bothwell. Seems he has been doing more than just plotting a kidnapping."

"Tell me what you know."

"Evidently he has a penchant for necromancy."

I sighed. "I heard rumors that he may be involved with the witches in some way. But necromancy? God's teeth."

"Two witnesses have confessed his involvement. Unfortunately, one is now dead."

"Agnes Sampson?" I guessed.

"How did you know?"

"His name came up during some of the witch interrogations."

"And you didn't think to investigate that?"

I straightened my cuffs in an effort to abate my rising agitation. "I had other business to attend to at the time. You mentioned two witnesses. Was the other Barbara Napier?"

He rubbed his chin. "Nay. This is where it gets interesting. Richard Graham has leveled the charges against him as well."

I searched my memory. "Why does that name sound familiar?"

"He was named during Geillis' interrogation. He too is a suspected necromancer."

I closed my eyes to the madness this was quickly becoming. It did not bode well for the earl to have two witches accuse him of involvement. But I wasn't sure how much credence would be put into their testimonies, especially since one of them was now dead. I opened my mouth to say as much but a coughing fit seized me, and I turned away from Blantyre.

"Perhaps you should go have a lie-down."

I coughed one last time, wincing at the pain that tore through my throat at the action. "I will be fine," I said, as I wiped my mouth. "Is this Graham fellow in custody now? I vaguely remembered a search being conducted for him when Seton first learned his name."

"Not anymore. He was questioned and released. Not enough evidence."

I frowned. "So, we can hold a woman in the tolbooth for months all because of a lover's mark on her neck, but this man, who seems to have knowledge of others using his craft, can walk free? I'm not sure I'm understanding the king's reasoning."

"You should know all of this. Where is your head?"

He was right. My thoughts had been elsewhere for a month now. I should have remembered all of this information that Blantyre shared with me now, but instead it was all a fog. I had been distracted.

We reached the king's antechamber when Blantyre placed a hand on my shoulder, stopping me. "I'm afraid I must insist you have a rest. Your cheeks are as flushed as a virgin bride and that cough sounds terrible. You do not want to pass your sickness on to the king."

He was right, but there was so much I needed to speak to James about. I took a breath to protest but was seized once again by another coughing fit. When I finished, I rasped, "I really need to speak to him."

Blantyre shook his head. "Impossible. But you can send him a missive, and I will see that he gets it." He turned me away from the king's door and gave me a little shove toward the corridor. "Ah, purely Providential," he exulted when he saw a maid walking toward us, a stack of linens draped over her arm. "Assist Sir William to his rooms," he commanded her.

Concern covered the young maid's face, but I tried to put her at ease. "I am fine. It is only a little cough. I can manage the walk to my rooms."

"Ye do look fevered, sir." She shifted the linens to her other arm then tucked a hand beneath my elbow. "Please allow me to accompany ye, and I will see that ye get a cold compress and some fresh mulled wine. Are ye hungry?" She turned to walk with me toward my rooms, clucking at me like a mother hen. I painfully turned my head and glanced at Blantyre. He chuckled in amusement then disappeared behind the king's door.

Grace, the maid Blantyre had so generously recruited to be my nursemaid, finished settling me in bed when there came a tapping on the door. She sighed heavily. "Ye will get no rest in this palace. There is always some mayhem occurring."

She opened the door to a worried Lady Beatrix who swept into the room, followed by her lady's maid, Fiona, carrying a tray in her hands. "William, my love. I came as soon as I heard. How are you feeling?"

I tried to look at her, but my head was now pounding, and I could barely focus on her face. A swath of peacock blue surrounded me, and the nauseating smell of lavender filled my nose. *When had the soft floral smell of Beatrix turned my stomach?*

I heard a clinking of earthenware as she sat down beside me.

"It's nothing." I squeezed my eyes shut and then blinked several times, feeling a burning behind my eyelids that wasn't there moments before.

"For the love of all that is holy, William, you are burning up with fever," she pronounced before even laying her cool hand to my brow. "Grace, gather a bowl of cold water and some cloths. We must get this fever down."

"Beatrix, perhaps you shouldn't be here. If I am truly sick with a contagious illness, I would never forgive myself if you fell ill as well."

She busied herself with the items on the tray and did not respond. She poured a splash of wine into a cup then held it to my mouth. "Drink this," she said as she tipped the cup. I took a small sip, but the action drove sharp pains into the back of my throat, and I began to cough once more. "I have brought some soup since you missed supper." Without warning, a spoon was brought to my lips, and I felt a watery substance being dribbled down my throat.

"Beatrix, please. I cannot eat right now," I sputtered. "My throat is extremely pained at the moment."

I heard what sounded like a stifled sob. "I just want to help, my love. You must eat to keep your strength up."

"I know, and I will," I assured her. "But I desperately need to get a message to His Majesty. Would you call my valet, Reeves, to scribe for me?"

"I can scribe for you," she offered.

I closed my eyes once more and licked my dry lips in an effort to stall. I could not have her scribe for me, for it was her that the missive was to be about. I needed to speak to James about my wish to be removed from consideration as Beatrix's suiter. I couldn't go through with the plans. Not after coming to the realization of my feelings for Ailsa.

I love Ailsa.

The admittance hurt my chest more that the ache I felt in my head and throat. Of course I loved her, but finally admitting it to myself underscored the heavy price I would have to pay.

She set the spoon back on the tray. "I'll find some foolscap," she said hesitantly. I heard the rustling of her skirts which led me to believe she had risen in defiance of my request.

"Beatrix, please." My voice was raspy and dry, and I licked my lips once again. "This is of a sensitive nature. Please call Reeves to assist me."

There was silence for a moment until I opened my eyes and saw her looking at me. Her eyes glistened with unshed tears. "As you wish," she finally whispered. Then turning to her maid, she said, "Fiona, fetch Sir William's valet."

Beatrix sat quietly beside me until Grace bustled back in, carrying a bowl full of snow, a pitcher of water and some clean cloths. The maid soaked the cloth in water then wrapped it around a handful of snow. She laid the wrapped snow on my forehead, and I felt myself sigh at the cool relief. Moments later, my valet entered with Beatrix's lady's maid.

"I suppose I'll leave him to your care," she told the man as she rose to her feet. "Reeves, be sure to call for me immediately once Sir William is finished writing his letter."

"Aye, Your Ladyship." Reeves bowed then went to work setting out the items needed to write my missive to the king.

There was another matter that I wished to discuss with James, and I decided to broach that topic first. That was the matter of Seton's questionable actions on the night that he arrested Mistress Blackburn. He had been caught in a lie of unfathomable proportions, making as if the woman had bitten him and bringing accusations against her that in reality, he was unprepared to defend. It was unwise, and I wondered at his lack of planning for such a desperate move on his part.

Regardless, it played in our favor. Mistress Blackburn had been released, and he now stood as an unreliable and incompetent accuser, and the king had no choice but to relieve him of the position of which he had been so hastily employed. This was my opinion of course, and I could only hope that James would see the man for what he was and agree to my wishes of barring him from his post.

I would address both topics in my letter to James and pray that he would be on my side concerning both.

~33~

February 1591

Ailsa

An early thaw had brought Mother and I out along the banks of the Water of Leith to gather *Salix alba*, willow bark. The trees would be sprouting in a few weeks, and I wanted to harvest the supple branches before the puffy silver catkins began to bloom on them.

The ice was melting, and the river rushed by in a cacophony of gurgling and swirling. The sun shone bright and warm, but it was still too early to see many signs of life along the river's edge, frogs and fish having not made an appearance yet.

We had cut two bushelsful, careful not to overload our baskets with more than we could carry. Mother lifted her basket onto her hip then ventured to the edge of the water and stood transfixed. I joined her once I had my basket, a little fuller than hers, hoisted into my arms.

"When I was a wee lass," my mother began, her eyes riveted on the rushing water below us, "My brother and I would toss leaves into the river, then watch them sail off on the ripples that carried them away. I liked to dream about where the leaves would go and what adventures they might see."

I stiffened at the mention of her brother, Rupert. I had not seen much of my uncle since I had learned of his betrayal of me. I imagined he realized his mistake in the signing of the marriage agreement with Seton and feared what the man might do when he didn't get what he wanted in the end.

My mother must have sensed my reaction because she turned to me, her faded gray eyes drinking me in. Her thoughts were coherent and on this rare occasion, she was fully cognizant of her surroundings. "Whatever happens, Ailsa, ye must not marry Seton." I felt the breath escape me in a harsh *woosh* as if I had been punched in the stomach. I didn't realize she even knew or understood about the predicament my uncle had put me in. "Rupert had no right to do what he did. He has always been a greedy man, and I can only imagine what money was traded in exchange for your hand in marriage to Seton." The pools of her gray eyes glistened under unshed tears. She reached up and brushed a wisp of hair from my eyes, tucking it behind my ear. She then ran her knobby hand along my braid and draped it over my shoulder before patting it down in a motherly fashion. "Do not marry that man to protect me or to prevent his harassments," she continued. "He is not worth losing your freedom. I'd rather die than see ye subjected to the likes of him."

A sob escaped my lips this time. I didn't know how she knew that I had considered marrying Seton. Perhaps it was *mother's intuition*. I didn't answer her but swallowed the lump in my throat and continued to watch the bubbling water rushing past.

A snapping of a twig behind us startled us both. We turned and found ourselves looking straight into the eyes of the very monster of whom we had just been speaking. A wide grin was smeared across his face, and his eyes danced with vile pleasure.

"'Tis a lovely day, is it not?" He dragged a deep breath through his nostrils. "I do hope it is this lovely tomorrow for our wedding day."

I felt my lip curl. My eyes darted behind him, looking for a way to flee. The aggressive river behind us gave us little way of escape should this man decide to fall upon us. I prayed Mother would not get it into her head to defend me to this man. I had learned my lesson when it came to speaking my mind to him, and I hoped that she had too. Fortunately, she stood as still as I did, gripping her basket and drawing ragged breaths into her aging lungs.

"Bailiff Seton, my mother is not well. Please allow us to be on our way so that we may deposit our willow branches and be about our business."

He furrowed his brow and eyed my mother. "She looks hale enough to me. But here, allow me to lighten the load of my future mother-in-law." He reached for her basket, but Mother shrank away from him. Apparently, there was no need to fear what Mother would say or do, she was terrified of this man now. She held firm to her basket, hesitant to relinquish her claim on it. "Come now, Mother Blackburn. Is that any way to treat your new son?"

"Ye are not my son."

He pulled her grip free from the basket of bark. The force of their tug-of-war sent her flying backward, and when the heel of her foot came down, there was no earth beneath for which it to land upon. Mother cried out as her foot slid down the slope, and she grappled at the ground to gain purchase.

"Mother!" I dropped my basket and reached out to her, grabbing her arm, and giving her a little tug to pull her back up the bank once more. Her knees landed hard on the still-frozen ground, and she cried out in pain. At least she was on solid ground once more, even if that ground now sent shooting pains into her joints.

"Bailiff, ye are a cruel man," I said bitterly. His brows shot up in innocence, but the gleam in his eye told me I spoke truth.

"Allow me." He strode forward and gripped Mother under her arm. She cried out as he squeezed her flesh within his beefy fist. He pulled her to her feet but did not release her once she steadied herself on her spindly legs.

"We shall be on our way." I glared, hinting for him to release Mother's arm.

"Aye, let us be on our way." He turned and tucked Mother's shaking hand into his elbow then bent and picked up her basket with his other hand.

"Your escort is not necessary."

"Oh, but it is, my sweet dove. This mystery brother of yours has failed to show, and there has been no proof produced otherwise that negates your uncle's right to control your marital prospects. You and I shall be wed tomorrow, whether you like it or not. I want to have a look around in the new home that I will be living in, so I will accompany you."

I gaped at him. "Your new home? The home I live in belongs to my mother, Bailiff Seton. Ye will have to provide me with a home." I tasted the bitterness of my own words. The act of even *pretending* I had any intentions of marry this man was like gall on the tongue.

He sniffed but did not reply.

As we made our way back to Fishmarket Close, I wondered what William would think if we happened upon him in the street. I had not seen him for several days and was disappointed that he had abandoned us. Perhaps abandoned was not the right word. We weren't his responsibility. He hadn't been charged with our keep. But I had fooled myself into thinking that he cared—if perhaps only a little—about my predicament with Seton, and now he was nowhere to be found.

I had even gone to his room on the High Street. The housekeeper, Mistress Kennedy, said she had not seen him in almost a week. I wondered what business of the king's kept him so occupied that he couldn't bother to leave the palace walls.

"You are deep in thought, my little dove."

My skin crawled with the pet name that Seton had taken to calling me. I did not answer him as we drew close to the door of our house. My thoughts now shifted from William to how I was going to keep Seton out of our house. I dreaded the thought of leading him right to our door. I had been so careful in avoiding him over the past week, and although I had not forgotten about my looming marriage to him, I had not seen him either and hoped that he had fallen off the face of the earth.

Mother had been quiet too, and I glanced at her now as we approached our home. She was limping, and I chastised myself for not paying more attention to her after her fall. I had been too preoccupied with my thoughts.

"Mother, are ye injured very badly?" My words seemed to snap her out of whatever reverie she was in. She looked at me with hollow eyes, but she did not respond. Terror gripped me, for I had seen that look before. The light had gone out of them, and she would soon be very confused.

Seton had finally released her, and I put my arm around her to hurry her toward the door. However, she bent over and pulled up the hem of her skirt to see the source of her pain. Blood oozed from a gaping wound that measured from her knee to her ankle. Clumps of mud and grass stuck to her skin.

"I'm bleeding," she began to wail. "I'm bleeding, and it hurts. It hurts."

With every repeated word she grew louder, and I could see Seton growing anxious. He shifted on his feet, and his face turned a bright shade of red. I had a decision to make. Should I risk the talk of the neighbors by allowing them to see Mother's unusual behavior or do I usher her inside and risk the chance of Seton gaining entry? I decided the latter was a far worse consequence. I tried to hush Mother softly but made no effort to open our front door.

"It hurts. There is blood on my skirts." She continued to cry.

"Can't you shut her up?" Seton asked. "She is drawing the attention of your neighbors."

Janet came out of her house and hurried toward us, carrying a clean wet cloth. "I heard a commotion in the alleyway. How can I help?"

Mother lifted her eyes to Janet, and I feared she would badger the woman. But my mother was always full of surprises. Instead of berating Janet she pointed a finger at Seton and wailed, "He pushed me!"

Janet looked up from her ministrations. Her brows deepened into a reprimanding scowl. "What?"

"He pushed me," Mother repeated. "He pushed me down the bank of the river, and I almost fell in."

"I did no such thing, you lying witch." Seton's anger was clearly visible.

I saw a small window of opportunity and seized upon it. "Bailiff Seton, Mother gets overwrought when she is tired. It would be best if ye be on your way as not to draw more attention to yourself." I pointed with my chin toward the main road, praying that he would take this way of escape I offered him.

"This is absurd." He stood with legs apart and fists clenched as if he were about to wrestle a wild dog. "You can rest assured, when we are married, this behavior will stop." He bared his teeth, and a vein in his neck bulged angrily.

Janet looked up at me in confusion. "Are ye to be married then, Ailsa?"

Not wanting to risk angering Seton further, I ignored her question. "Does the cut look deep, Janet?"

"I think it might need a stitch or two. How did ye say this happened?"

I snuck a glance at Seton out of the corner of my eye.

"Mark my words," his voice shook. "She will be dealt with." He turned, but before plodding off, he said, "I'll see you on the morrow, Ailsa. Bright and early at St Giles Kirk. And do not even think about not showing." My momentary relief at his parting was negated by his churlish reminder.

"Janet, ye don't know how thankful I am for your questions."

She looked at me with concern. "Are ye really going to marry that man?"

"Not if I can help it." I bit my lip. My insides still quivered from Seton's threats, but a plan was beginning to form in my head. "Let's get Mother inside, so we can treat her wound." I wrapped my arm around Mother's waist again. "I could use your help if ye don't mind. Ye heard what that man said. If I am forced to marry him, that just might be the end of my mother."

Janet gasped at my pronouncement. "What a horrible man."

"Aye. Come inside, and I'll tell ye how ye can help."

~34~

March 1591

William

I awoke to the soft hum of ladies' voices chatting softly somewhere close by. I opened my eyes to behold Beatrix sitting across the room with a young companion I did not recognize. They were stitching fabric, and Beatrix paused when she heard my movement.

"Hattie," she said, handing the lass her needlework, "please take our things to my rooms and notify His Majesty that Sir William is awake." The other woman looked up sharply, then seeing I was indeed awake, she moved quickly to fulfil her Lady's request. I watched Beatrix as she rose slowly from her seat and walked toward me, bringing her chair with her. She set it down gently, and when the other woman had departed, she looked back at me and smiled weakly. "Hello, William."

"What time is it?" My mouth was dry, but I noticed that the soreness in my throat was considerably more tolerable. In fact, I barely felt a twinge when I swallowed.

She chuckled. "Perhaps you should ask what day it is instead. You have been asleep for several days."

Alarmed, I pushed myself up onto my elbows. "Several days?" I echoed.

"Aye. Your fever broke last night. We really feared for your well-being."

I blinked at her, trying to process the information. "You did?"

Her mouth curved upward as if she were still smiling, but her eyes showed no happiness. "Aye."

"You have a new maid. Where is Fiona?"

"Dead," she said simply, as she poured wine into an earthen cup.

"Dead?" I felt like one of those exotic birds. All I seemed capable of doing was repeating information.

"She took ill a day after we began tending to you. Only she wasn't as fortunate as you. She was gone within a day." Her voice wobbled on her last words.

"That's awful." I took the cup she offered and drank heartily. "I didn't realize how serious this illness was."

"No one did, at first. His Majesty has lost three servants so far, and Thomas Hamilton has taken to bed now as well. However, he is expected to recover."

I laid back against my pillow. "That is a relief."

She didn't say anything for a few moments, but when I opened my eyes, she was staring at me, a sadness pulling at her lips. Panic overtook me. Had someone else died? Were the king and queen all right? And Ailsa?

"William, there is something I need to speak with you about, but I wonder if I should wait until you are fully recovered."

"I am recovered enough to talk about anything you wish." I raised myself up in the bed further. She fluffed my pillow and adjusted it for my comfort. She didn't say anything further, and I was beginning to think she had decided against it. I couldn't take the anticipation. "Is the king well?"

"The king is well," she said flatly.

"And the queen?"

"Both king and queen are well," she rebuffed. Then suddenly she said, "I want to release you from—" she paused and swallowed, then wet her lips before continuing, "from any understanding we may have had."

I looked at her, surprised. I was sure I understood her meaning but wasn't sure what had brought this about. "Do you refer to our presumed betrothal?" She sniffed lightly and dabbed at her nose with a lace handkerchief, then nodded quietly. "Is there someone else you wish to marry?" I had always thought there may be something between her and Blantyre. I couldn't help but wonder even now.

She laughed softly again. "You men and your pride. I suppose that would be your first thought." She adjusted her skirts, brushing at an unseen speck. Lifting her chin slightly, she said, "I do have other admirers you know, but this has more to do with your other love interest, not mine."

I stared at her blankly. "To what do you refer?"

She took the cup from my hand and set it aside. Pausing another moment, she shifted in her seat. "I refer to your lady friend, Ailsa Blackburn."

The sound of Ailsa's name on Beatrix's lips sent an odd shiver through me. "Has something happened?" I asked cautiously.

She stood and drew away from me, coming to a stop in front of my desk. She pushed a piece of foolscap aside idly, then fiddled with a quill that laid ready to be put to use.

Without turning back to me, she whispered, "You talk in your sleep, William."

I stared at the back of her head as if her curls had turned to snakes and were now doing a dance on her head. "I talk in my sleep?" There I went again, the fever must have stolen all my intelligent speech and left me with only the capability to mimic.

She turned slowly toward me. Her eyes were wet and devoid of their typical mirth. Blotchy red patches now covered her neck. It was as if the color had drained from her face and was now pooling on her creamy skin, right above the deep neckline of her cerulean blue dress.

She opened her mouth as if to explain but then closed it again. I wanted to ask her what I am to have said, but I was afraid to hear the answer. So, I waited. Waited for her to show the courage that I apparently lacked. But without a word she came and stood over me, and I watched as she bent and gave me a chaste kiss on my forehead.

The faint scent of lavender filled my nose again. However, this time it brought only memories instead of the nausea I experienced that first day I was sick. It was astonishing how a few simple words could change your life completely and make you see things in a different light. Beatrix was no longer a dilemma to be solved, but a pleasant recollection to look back on fondly. She brushed the back of her hand against my cheek.

"Farewell, William."

I watched her hips sway under her farthingale and heard her skirts swishing across the wooden floor as she left me lying there to contemplate my own state.

"His Majesty has sent me to check on you," Blantyre announced sometime later. Grace had brought me a bowl of soup, and I was enjoying it most eagerly having not eaten in several days.

I looked up from my bowl, taking particular notice of the scowl on Blantyre's face. "Is something amiss?" I tilted the bowl to drain the remaining contents, sledging the bottom with my spoon.

"You know what is amiss, Broune." He sat down beside my bed and folded his arms over his chest. He looked agitated and it probably wasn't from his unappealing whey-colored doublet that hung open in disarray.

Setting the bowl down, I silently picked up what remained of my bread and shoved it into my mouth. I was in no mood to squabble with him over Lady Beatrix's hurt feelings.

"What's done is done, Blantyre," I said around the bread. "I have no control over what I said in my sleep. It is not how I would have liked to have broken the news to her, but there is nothing to be done for it now, and I'm glad it's done."

He gawked at me. "You hurt her terribly," he fumed.

"And I am sorry for that," I countered. "But it is done, and I haven't the heart to try to win her back. Look on the bright side, now you can pursue her. You know you have wanted her for months."

"That's beside the point," he thundered. My eyebrows shot up in surprise, not at the truth of my accusation, but at his admittance to it. He stood to his feet. "If you weren't my friend, I'd have half a mind to challenge you."

I sighed and turned to Grace who had taken up permanent care of me. I nodded toward the tray on my lap, and she took the hint, removing it immediately.

"But you won't because you know it is the right thing for me to do. And you know I am the better swordsman."

"Humph," he mumbled as he stood and walked to the end of my bed where he strode back and forth. "How can this be the right thing for you to do? You are giving up a title and money. Money, man! You would never want for anything. Your children would never want for anything. And she is beautiful. You're going to regret this decision," he said in finality as he chewed on his thumbnail and continued to pace.

Perhaps I would regret it, but I wasn't about to admit that to him. Instead, I said, "What day is it?"

He stopped shuffling his feet and glared at me. It's Sunday."

"What day of the month is it?"

"It's the third day of March. Why?"

"Deuce it." I threw back the blankets and swung my feet over the side of the bed. The cool air hitting my bare skin raised gooseflesh all over my body.

"God's teeth, William!" Blantyre held his arm up to shield his eyes. "Have you forgotten you wear no clothes?"

"Nay, but I forgot about your sensitive eyes." The jest solicited a chuckle from him.

"Where are you going? What has you in such a dither?"

I pulled my breeches on then looked around for my tunic—any tunic—that I could wear until I could get some proper clothing. The clothes I had worn on the day I fell ill were nowhere to be found. "Where are my clothes?" I bellowed.

Blantyre stood transfixed at the foot of my bed. "Your maid probably took them to be laundered. Calm down. What is the rush?"

I shoved my feet into my boots then stood on shaky legs. After days abed, my feet refused to cooperate. I fell back onto the bed and cursed as I scrambled to stand again. Taking a slow, wobbly step, I gained confidence and strength with every step toward the door.

"Now hold a minute!" Blantyre stopped me, laying a hand on my shoulder. "You can't go out there without a shirt on. What has gotten into you?"

I looked down then at my bare chest. "I've got to get to Ailsa. She was to marry Seton on the first day of March if her brother did not reach Edinburgh in time. Do you know if Nicholas Blackburn has come into town?"

Blantyre stared at me as if I had just inquired whether the Queen of England had come for supper. "I know not," he finally responded.

I ran a hand through my hair. "I need my clothes!"

"All right, man," he said, holding his hands up in a calming fashion. "I'll call for someone to fetch your valet." He moved toward the door then stopped before opening it. "I almost forgot." He reached into his pocket and pulled out a missive sealed with an unknown stamp. "Hamilton heard you were recovering and sent this. I believe it has to do with Bothwell."

I took the letter but did not open it. "Bothwell is the least of my worries right now." I stared at Blantyre, waiting for him to leave and find me some clothes.

He turned back toward the door. "What will you do if she has already married him?"

What would I do indeed? A hundred scenarios ran through my mind, including thoughts of snapping Seton's head from his body, and pulling him asunder, limb by limb. Instead, I settled for something more plausible, like stealing Ailsa away and fleeing to England.

"I'll worry about that when the time comes. Now fetch my valet and make haste."

~35~

March 1591

William

I did not get far. I made it down the hallway toward the front of the palace when a footman approached me. "Sir, His Majesty has requested your presence. He is in his antechamber."

Knowing I had no choice, I frustratedly turned and retraced my steps and soon found myself in the king's chamber. His Majesty sat at leisure playing some game of cards with two of his English favorites, Robert Bowes and Roger Aston, and the Chancellor, Lord Thirlestane. I avoided Thirlestane's eyes, as it was his position that James had promised to me, should I conduct the witch trials of North Berwick to his satisfaction.

"My friend is back from the dead." James motioned for the young boy who held his cards to lay them upon the table. He leaned back in his chair to inspect me. "You do look a little worse for wear, William. How are you feeling?"

"I have been better, Your Grace." I swept a glance toward the other players and noticed that their round must be over, as they had all laid their cards down and turned their attention to me.

The king waved a hand to a nearby chair. "Come, sit, have a drink with us. We were just finishing our fifth round of Maw. Thirlestane has jinked it again."

I felt my throat tighten at the thought of being delayed. The king loved cards and particularly this game. Play could go on half the night.

"I do not wish to disrupt your game, Your Grace. I have some business to attend to and would like to see to it before sundown. If I may be excused—"

"Nay, you may not."

Aston, a small-statured man with hands bearing neatly trimmed nails and skin as delicate as any woman's dealt the cards for the next round, laying a hand for me at the empty seat. "Sit," The king commanded.

I took a deep breath then sat down, picking the cards up with hesitation. Bowes spoke up. "Rumor hasss it that you are the lead inquisitor in the current witch trialsss." The man eyed me; his lengthy drawing of syllables accented his interest in my occupation.

"Aye," I said, not elaborating. I arranged my cards in my hand as the king grunted beside me. I snuck a look at him from the corner of my eye and noticed the smirk that had settled on his lips. His card holder was arranging His Majesty's cards as well, so James took a swig of wine while he waited.

"Have you worked closely with Deputy Bailiff Seton then?"

At the mention of Seton, I felt my insides tighten. Straightening, I tried to squelch my disgust. "I am acquainted with him."

"Are we here to talk business or enjoy the game?" James quipped. We began the round and the fast-paced play had my head spinning. "William, if you had that card in your hand all along you could have robbed the pack at the beginning. Are you not thinking clearly?" The king, who depended heavily on others to hold his cards and sometimes give him suggestions as what to play, was always quick to point out the mistakes of others. That was one reason why I did not enjoy playing games with him.

"Your Grace, I just drew that card."

"You should cut the man some slack, Your Majesty. Didn't you say he has just recovered from a most debilitating illnessss?" Bowes leaned with one elbow on the table and casually tossed down a card.

"Humph," James mumbled. The play continued, and within

minutes, the round was over, and Thirlestane had won the first trick. The game continued for three more rounds with Thirlestane winning another and His Majesty taking the next two.

After Bowes took the fifth trick, I saw my opportunity. Knowing how much the king hated wasting his time on those he felt were not worthy opponents, I made my move.

"Your Grace, as you can see, I am not feeling my best. I fear the fever I sustained for several days has affected my thinking. I beg to be released so that I may see to my errand."

"Nay, you may not leave. I have a matter of importance to discuss with you. Gentleman," he turned to the other three men, "please excuse me and Sir William." The men stood, and the Groom Porter, who had been standing behind the king's card holder, began gathering the cards and what booty the king had accumulated.

It wasn't until the room cleared and I was left alone with the king that I remembered the missive that I had sent to him that first day I had fallen ill. I hoped now that this is what he wished to speak with me about. Perhaps he had already sacked Seton and had sent him back to North Berwick, well away from Ailsa and any further meddling.

I stood waiting for the king to start the conversation. But once he opened his mouth, I wished I were anywhere but here standing before him.

"It has come to my attention that you have laid aside any intentions toward Her Majesty's lady-in-waiting, Lady Beatrix Ruthven, before receiving pardon from me to do so." His brow had sunk to a deep valley between his eyes, and his downturned mouth made it clear what he thought of my decision.

"Your Grace, apparently I talk in my sleep."

His brows lifted at that, and his melancholy eyes took on a look of astonishment. "Most interesting. And what did you say in your sleep?"

"I do not know. But evidently it had something to do with Ailsa Blackburn, the scribe's daughter of whom I wrote to you."

The king stepped closer to me; his shoulders sagged in relief. "Ah, it was only some feverish mumblings. Surely Lady Ruthven can forgive your incoherent gumming and make concessions." He laid a hand on my shoulder and squeezed in a satisfactory conclusion. When I did not answer, he dropped his hand. "Did you admit to having feelings for this woman?"

"Nay, I had just awoken from several days of fevered sleep. My thoughts were not coherent, and I was incapable of making much of an argument." I failed to mention how little of an argument that would have been.

"Well then, there you have it. Explain to her that you would like a chance to woo her once more. According to Her Majesty, the woman dotes on you something terrible."

I stood staring at the toe of my left boot, noticing there was a scuff mark there that Reeves had missed when polishing them. I looked to the other boot to see if there were similar marks, but the king's voice disturbed my thoughts.

"William, you will speak with Lady Ruthven. I am most aggrieved at this development, and Her Majesty is very disappointed as well. We take great interest in the well-being of our friends. This is for your benefit, and you will not put off the bride that we have chosen for you."

I lifted my eyes to the king, feeling the weight of his pronouncement. I considered the danger in contradicting him. We had been friends for a long time, and I usually went along with any job he tasked me with or any plan he had for me. Everyone did. But how far could I push this issue and what would be the consequences should I anger him? I took a deep breath before summoning the strength to answer.

"Your Majesty, I appreciate your interest in my affairs. You have been most gracious to me and allowed me opportunities, many of which I did not deserve. I will be forever grateful to you and Her Majesty for your benevolence. However, as I told you in my letter, I cannot see this betrothal through, nor do I wish to." I paused, unsure of how he would receive my next words. "I love another and therefore cannot attach myself to Lady Ruthven and subject her to an unhappy marriage."

James stared at me in disbelief. His nostrils flared, and his lip curled slightly as if in disgust. "What on earth does love have to do with it?" His voice heightened into a shrill ring. "You came from nothing, you *had* nothing until I gave you a position at my court." I flinched as if it were his fist hitting me instead of his words. It was true, I had been a beneficiary of his good will only because of the connections my father had to his mother. I was not born into this noble life, and for the first time, I felt uncomfortably out of place here. I also felt suddenly aware that our friendship had only been one of convenience, built upon what I could do *for* him. Now I stood questioning the depth of our friendship.

"You will continue to have nothing if you insist on refusing the hand of benevolence that has been proffered you." He turned his back on me and strode across the room. James drew near the window and stared blankly out for a moment. Then with renewed vigor, he continued his lecture. "Who is this woman? How will she fit into your life here? You have ambition, William. Do not throw it all away for a chit of no consequence. What would your father think? Evidently you have not sought his counsel, for I believe him to be a man of common sense that would not approve of this match."

At the mention of my father, I felt my resolve strengthen. He too had come from nothing and made a name for himself at court by the power of his own good character. And he too had married a woman that many thought to be beneath him, and it had not damaged his reputation one bit as far as I could tell. However, one thing separated my father from me in this situation, and that was that I would marry for love. I would not live with the regret and sorrow that he had lived with all those years simply because he had not taken hold of the opportunity when it presented itself to him.

"Actually, I *have* spoken with my father, and he supports my decision."

James jerked his head toward me, his mouth gaping.

"Unbelievable." He scratched the whiskers on his cheek then stroked his beard thoughtfully. Turning back to the window, he leaned an arm against the wall and spoke nothing for the space of several minutes. I watched him, trying to determine what thoughts were running through his mind. The silence was like a clamoring bell, and the longer he stood thinking, the more anxious I became.

A knock interrupted our ruminations. I had hoped that the interruption would be my means of dismissal. However, when David Seton appeared at the door dressed in what looked to be a new doublet and trunks, with his straw-colored hair pulled back into a slick queue, irritation pricked at me. Were these the fresh garments of a newly-married man? And what's more, had the king not taken my counsel concerning him?

"Ah, Bailiff Seton," James was saying, motioning the man into his chamber and waving the guard away who had let the blackguard in. "Do join us."

Seton crossed the room and bowed majestically before the king. His apparel may have improved considerably since the first time I saw the man, but he still looked like a rat in men's clothing. A strand of hair had pulled loose from its tie and hung unstylishly out of sorts above his left ear, and his hose bore a tiny hole above his right knee. I tamped down the urge to point out his unkempt appearance.

"Your Majesty, I hope I am not disturbing you." He took James's hand and kissed the ruby ring the king wore on his third finger.

The king cleared his throat. "I was just having a most interesting conversation with an old friend." He motioned toward me. "I do believe you know Sir William Broune."

Seton turned, and the smile that had graced his lips fell instantly. "We are acquainted," he said, as his eyes roved over me from head to heel.

I wanted desperately to ask him about his nuptials and whether they had actually taken place. But given the fact that Ailsa was a sensitive topic with the king at the moment, I refrained. In addition, I didn't want to give James the impression that my accusations against

Seton had anything to do with my feelings toward Ailsa. For they did not. I had not liked the man from the moment I met him.

I nodded to him but did not speak. Instead, I allowed Seton and the king to discuss whatever it was that had brought the bailiff here. The tension in my chest brought on by my urgent desire to go find Ailsa was abated slightly by my curiosity of what Seton had to say.

The old, drafty castle was constantly at battle with the fire that burned in the hearths. I strode to the waning flames and stoked them vigorously. With an ear open to their conversation, I pretended to be preoccupied with my task.

"Your Majesty, I have here a warrant for the arrest of a woman who has broken a legal agreement." His voice was smooth, and I got the distinct feeling that he was looking at me to get a reaction.

I straightened and turned to look at him. I measured the weight of the poker I held in my hand and considered whether it was heavy enough to knock the man out, should I decide to hit him with it. Of course, any violence in the king's presence would most assuredly mean my immediate imprisonment, but the result would have almost been worth it.

I stepped forward before the king could respond. "I do hope you are not referring to the agreement that Rupert Marley and you entered into on behalf of his niece. I have filed a Stay of Pursuance on that bond, and you still have three days before you can act upon that contract any further."

"I do indeed refer to that pact." Seton took a step closer to me. "You have been sticking your nose into my business for a while now. I wouldn't doubt if you know where my betrothed is. In fact, I would venture to say that you have probably assisted her in some way." He pushed his fist into his other hand, and I could hear the joints of his finger bones crackling under the pressure.

The king looked from Seton to me. "Bailiff Seton, Sir William has been ill for the past several days. I doubt he knows anything about your betrothed."

Seton didn't take his eyes from me but spoke to the king from the corner of his mouth. "This is an interference that has been in the works for some time now, Your Grace. My betrothed did not show up on our wedding day, and I am sure that Sir William knows something about that, regardless of his illness."

"I do not know where she is," I said bitterly. I still gripped the iron poker in my hand and fought the urge to bludgeon the knave through his piggish skull.

James shook the fog from his head. Frowning, he said, "Whom is this chit that he speaks of, William?" The king turned his eyes on me, and I could feel my dignity slowly seeping out of my pores.

"Ailsa Blackburn, Your Grace." I looked up into the king's face, hoping to find a sliver of decency there. Would he call me out in front of Seton and demand I give my lover up in the name of justice?

"Ailsa Blackburn?" he said slowly, understanding dawning on him.

"Aye, Your Grace," Seton and I answered at the same time. The bailiff scowled at me but remained silent.

James turned his back on us and strolled across the room. When he reached the end, he turned and ambled back. He crossed one arm over his chest and pulled at the lobe of his ear with his other hand. Finally, he said, "When did you say the Stay of Pursuance expires?"

"In three days, Your Grace." I studied him closely. Seton had presented the king with the perfect opportunity to rid me of Ailsa, in order to bring Beatrix back into the picture for me to marry her as he and the queen wished.

"And what had you hoped to accomplish during the interim?" The king's eyes danced with mischief, but I would not give him the pleasure of seeing me squirm.

"She had hoped that her brother would reach Edinburgh from London, in order to verify that her uncle has no legal right to enter into any agreement on her behalf."

"Your Grace, I do not believe this brother actually exists. It is my belief that Mistress Blackburn has made the story up in order to be released from the agreement."

James lifted his brows at that. "Do you really want to marry a woman that would go to such lengths to avoid binding herself to you?"

Color crept up Seton's ears, burning a crimson red. He opened his mouth to rebuff the king's question but then changed his mind and closed it again. He balled his hands into fists at his side, then finally said, "I think she can be made to see reason."

I would have lunged at him, but the king's words cut through the air, bringing me to a halt. "You have three days. Three days to find the chit and bring her to me. I want to hear for myself about this brother of hers. I will not sign the arrest warrant, Seton. One of you will need to find her and bring her here on her own accord. I want to see this woman for myself and see what it is about her that has two grown men squabbling over her."

"But Your Grace, the warrant will draw her out. It will force others to give her up or face punishment for aiding her."

"She has broken no law yet, Seton. Let it be known that the king has requested her presence in his privy chamber. I will decide the matter then. That is all."

The king waved us both away in dismissal, but I held back until Seton had departed.

"Your Grace—"

"I'll hear no more about it, William. I will decide once I have met the woman."

"But," I hurried to append, "please keep in mind that this is the same woman whose mother was arrested by Seton and charged with witchcraft only weeks ago. There is no love in his heart for her. He merely wishes to possess her like an object that can be bought and sold."

James looked at me with his flaccid blue eyes. "As long as he can provide for her, that is all that matters. Besides, I would think a marriage to the daughter would protect the mother from any further accusations." James heaved a sigh. Clearing his throat, I sensed his attempt at making peace. "I leave for Falkland Palace in the morning. Send word to me there when you have found her." He held a slender finger up to me in warning. "Do not do anything in haste concerning this woman, William. If I find that you have attached yourself to her before I have had a chance to make a judgement, there will be ramifications."

My knock sounded hollow, and I shifted my weight as I stood waiting for Ailsa to answer the door. An overwhelming sense of dread filled me the longer I stood there with no answer from within.

"Ye are not the man she was to marry." Startled, I turned abruptly. A young woman stood on her threshold two doors down, holding a small child on her hip. Her mousy brown hair was pulled back in a severe knot but wild tendrils fell over her eyes, and she brushed at them with the back of her hand.

"Nay, I am a friend. Have you seen Ailsa then?"

"Not in a couple of days." She shifted the child nervously from one hip to the other, and I noticed her gaze would not meet mine. She knew something.

"Do you have an idea of where she has gone? Is Mistress Blackburn with her?"

"Now why would I tell ye anything? How do I know that ye are not in cahoots with that nasty man who threatened her and is trying to force her to marry him?" The child began to whimper, and she shifted his weight once more.

"Don't lump me in with his lot," I said, with a little more force than necessary. She took a step back, sinking into the safety of her doorway.

"Please, Goodwife. I am trying to help Ailsa. If you could just tell me where she has gone. Has her brother arrived from London yet? Can you at least tell me that?"

"I don't know about no brother," she said. "Good day to ye." She curtseyed slightly then closed the door in my face. I stood there for a moment, contemplating my next course of action. Relief flickered in me when I heard the woman's door open once more. Perhaps she had changed her mind and would help me after all.

"Go on with ye," shouted her husband. "We don't need your kind lurking around here."

"My kind?" I spat out the words. "What is that supposed to mean?" I took a step forward and the man moved out of his house.

I turned and walked away from the man before a fight could ensue. "And don't ye show your face around here again," he called, as if he thought he had scared me away. I wasn't afraid of him. I was just afraid for Ailsa.

~36~

March 1591

William

I returned to my room on the High Street well after sundown. I had no luck in finding Ailsa and no idea where else to look for her.

"Sir William." Master Gordon, the bookseller, stopped me on the stairs leading up to my room when I arrived home. He was just closing up shop when I stepped inside the building, and he shuffled over to me, his wife holding his arm for support. "The missus happened to remember another friend of Ailsa's. Perhaps you could find her there if you've had no luck thus far."

I had approached Gordon earlier in the day. I remembered that he had known Ailsa's father and thought he may know of other acquaintances of hers or her family's.

"I have had no luck, Master Gordon. I've walked the length of this city, from the Grassmarket and Castlehill to the Canongate and Holyroodhouse, to no avail. I would appreciate any other suggestions you have to offer."

Mistress Gordon reached out a hand to me. "Ye need to take care of yourself, Sir William. We can hear the tiredness in your voice. Get some rest. I'm sure Ailsa is resting peacefully at the McMurray's home. Bess is Ailsa's closest friend, and I cannot believe Martin didn't think to mention her when ye asked about Ailsa's friends earlier."

"My mind is getting old, dear one." Gordon said in his defense.

I rubbed a hand over my eyes. They burned and felt like they were full of sand. "Bess McMurray? Where does she live?"

"Master McMurray, her father, is a chandler. His family lives above his shop on Grey's Close."

"The chandler shop," I repeated. I turned wearily to go back out, but Gordon stopped me.

"Ye are about to fall over, man. Ye should take my wife's advice and get some rest. Mistress Gordon gives excellent advice, and I am wont to follow it whenever she gives it." He eyed me and tilted his head toward his wife as if to communicate some mental male message to me.

"As if ye ever follow my advice willingly, husband!" The woman swatted her husband on his arm and chuckled sweetly. "Ye do beat all, my love."

I took a deep breath and considered the Gordons' suggestion. I wanted desperately to find Ailsa, but I felt like I was about to collapse. My health had not completely recovered, and my body was fatigued. My brain told me I could help Ailsa better if I didn't drive myself into the grave in the meantime.

"Here, dear." Mistress Gordon fished in a basket that hung from her arm. She drew out a small package and thrust it toward me. "We had a meat pie left over from lunch. Eat this and build your strength up."

I took the pie from her hand. "Thank you, Goodwife. I appreciate your concern."

"Aye, well. Ye need to be at your best if ye are to help Ailsa. We have known her since she was a wee thing trailing behind her father as he conducted his business in town. If she is in danger from this bailiff as ye have said, then ye must take care."

I ate my meat pie then fell into bed exhausted not long after. I felt as if I had just closed my eyes when I heard a soft shuffling sound at the door. I reached beneath my pillow, feeling for the sgian dubh that I kept there. I wrapped my fingers around the knife, taking comfort in the smooth dips and curves of the Celtic knotwork that had been fashioned into the handle. Then I waited to see who was intruding.

The light of the moon was hidden in cloud cover, making it difficult to see in the darkness. A faint glow through the single window was the only light to be had, and as the figure pushed the door open, I could not make out the form. I gripped the sgian dubh tighter. Had Bothwell sent someone to spy on me? Hamilton's letter, which I had finally read as I ate my supper, had indicated that several witnesses had come forward now to say that Bothwell had been involved in some mischief intended to stir up trouble for the king. Hamilton had provided the names of several people for me to talk with who could give me more details about Bothwell's crimes.

The figure stumbled quietly across the room. I blinked several times, trying to force my tired eyes to focus and make out some attribute that might help me identify them, should they try to rob me— or harm me. The body—whoever it was—made their way toward me. As they drew closer, I heard a thumping noise as they fell forward, grabbing the table to steady themselves. They had tripped over my boots that I—for probably the first time in my life—had not set neatly beside my bed.

I held my breath and watched as the person felt around on the table as if looking for something. "Hmm," I heard them mumble softly in confusion as they gave up their search on the table and moved toward the bed. I stiffened in anticipation, awaiting the moment when I would make my move before they could discover me.

The intruder walked to the side of the bed and removed their cloak. Tossing it onto the foot of the bed, they sat down and bent over, as if they would remove their boots. I breathed a prayer of thanks that I had the foresight to scoot to the far side of the bed to avoid being sat on.

I heard their boots drop to the floor, and they let out a little sigh. Sitting on the edge of the bed for a moment, they sat in complete silence, not moving, as if they were contemplating their next action. I braced myself and as the body made as if they would lie down on the bed, I made my move.

In a flash I threw my arm around the intruder and pushed the knife against their neck. I covered their mouth with my other hand, so they couldn't cry out. Their cries were muffled by my hand, but their body wiggled violently as they tried their best to slip from the hold I had on them.

"Who are you? Who sent you?" I asked into their ear, aware that I had not removed my hand so that they could speak. "Give me your name and the name of the person who sent you, and I may consider giving you a chance to repent before I cut your throat." More muffled cries ensued, and I found although I was much larger than the intruder, they were hard to hold onto in their thrashing about.

I expected the hard, muscular body of a male youth. What I held in my arms though was the soft, curved body of a woman, or a wildcat perhaps. That remained to be seen.

The woman jerked so violently that her hair fell lose from where she had it tied at the nape of her neck. But in the same moment that her locks fell about her shoulders, she drew back her arm and elbowed me right in the gut. I felt the air gush out of me at the unexpected motion and I almost—*almost*—lost my grip on her. Just then the sweet smell of heather wafted under my nose. I loosened my grip slightly but did not release her.

"Ailsa?"

She jerked once more and moaned an answer into my hand before I removed it from her face.

"Mother of God, William!"

The profane exclamation startled me, and I released the remaining hold I had on her.

"Ail—"

But before I could say another word, she had turned in my arms and flipped me onto the bed, pinning me down as she sat on top of me. How this petite woman could easily wrestle my towering height and weight that was twice her size so easily was a testament to how completely besotted with her I actually was.

"Are ye trying to kill me?"

"I thought you a spy."

"A spy! Ha!" She peered down at me, and if the faint moonlight hadn't indicated the annoyance on her face, the sound of her voice would have. "Where have ye been?"

I tried to sit up, but she held me down firmly, and I gave up the struggle immediately. If she thought this was some kind of punishment, she had a lot to learn.

"I fell ill while I was at Holyroodhouse. I couldn't get out of bed for several days and slept incoherently most of the time. Several people died from the same illness I had. It was very serious."

A faint mewing slipped from her lips, and I felt her grip ease. "Oh," she finally said. "I'm so sorry."

I held the gaze of her unfocused eyes and watched as several emotions flickered across her face. I was a cad for playing on them, but I couldn't help myself. "I almost died," I said pitifully.

A slight intake of her breath led me to know that my emotional dagger had hit its mark. She leaned forward, placing her small hand on my bare chest. When her skin touched mine, she tried to draw back, but I grabbed her hand and held it steady. She wasn't getting out of this situation she put herself into that easily.

She yelped. "Ye don't have a shirt on." She tugged once more, trying to free her hand from my grasp.

"I don't have *any* clothes on, Ailsa. You have disturbed a weary man's sleep."

She wiggled harder then, and I released her hand so that I could lay my hands on her hips. "Shh," I soothed, and she finally stopped squirming.

"I thought ye had abandoned me, William Broune," she whispered into the dark. Her voice cracked when she said my name, and a tiny hiccup escaped her.

"I'm sorry. I should have sent you a message when I first fell ill.

But there were a few other matters that I needed to attend to, and they were first and foremost on my mind."

"Such as?"

I chuckled. "Such as Lady Beatrix Ruthven."

At the sound of Beatrix's name, Ailsa stiffened and tried to remove herself from off of me. I gripped her hips tighter.

"Why ye little—"

"Hush, Ailsa, and let me tell you why." She stopped wriggling once again. "I had to tell the king that I could no longer pursue his wishes for the two of us to wed. I told him I loved someone else, and therefore I could not marry her."

Silence ensued as Ailsa took in what I said. Finally, she said softly, "Ye love someone else?"

"Aye. Can you guess who that is?"

She giggled then slapped her hand over her mouth. Another hiccup escaped and then a sob. "Oh, ye impossible man."

I wrapped my arms around her as I sat up. Holding her tightly, I kissed her, drinking in the sweet smell of her hair. I inhaled deeply then nuzzled against her, running my fingertips down the slender column of her neck. I resisted the urge to touch every inch of her body, to run my hands over every alluring curve and to taste the salt of her enticing skin. All my senses were alert to her, every receptor begging for more sensation. Like a lodestone drawing iron, her pull on me was hard to resist, and I fought the urge to take her and make her mine right there upon the bed. At a painfully slow pace, I trailed kisses down her neck, determined to not rush the feast set before me. When I felt her trembling beneath me, I paused. "You are cold."

"Not anymore," she said, more than a little breathless.

"I should start a fire." I moved to pull away.

"Ye already have. Don't ye dare stop now."

I chuckled, and I could feel her smile against my mouth. I leaned back on the bed and pulled her with me, my lips never leaving her skin. I rolled her over onto the bed as I bit softly against the lobe of her ear, the base of her throat, the smooth roundness of her shoulder.

The soft sounds that escaped her left me breathless too. I would have continued my trek downward until Ailsa sighed and laid her small hands against my chest to get my attention.

"William," she said quietly, "what am I going to do?" She pushed me back against the bed and sat up, propping her head upon her arm to look at me. Her hair brushed against my chest, driving maddening thoughts into my head. I twirled a strand of chestnut curls around my finger, while hers stroked lightly against my skin.

"We'll figure out something," I said, trying to clear my head. I dropped back onto my pillow, dragging deep breaths into my lungs to slow my pulse. Our problem loomed above us like a threatening storm cloud, yet I didn't want to think about that at the moment. Her hands on me sent white hot sparks shooting to my core and my flesh ached from the heat of her. All I wanted to do was succumb to the purifying fire that was Ailsa.

Lying as we were, the faint glow of moonlight cast silvery shadows across her face, illuminating her amber eyes and soft mouth. She pinched her bottom lip between her teeth before speaking. "I'm sorry for dragging ye into this."

I lifted my head to get a better look at her. "Do not apologize for something in which I willing entangled myself."

"Aye, but the fact remains that ye had a path laid out before ye, simple and tidy."

"There was nothing simple about my life. Every move has been skillfully planned, every word considered, every thought carefully constructed. In fact, very little about my life has actually been ordered by my own hand."

"Yet, ye've managed to do quite well for yourself. I don't know why ye'd want to throw it all away." She looked away from me then as her breath caught on her last words. I watched her silently for a moment before reaching up and stroking the back of my finger across her cheek.

"I'd give my own life's blood if it meant it would make you happy. I'd abandon any scheme, forfeit any honor, surrender any possession, if that is what you asked of me."

She touched a single fingertip to my lips to stay my words. "I would never ask that of ye." Brushing her finger across my lips, she then laid her palm against my face. The whiskers there scraped her soft palm. "But ye have no idea how glad I am of your devotion." With the pad of her thumb, she then traced my chin, studying it intently. "Ye have an indentation here."

"Aye" My mouth quirked, and she dipped her head shyly.

"I'm sorry; I can't seem to stop touching ye."

"I'm rather enjoying it."

She dropped her hand from my face and rested it once again upon my chest. Her touch drifted down the hard plane of my abdomen and sent another bolt of energy through me. In the stillness of the room, I was sure she could hear my heart pounding out a frenzied tattoo. "Are you trying to drive me mad?"

"What do ye mean?" She stopped when understanding took hold. "Oh." She pulled her hand away and pushed herself up. Abruptly, she asked, "Why did ye not start a fire earlier?"

"I was too tired. I walked this city all day looking for you."

She ran the back of her hand across my cheek one last time, and I felt my body shiver again in response. "Ye are cold as well. Let me start the fire." She removed herself from the bed and wrapped her cloak about her once more. She had no idea what she did to me. But I would let her think it was the cold. "Where did you place the candle? I couldn't find it on the table when I came in."

"It's here." I lit the candle and handed it to her. While she was pushing the kindling around in the hearth, I dressed.

"Have you been staying here?" I asked as I pulled my tunic over my head and reached for my breeches.

"Aye," she responded, not turning around. "Nick has not come. I ran out of time and had to do something."

"If you have been staying here, why was there no fire banked?"

"I didn't want to leave any evidence behind of my being here. The first night I didn't even light a candle for fear of being discovered."

"You must have been very cold," I said, standing close behind her now.

She turned suddenly, surprised at my proximity. "Aye, it…I was cold." She stumbled over her words. I nodded in understanding, taking great pleasure in making her squirm. Now that the darkness had been dispelled, her courage had fled and her shyness had returned. I ran my hands up and down her arms several times in an effort to create friction to warm her. Then I took her hands in mine and laced my fingers between hers. I pulled her closer.

"Where is your mother, Ailsa?" I brought her hands to my lips and kissed them to encourage warmth.

"She is with my friend, Bess, and her family. I thought it best we not be together in case Seton found us. If one of us was discovered at least the other would be free."

"Mm hmm," I answered, not taking my lips from her hands. I kissed the inside of her wrist and a little squeak escaped her lips.

"What am I to do now, William? Nick still has not come. I can't stay in hiding here forever."

I leaned my forehead against hers and closed my eyes. "I wish I could say we will marry, but that is not possible right now."

She stiffened and pulled away from me. "What kind of game are ye playing?"

I caught her by the shoulders before she could get away from me. "It is no game, Ailsa. But the king has warned me that I am to bring you before him and Seton so that he can make a decision as to whether he will hold you to the agreement your uncle made."

Ailsa gasped. "Ye wouldn't!" She jerked away from me, a look of fear in her eyes. "I will not go, William. I will not allow another man to force me into a marriage that I do not want. I do not care if the king of Scotland says I must. I will not marry that man." Her words rushed out, and every syllable tore at me.

"Ailsa, I understand. But if I marry you before the king has had a chance to make his pronouncement, I risk judgement on my head."

"So, it's my freedom for yours, is it?"

I stood stunned at her words. She could have carved me from chin to groin with a dagger, and it could not have hurt more. But I supposed that was exactly what I was saying. I was so concerned at the king's reaction, that I forgot that he was just as likely to rule in Seton's favor as in mine. In fact, given the fact he wanted me to marry Beatrix, it was likely I would not be the winning party in a judgement where Ailsa was concerned.

Silence hung over us as Ailsa put a kettle of water on the fire and prepared to heat the spiced wine. Once it was ready, I sat down across from her with a small package in my hand. I held the peace offering out to her, and she eyed it as if it were a dead rodent.

"What is that?" She poured the wine into our cups and set one down in front of me.

"A promise," I said, not taking my eyes off of her.

She unwrapped the parcel and drew a sharp breath at the sight of the brooch within. Covering her mouth with her hand, she spoke barely above a whisper.

"*Of earthly joys thou art my choice*," she intoned. She stared at it for several moments, rubbing her thumbs over the inscribed words. "'Tis beautiful. But are ye sure this is what ye want? Am I truly your choice?"

I took her hands in mine. "You have gotten under my skin and into my blood. You've messed with my head and sometimes you've even stolen the breath from my lungs." Her mouth fell open, but I continued before she could say anything. "Yet I have never felt more alive than when I am with you." Her lips began to tremble, and I pulled her closer. "And if you will have me, I'd like to spend the rest of my life showing you just how sure I am of my choice." Then I kissed her. Slow and long and until I almost forgot why we were here. When I drew back, her eyes were shining with unshed tears.

She lifted the heart-shaped piece from the cloth and held it up to the candlelight. When the illumination of the flame hit the garnet, it gleamed a fiery ray of light. She pinned it on her dress, right above her heart. "I will never take it off."

I admired the jewel for a moment, then said, "That is my promise to you, Ailsa. No matter what happens know that I want to make you my wife. It may not happen when I want it to, but I will make it happen, you have my word."

A sob escaped her lips, and she reached a small, shaky hand and wiped a tear from her eye. "I will hold ye to that, William Broune. Ye will never be free from me now."

I took a sip of wine, and we drank in silence for a spell until Ailsa remembered something of interest.

"There has been another arrest on witchcraft charges," she said as she took another drink from her cup.

"Who is the unlucky person this time?"

"Euphame MacCalzean."

I looked at her in surprise. "Effie? Really?"

"Ye know her then?" She held her cup gingerly in her hands and blew gently on the hot liquid within.

"Aye. She was involved in a lawsuit some years back involving Beatrix's uncle, Archibald Ruthven."

"She is the sister-in-law to Seton, married to his first wife's brother," she stated matter-of-factly.

"How do you know that?"

She didn't answer for several moments, only sat drinking her wine. Then she looked at me almost sheepishly and said, "I visited her in the tolbooth."

"You what? How on earth did you get in?"

She shifted uncomfortably in her seat but did not look at me. Finally, she said, "I sort of bent the truth a little."

"Really? And what truth was that?"

"I may have told the Mistress McCollum that ye sent me to minister to the new prisoner."

I stared at her incredulously. "You lied to the tolbooth gaoler to convince her to let you in?" I laughed dryly and shook my head in disbelief.

"Please don't say that. I am ashamed of my falsehood, but I needed to get information. I actually went there to see if she had seen or heard from ye. I could trust her, for she seemed to be keen on ye the night we visited there to see Geillis."

"Keen on me? The woman is old enough to be my mother."

"All the same. She was cooperative with ye that night, and I sensed she had a soft spot for ye. I hoped that she would know something about where ye had been or maybe even seen ye. I just happen to be there when Euphame was brought in."

"You are very lucky that Seton didn't take you right then." I set my cup down a little harder than I intended, and the whole table shook under the force.

"Aye, but he isn't the one who brought her in. I suspect he was too much of a coward to actually do the arresting, seeing how she is family. What monster has his own in-laws arrested?"

"We *are* speaking of Seton. So, what happened next?"

"Mistress McCollum said she hadn't seen ye, and that is when I got the bright idea to tell her that was too bad, for I had hoped that ye had told her about me coming and that ye wanted me to see to the needs of the new prisoner."

"And she just let you right in?"

"Aye. She said she'd do anything for Sir William." The smug little expression on Ailsa's face was actually adorable, but I scowled to cover my amusement.

Ignoring her teasing, I said, "So, what did you find out from speaking with Effie?"

"Well, as ye know, she is a woman of some means. She told me that a couple of years ago, Seton's mother-in-law passed away. When she died, she left a good sum of money for Euphame and her husband, but her husband's sister received only a small portion. Seton and his wife were offended at the affront, and he and Euphame have been at odds ever since."

"So, if Seton has a wife, why is he pursuing you?"

"I asked Euphame the same thing. I hoped for an instant that I had found my way of escape, but alas, his wife gave up the ghost about a year or so ago. He is a free man."

I let out a low growl at that and pushed myself away from the table. "He may be a free man, but you are not a free woman." Leaning against the counter, I crossed my arms in front of me and looked at her. She refused to meet my gaze, and I was forced to go to her. "We'll figure out something, my sweetling. Why don't we get some sleep now, and we can talk further in the morning?"

Ailsa jerked her head toward me at that. "Sir, ye may have declared your love for me, but—"

"Relax, I was planning to sleep on the floor." Her shoulders sagged in apparent relief, and she blushed prettily at the misunderstanding. "If I may have but one blanket from the bed, I will lie here in front of the fire."

She nodded her head and watched as I pulled the counterpane from the bed.

"William," she spoke slowly as if she deliberated her words. I turned and looked at her, and her face had gone pale. "Do ye suppose that the Earl of Bothwell is a witch? Perhaps when the prisoner said *he will be taken*, she meant *killed*."

I paused, feeling like all my blood had drained from my body. "Murder is certainly within Bothwell's repertoire."

She worried her bottom lip between her teeth. "That would explain much."

My curiosity was piqued. "Did Euphame tell you something about the earl?"

Her brows drew together into a confused line, and she blinked as if deep in thought. "Actually," she said, as if puzzling out an intriguing riddle, "it wasn't *my* conversation with Euphame that shed light on the subject."

~37~

March 1591

Ailsa

William stared at me, his counterpane hanging in mid-air. He dropped the blanket and grabbed a chair from the table then turned it around and straddled it, in order that he might lean upon the back. "Start from the beginning," he urged.

I sighed and rubbed a hand across my forehead. The last few days had been so worrisome that I hoped I could remember everything that I had witnessed at the tolbooth.

"I only spoke to Euphame for a few minutes. Of course, she denied knowing anything about the witchcraft of which she was accused. She opened up freely to me about her family troubles though. She believes the accusations have something to do with the money and the land that she owns. She said her arrest is a deliberate attempt to get her out of the way and take her wealth."

"She has had a lot of family issues from what I understand," William threw in. "But I knew nothing of her relation to Seton. It is believable though that he would try to get rid of her. Look what he did to your mother."

"Aye. But I didn't get much further than that in our discussion, for shortly after entering her cell, Mistress McCollum came back and hurried me out. She said a representative from the king was there to question Euphame, and I would have to cut my visit short."

"A representative?" William questioned. "Who was it?

I shook my head in recollection. "I didn't recognize him, and he didn't say his name. But he had a very odd speech. He was English, but there was something about the way he spoke that made me think he might have some type of impediment."

William's forehead crinkled in thought. "Did he draw out his sounds at the end of his words?"

"Aye, that's it. Perhaps not an impediment, but a very unusual way of speaking. A little unsettling."

William stood then, shoving the chair away from himself. "He did seem awful curious about my job as the king's inquisitor. He kept asking me questions this afternoon."

"Who? Who is he?" I watched as William paced back and forth in front of the door, rubbing the dark stubble that had begun to grow on his cheeks. The floorboards groaned under the weight of his steps, and each one creaked out a different note.

"Robert Bowes. He is an English diplomat. He was playing cards with His Majesty when I went to speak to the king."

"Well, I departed immediately once Mistress McCollum warned me of his coming. But what she didn't know was that I actually didn't leave the tolbooth. I had pressed myself into a small recess in the wall under the cover of shadow and listened to his inquisition."

William stopped pacing and looked at me. "Ailsa Blackburn, you are going to find yourself in a lot of trouble one of these days. What you think is cunningness is actually ill-judgement. You are playing with fire where the witches and the king are concerned. I would advise you to be very careful."

I stood and went to him. "Your concern is admirable. Truly." I kissed him on the cheek, but when he tried to wrap his arms around me, I pulled away quickly. "Anyway, I heard this man ask Euphame about her connection with the Earl of Bothwell. He wanted to know what her involvement was with the wax statue, and what words exactly were spoken over the figure on the night Bothwell brought it to her and Geillis." I paused my story. "Do ye remember Barbara and

Agnes talking about a wax figure?"

He nodded thoughtfully. "Aye, it was an image to represent His Majesty."

"Exactly. This Bowes fellow claims that Euphame was involved with the enchantment and that she and Geillis were given the figure to roast upon the fire. He also told her that Barbara had already confessed that the purpose of roasting the figure was so that another should rule in His Majesty's place."

"So, Bowes thinks that Bothwell put the women up to this scheme. I wonder if he did it to put himself in James's place."

"Does it really matter who he wanted in the king's place? It is still treason nonetheless."

"True. And the method by which they have chosen to bring about this means is treacherous indeed. From my understanding, when the wax figure begins to melt, the subject it represents feels the pain of it."

I covered my mouth in horror. "'Tis truly an evil endeavor. And to think, I once believed Geillis to be innocent in these matters."

William put his arm around my shoulder. "You are a compassionate woman, Ailsa. You want to see the good in people. That is an admirable quality. But the problem is we do not know who to believe. There are so many accusations flying around at the moment. And people will say just about anything to relieve the pain of their interrogations. Seton is a vile man who will stop at nothing to get the confession that he desires. I pity Mistress MacCalzean when Seton gets his hands on her. If there is underlying malice in his heart toward her, she doesn't stand a chance."

I shook my head in dismay. "Bowes also claimed that Euphame and Geillis roasted a black toad that had been given them by none other than Dr. Fian. They hung the toad for three days and collected the juice in the shell of an oyster. And he claims that she asked an attendant in the king's chamber for a piece of clothing belonging to His Majesty to use with the image. The hope was that the bewitching would cause the pain of needles upon His Majesty and bring about his death."

"Who is this attendant?" William asked in alarm.

I shrugged. "I know not. He may have said her name, but it didn't stick with me."

Worry overshadowed William's face. "Is it any wonder that the king is so paranoid? The man sleeps with one eye open."

"Do you think the Bowes fellow is on the king's side? He is an agent of the Queen of England, after all."

"I'm not sure. But it does sound as if he has it out for Bothwell. I wonder if he is using these witch trials to pin accusations on the earl for political reasons or if there is some truth in Bothwell's involvement? And where is he getting all of this information? I sure missed a lot while on my sickbed."

"Everyone in Edinburgh knows the earl. He is a notorious blackguard," I said.

William nodded in agreement. "Aye, that he is. But why go about it by such arcane means? Bothwell has never been one to shy away from a fight. And he has plenty of backers, especially from the border earls. He could probably take the throne by force if he really wanted to."

"Then perhaps it is time to take these accusations against the earl a little more seriously. But it better be looked into quickly. It seems that all the witnesses against him are being burnt at the stake." I shuddered simply speaking the words.

~38~

March 1591

William

Two nights later I returned to my room on the High Street to check on Ailsa and bring her a few items to make her more comfortable. But as I made my way up the stairs to my room, I ran into her coming down the steps.

"William, I was just about to go out."

"I can see that." I stopped two steps down from her so that my eyes could be level with hers, and she swayed away from me and our close proximity.

"I was going to check on my mother and see if Nick has come yet."

"Didn't I ask you to stay put and out of sight? I laid my hand against the wall beside us, blocking her from moving any further down the stairs.

"Aye, ye did. But I cannot stay cooped up here for the rest of my life. I have some things I need to take care of."

"It is not for the rest of your life. It's only until your brother arrives."

She pulled her earasaid tighter about her and lifted her chin. "Well, how will I know if he has arrived if I don't go and check? He doesn't know where I nor my mother is. If our hiding places are good, he will never find us."

"You've got a point," I said, not removing my arm. "But it is getting dark. The more dangerous for you to be out and about." I leaned closer to her, and she laid her hands on my chest to keep me at a respectable distance.

"I have survived twenty-one years without your protection, William Broune. And walking in the dark unaccompanied has never been a problem before. Now if ye will excuse me, I have some business to take care of." She pushed against my chest, her small hands unable to budge the mountain before her.

"Ah, but you have never been engaged to a blackguard before. And you've never been in hiding for fear of your life. Perhaps you should heed my warning and make your way back up these stairs." I nodded toward the landing, refusing to move out of her way.

She huffed but turned and traipsed back to the top. When we reached my door, she said, "When this is all over, I'll trudge about wherever and whenever I please."

I stuck the key in the lock and replied, "When this is over, you will be my wife, and you won't *want* to leave my room." I pushed the door open and motioned for her to enter.

Something like the cross between a muffled scream and a pout came out of her mouth. "Oh, ye impossible man."

"Aye, you've said as much before," I retorted, shutting the door behind us. I placed a package on the table. "There is a jar of honey and some lemon wafers in the package for you. I also brought you a journal and some more ink."

Ailsa rushed to the table to open the items. Laying the honey and wafers aside, she grabbed the pot of ink and the journal and immediately sat down to write something.

"Well, that was quick. You already have something you want to jot down?"

"Aye," she said, not looking up from her task. "I want to make my list of reasons why I dislike you while they are fresh in my mind."

I chortled and sat another package down on the table.

"What's that?" she asked, looking up briefly from her writing.

"They are signed and sealed affidavits from several witnesses who claim to have knowledge of the Earl of Bothwell plotting against the king."

"Ye think that the Earl of Bothwell is the plotter the prisoner spoke of?"

"I have my suspicions."

"Were ye able to collect all of those today?"

"The past two days. But I can't leave them at the palace. As you know, there are those even in the king's court who cannot be trusted."

"It must be nice to be able to move about the city and not be cooped up indoors all day," she said sardonically as she continued to write.

"I *have* been cooped up indoors for most of the past two days. Barbara Napier has been on trial."

Ailsa stopped writing and lifted her eyes from her task. "Barbara?" She swallowed hard. "Have ye reached a verdict?"

I blew out a frustrated breath and sat down across from her. "We did, but it wasn't what the king wanted."

"What? What does that mean?"

"We didn't feel there was enough evidence to convict Barbara of witchcraft. The king disagreed and told us to search our hearts. He then adjourned the hearing until three days hence."

Ailsa stared at me, her pen suspended in mid-air and dripping ink onto the page on which she was writing. "He won't take any other answer but execution, will he?"

"I'm afraid not."

"But what will ye do, William? Ye can't convict a woman just because the king wants ye to."

I closed my eyes and ran a hand across my forehead. I had been asking myself the same question for two days to no avail. My mind went back to Agnes' trial and subsequent execution. That woman had ensnared herself, and I still dealt with the guilt of the conviction I helped hand down.

"I don't know, Ailsa," I finally said. "Sometimes I wish I had never come to court at all."

Ailsa tore the page on which she had been writing from her journal and neatly folded it. She reached out her hand and laid it atop mine.

"It is a difficult position ye are in. But I believe ye will do the right thing. She pulled my hand to her lips and kissed it softly. "Ye have a good heart, and ye will do the right thing," she said again. I watched as the little wisps of her hair brushed against the top of my hand and sent a surge of heat up my arm. Her faith in me was overwhelming— and humbling.

She handed the missive that she had torn from her journal to me, and I stared at it dumbly.

"What's this?"

"It is a letter instructing the reader that they may trust ye."

"I looked up at her in surprise. "What?"

She sighed. "It is a letter for ye to show the McMurrays. When ye go to check on my mother, they will not trust ye are who ye say ye are, for I have told them about David Seton, and they know the threat he is to me. They will be suspicious of ye, and therefore the letter will set their minds at ease, and they will know they can share information with ye about my mother. They may even let ye see her, although I wonder now if that is a good idea."

"Do you think it will upset her to see me? She may question where you are."

"That's what I am thinking too. Just make your inquiry discreetly. If they say she is all right then I trust them."

I tucked the missive into my pocket and grabbed the affidavits from the table. I slipped them into my desk drawer for safe keeping, along with the previous letters that Hamilton had sent concerning Bothwell. Spying the key that Bothwell had left on my table, I tucked it inside the stack of letters as well.

"If I am to go, I should leave at once. I am to host supper in the king's absence for a few of the dignitaries that are at court."

"Then ye best leave straightway. For the letter will also prove your identity to my brother, in case ye meet him when ye go check on our house."

"All right, but you will owe me a favor when I see you again." I kissed her quickly as I tried to repress the smile playing on my face.

I knocked thrice before someone answered at the McMurray residence. When the door finally opened, a short, middle-aged man stood before me. Worry lines creased his forehead, and his faded eyes studied me cautiously.

"May I help ye?"

"Good day to you, sir. My name is William Broune, and I am a friend of Ailsa's. She has asked me to check on her mother." I dug in my pocket and produced the slightly creased letter penned by Ailsa. "She has written a letter of introduction for me." I handed him the missive and watched as sure and steady hands unfolded the paper.

"How do I know that ye didn't pen this letter yourself?" His question surprised me, and I was momentarily speechless as I was not prepared for such a doubt.

But before I could recover the use of my tongue, a young woman stepped up behind him holding Sadie in her arms.

"Let me see it, Father. I know Ailsa's handwriting. I'll be able to tell if the letter is authentic."

"But ye cannot read, child," her father said.

"Aye, Ailsa has been teaching me. I've come a long way." She smiled a bright, pretty smile that made her eyes light up. A little dimple dented her cheek.

He handed the letter to his daughter, and she shifted the cat in her arms so that she may scan the contents of the missive more easily.

"You must be Bess," I said as she perused the note.

"Aye," she responded, looking up at me from under long, fair lashes. "And ye are indeed William Broune. I have heard much about ye."

Her father looked from her to me in confusion. "Is it safe, dear heart?"

"Aye, Father."

Master McMurray opened the door wider and motioned for me to enter.

"Forgive me, sir. But I think it best if Mistress Blackburn not see me. We felt it might disturb her and start her asking questions about Ailsa. Perhaps even upset her."

"True, true." He bobbed his head in agreement.

"I merely wish to check on her well-being to set Ailsa's mind at ease. How does the mistress fair?"

Bess lowered her voice. "She is tolerable. But Mistress Blackburn is beginning to question more and more where Ailsa is and why she cannot go home. I do hope that Nick arrives soon. Have ye heard any word?"

"Nay, but I am going to check their house to see if there is any sign of him there. Is the mistress in need of anything?"

"Ye are kind, but nay, she has all she needs."

"Then I shall take my leave, for I have other business to attend to." I bowed to them and turned to depart.

"Please give Ailsa all my love, and please take care of her." Bess pleaded as I turned away.

I turned in the direction of Fishmarket Close, still thinking about my conversation with Bess. Ailsa was teaching her to read. I smiled to myself, a mixture of pleasure and pride swelling in my chest. This woman would never stop amazing me. I removed her letter once more from my pocket and unfolded it, curious as to the handwriting that Bess had come to recognize.

"Is something amusing, Sir William?"

I jerked my head up just in time to see Seton step out of the shadows, and I noticed he wasn't alone.

~39~

March 1591

Ailsa

William never came back.

I made my way along the alley toward Grey's Close. The faint, gray streaks of early dawn bled over the horizon and I hurried along in the shadows so as not to be seen on the street when the sun came up. My heart was pounding and hundreds of scenarios were galloping through my mind. Perhaps Mother had fallen ill. Or maybe news had come that Nick would be delayed further. Even the possibility that William had simply forgotten about me and gone on to the palace to see to his duties had crossed my mind. But all of these situations did not account for the very simple fact that he had not returned. And now here I was seeking answers from the McMurrays, all the while pushing that gnawing fear of the worst to the back of my mind.

I stumbled along blindly until, in my haste, I stepped into a ditch full of only God knows what—probably mud and excrement, if I had to guess—and lost my balance. My foot sank into the mire, causing me to almost fall flat on my face. I stretched out a hand to steady myself and, in the process got my hand caught in my earasaid and pulled the garment down into the mud with me. Tangled in a mess of mud and cloth, tears of frustration finally spilled over. By the time I arrived at Bess's house, I was thoroughly sopped.

"Look at ye!" Bess exclaimed as she opened to me. "What has

happened?" She pulled me into her room and began removing my muddy clothing. "Ye look as if ye have been brawling at the—" I burst into tears, and she stopped her lecture. "Shh, there now. 'Tis all right. We'll get ye cleaned up."

I allowed her to pull the cold, wet clothing from my body. When I had regained my composure, I said, "Is Mother well? I have been worried about her."

Bess looked at me strangely. "Aye, she is well. Did Sir William not relay our message yesterday eve?"

"So, he was here?" I couldn't stop the shaking in my voice.

"Of course. It was ye that sent him, was it not? He is a fine specimen of a man, Ailsa. I can see why ye are taken with him." She grinned with teasing in her voice, but when she saw the worry on my face she ceased. "What is it?"

"He never returned. He was supposed to get word to me of Mother before he went on to the palace, but he never came. I don't even know if he made it to our house to see if Nick has come. I fear that something has happened to him."

"Nonsense," Bess tried to sooth. "He probably lost track of time. Those courtiers are forever dining and reveling. I'm sure he has just been delayed."

"Nay, Bess. I know him," I said vehemently. "He understood how anxious I was about Mother. He would not have left me to worry all night, knowing that he had instructed me not go out and check on her myself." I shook my head. "Nay, something has happened. I feel it."

Mistress McMurray appeared in the doorway with a tray of hot drinks. "Your mother thought she heard your voice, Ailsa. Should I tell her ye are here?"

I swallowed the lump in my throat. "Nay, I need to find William. As long as I know Mother is well, that will suffice for now."

Bess furrowed her brow in concern. "Ailsa, ye can't go out. Daylight has broken, and ye might be seen on the streets by Seton."

"I'll keep my face covered. I must go. William has defied the king by helping me, and he may be in danger."

"Your clothes? I can wash these but they won't be dry for a good while," Mistress McMurray said.

"She can borrow something of mine," Bess said in a hurry. Looking back to me she explained her ambivalence, "I don't like the idea of ye wandering the city trying to avoid the prowling eyes of David Seton, but I understand why ye must." She took a shaky breath. "Ye must find William."

I pushed the sleeves of Bess's frock up to my elbows and lifted the skirts from the ground, so I could walk without tripping. Bess was a good three inches taller than me and her clothing hung on me like a window drapery. I carefully picked my way around the puddles this time, determined not to soil her dress. By the time I reached the mercat cross the sun was peeking through the clouds. The swallows that had flown north for the summer with their sweet chirping and whirring noises could be heard even over the bustle of the merchants setting up their shops. Small bonfires dotted the area surrounding the Luckenbooths, and the aroma of roasting meat made my mouth water.

However, there was no time to stop and enjoy the sounds and smells of the early spring day. I quickly scanned the mercat cross for Gerald, the young boy who sometimes ran errands for me. He was always about, for his father was the blacksmith and had a shop a stone's throw from the center of town.

I spotted the boy a little way's off, kicking a ball about with his sister. I stepped up beside him. Producing a coin, I waved it in front of him.

"I have a job for ye, Gerald."

The young boy's eyes widened into goose eggs. "Mistress Blackburn! I haven't seen ye and your ma around for days. I was worried about ye."

"That is very kind of ye." I touched the boy's chin with my thumb. "Can ye run an errand for me?"

He nodded his head. A mess of thick, honey-colored curls fell into his eyes.

"I want to come too." Gerald's sister, Miriam, spoke around the thumb she had stuck in her mouth.

"Ye can't, Mir. This is big boy stuff," he said soothingly.

"That's right. And it requires your utmost discretion, Gerald. I have a letter for ye to deliver. It needs to go to Holyroodhouse, but ye cannot tell anyone who sent the missive. My life and the life of someone I care about depends on it. Can ye do that for me?"

Gerald blinked up at me, his eyes having grown even rounder. "Aye, Mistress. I will not tell a soul."

"Good boy. Now, take this letter to the palace. Make sure they know that it is for Lord Blantyre's eyes only. Can ye remember that name?"

"Lord Blantyre," Gerald repeated.

"Aye. And when ye have delivered it, take this coin and buy something lovely for ye and your sister."

Gerald took the letter and the coin and grinned mischievously. "I am the best secret-keeper in Edinburgh, Mistress…erm…what is your name?" He snapped his fingers as if trying to remember the name of the sender that he was supposed to forget.

I smiled at his boyish humor. "Now go. The letter is to be delivered at once."

"Aye," he said excitedly. "Miriam, run back to Da and stay there. I'll be back in a trice."

His sister whimpered momentarily, then turned and ran off, presumably back to her father's forge. I watched the boy disappear into the crowd, noting how nimbly he worked his way through the throng of market-goers that were already starting to gather. I breathed a prayer that he would reach the palace without issue and that Lord Blantyre would help me. William had told me how they were boyhood friends and that he trusted him more than anyone else at court. I hoped that he could still count on his friendship. He was the only person I could think of who may know where William was. I was putting all my eggs in one basket by contacting Blantyre, and I hoped it was not a mistake.

I wanted to check on our house and see if Nick had arrived yet. I turned to make my way to Fishmarket Close and ran right into the arms of David Seton.

"There you are, my little dove." He reeked of ale and swayed on his feet when I turned and bumped into him.

Pure fear gripped me but I tried to keep my voice calm. "Bailiff Seton." My first thought was to run, but he stood too close and I was within his reach. "Do ye never sleep?"

His brows shot up and he truly looked injured at my tone. He tilted toward me and I put out a hand to keep him from falling into me. "I have been looking for you for days but I couldn't find you." His voice warbled as tears welled up in his blood-shot eyes and he sniffled, swiping his sleeve across his nose.

He was drunk. I glanced around, seeking some face in the throng of marketers that I could motion to for help. But no one seemed to pay us any heed.

He laid his hand on my shoulder. "Please, I need to speak with you. Come sit with me. Let us talk."

There was no way on earth I was going anywhere with this man. No matter that his drunken stupor had rendered him a blubbering bairn. I didn't trust him and seeing Seton completely in his cups almost disturbed me more than seeing him sober. His new gentleness was unnerving.

"Bailiff Seton, I have much to do. Please, say your piece so that I may be on my way." Did he even remember that there was a warrant out for my arrest?

"Come, my little dove. Your lover has been arrested. It is time you come to me, your betrothed."

William arrested? That couldn't be. He was the king's man, the king's own inquisitor and childhood friend.

"Ye are lying," I said, trying desperately to maintain my composure.

He blinked at me slowly, as if trying to process my accusation. Then he said, "William Broune is this very hour in the tolbooth, arrested on a charge of treason for disobeying the king's orders. He was found with a letter from you in his possession. He was to bring you immediately to the king when he found you, but instead he has hidden you away, presumably to have his way with you. The king will not be happy."

His words tore at me. The thought of William's punishment due to my dilemma weakened my knees. I could not live with myself if he came to ruin because of me. My vision clouded with the picture of William's head on a pike, a feast for the crows. A traitor's death. I swallowed the cry that rose in my throat.

He leaned toward me again, his eyes falling on my mouth.

My stomach lurched, but I easily stopped him with my hands on his chest. "Not here." I pretended shyness, in hopes of dissuading him. "Not in public, Bailiff."

His bottom lip trembled. "What does that snake, William Broune, have that I don't?" He sounded like a love-sick sop and I resisted the foolish urge to laugh in his face.

Instead, I said, "What do ye have against Sir William?"

He laughed sardonically. "What *don't* I have against him? The self-important man has looked down his nose at me since the first day I met him. He is no better than me. He is the son of a cleric and a palace maid and the only reason he holds his position is because the king is too sentimentally attached to those men he grew up with since boyhood. He is haughty and rude and dressed too prettily for my liking."

He sounded like a spoilt child tattling to his mother.

"So ye are jealous of his good looks then? Or is it his position at court that ye want?" I tried not to sound mocking, but his hatred for William was astounding.

"Hardly," he scoffed. "But he won't look so meticulous once we're done with him. His time in prison will do wonders for his perfect appearance. And his position at court will soon be coming to an end as well. The new king doesn't care for Broune either. But I venture to say, he won't be around long to worry about it anyway." A hysterical sort of giggle bubbled out of him before he covered his mouth with his hand. That did nothing to stifle his drunken laugh.

"The new king?" I asked, hiding my alarm. "So, he's really going through with the kidnapping?"

Seton stilled, and his face lost all expression. "How do you know about that?"

He spoke of Bothwell, but I didn't want to let on that William was suspicious of the earl. I chose my words carefully, not mentioning Bothwell directly.

"Everyone knows about the kidnapping plans. It is general knowledge. The question is whether he will actually go through with it."

"You might want to be careful of what you say, little dove. Lord Bothwell doesn't take too kindly to those who underestimate him."

My eyes widened at his admittance. "Lord Bothwell?" As if just realizing what he had done, he released my shoulder and ran his hand through his hair nervously.

"I shouldn't have said that," he mumbled under his breath.

"Have ye become a traitor then, Bailiff Seton? A traitor to His Majesty, King James?"

That sobered him a little. "I am loyal to myself alone. And the earl has given me a fair wage to dispose of certain—undesirables."

I tried to tamper my panic. I needed him to talk, to tell me any details that I could share with William. "What kind of undesirables? Like whom?"

He laughed, stepping closer to me once more. "Your peacock for one. Do you know that man actually had the nerve to try to convince the king to be rid of me?" His chin began to quiver. "I had to do a lot of talking to persuade His Grace of the benefits of keeping me on the witch hunts. And the earl doesn't trust him. He wanted him to do some legal work for him, but he has changed his mind. I was more than happy to oblige the earl's request to get Broune out of the way for good."

The ale had sure loosened his tongue. I was only too glad to be here to exploit it.

"Why would the earl come to ye for assistance when he can do it himself?"

A madness rounded his eyes. "You doubt my word? See here." He shook a leather pouch in front of my face, and I could hear the coins clinking inside. "This is real gold. A gift from the earl for my pledge of assistance. I could dress like a peacock too since that seems to be your preference." He leaned closer and rubbed his face against mine, taking a deep breath through his nostrils. He planted a peck on my lips and grinned childishly. He then straightened suddenly and said, "And I most certainly can afford a home for us to begin our new lives together, so your mother can stay put. There will be no need for her to live with us."

How dare he try to cast off my mother. I glanced down at the leather pouch he clutched in his hand. "That purse means nothing. It could have come from your own coffers for all I know."

He scoffed. "Oh, I assure you it didn't. Look." He held his corpulent hand in front of my face. On his shortest finger sat a gold ring inlaid with a small ruby.

"F.S.?" I squinted to make out the inscription.

"Francis Stewart, the Earl of Bothwell. But never mind him. All you need to know is that I can keep you in true comfort." He leaned in again and I took a step back to avoid a repeat kiss.

"Bailiff Seton, I really must be on my way. Can we chat later?"

He dropped his beringed hand and stared at me as if he forgot what he was talking about. He was so engrossed in bragging about his own exploits.

"No, I want to talk now. You were supposed to marry me." He stopped talking then, and a light of understanding seemed to dawn in his eyes. It was clear the moment he remembered my crime. "You have broken our contract." His voice rose into a mournful whine. He was still not clear-headed. I wondered if I could play on his ale-soaked emotions.

"I need more time, Bailiff. My trousseau isn't ready yet. Don't ye think the wife of the Deputy Bailiff should be well outfitted with new dresses? I want to look my best so not to embarrass ye."

"You could never embarrass me, my little dove." He reached a finger up and ran it down my cheek. "How much time do you need?"

"Another week, my lord." I tamped down the bannock I had eaten for breakfast. All this pretending was going to make me ill. But if it worked, it would be worth it.

"I can't wait that long, my little dove. I'll give you three days."

If he called me *little dove* one more time, I really was going to lose my bannock. "Ye are too kind, Bailiff. I don't know what I have done to deserve your attention." *But I repent of it*, I secretly thought to myself.

He grinned at me again, his blood-shot eyes looking glassy. "Then you will meet me at St Giles to exchange our vows? In three days?" He looked so hopeful, I almost repented of my deceit.

"I would love to be wed at St Giles," I said vaguely. He tried to lean into me once more with lips puckered. "Bailiff, please. Let's keep our kisses for the wedding day."

His bottom lip protruded like a child who had been told no. I patted his arm reassuringly and turned him around to be on his way.

"You won't forget, my little dove? Our wedding at St Giles in three days."

"Believe me, Bailiff. I will not forget."

I watched as he stumbled on his way down the High Street, stopping once to look back at me. I waved sweetly and motioned for him to go on. I quickly turned in the opposite direction. I hoped I could reach the McMurrays' house before Seton sobered and realized what he had done.

~40~

March 1591

Ailsa

The silence was driving me mad. I heard the ringing of the curfew bell, and the night watchman call out at some point in the night. But then there was silence. Even the scurrying of a mouse would have been more tolerable than the eerie quiet that seemed to hang in the air like a terrible miasma.

Yet the quiet was safer than the alternative. And though I shivered in the stillness of William's chamber, I listened for the pounding of footsteps or the raising of voices. Anything that would indicate to me that my whereabouts had been discovered. For if the king's own man had fallen into the hands of David Seton, what was to keep me from the same fate?

I curled myself into a ball, pulling my knees up to my chest in an effort to maintain my body heat. I balanced my journal on my knees and the pot of ink on the lumpy straw mattress, careful not to spill ink on William's bed. I checked my list against the inventory in my head. Only a few amber crumbs of the dried poppy tears would be needed in order to make my tincture. Of the herbs and flowers we grew in our little garden, the poppy had some of the most powerful affects. I used it sparingly, which provided enough for what I needed now. Great care must be taken with the use of the poppy tears, for too little would bring a man out of his stupor too soon, and too much could kill him. I scratched the words *Papaver somniferum* upon my page, enjoying the sound and look of the Latin words for opium poppy.

I strained to see the words in the weak light of the moon and drew the page closer to my eyes in order to add my next item. I was convinced I had everything I needed to carry out my plan. The only thing to be done now was gather the plants and pods I needed and make the sleeping potion that could be added to the tolbooth guard's ale.

I heard the creaking of a floorboard on the other side of the door. I threw my earasaid over my head and wrapped it around my face. Carefully setting the pot of ink aside, I scrambled to the corner of the room and pressed myself into the deepest recesses of William's chamber. I waited, desperately hoping against all hope that it was William at the door.

The body shifted, and I heard a soft clicking sound as if the clogs of a clock were being pushed about. But by the time my mind registered that the sound I was hearing was a lock being picked, the door creaked open slowly. From my shadows I could see a man step into the room, and the faint moonlight that lit his features revealed it to be Lord Blantyre.

I relaxed my shoulders and let out the breath I was holding. "I scarce believed ye would come," I heard myself saying.

A soft sigh escaped his lips, but he didn't speak. He closed the door behind him and locked it again. He moved no further into the room, and for a moment, I feared that I had mistaken the man's identity.

When I didn't speak again, he said, "I vacillated on whether to come. You are a wanted woman, Mistress Blackburn."

From my place in the shadows, I shifted uncomfortably. "If ye fear for your own safety, then look not upon my face. Say ye have not seen me when ye are asked. But for the sake of our mutual friend, please help me." My words were raw with emotion, and I hoped that Blantyre could hear the desperation in them.

"Aye, you bring up a good point." He finally moved forward and pulled a chair away from the table to seat himself. "I risk a great deal coming here to meet you. The king has taken a great interest in the woman who has drawn away his friend's affections from the Lady that His Majesty would have him marry. And since William's arrest, he has signed a warrant for yours as well."

I swallowed hard, not sure of Blantyre's opinion of me. I was beginning to realize that, although he was a friend of William, that didn't make him a friend of mine.

"I have done nothing untoward. William is a grown man. He may cast his regards toward whomever he pleases. No one twisted his arm."

He chuckled at that, a dry, cynical laugh. "Nay, I dare say, it wasn't his arm you twisted." He reached toward the candle that sat in the middle of the table and struck the flint to light it. A golden flame ignited, casting his long, thin face in a more contemptuous light. "Why are you in the dark, Mistress Blackburn? And why do you have no fire in the hearth?" He pulled his cloak tighter around him, looking toward the hearth.

"I do not wish to be discovered. I light not the fire for warmth nor sustenance for fear that the smoke or the smell might give me away. I can only imagine what William is currently suffering."

His brows burrowed into a deep line, and he leaned his elbows on the table. "That is the only reason I am here. Not to help you but to help him."

"Ye help him by helping me." I glared at him from my corner. It was going to be harder to convince him than I thought.

"Step away from the shadows, lass. Come, sit." He motioned toward the chair that sat across from him. I crept toward the table and removed the covering from my face. As I drew closer, I noted the worry etched into the lines about his eyes. "I received your note before I even heard word of William's arrest. I had been away with His Majesty at Falkland Palace."

He slouched in his chair, his arched back giving him the appearance of a hunchback. He bounced his leg up and down in a nervous tick.

"I was informed of it after I had sent you the missive. Surely the fact that Seton has arrested the king's friend is a defiance of His Majesty's orders as well. Weren't both William and Seton charged with finding me and sending word to the king immediately once located?"

"Aye. That is one point in William's favor. But I would venture to say that William's direct disobedience at finding you—then hiding you—will not bode well for him."

"Which is why we must help him." I felt my vehemence heating my words. "Seton will stop at nothing, and His Majesty will play right into his hands. It seems he has done so for months now."

Blantyre straightened. "What did you have in mind?"

I lowered my voice. "I want to break him out of prison."

Blantyre choked as if he had swallowed a chicken bone. "Break him out of prison! You can't be serious!" I didn't reply. "What the deuce? You *are* serious." He stood abruptly and moved across the room. Drawing the ladle out of a bucket, he drank deeply. "Have you any wine?"

I moved toward a shelf from where I had seen William pull bottles before. "He has only whisky," I said, grabbing a cup and bringing the bottle back to the table. He poured himself a dram and shot it straight back.

"You are talking about committing treason, you know that right?" He took another swig and swallowed it just as quickly. Dropping the cup on the table, he wiped his mouth on his sleeve.

"My lord, Seton has entered into an agreement with my uncle that has bound me to him irrevocably. My uncle had no right to do so, and William has been trying to assist me in freeing myself from this bond. The bailiff has been hunting me like a hound since the agreement was made. Somehow Seton caught William with a missive signed by me which was intended to protect me. I don't know how it came about that it was found, but now William is in danger, and I cannot live with myself knowing that it is because of me that he has come to this trouble."

Blantyre's eyes hardened, and he leaned forward even further until his face was within a hair's breadth of mine. "Let me be perfectly honest with you. I care not what Seton's intentions are toward you. William is an idealist that has entangled himself in a winch's troubles. Now, he fancies himself in love with you and has thrown away any hope of happiness and success of which he ever had a chance. As far as I am concerned, this is the perfect solution to make him see reason."

I stared at him, feeling my face burn under the light of this truth. "Ye seem to be under the impression that William is merely being held to be kept out of the way. There is real danger here that I do not think ye understand. He is a pawn being used to bring about the Earl of Bothwell's plan."

His reaction was gratifying, for the smirk he held in place fell sharply. "What do you know of Bothwell?" The curl of his lip when he said the earl's name spoke volumes as to the dislike he had for the man.

"I know that he has been accused by several people of necromancy and of using his craft in order to bring about the fall of King James. I know that he intends to get His Majesty out of the way so that he may set himself upon the Scottish throne. And I know that he has a strong disliking for William and has every intention of removing him and several others at the king's court from their positions. It seems he does not fancy them. Are ye one of those people, Lord Blantyre?"

"God's teeth. How did you come about this information?"

"It seems that David Seton's tongue cannot keep its secrets when he is drunk."

His face softened. "He saw you then? How did you get away from him?"

I looked away, uncomfortable at this sudden concern. "Turns out the bailiff is a tongue-wagging fool when he is drunk."

He laughed, and I saw the flame of the lone candle on the table flicker from the force of his breath. But the sound he made was eclipsed by a noise on the landing right outside the door.

"Hush." I laid my hand upon his sleeve to get his attention.

"Someone is here." We both strained at the muffled sounds until the heavy footsteps moved down the hall.

"A neighbor," Blantyre explained. I looked at him, feeling my heart in my throat.

"What we do, we must do quickly. Are ye willing to help me or nay?"

His face was unreadable, and I silently breathed a prayer for his cooperation. If he refused, I wasn't sure I could do it alone.

"Tell me more about this plan of yours to get William out of the tolbooth."

I quickly retrieved my notes. "Can ye get your hands on a good bottle of port, my lord?"

~41~

March 1591

William

I suppose I should have been thankful that I wasn't chained to the wall like the accused witches. But my gratitude ended there. Not even a bench had been provided for me to sit upon and no blanket or bedding given for the sake of my warmth. There were no books to occupy the mind nor pen and paper to occupy my hands. And to top it off, the bucket provided for my relief had not been emptied since the last occupant of the cell had made use of it. The place stank of excrement and vomit, and the odor turned my stomach more times than I could count.

It was a wonder then that my stomach found itself continuously hungry. But the gruel and bread that had been offered me to sup upon was deficient: the former being cold and the latter stale. On more than one occasion I found myself wishing for one of Ailsa's loaves that she snuck to the witches. A little note written in her hand would have nourished my soul more than the bread filled my belly. But alas, she was not here, nor her bread, and I lamented the fact that I had no way of getting word to her of my arrest.

I reached into my pocket and pulled out the handkerchief that I had kept with me since the day it was given me. Although I had washed it, I still imagined it smelt of the herbs that Ailsa kept hanging in her house. The sweet smell of lemon balm and the piquant odor of the valerian root. The aroma still triggered memories of her skin and of her hair. I tortured myself by holding it once more to my nose and breathing in her essence and remembering the feel of her on top of me as she pinned me to my bed. I closed my eyes in a silent plea, beseeching the Almighty to protect her and keep her from Seton's reach.

I sat in a corner, my back against the cold walls of my prison cell. The slimy, wet stones did nothing for my comfort, and I shifted my weight in order to ease the stiffness in my bones. I had just begun to nod off when a sound at the great oak door of my cell startled me awake.

"'Tis me, Sir William," Mistress McCollum called out as she fumbled with the key to my lock. The door swung open, and I beheld the woman's face, pinched with worry for my well-being. "I've brought ye some water and a cloth to clean yourself up. Ye are going to see the king today."

I straightened. "The king has returned?"

"Aye. Now let us pray that he gets this whole mess straightened out." She lowered her voice. "And that he will finally see Seton for the snake he is."

I looked down at myself and studied my state. My breeches, which had sustained a tear when Seton had seized me two days before, were now bloodied and soiled. There was no cleansing them from the grime I had collected from the floor. My linen tunic was also sullied. The condition of my dress was enough to drive me mad. And it probably would have, had I not been more concerned about Ailsa's safety, and what might have become of her in the ensuing hours since my arrest. My only hope rested in the fact that had Seton found her, he surely would have ran to tell me about it.

And as if thoughts of Seton charmed him into being, the man appeared in the doorway. "Thank you, Mistress McCollum. That will be all we require."

The woman jumped when Seton spoke, not realizing he had appeared. The hard expression on her face solidified her thoughts about the man, and she raised her chin in defiance.

"Ye should at least let the man change his clothes for such an important meeting."

Seton pushed himself away from the door frame and stepped into my cell. Scuffing his feet across the floor, he came and stood over me.

"Nay, I don't think I shall." Mockery danced in his eyes and a little grin spread across his face. "Let the king see the proud peacock for what he truly is: the son of a palace maid, lower than dirt, and no better than me."

Mistress McCollum sniffed at that and unleashed all her wrath upon him.

"I never pegged ye as a jealous man, Bailiff Seton. But that green-eyed monster has consumed ye. Is that what this is all about?"

Seton turned on her and was before the older woman in an instant.

"Do not question my authority. Mind your own business, mistress, or you might find yourself tied to a stake." His face was mere inches from the gaoler's, and the fear that crumpled her brow was distressing. "Now, run along and make sure that all is ready for the prisoner to be transported to the palace."

Mistress McCollum stole a glance at me before departing. I nodded gratefully to her then turned my attention toward my ministrations.

Seton stalked back to me. "Has Ailsa tried to make contact with you?"

I continued to wash my face and neck, disregarding his question.

"I have seen her," he said, trying once more to get a reaction out of me. "I've felt her softness within my hands and smelled the sweetness of heather in her hair. I've even kissed those tender lips. She is tantalizing, is she not?"

I scrubbed my skin harder, as if his disgusting words clung to me. When I did not respond, he tried another tack.

"Oh, I almost forgot to mention. She's agreed to be my wife. Seemed most eager to do so. She is preparing her trousseau this very moment."

I laughed. "You must have been dreaming. Either that or you were drunk. She would never agree to marry you." Even as unlikely as his words were, I could feel the fear creeping up within me. I had no way of contacting her. Had she felt this was her only option?

His face was expressionless. "So, what if I were a little drunk? We worked our issues out, and soon, very soon, she will be in my bed and—"

I didn't let him finish. I hurled the dirty water from my bowl into his face and lunged at him. I knocked him in the head with the bowl, and he shook his head heartily, sputtering water and sliding on the slippery, wet floor. He fell hard onto his knees, and I saw my opportunity. I threw myself upon his back and wrapped my arm around his neck.

"Jamison," he squawked, calling for the guard that stood watch right outside my cell. I squeezed harder, trying my best to cut off any air that could still seep into his lungs. Seton pushed himself to his feet, grappling my arm in an attempt to loosen my hold. The cell door slammed open, and Jamison stalked toward us, club in hand. Then a severe pain struck me in the back of my head. The last thing I remembered was sliding down the wall, the feeling of sharp stones scraping against the flesh on my back.

The pain in my head was excruciating. I opened my eyes to behold fuzzy red pomegranates and pale green pears entwined with leaves and vines and the tail feathers of a strutting pheasant and its mate, parading across the ceiling. Holyroodhouse. I was in the king's antechamber at Holyroodhouse.

I sat up. Making a move to lay my hand on the back of my head, I was alarmed to find that my hands had been tied together. My back was burning, my head pounding. I licked my lips noting the dryness in my mouth and looked around. I thought for a moment that I was alone. But as I began to stir a voice called out to me from across the room.

"You got yourself into a messs." Bowes' unmistakable serpentine drawl besieged my ears.

"Where is the king?" I said, still trying to get my bearings. I sat up straighter and stretched my legs until my feet reached the floor. My head was pounding, but I would not let that deter me. "I must speak with His Majesty."

"In due time, my good man." Bowes reached a cup of amber liquid toward me, and I took it with both hands.

I downed the liquid then handed the cup back to him. "I didn't even get to enjoy my carriage ride."

Bowes chuckled and took the cup from my hands. "Yesss, that was quite a scrape with the bailiff. Next time you might want to forego the kerfuffle with an ox." He strode across the chamber and placed the cup on a silver tray and filled it again.

"It was two against one. Just wait until I catch him alone."

Bowes looked amused. "Well, either way, I am glad for this opportunity to speak with you momentarily. Seton is with His Majesty now, so we haven't much time."

I tried to focus my eyes on the Englishman. There were two of him in front of me, and I needed to see only one. I squeezed my eyes together tightly then opened them again, but the man and his ghostly counterpart still stood before me.

"What is this about?"

He came back and sat down beside me, handing me a small tray of cheese, bread, and fruit. I grabbed the cheese and stuffed a wedge into my mouth.

"I suspect that our bailiff is not as innocent as he is trying to make himself out to be." I stopped chewing and stared at him. "I have reason to believe that he is working with the Earl of Bothwell to remove certain, shall we say, *unwanted* personsss from Bothwell's path."

I popped another wedge of cheese into my mouth and followed it with a grape. "What proof have you of this scheme?"

"None." Bowes flicked a piece of dried mud from his boot then brushed off his hands.

"Then why do you suspect him?" I said around a mouthful of food. I was having trouble following this conversation.

"Large sumsss of money have passed through the earl's handsss lately. He has sold off one of his estatesss, and not long after, the bailiff bought a home on the other side of town."

As much as I wanted to find any evidence that Seton was a criminal, I hardly thought this constituted any wrongdoing. "I doubt that will hold up in court."

"Then there is that small matter of Bothwell's fraternizing with the witchesss. Did you find out anything about that when you met with him?"

I almost choked on the bread I was chewing. "I would ask how you know about our meeting, but that would make it sound like I was hiding something."

Bowes laughed again, but his amusement was curbed. "You know His Majesty has everyone watched. Everyone is followed. Even his closest of friendsss. I'm sure there is someone watching me as well. After all, I am a foreigner."

No, I did not know. Then again, perhaps I did know and had forgotten. I couldn't seem to make sense of anything at the moment. I felt like one of those fools that served at the Queen of England's court. The people who were employed to say and do silly things for the queen's amusement.

"I have never given him a reason to have me followed," I finally said. "Not until I defied his wishes for my marital aspirations."

"Ah, yesss, Mistress Blackburn." He snuck a grape from my tray and popped it into his mouth. "She is a lovely creature. I'd hate to see her tied to a man like David Seton. But it is no use, for you shall surely never marry her."

I stiffened at his pronouncement. "We'll see about that," I dared, determined that I was going to make my own choices.

"Suit yourself," Bowes replied. "It really doesn't concern me. But what does concern me is Bothwell. As you know he has made several attempts to lure my mistress into an agreement concerning the border earlsss. Queen Elizabeth doesn't trust him. For example, look at how he reacted to the execution of your Catholic queen. He was ready to go to war."

I stared at him without reply. While the king put on the appearance that he was distraught over his mother's death, Bothwell had suited up, ready to call down all the forces of Scotland on the English queen in retaliation. It was theatrical, but I was sure the brute would have followed through if he had the backing.

The pain in my head was excruciating, and this conversation was not making it any better.

"So, what do you wish me to do? I have no knowledge of Seton's connections with Bothwell, and as you can see, I am currently in no position to help myself, let alone anyone else."

"No, but you do have information about Bothwell and the witchesss. Mention that to His Majesty. I believe it will help your cause."

"And I suppose it wouldn't hurt yours either."

He opened his mouth to say something more, but just then the door opened, and a servant appeared in the doorway.

"Sir William, His Majesty asked me to check on you and see if you were awake. He wishes to speak with you."

Bowes held out a hand to me, and I grasped it with both of mine, accepting his offer of assistance to stand. For a moment the room did a dance about me, and I closed my eyes once more to gain composure.

The footman, whom I did not recognize, led me through the king's bedchamber and into his closet on the other side. I concentrated on putting one foot in front of the other, focusing on my balance and making sure I didn't fall on my face. The king sat behind a large desk with two stacks of antiquated books piled high in front of him. A small opening between the stacks revealed the king, deep in thought, with his head bent toward his notes. Blackened fingers shuffled his foolscap about as he dipped the nub of his quill into the pot of ink in front of him.

The footman announced my arrival, but the king did not lift his head. He was writing furiously, and there was no dissuading him when he had set his mind to something. The servant waited an extra beat for the king's next instruction, but when His Majesty did not answer, he stepped back into his place along the tapestry-covered wall.

Seton was nowhere to be seen unless my blurred vision was playing tricks on me again. I silently hoped that he had slipped out of the door on the opposite end of the room. I was surprised to find that he did not wish to be a part of this interview, but perhaps James had forbidden it.

I stood in silence with my hands bound, observing the ornately covered floors. The rich carpets of plush scarlet and gold pile that usually covered the wooden planks now looked dull and unimpressive to me. The heavy velvet curtains were drawn aside to let in the early spring sunlight, the only source of brightness in the drab room. A portrait of oil on canvas in the likeness of James's grandfather, the fifth James, hung behind the king's desk, a silent sentry of the current king's thoughts and scribblings. I tried to focus on him in an effort to calm my nerves and quell my jumbled thoughts.

My body ached, and after standing unnoticed for several minutes, I cleared my throat. The action had the desired effect, for James lifted his head suddenly, his eyes vacant of anybody or anything that was not a part of his current deliberations.

"Ah, William. I am glad you have come. I have begun a dissertation on the various arguments concerning sorcery and demons and the like. I have been reading on several clerical accounts, but I want to include some judicial studies as well. You are just the person with which to have that dialogue."

I was stunned into silence. I stood here, bloodied, filthy and injured, with hands bound and clothing askew, and he wanted to chat about court cases? When I did not answer, he looked up again with brows furrowed in irritation.

"Your Grace," I began slowly, holding out my arms. Comprehension arrested him, and he motioned to the footman.

"Cut Sir William's bindings." If I had hoped for compassion or an apology, I would have been sorely disappointed. The king pointed to an armchair opposite his. "Sit."

I rubbed my wrists where the ropes had chafed my skin. I then sat carefully, and the king finally turned his attention fully on me. As if he had forgotten his first trail of thought, he said, "I am very disappointed."

I shifted in my seat, prepared to weather any verbal blows the king might deal me. I was having trouble organizing my thoughts, but I remembered that I had disobeyed his order concerning Ailsa, and I was fully prepared to suffer the consequences for my actions. What I was not prepared for was the king's accusations of duplicity.

"You have betrayed that unspoken oath that we have shared since boyhood."

"Your Grace?"

"I have suffered many betrayals in my lifetime, and many at the hands of blood relatives. But an oath of friendship between brothers," The king broke off his accusation, his voice beginning to shake under the implications.

"Your Grace, I, I can explain," I fumbled. My tongue felt thick and stupid in my mouth.

"Don't!" he shouted, holding up a hand to silence me. "Don't preen my feathers with pretty words and excuses, William. I gave you an order, and instead, you ignored it to satisfy your own lust."

"It wasn't like that, Your Majesty."

"No? Do you deny that you disobeyed my order so that you may take David Seton's betrothed to bed and defile her?"

Dazed, I felt the blood drain from my face. I rubbed a hand across my forehead trying to conjure my memories. I didn't think I had defiled her. Surely, I would have remembered that. I finally settled for, "She is not his betrothed."

"But you have disobeyed my orders for this winch, nonetheless." The king pushed himself away from his desk and stood on his stick legs. "You, who have been my friend for almost longer than I can remember, sacrificed that honor and friendship for a common doxy."

"I must request you stop insulting the woman I love." I said with a calmness I did not feel. I clenched my jaw, making my teeth hurt, and my head ache even more. "I am going to marry Ailsa Blackburn. I have made my choice, and if that means living the rest of my life in a derelict hovel on the outside of town, then so be it."

The king's eyes widened in outrage. "This is no longer about you, William. This is about me," he roared. "This is about you disobeying my orders and about your affiliation with Bothwell, whom you know I do not trust."

Fear gripped me, causing my blood to run cold. "Bothwell?" I choked the earl's name. "What have I to do with Bothwell?"

James leaned forward, resting his knuckles on the top of his desk. "Do you mean to insinuate that you have had no dealings with the Earl of Bothwell? Do not lie to me, William. My heart cannot take such blatant dishonesty."

"I do not lie. I am not working with the earl to—" I paused, trying to determine the word I wanted to use, "to undermine you. At least not willingly." The last words came to mind as an afterthought, for I wasn't sure now that the dealings Bothwell tried to involve me in were not in fact something to do with his kidnapping schemes.

"What the deuce is that supposed to mean? Not willingly?"

I sighed heavily, gingerly running a hand over the lump I could now feel growing on the back of my head. I looked up into the king's face and noticed the dark smudges under his sunken eyes. He looked like I felt: worn, haggard, and greatly in need of a drink.

"The earl sought me out some time ago. I think he needed an advocate to do some legal work for him."

"You think? You do not know why he sought you out?"

I rubbed my hand across my face once more, willing my mind to think clearly yet knowing it would not cooperate. "If I remember right, he was preparing to take on more business and was worried that the transfer of power might be contested."

"Transfer of power? And you didn't think that sounded suspicious?

Really, William? This convenient lack of memory is most troublesome."

"It cannot be helped, Your Grace. I fear I have sustained a rather serious injury when I was hit in the head in the tolbooth."

The king eyed me suspiciously. "Well, it must be helped. What else did he tell you?"

I swallowed hard, grasping at words and phrases that were floating around in my mind and trying to string them into an intelligible sentence.

"He was not quick to divulge the particulars to me. Perhaps he didn't know if he could trust me. We didn't finish the conversation because we were interrupted by a visitor. I never got to meet with him again."

The king crossed his arms and looked down at me. His mouth pulled into a frown, and disbelief was written all over his face. "Seton says that you and the earl have met on several occasions."

"He lies!" I started out of my seat, and the sudden movement sent my body swaying. I gripped the front of the king's desk to steady myself. "I cannot believe you would take the word of this knave over the word of your friend." The king took a step back, a darkness overshadowing his face. The air between us grew heavy with the accusation, but I would not back down.

"I advise you to remember your place, William Broune. The bailiff has pointed out to me that you have begun to overstep your station. We may be friends, but you are first and foremost my subject, and I will have your respect."

"And that is something I cannot presently offer you." I bit the inside of my cheek as soon as the words slipped off my tongue, but there was no taking them back. The king staggered at the slight before bellowing his response.

"Guards!"

Four men armed with halberds in hand and swords at their side rushed forward. I hadn't even noticed them standing watch, two at each door. Their yellow padded doublets and russet trunks flashed briefly in front of me before I registered what was happening.

"Your Grace!" I tried, twisting around to look at his face. "Your Grace, please. I have more to say to you." The words were muddled in my mouth. The king had turned his back on me. He was leaning now against a windowsill and staring out into the courtyard.

"You have wounded me greatly, William. It will take some time to recover from this most vexing injury. I will send for you when I have recovered and when your memory is more willing to cooperate."

It was the last thing I heard before being spirited back to the tolbooth.

~42~

March 1591

Ailsa

Lord Blantyre returned the next evening with two bottles of the finest port that I had ever seen. "If it ever gets around that I was the one who supplied you with these—"

"I won't betray ye if that is what ye are worried about." I took the bottles and set them on the table along with the tincture that I had made. He watched as I took a small needle and drew it across the wax seal. I peeled the wax off then took the needle and began to dig out the leather knot that had been stuffed into the mouth of the bottle. Pulling the knot out slowly as not to tear it, I laid the leather piece aside.

"Is this safe? I don't want murder added to my list of offenses if you get caught."

"'Tis safe when used in the correct quantities." I carefully poured the poppy-tear elixir into the first bottle and gently swirled the contents. "There is very little change to the color of the wine and it cannot be detected by scent if you use the correct amount." I held the bottle out to Blantyre for him to smell. He brought his nose close to the opening and sniffed strongly. "There is a taste of bitterness in the tears of the poppy, but as long as ye don't add too much, the flavor is barely detectable."

He handed the bottle back to me, and I stuffed the leather knot back into the mouth of the bottle. I proceeded to do the same to the second bottle, then sealed them both with a fresh wax closure.

Blantyre shifted beside me. "You are not going to like this, but I'm afraid I am not going to be able to accompany you to the tolbooth."

It felt as though my heart had fallen into my stomach. My first instinct was to react spitefully. "Why not? Ye never struck me as a milk-livered craven, my lord."

Blantyre let out a short breath. "Mistress Blackburn, I have duties at the palace that I cannot evade." He pulled out a folded piece of paper and held it out to me. "I have written down for you the times of the changing of the guard at the tolbooth, and when Mistress McCollum will also be on duty, since you are sure she will assist you."

I unfolded the paper and looked at the notes he had written. I felt tears pushing against my eyes. I had been nothing but a tangled ball of emotion since all of this had begun, and it seemed that tears were an instantaneous reaction to almost every disappointment.

"Thank ye, my lord." I tucked the notes into my pocket and began stuffing the bottles into my basket along with items I thought I might need to minister to William. A bar of lye soap, fresh bandages, and a few healing herbs in case there had been any altercations while he was within Seton's custody. A meat pie, a fresh loaf of bread and a small jug of ale were also tucked inside. All covered with a clean, linen tunic. I would have taken breeches and doublet too, if I thought it would fit inside the basket. I remembered the conditions of the tolbooth cells, and if William hadn't driven himself mad yet with concern over the state of his dress, it would unnerve me to see him in any condition other than perfect.

"Where will you go once you have sprung him from the tolbooth?" He fidgeted with his thin mustache that he had waxed to a fine point. He seemed as nervous as I was, which surprised me since he would not be risking *his* skin should I get caught.

"We will go to the McMurrays' and wait for my brother Nick to arrive. He should be here any day now that the snow has melted. My mother and I will return to London with Nick. Things have become too dangerous for us here in Edinburgh. William will accompany us. That is, unless he wishes to stay here." My voice failed me on those last words. The thought of William not wanting to go with us had never even crossed my mind.

Blantyre's eyes tightened on me. "You must convince William to leave with you. I did not wish to alarm you and cloud your thinking with worry, but there is to be a trial. William has been charged with treason."

"What? Ye should have told me."

He continued to twist his whiskers. "It is as I have said. I did not wish to worry you. But now you know the seriousness of his crimes, and you must talk some sense into him if he shows the slightest desire to stay behind."

"There is no crime, Lord Blantyre. William is innocent."

"Fine. Then leave him where he is. Allow justice to take its course, and he will be a free man legally when it is all over." The heat in his voice was understandable, and suddenly all my reasons sounded like folly.

"It will never be over, my lord. At least not for me. But ye are right. Perhaps I should leave William where he is, tell him I am going to England, and when he is a free man, he can find me." The words tasted like bitter herb upon my tongue, but Blantyre was right. If I took William away to England, he might never be able to return to Scotland. His aging father was still in St Andrews. He would not want to risk never seeing him again. They were very close. And his great position at the king's court and all that he had worked so hard to build would be razed as if the Great Alexander of Macedon had pilfered it himself.

I sat the basket back on the table and stared at it. After a moment's hesitation I said, "Ye are correct, Lord Blantyre. Now what am I to do?"

The man turned away from me and looked down at the floor. "I too am torn, Mistress Blackburn. I lack faith in our justice system, and I do not trust Seton to not have some false evidence planted to ruin my friend. As much as I would like him to stay, there is really only one choice."

I sighed heavily. "We are going in circles. I cannot think straight, and ye are not helping. I will leave it up to William when I get there." I glanced toward the window where the light was quickly fading. "It's almost time."

"Then I shall leave you with a wish for success." Blantyre reached for the coin purse he had tied at his waist. "Here, take this in case you run into any trouble and need a little extra." He handed me the leather pouch.

"For a bribe?"

"Or should you find yourself halfway between here and London, and your bellies are empty. Use it how you see fit."

"Thank ye, my lord." I laid my hands on his shoulders and kissed his cheek quickly. A crooked smile pulled at his lips.

"I would have liked to have known you under different circumstances, Mistress Blackburn. I think we may have gotten on quite well."

I felt the color burn on my cheeks but smiled nonetheless. "Perhaps."

He left then, and I felt the weight of what I was about to do press down on my chest. I took a deep breath then threaded my arm through the handles of my basket and lifted it onto my arm. But as I was about to open the door, I remembered something that I had almost completely forgotten in all the bustle. I thought about the papers and letters that William had stuffed into the drawer the day he was arrested. There was information in there pertaining to the Earl of Bothwell. Perhaps there was something inside that could buy his freedom.

I grabbed the bundle of documents then pulled a folded letter from my own pocket and tacked it to the top of the pile, underneath a key that William had attached there as well. I had written down every detail of my conversation with Seton. It would be the word of a wanted woman against that of a supposedly respectable bailiff, but I had to try. I had to get the confession into the right hands and hope that it would at least be enough to raise suspicions and spur further investigation.

I stuffed the bundle into the waistband of my skirts, then pulled my shawl tighter around me. Looking once more around the room, my eyes landed on a small, red tin that sat on the shelf above the counter. I hurried to it and pulled it down, barely able to reach it, even standing on the tips of my toes. Memories flooded back to me of the day when William had prepared the hot cacao for me. That was also the day that I first realized my feelings for him. The recollection made me smile, but I also found my cheeks damp with the precious memory.

I stuffed the tin inside the basket and covered the items once more with the linen tunic. Taking one last glance around the room, I pulled the door closed behind me and locked it up. I would not look back.

~43~

March 1591

Ailsa

By now the sun was almost gone, and the shadows of dusk were beginning to dance across the streets of Edinburgh. I slipped through the shadows comfortably, for I had become adept at moving around in the dark. But I mustn't grow too confident. One little slip up could find me in a cell of my own, for Seton was always watching. It seemed he never slept.

Which is why when I heard the dreaded sound of someone calling out my name minutes later, I felt the hairs on the nape of my neck stand on end. I quickened my pace, but it seemed the voice calling out to me was aided by a horse and wagon, which brought the body closer to me, and I could not outpace it. I slipped between two buildings and stopped in the shadows to listen for the sound of hoofbeats to clop past me.

However, the voice sounded vaguely familiar, and as he drew closer and called out my name again, this time accompanied by a lecturing older-brother tone, my heart leapt at the sound, and it was all I could do not to cry out in ecstatic jubilation.

"Nick!" I cried, stepping out of the shadows, at once not caring who saw me. It was foolish, but the excitement of hearing my brother's voice and seeing his beautiful face so overpowered me, that it could not be helped.

"Baby sister." He wrapped his arms around me and squeezed tightly. I buried my face into his shoulder and breathed in the familiar scent of perspiration, horse flesh and whisky. The relief of feeling his arms about me broke something inside, and I could hold back the tears no longer. I began to sob onto his woolen coat as he rubbed his hand up and down my back soothing me with soft words.

"Where have ye been?" I said, a little more forcefully than I wished.

"The roads have been impassible since the middle of February. Then, once the snow and ice melted, the mud became so pliable that the wheels of the coach consistently got stuck. On bad days, it would take us three hours just to go a mile down the road." I continued to snivel onto his coat. "Hush now, all will be well. I made inquiries at the alehouse and found that I am not too late after all. Ye have not been joined with the bailiff yet. That is good. But ye are also a wanted woman now, by the king's decree, and that is not good. We must get mother quickly and set out immediately. I had hoped all could be resolved with the bailiff in a cordial manner. But now that there is a warrant out for your arrest, we will need to alter our course."

He untangled himself from my arms and adjusted his coat accordingly. Wiping the wetness from my tear-stained face, he put on a smile. But I was not so quick to share my own.

"Nick, there is something that I must do before I leave Scotland."

"Well, then, let's get to it and get it taken care of. Come." He pulled me toward the wagon that he had been driving, but I tugged my sleeve away from his hold.

"Ye don't understand. There is *someone* I must see. Someone I must *get* before I can leave."

Nick stared at me briefly. "Who is it? Ye haven't taken it into your heart to help these accused witches, have ye? That sounds exactly like something ye would do."

I laughed nervously. "Nay, he is not a witch."

Nick's eyebrow shot up in interest. "He?"

"Aye. He has been falsely accused of treason, and it is all my fault.

I must help him."

"Ailsa, that is very noble of ye, but we haven't the time. I want to be well on our way back to London before the sun comes up."

"Then ye will just have to take Mother and go." I refused to take another step forward. "I cannot leave William behind. At least, not without giving him a chance at escape."

"Who is this William? Why are ye responsible for his treasonous charges?"

I began walking toward the tolbooth once more. "Come, I will tell ye all about him as we walk. As ye have already said, we haven't got much time. I will explain as we go."

But Nick stopped me before I could take another step. "Here Ails, I know it's not far, but ride with me in the wagon. 'Twill be safer."

Hiding my face within the folds of my shawl, I jumped down from the wagon. "Wait here," I instructed Nick as my eyes darted up and down the street watching for prying eyes.

"I will not! I'm coming with ye."

"Just wait until I make sure that Mistress McCollum is still on duty. I'll come and get ye if it is clear."

But caution turned to alarm as I opened the door. A woman stood within the receiving room, pulling on a set of gloves over her slender fingers. She wore a gown of apricot silk with tiny green bows and seed pearls sewn upon it. She looked like a lovely garden blooming in the first rays of spring. A short lace ruff stretched around the back of her neck and lay open in the front revealing one simple jewel: a pink, tear-shaped pearl of exquisite beauty.

The woman's eyes widened when she saw me, and I cursed myself for carelessly being discovered. "Lady Ruthven." I breathed her name as if in prayer, for indeed I did pray that she would have mercy on me and not reveal my presence to Bailiff Seton nor the king.

"Mistress Blackburn." She blinked at last, as if recognition had finally found her. "If one didn't know any better, they would think you and I have an affinity for the tolbooth, for we both seem to make a habit of meeting each other here."

I swallowed, feeling my legs grow as weak as willow branches. "Are ye here to see Sir William then?"

"I am," she said as she pulled on her other glove. "It is a pity that such a glorious man has been brought so low." She looked at me then, braising me with a hot stare that swept the length of my body. "It is only fortunate for me that I removed myself from his company before I too might have been caught in some false accusation."

Hope blossomed, creating a lump in my throat. "Ye believe him to be innocent then?"

"Aye. But what I believe will not save him." She stopped then, her voice catching on a note of emotion. "Only God can do that for him now."

At that moment Mistress McCollum came through the door that led to the upper block of cells. She stopped suddenly when she saw Lady Ruthven and I exchanging words.

I stilled my heart and grasped my brooch that William had given to me. Rubbing my thumb over the inscription and around the tiny garnet, I drew strength from the words on the ornament and the man who had given it to me.

"Lady Ruthven, if ye believe Sir William to be innocent, then I must ask ye not to reveal that ye have seen me here tonight. I might be able to help him, but if it is reported that I was here, it might make matters worse."

"You have definitely made matters worse for him. But your secret is safe with me." The emotion was thick in her voice, and I wondered if she hated me for the role I had unwittingly played in the dismantling of her betrothal to William. "I must go," she said, hurrying toward the door.

I considered momentarily how she had snuck here on her own in the dark. She had been so worried the night she and William had accompanied me here to see Geillis. Perhaps it wasn't the dark that had worried her, but me with William. How right she had been.

Then a thought struck me. "Lady Ruthven, how possible is it for ye to get an audience with the king this evening?"

She tilted her head, and compassion filled her eyes. Her voice softened, and she said, "I have spoken with His Majesty already. There was nothing I could say that would prick his heart."

I stepped closer to her, reaching into the waistband of my skirt. "What if you could show him proof of William's innocence?" I pulled out the bundle of letters and held them carefully in my hands. She looked down at the missives, and her eyes widened.

"What is that?" Her voice shook, and I lifted them to her.

"These are letters and signed affidavits that prove that William has been investigating the Earl of Bothwell for some time now. And there is a signed letter from me, recording a confession that was made to me by Deputy Bailiff David Seton, proving that he has been working for the earl to get William and other courtiers out of the way to make room for Bothwell to take the throne."

A small intake of breath was all I heard before tears flooded her eyes. "I've prayed for a miracle, but never did I believe it would come from your hands." She took the letters from me and tucked them into her cloak. "I will take them straightway to His Majesty. Nay," she corrected, her head shooting up. "I will take them to my Lady, the queen. She is very persuasive with her husband." A small smile brooked her lips. She reached out and squeezed my arm in relief. "Thank you."

"Mistress Blackburn, if ye are discovered here it will be the end of your freedom." The gaoler warned in her gentle voice that she only reserved for people whom she liked. She looked frazzled, her wiry, gray hair springing out from under her cap in all directions, and the bags under her eyes looked to hold a least a week's wage of coin.

"Mistress, if ye please, I must see William. I have a plan to help him escape. Now I know that puts ye at a great disadvantage and in much danger. I am willing to compensate ye for your assistance." I held up the coin pouch that Lord Blantyre had given me.

She held up her hands in refusal. "I cannot take your coin. Sir William is a man I respect greatly, and he has been wrongfully accused. But against Bailiff Seton, there is no defense. Do what ye must, for if he stays here, he will surely die. But I cannot take payment for it."

I tied the coin purse back on my belt with shaking hands. "Thank ye, mistress. Now I will fetch my brother, and we will retrieve William as quickly as possible."

"Your brother? Why, the bailiff would have us all believing that your brother was a myth."

I smiled broadly at her. "He is very real, I assure ye, and he has just arrived. And not a moment too soon. Let me get him, and ye shall see."

When I returned with Nick a moment later, the gaoler was still anxious. "How will ye get past Jamison? He and Bailiff Seton are as thick as thieves. The bailiff has the guard in his pocket. I don't think even the coin in that purse of yours will convince the man to help."

"Do not fret, mistress. I have a plan." I pulled back the linen tunic to reveal the bottles that Lord Blantyre had given me. "There is enough poppy tears in these two bottles to fell a horse. At least for a few hours. Long enough to get William out and be long gone before he comes to."

Compassion filled the older woman's eyes. "Mistress, there is something that ye must know before ye proceed. Sir William is," she paused, evidently struggling with her next words.

"Please, Mistress McCollum, we haven't much time. What is it?"

"Sir William has an injury. To his head. It has rendered him confused at times. It has also affected his eyesight. He said he sometimes sees two of me when I come to bring his food."

My chest tightened. Would he even know me? And would he be able to think clearly to make a decision on whether to stay or go?

"Well, it is a good thing that my brother arrived when he did. We may have to carry him out, but we will get him regardless."

~44~

March 1591

William

Beatrix came bearing news. I was being charged with treason, and there would be an assize two days hence. Sir Jonas, an advisor with whom I had worked on several cases the last couple of years, had been sent to defend me. Yet I still had not been allowed to send for any evidence with which I might make my case and prove my innocence.

Only a half hour had passed when I heard noise once more outside my cell door. But when nothing came of it, I settled back down onto my spot on the floor, determined to get some rest before Sir Jonas came to see me again in the morning. A little while later, I heard the noise again, but this time it was accompanied by the opening of my cell door.

My eyes had been playing tricks on me ever since my fight with Seton, often rendering my sight fuzzy or duplicating people who stood before me. But now I was sure my eyes were playing the cruelest of tricks on me yet. For there within the door frame stood the most beautiful pair of amber eyes accompanied by a golden face enshrouded with wisps of coppery tendrils of chestnut hair.

I blinked, whether unwilling or unable to believe that she stood before me now, I knew not. But when she spoke my name, I realized I wasn't dreaming, for my ears had not deceived me the way my eyes had.

"William!" She hurried across the room to where I lay on the floor. Falling to her knees, she grasped my face in her hands. "What have they done to ye?" She kissed my forehead, then both of my eyes, then pulled back to look at me again.

"Kiss me like you missed me," I said, eliciting a chuckle from the man who stood behind her. She laid her lips to mine, and the heat was better than any fire I could have asked for in this freezing cell. I wrapped my arms around her, placing one hand behind her slender neck to steady her trembling body. I drank her in, like a man thirsting for water in the desert. The softness of her skin under my fingertips thawed my frozen limbs, and I fought the instinct to press my body to hers and finally claim what Seton could only fantasize about. Her lips on mine were a dream come true, and if this were to be my final days, I would hold this one memory in my heart until my last dying breath.

Behind Ailsa, the young man cleared his throat. He had the same amber eyes as Ailsa, though they lacked the fire hers held. His hair was lighter, and he had whiskers that were brushed into the pointed style of the English beard. Even with the facial hair, there was no mistaking the resemblance.

"Are you Nick?" I asked, reluctantly pulling away from Ailsa.

Ailsa turned to look at the man. "Indeed. Can ye believe it? The fabled brother has come at last." She then began digging in her basket. She pulled out a clean tunic for me. I almost wept at the sight. She hurriedly pulled the dirty one over my head and shoved it into her basket. "I brought soap for ye to wash, but I see there is no water. It will have to wait until later." She then pulled out a bundle tied with jute and unwrapped it. Within was a meat pie and a fresh loaf of bread. I did weep then, thanking the Almighty for granting my wish. "What is wrong?" She asked as she pulled a jug of ale from her basket and removed the stopper.

"I have been praying for one of your loaves of bread, like those ye made for the witches." I sank my teeth into the tender dough and sighed contentedly.

"So, she did involve herself somehow with those witches," Nick said, laughing.

"Nick, check on the guard, please." As she gave this instruction, she produced a ring full of keys and quickly shoved the correct one into the shackles that held me bound to the wall.

I stared in disbelief. "Where did you get that? No, *how* did you get that?"

"He is sleeping happily just as ye said he would. That stuff worked fast," Nick observed.

"Aye, and he should be in a comfortable stupor for several hours, but we still don't want to dally." Looking up at me, she said, "I can explain once we are far away from here." She finished her task, then handed the keys back to her brother. "Nick will put the keys back where we found them. The man won't know what hit him, nor will he know what has happened to ye."

"I almost wish I were here to see his reaction," Nick said from the doorway.

"Are ye able to walk? Mistress McCollum said that ye have been having some issues with your eyes."

"Aye, I can walk, but ye might need to guide me down the steps. I see double sometimes." I shoved the last of the meat pie into my mouth and washed it down with ale.

Ailsa stood and offered a hand to help me up. She then pulled my arm over her shoulder. "Lean on me."

We walked through the door, and Nick closed it behind us, securing the lock once more and attaching the keys back on the guard's belt.

Once we reached the receiving area, Mistress McCollum stood waiting. Her face was taut with worry, and even in the candlelight, I could tell that the color had drained from her cheeks.

"Sir William, I do wish we were parting on more amiable terms. But ye must hurry, away from this place and that horrible bailiff."

I reached out and took the older woman's hands in mine. "I am much obliged to you, mistress. But how will you explain my escape?"

She looked from me to Nick, then back at me again. "I have been thinking about this. Ye will just have to hit me."

Nick and I looked at each other then back to her. "Hit you?"

"Mistress, I've never hit a woman in my life," Nick objected.

"Nor I," I said. "And we are not about to start now. Let us tie you up. You can tell the bailiff that a man in a dark cloak overpowered you and took me."

"I have a better idea." She hurried toward the door and slipped out.

"Please hurry," Ailsa said, more to herself than the missing woman.

When Mistress McCollum came back inside, she was covered in dirt and grime. Three questioning faces turned toward her. She chuckled. "I can't be looking like I was overpowered without putting up a fight. A good role against the wall outside does the trick." She reached down and took a handful of her bodice in each fist. Pulling in opposite directions, she ripped her dress, a satisfied look settling on her face. "Now if I just had some blood." She looked up at me, and I raised my brow to her in question.

Nick stepped forward. "Here," he said tapping his chin. "Split my lip open and it will give ye the blood ye need."

"Nay Nick!" Ailsa cried out, stepping between her brother and the large woman.

"'Tis all right," said Nick. "I'm used to it. A fight breaks out at least twice a week in the theater where I work. I can handle it. Go ahead, hit me right here."

The gaoler looked at Ailsa, then to me.

"His lip won't give you the blood you need. You'll need to bloody his nose," I instructed.

Ailsa let out a small gasp, but before she could protest further, Mistress McCollum balled her hand into a fist and punched Nick, spilling blood down his face. She then wiped her bloodied knuckle on the top of her bodice. Nick pulled at the torn piece of dress, dabbing at his bloodied nose.

"I've never been clouted by a woman before." He grinned. "At least, not one with so much strength."

"Tie her up quickly so we can go."

Beside me, Ailsa stiffened, her body beginning to tremble with the unusual events. "Not too tight," she insisted. "I don't want her injured." When the woman was comfortably tied, Ailsa bent and kissed the older woman on the cheek. "Thank ye for everything." The woman nodded then positioned her body so as to be believable when Seton arrived.

"Lie down in the back of the wagon, and I will cover ye up." Nick motioned to the horse-drawn wagon that sat right outside the door of the tolbooth, and I climbed in with his and Ailsa's assistance.

Ailsa spoke quickly. "William, I have put ye in a most dangerous predicament, and now ye have a hard decision to make. Do ye want us to return ye to your room above the bookshop, or do ye want to go with us to England? I know it is a sacrifice to ask this of ye."

"I will go with you, of course," I answered immediately, not needing time to ponder the decision.

"But, what about your father? What about the life ye have built here?"

I pulled her hand from the back of the seat where it was gripped tightly. "Ailsa, my life is wherever you are. If you are not with me, then my life will not be worth living." I kissed her hand and released it, knowing there was little time to spare.

A smile spread across her face. "I was hoping ye would say something like that." She sat down, and Nick began spreading out a large tarpaulin over the back of the wagon to conceal me. Ailsa continued talking. "With the help of Lord Blantyre, I have gathered a few of your possessions, including some of your finest pieces of clothing and brought them to our house. We will need to go to the house, Nick, and pick up our things."

"Ailsa, ye know our time is limited."

"It cannot be helped. We are leaving our lives behind, Nick. Ye must allow us this one concession."

Nick sighed, and I heard him snap the reins to set the cart in motion. We jerked forward, and I measured the distance blindly from beneath my cover, making note of how far we traveled and where we turned.

I also thought about my father. I would write to him when we reached London. He would understand the choice I had to make. Still, that didn't assuage the ache I felt in my chest at the thought of being so far away from him. He was getting older, and I had hoped one day to convince him to come live with me in Edinburgh when he was no longer able to care for himself.

We didn't have far to go, and I soon felt the wagon pulling to a stop.

"Ailsa, ye must make haste." Nick was telling her. They both stepped down from the wagon, and I waited in hiding for them to return. But within minutes the sound of hooves pounded in my ear as a horse and rider approached.

Nick was placing a second trunk into the back of the wagon when I heard the voice of Seton accosting him.

"Ho there! What are you doing?"

Nick continued his task, shoving the trunk toward the back of the wagon and adjusting the cover to conceal both me and our belongings.

I could hear Nick brushing off his hands, then turn to address the intruder.

"Who are ye?" Nick said with irritation in his voice.

"I'm afraid I must ask the same of you. I am the bailiff, David Seton, and ye are removing the property of a person who has a warrant out for her arrest. What is the meaning of this?"

Surely Nick had figured out with whom he was speaking, yet he gave no indication of alarm. "A warrant? Of whom do ye speak? My mother or my sister? For neither are likely to break the law and require arresting."

Silence followed for a split second as this information must have been settling into the bailiff's thick head. I wondered where Ailsa was.

Seton was sure to check her house if he thought her inside.

"Ailsa Blackburn is wanted for questioning by the King of Scotland himself," Seton said with a growl. "And she is thought to have ties to a traitor who even now awaits his trial at the tolbooth at the mercat cross."

So, Seton did not know of my escape. A slight sigh of relief escaped me as I continued to listen.

Nick acted nonplussed. "A traitor ye say? I have no knowledge of such ties. Who is the blackguard that would accuse my sister of such nonsense? They surely do not know her very well." Nick was good. Ailsa had told me that he had been employing himself at a theater in London, working with the playwright, Christopher Marlow. The acting lessons were paying off. He sounded very convincing.

The sound of boots scratching dust reached my ears as Seton evidently dismounted his horse. "Well, you can believe it, sir. It is true. And I should know, for I am betrothed to your sister, per your uncle's agreement."

"My uncle?" Nick laughed. "Ye mean Rupert Marley? He may be my mother's brother, but he hardly has any say in whom Ailsa marries. From my understanding, my sister did not agree to this betrothal."

Seton's voice sounded nearer now. "So, you have seen her? You have talked to her? Sir, if you are hiding the lass then you shall be called into question as well."

"I merely speak of the letter that Ailsa sent to me, asking for my assistance. But I have not been able to find her since I arrived in Edinburgh. She is not here, nor does it look like she has been for quite some time."

"We'll see about that." Heavy footsteps sounded as Seton walked down the close and into their house.

"Hold tight there, Will," Nick whispered. "Do not fear. Ailsa has stepped into a neighbor's house. As long as she stays put, I think we will be all right."

I silently thanked Nick for the information, then listened as he too, walked down the narrow alleyway, presumably toward their house. Minutes later, both men were back outside, and Seton's voice could be heard loud and clear.

"Why are you taking things from this place, Master Blackburn? If you do not know where your sister or your mother is, what are you planning on doing with their things?"

"I never said I did not know where my mother is, Bailiff Seton. She is visiting my uncle in London and is very anxious to hear news of Ailsa's well-being. Now, if ye will excuse me, I need to finish up here so that I may make some inquiries and see if I can track my sister down."

"You're telling me that you have not seen your sister since you arrived in Edinburgh? You do not know where she is?"

A note of amusement played in Nick's voice. "If I knew where she was, there would be no need to try to track her down, now would there be, Bailiff Seton?"

"Humph," Seton grunted. "You will do well to remember that if you find your sister, you are under obligation to the crown to report her."

"Right," Nick chuckled.

Just then, the thundering of more horses approached. This was it. My escape had been discovered.

"David Seton?" A voice boomed. I wanted desperately to make myself known. To make it look like it had all been my idea, and Nick was innocent in the matter. But if I was discovered in his wagon, a simple excuse would not suffice.

"By orders of His Majesty, King James, ye are under arrest." More scuffling of boots against gravel could be heard, and Seton cursed.

"What is the meaning of this?"

"Are ye David Seton, Deputy Bailiff from Tranent?" the voice asked.

"Aye."

"And are ye in possession of a gold ring which bears a single ruby and the letters F.S. on it?" the voice asked again.

"Why do you ask?" Seton's irritation scratched in his voice, and it was apparent he was getting impatient.

The shuffling of feet and bodies could be heard. Then, "You have no right!" from Seton. I imagined them pulling the ring from his finger.

"Because this ring was a gift from His Majesty to Francis Stewart, the Earl of Bothwell. We have sworn written testimony that ye are bearing such ring and have been working secretly with the earl to the detriment of His Majesty's kingdom."

A sound of a fist hitting flesh resounded in my ears, then much scuffling. It only took seconds for the men to apprehend Seton. I could tell by the way he spoke to Nick.

"Your sister will pay for this little trick." His voice shook with anger. "And remind her that her lover is still in the tolbooth and will get what's coming to him too."

I could hear the strain in his voice as he shuffled away. The sound of pebbles crunching under hooves could be heard, and I felt the tension in my neck easing as the danger rode away.

Nick let out a breath. "I can't believe that just happened. Are ye all right, Will?"

I had never been called *Will* in all my life, but at this moment I didn't care. Ailsa had not been discovered, and Seton had been arrested. And as crowning joy, he didn't know I had been sprung from the tolbooth. Oh, to be a mouse in the room when that was discovered!

Ailsa's voice shook with emotion. "That was fast! Lady Beatrix was right about the queen's influence."

"Lady Beatrix?" I sat up straighter. "What does she have to do with this?"

"I'll explain later." Ailsa laughed. "For now, let's go get mother and leave this place for good." Turning back to Nick, she said, "Do ye think it's safe now for William to ride up here with us?"

I spoke up from my hiding spot. "Nay, I am still an escaped prisoner, and you are still a wanted woman. I think it's best if I stay hidden until we are safely out of Scotland."

Ailsa frowned, but I could soon tell she was back in high spirits as she chatted with Nick.

"Will it be hard to find lodging in London, do ye think?"

"Nay. And with Will's knowledge and my connections, I wouldn't be surprised if he is invited to court within days of our arrival. The queen is very keen on the comings and goings of her cousin's Scottish subjects. Especially ones with close ties to the Scottish king."

Nick snapped the reins, and we lurched forward once more. A new anxiousness gripped me as we bumped along the roads of Edinburgh. Only time would tell if I was being thrown out of the kettle and into the fire. But it didn't matter. I had the woman I wanted and the clear conscience I desired. I would need to write to Father and finally answer his question. *Aye, Father, she is enough.*

~Epilogue~

London, July 1603

William

"We shall be late if we do not leave within the next five minutes, my love." I sat between our eight-year-old and our six-year-old, trying my best to keep the boys' costumes intact. Tom, the oldest of the two, kept pulling at his lace ruff and making faces. Our younger son, Will, thought it was great fun and liked to imitate his older brother. He had already pulled his ruff off twice.

"I dislike these collars," Tom complained. "They make me itch."

"Ahh, but you look so handsome in your new doublet and ruff," I soothed, playing on the boy's vanity. Although he was not my namesake, he was the mirror image of me with his dark, curly hair and blue eyes. And he had all of my attributes, including a penchant for looking his best. Ailsa cried foul the first time the boy asked if he could shine the buckles on his shoes.

Thinking of Ailsa seemed to summon her to the doorway. She stood there holding little Isobel's hand, the three-year-old's face streaked with fresh tears.

"What is it this time? I asked, rushing toward them and scooping Isobel up into my arms. She squealed as I blew a raspberry under her ear.

"She didn't want to wear the pink ribbons in her hair. She wanted the blue."

"So why didn't you just allow the blue?" I wiped a thumb across the cherub's cheek to brush away the residue of tears then tapped her on the nose.

"Because the last time she wore the blue ribbons she yanked them out of her hair and gave them to Sadie to play with. By the time the cat was through with them, they were nothing but shreds. She even got the cat in trouble; Mother scolded Sadie instead of Isobel."

"I am surprised Sadie can even gather the strength to move, she's so old. Even your mother gets around better than her."

"Cats live forever, dear."

"Will Sadie live forever, Papa?" Will's big brown eyes widened in amazement upon overhearing our conversation.

"All animals die," Tom said matter-of-factly. "It's a fact of nature." The boy pulled at his ruff once more, looking down at his little brother without sympathy.

"Is Sadie going to die, Mama?"

"Aye," replied Tom.

"No, she won't," Will cried. "Mama, tell Tom that Sadie isn't going to die."

Casting a glance at Ailsa, I could see her tolerance was quickly fading.

"All right boys, let's let Mama get her shoes on. Your grandfather will be here any minute."

"Grand Poppy!" Isobel shrieked, clapping her hands. I ushered the boys toward the door and was stopped by a dramatic clearing of the throat.

"Have ye forgotten that I need assistance?" Ailsa looked at me with one brow raised, then down at her bulging belly.

"I'll help you, Mama," Will chirped, running to fetch his mother's silk slippers from the other side of the room.

"Let's hope I can even get them on my feet," Ailsa quipped. "My feet are so puffy. I do wish King James's coronation would have come after the birth of this baby. Then perhaps I wouldn't look like a bloated globe."

"What's a globe, Mama?" Will piped up.

"A very round ball." Ailsa chucked the boy under the chin, and he grinned up at her, revealing a gap where a tooth had once stood.

"A ball!" Isobel squealed, and Will puffed out his cheeks and began prancing about the room with his arms bent out in front of him, indicating a very round belly.

"I guess now is the time to ask the question that has been on everybody's mind. Are ye nervous about seeing the king again after so many years?"

"Well, he has been in England for two months now, and I've managed to steer clear of him thus far. Maybe he won't notice me." I set Isobel down, and she immediately ran to her brother, clapping her hands and dancing.

"Aye, but it's no wonder. The man is afraid of his own shadow. He never goes out, and if ye aren't at court, then I suppose he won't see ye."

"I never had to be at court when the queen was alive. She gave me a job to do, and I did it. And she paid me. There was no need to be constantly under foot with my hand held out begging for favors."

"That's why she liked ye so much. That and your dashing good looks."

"That's not true."

"'Tis so. And your father agrees with me."

"He always agrees with you." I scowled.

"That's because I'm his favorite," she replied sweetly. "Anyway, let's hope the queen's successor will remember how valuable ye can be as well." Ailsa held out her own hand, silently asking for assistance to help her stand.

I pulled her to her feet and wrapped my arms around her. She may have felt like she was as big as a globe with all its countries and oceans painted on it, but I could still wrap my arms about her and she still felt slight in my arms.

She nuzzled her nose into my neck and breathed deeply. "Do ye think he has forgiven ye?"

I was silent for a moment, thinking about all that had passed between the king and I before we left Scotland. "Well, he forgave Bothwell over and over again. Every time the man committed some crime against His Majesty, he would just sneak in to see the king and beg for forgiveness. James would always give it. Perhaps I could do the same."

"But ye aren't very good at begging, dear." She looked up at me, and those fiery eyes sent a spark right through me.

"I only beg when it's something I really want." And I bent my head and kissed her, wishing there wasn't a new king to coronate and that we could just stay home.

~*Historical Notes*~

King James VI

King James's obsession with witches began when his new bride's ships were waylaid by storms on her voyage from Denmark in the autumn of 1589. Queen Anne was forced to land in Norway where she tried unsuccessfully to set sail again. When it became apparent that she would need to stay the winter in Norway, James decided to rescue her by sailing himself to Norway to retrieve her. He returned with her to Denmark where they stayed the winter. It was during their time at the Danish court that James was first introduced to the idea that witchcraft may have been responsible for their ill-fated efforts.

Around the same time of Anne's first attempted voyage, troubles were brewing off the coast of Scotland as well. Storms were responsible for the wreckage of a ship that killed a lady-in-waiting, Jane Kennedy, and her servant, whom James had appointed to wait for their new queen's arrival.

The following year, the Copenhagen witch trials began in which several women were accused of having used witchcraft to terrorize Queen Anne's ships. More than a dozen people were executed by burning due to the outcome of these trials. Five months after the first accused witch was burned at the stake in Denmark, Geillis Duncan was arrested in Scotland and the North Berwick witch trials began.

David Seton

Deputy Bailiff David Seton was indeed the man responsible for the arrest of the first accused witch in the North Berwick witch trials. However, the facts behind his part in my story end there. Although several historians are of the belief that his issue with Geillis was driven more out of lust, I have read nothing more of his involvement with the trials other than his arrest and interrogation of Geillis. However, he was indeed the brother-in-law to another of the executed woman accused of witchcraft, Euphame MacCalzean. Euphame's husband was the brother of Seton's wife. From my research, records do not indicate whether his wife was still alive during the time of the witch trials.

Francis Stewart, 5th Earl of Bothwell

One person that appears to have been involved in some pretty shady dealings during this time was the fifth Earl of Bothwell, Francis Stewart. Francis was the nephew of the infamous 4th Earl of Bothwell, James Hepburn, the third husband of Mary, Queen of Scots. He was also a cousin of King James by way of a shared grandfather, James V.

This 5th Earl of Bothwell was a trouble maker on all accounts and was truly a thorn in James's side. Before the witch trials, he had already attempted to kidnap the king. He and his accomplices stood trial for their crimes and were found guilty but the sentences were never carried out.

After the witchcraft accusations began, he continued to harass James and even attempted another kidnapping. He was arrested, and this time the crime of necromancy was added to his list of offenses. Of course, he denied the charges. While imprisoned in Edinburgh, he escaped and was continuously on the run and wreaking havoc until he eventually fled to Italy, where he lived out the remainder of his days.

Bothwell's name comes up quite a bit in the North Berwick witch trials narrative, and some historians believe he is the "devil" that many of the Scottish witches pledged fealty to at the Kirk of North Berwick. Even in later years after fleeing to Italy, letters were found in his possession that alluded to his dealings with necromancy and other sorceries.

Tea and Cacao

Ailsa uses several types of herbal teas in The King's Inquisitor and the drinking of tea is mentioned several times. I believe it important to point out that the drinking of tea as we know it today was actually not enjoyed by the Scots until about the middle of the 17th century. And although herbal concoctions for ailments have been around for centuries, they were not necessarily known as what we now call *tea*.

Ailsa enjoy a cup of cacao in this story as well. Though not the sweet, chocolaty drink we now know it as, hot cacao was already in Europe by this time thanks to explorers of the New World such as Hernando (later known as Hernán) Cortés. It would have been prepared in a similar way as described in the story. However, I have found no evidence supporting or refuting whether it would have been available to Scots by the end of the 16th century, so this is just another example of my imagination at work.

~*Author Acknowledgements*~

A huge thank you goes out to my editor, Janice Broyles, for her never-ending patience and wisdom. Thanks for letting me bounce ideas off of you, even when I am totally wrong.

I also owe a mound of gratitude to Julia Bracewell, Heather Carter, Laura Loney, and Catherine Meyrick for your fathomless historical knowledge. You understand the importance of accuracy in historical fiction and the struggle that can entail! I am forever grateful for your insight that helped make The King's Inquisitor the best it can be. Thank you!

Thank you for your purchase!

If you enjoyed **The King's Inquisitor,**
Read the first book of Tonya Ulynn Brown's Stuart
Monarch series:

The Queen's Almoner

Visit the author online at www.tonyaubrown.com